RACHEL BOWLBY is Northcliffe Professor of Modern English Literature at the University of London. She is the author of *Virginia Woolf: Feminist Destinations* and *Freudian Mythologies: Greek Tragedy and Modern Identities*, and the editor of two volumes of Woolf's essays for Penguin.

OXFORD WORLD'S CLASSICS

*For over 100 years Oxford World's Classics have brought
readers closer to the world's great literature. Now with over 700
titles—from the 4,000-year-old myths of Mesopotamia to the
twentieth century's greatest novels—the series makes available
lesser-known as well as celebrated writing.*

*The pocket-sized hardbacks of the early years contained
introductions by Virginia Woolf, T. S. Eliot, Graham Greene,
and other literary figures which enriched the experience of reading.
Today the series is recognized for its fine scholarship and
reliability in texts that span world literature, drama and poetry,
religion, philosophy and politics. Each edition includes perceptive
commentary and essential background information to meet the
changing needs of readers.*

OXFORD WORLD'S CLASSICS

—

VIRGINIA WOOLF

Orlando
A Biography

—

Edited with an Introduction and Notes by
RACHEL BOWLBY

OXFORD
UNIVERSITY PRESS

OXFORD

UNIVERSITY PRESS

Great Clarendon Street, Oxford OX2 6DP

Oxford University Press is a department of the University of Oxford.
It furthers the University's objective of excellence in research, scholarship,
and education by publishing worldwide in

Oxford New York

Auckland Bangkok Buenos Aires Cape Town Chennai
Dar es Salaam Delhi Hong Kong Istanbul Karachi Kolkata
Kuala Lumpur Madrid Melbourne Mexico City Mumbai Nairobi
São Paulo Shanghai Taipei Tokyo Toronto

Oxford is a registered trade mark of Oxford University Press
in the UK and in certain other countries

Published in the United States
by Oxford University Press Inc., New York

Biographical Preface © Frank Kermode 1992
Introduction, Select Bibliography, and Explanatory Notes © Rachel Bowlby 1992
Chronology © David Bradshaw 2000

The moral rights of the author have been asserted
Database right Oxford University Press (maker)

First published as a World's Classics paperback 1992
Reissued as an Oxford World's Classics paperback 1998
Reissued 2008

All rights reserved. No part of this publication may be reproduced,
stored in a retrieval system, or transmitted, in any form or by any means,
without the prior permission in writing of Oxford University Press,
or as expressly permitted by law, or under terms agreed with the appropriate
reprographics rights organizations. Enquiries concerning reproduction
outside the scope of the above should be sent to the Rights Department,
Oxford University Press, at the address above

You must not circulate this book in any other binding or cover
and you must impose this same condition on any acquirer

British Library Cataloguing in Publication Data

Data available

Library of Congress Cataloging in Publication Data

Data available

ISBN 978-0-19-953659-7

7

Printed in Great Britain by
Clays Ltd, St Ives plc

SHEFFIELD HALLAM UNIVERSITY
WL
828
Woolfv
ADSETTS LEARNING CENTRE

CONTENTS

ACKNOWLEDGEMENTS

FOR their genereous help and suggestions, I thank especially Julia Briggs, Bet Inglis, Peter Nicholls, and Nigel Nicolson.

BIOGRAPHICAL PREFACE

VIRGINIA WOOLF was born Adeline Virginia Stephen on 25 January 1882 at 22 Hyde Park Gate, Kensington. Her father, Leslie Stephen, himself a widower, had married in 1878 Julia Jackson, widow of Herbert Duckworth. Between them they already had four children; a fifth, Vanessa, was born in 1879, a sixth, Thoby, in 1880. There followed Virginia and, in 1883, Adrian.

Both of the parents had strong family associations with literature. Leslie Stephen was the son of Sir James Stephen, a noted historian, and brother of Sir James Fitzjames Stephen, a distinguished lawyer and writer on law. His first wife was a daughter of Thackeray, his second had been an admired associate of the Pre-Raphaelites, and also, like her first husband, had aristocratic connections. Stephen himself is best remembered as the founding editor of the *Dictionary of National Biography*, and as an alpinist, but he was also a remarkable journalist, biographer, and historian of ideas; his *History of English Thought in the Eighteenth Century* (1876) is still of great value. No doubt our strongest idea of him derives from the character of Mr Ramsay in *To the Lighthouse*; for a less impressionistic portrait, which conveys a strong sense of his centrality in the intellectual life of the time, one can consult Noël Annan's *Leslie Stephen* (revised edition, 1984).

Virginia had the free run of her father's library, a better substitute for the public school and university education she was denied than most women of the time could aspire to; her brothers, of course, were sent to Clifton and Westminster. Her mother died in 1895, and in that year she had her first breakdown, possibly related in some way to the sexual molestation of which her half-brother George Duckworth is accused. By 1897 she was able to read again, and did so voraciously: 'Gracious, child, how you gobble,' remarked her father, who, with a liberality and good sense at odds with the age in which they lived, allowed her to choose her reading freely. In other respects her relationship with her father was difficult; his deafness and melancholy, his excessive emotionalism, not helped by successive bereavements, all increased her nervousness.

Stephen fell ill in 1902 and died in 1904. Virginia suffered another breakdown, during which she heard the birds singing in Greek, a language in which she had acquired some competence. On her recovery she moved, with her brothers and sister, to a house in Gordon Square, Bloomsbury; there, and subsequently at several other nearby addresses, what eventually became famous as the Bloomsbury Group took shape.

Virginia had long considered herself a writer. It was in 1905 that she began to write for publication in the *Times Literary Supplement*. In her circle (more loosely drawn than is sometimes supposed) were many whose names are now half-forgotten, but some were or became famous: J. M. Keynes and E. M. Forster and Roger Fry; also Clive Bell, who married Vanessa, Lytton Strachey, who once proposed marriage to her, and Leonard Woolf. Despite much ill health in these years, she travelled a good deal, and had an interesting social life in London. She did a little adult-education teaching, worked for female suffrage, and shared the excitement of Roger Fry's Post-Impressionist Exhibition in 1910. In 1912, after another bout of illness, she married Leonard Woolf.

She was thirty, and had not yet published a book, though *The Voyage Out* was in preparation. It was accepted for publication by her half-brother Gerald Duckworth in 1913 (it appeared in 1915). She was often ill with depression and anorexia, and in 1913 attempted suicide. But after a bout of violent madness her health seemed to settle down, and in 1917 a printing press was installed at Hogarth House, Richmond, where she and her husband were living. The Hogarth Press, later an illustrious institution, but at first meant in part as therapy for Virginia, was now inaugurated. She began *Night and Day*, and finished it in 1918. It was published by Duckworth in 1919, the year in which the Woolfs bought Monk's House, Rodmell, for £700. There, in 1920, she began *Jacob's Room*, finished, and published by the Woolf's own Hogarth Press, in 1922. In the following year she began *Mrs Dalloway* (finished in 1924, published 1925), when she was already working on *To the Lighthouse* (finished and published, after intervals of illness, in 1927). *Orlando*, a fantastic 'biography' of a man–woman, and a tribute to Virginia's close friendship with Vita Sackville-West, was written quite rapidly over the winter of 1927–8, and published, with considerable success, in October. *The Waves* was written and rewritten in 1930 and 1931 (published in October of that year). She had already started on *Flush*, the story of Elizabeth Barrett Browning's pet dog—another success with the public— and in 1932 began work on what became *The Years*.

This brief account of her work during the first twenty years of her marriage is of course incomplete; she had also written and published many shorter works, as well as both series of *The Common Reader*, and *A Room of One's Own*. There have been accounts of the marriage very hostile to Leonard Woolf, but he can hardly be accused of cramping her talent or hindering the development of her career.

Preface

The Years proved an agonizingly difficult book to finish, and was completely rewritten at least twice. Her friend Roger Fry having died in 1934, she planned to write a biography, but illnesses in 1936 delayed the project; towards the end of that year she began instead the polemical *Three Guineas*, published in 1938. *The Years* had meanwhile appeared in 1937, by which time she was again at work on the Fry biography, and already sketching in her head the book that was to be *Between the Acts*. *Roger Fry* was published in the terrifying summer of 1940. By the autumn of that year many of the familiar Bloomsbury houses had been destroyed or badly damaged by bombs. Back at Monk's House, she worked on *Between the Acts*, and finished it in February 1941. Thereafter her mental condition deteriorated alarmingly, and on 28 March, unable to face another bout of insanity, she drowned herself in the River Ouse.

Her career as a writer of fiction covers the years 1912–41, thirty years distracted by intermittent serious illness as well as by the demands, which she regarded as very important, of family and friends, and by the need or desire to write literary criticism and social comment. Her industry was extraordinary—nine highly-wrought novels, two or three of them among the great masterpieces of the form in this century, along with all the other writings, including the copious journals and letters that have been edited and published in recent years. Firmly set though her life was in the 'Bloomsbury' context—the agnostic ethic transformed from that of her forebears, the influence of G. E. Moore and the Cambridge Apostles, the individual brilliance of J. M. Keynes, Strachey, Forster, and the others—we have come more and more to value the distinctiveness of her talent, so that she seems more and more to stand free of any context that might be thought to limit her. None of that company—except, perhaps, T. S. Eliot, who was on the fringe of it—did more to establish the possibilities of literary innovation, or to demonstrate that such innovation must be brought about by minds familiar with the innovations of the past. This is true originality. It was Eliot who said of *Jacob's Room* that in that book she had freed herself from any compromise between the traditional novel and her original gift; it was the freedom he himself sought in *The Waste Land*, published in the same year, a freedom that was dependent upon one's knowing with intimacy that with which compromise must be avoided, so that the knowledge became part of the originality. In fact she had 'gobbled' her father's books to a higher purpose than he could have understood.

Frank Kermode

INTRODUCTION

WHAT is *Orlando*'s editor to do? She—but there is every doubt of her sex—finds herself in the hopeless situation of dealing with a book which is already a parody of the kinds of scholarly enterprise which her introduction might try to emulate. The novel—but is it a novel?—satirizes the conventions of biographical and historical writing, and—worst of all for the immediate undertaking—it even includes parodies of the conventional front and back, the preface with acknowledgements and the index of names, not to mention a couple of spoof footnotes put in as it were to boot by the pseudo-editor of the pseudo-biographer.

The editorial problem is compounded by the fact that these are not isolated elements, for which separate commentary on, say, 'humorous aspects' might be appropriate while leaving the body of the book and its message or merits intact. Right from the start—the very first sentence muddles the expectations of reading by stopping to fuss over the validity of a masculine pronoun—the biographer-narrator is teasing us, making us aware of his—though once more, there is every doubt of his sex—activities in such a way as to draw attention to his being anything but an objective reporter of given facts, even when he is following proper biographical practices to the letter. Here again, the would-be editor is doomed if she imagines she can come along and sort all this out, neatly restoring all the planks and joistings of a solid narrative and well-covered biography that the book she is dealing with has just loosened up, showing them to be much less sturdy than they seemed.

Introduction

As a last scholarly resort, the editor may head towards that thing called 'other evidence', located outside that other thing called 'the text itself', in other words to that traditional locus of verifiable backgrounds and intentions which can always be counted on to yield some plausible quotation to bolster up an otherwise collapsible argument. But there she finds herself no more securely placed. There are some minor but no doubt honourable satisfactions to be gained from the careful picking up of piecemeal evidence—burrowing around in the chippings of diaries and letters as Orlando's biographer tells us he does among certain 'tantalizing fragments' (p. 122). It is from these that he pretends to reconstruct his account of the revolution in Constantinople, including the revolution in Orlando's sex; and since he lets all the gaps show, rather than welding them into apparent coherence, the inference to be drawn for the value or pertinence of such endeavours is not encouraging. In this particular instance, moreover, it is not only that the method comes unstuck, but also that almost everything Woolf says about *Orlando* and her plans for it seems to reinforce the stance, or anti-stance, suggested by the novel itself.

In her allusions to *Orlando*, Woolf comes back repeatedly to words such as 'wild', 'satiric', 'joke', 'fun', 'escapade', 'fantasy'—words which she never normally uses about her projects for writing and which seem to mark off this novel as an experiment in a rather different mode from the kind she undertook in what it then seems preferable to call her more 'serious' fiction. 'I want to kick up my heels and be off', Woolf remarks in her diary when she is getting out her first conception of the novel, and there the phrase nicely evokes the way that *Orlando* is both running away from it all, a gleeful escape from confinement, and something 'off', offbeat and off-beam, a little risqué for the safely tethered novelist. In both senses, *Orlando* is Woolf showing 'off'. Here is the diary entry in more detail:

No attempt is to be made to realise the character. Sapphism is to be suggested. Satire is to be the main note—satire & wildness. The Ladies are to have Constantinople in view. Dreams of golden domes. My own lyric vein is to be satirised. Everything mocked. And it is to end with three dots ... so. For the truth is I feel the need of an escapade after these serious poetic experimental books whose form is always so closely considered. I want to kick up my heels & be off. I want to embody all those innumerable little ideas & tiny stories which flash into my mind at all seasons. I think this will be great fun to write; & it will rest my head before starting the very serious, mystical poetic work which I want to come next.[1]

Satire, Sapphism, Constantinople, and a host of other 'tiny stories' all duly turn up in *Orlando*, as well as the absence of realism in the portrayal of the central character and the mockery of 'my own lyric vein' (the 'Time Passes' section of *To the Lighthouse*).

   A glance at the initial reception of the book when it was published in 1928 seems to confirm its success in the author's own terms, as critics echo the phrases of exuberance almost as if they had been looking over her shoulder as she sat writing her diary. This is Conrad Aiken in the Chicago *Dial*:

The tone of the book, from the very first pages, is a tone of mockery. Mrs Woolf has expanded a *jeu d'esprit* to the length of a novel. ...
   There is thus an important element of 'spoof' in *Orlando*: Mrs

---

[1] *The Diary of Virginia Woolf*, ed. Anne Olivier Bell and Andrew McNeillie, 5 vols. (London: Hogarth Press, 1977–84), iii. 131.

Woolf apparently wants us to know that she does not herself take the thing with the least seriousness—that she is pulling legs, keeping her tongue in her cheek, and winking, now and then, a quite shameless and enormous wink.[2]

Or Raymond Mortimer: 'The first thing to say about the book is that it is a lark. The preface is a parody of prefaces and the whole book is written in tearing high spirits.'[3]

But the larking around and the leg-pulls were not always left at that: some reviewers went further. Desmond MacCarthy saw *Orlando* as more than a diversion: 'In *Orlando*, which is pure fantasy, she appears to have found herself more completely than ever before.'[4] Then there is the letter from Vita Sackville-West, finding herself 'completely dazzled, bewitched, enchanted, under a spell. It seems to me the loveliest, wisest, *richest* book that I have ever read,—excelling even your own Lighthouse.[5] Admittedly, Sackville-West, to whom the book was dedicated in recognition of her crucial part in its conception, could hardly have been a more interested reader. From the other side, Arnold Bennett, never a great admirer of Woolf's work (as she was not of his), characterizes *Orlando* as 'a very odd volume'. Beginning with an evocation of how everyone is talking about the book, Bennett then denies the importance which that fact might suggest. His comment that 'You cannot keep your end up at a London dinner party these weeks unless you have read Mrs Virginia

[2] Robin Majumdar and Allen McLaurin (ed.), *Virginia Woolf: The Critical Heritage* (London: Routledge and Kegan Paul, 1975), 235.

[3] Ibid. 241.

[4] Ibid. 222.

[5] Louise A. DeSalvo and Mitchell A. Leaska (ed.), *The Letters of Vita Sackville-West to Virginia Woolf* (New York: William Morrow and Company, Inc., 1985), 288.

Woolf's *Orlando* ' immediately relegates it to superficiality, ephemerality, and snobbery, all three at once. But Arnold uses the very same vocabulary to talk about what he does not like as do those who see these qualities as positive: 'a play of fancy, a wild fantasia, a romance, a high-brow lark'.[6]

It may seem odd that both detractors and advocates agree with the author herself and with the book's dedicatee about the kind of thing *Orlando* is. We might then wonder whether this disagreement of value over a matter where there is apparent consensus does not suggest some further questions about fantasy and parody, kicking heels and pulling legs: about whether the very playfulness of fantasy may not, sometimes, be a way of saying the most serious things. (This might explain too why those who dismiss *Orlando* because it is 'only' a lark do not always simply say that and no more, but see a need to condescend to it too: 'The succeeding chapters are still more tedious in their romp of fancy';[7] 'an addiction of parenthetical whimsicalities that are not particularly effective'.[8])

This agreement over the style coupled with a division of critical estimates has continued to characterize writing about *Orlando*, though with less disapproval on the negative side and more elaborate argument on the positive. One recent example of the dismissive mode which Woolf partly adopts herself—*Orlando* as a respite from the serious work—is Susan Dick's book, which slips a solitary paragraph on *Orlando* into a brief section entitled 'From *To the Lighthouse* to *The Waves*'.[9] At the other extreme is

---

[6] *Critical Heritage*, 232.
[7] Arnold Bennett, *Critical Heritage*, 233.
[8] *New York Times*, *Critical Heritage*, 231.
[9] Susan Dick, *Virginia Woolf* (London: Edward Arnold, 1989), 59–60.

Introduction

Susan Squier, who sees *Orlando* as nothing less than Woolf's 'literary emancipation', in which 'she confronted the influence of both literal and literary fathers to reshape the novel, and so create a place for herself in the English novelist tradition which was their legacy to her'.[10]

This is a large claim; but if it seems too much for a joke, serious scholars might be reassured by this other diary entry in which Woolf too seems to have rather grander designs for what she had first conceived as her escapade:

One of these days, though, I shall sketch here, like a grand historical picture, the outlines of all my friends. . . . It might be a way of writing the memoirs of one's own times during peoples [*sic*] lifetimes. It might be a most amusing book. The question is how to do it. Vita should be Orlando, a young nobleman. There should be Lytton [Strachey], & it should be truthful; but fantastic. Roger [Fry]. Duncan [Grant]. Clive [Bell]. Adrian [Stephen].[11]

This is an interesting passage, because while on the one hand it could hardly be more direct in its prefiguring of *Orlando* (Vita and the book's hero(ine) are named and identified), on the other it adds a whole list of Woolf's friends who do not in fact come to feature in the book she began a few weeks later. The last part, suggesting an exploration of the lives of a group of friends, could be read in fact as another adumbration of Woolf's next novel, *The Waves*, which, in its difficulty and its studied seriousness, might seem to be the one most diametrically opposed to the lighter tones of this one. But what this passage then brings out is what is none the less shared between the two—and between *Orlando* and others of Woolf's novels.

---

[10] Susan Squier, 'Tradition and Revision in Woolf's *Orlando*: Defoe and "The Jessamy Brides" ', *Women's Studies*, vol. 12, no. 2 (1986), 167.

[11] *Diary*, iii. 156–7.

Introduction

The casual 'one of these days' proposal expressly brings together memoirs and history, individual and collective stories, as related concerns, while 'Vita . . . as a young nobleman' adds two more questions: sexual identity (the woman as the man) and the novel as a personal testimony of love (Vita). Taken together, these four elements, two on each side, would seem to put forward once again the opposition between serious work (preserving a record, maintaining things in their place) and fun (the 'off' fantasies of love and sexual play). Susan Squier reinforces her case for the significance of the novel by a gentle relegation of the second strand. As though giving more weight to the soft implications of Nigel Nicolson's description of it as 'the longest and most charming love-letter in literature',[12] she calls it 'a serious work of criticism as well as a love-tribute'.[13] Yet the most serious, and wildly romantic contribution of *Orlando* might be its more dramatic suggestion that there is far more connection and interchangeability between these two than the conventional division would indicate.

This bringing together of work and love, of what is serious and what is fun, applies also, as we shall see, to the other kinds of division the novel addresses—between periods of history and phases of people's lives; between words and what they talk about; and, most of all, between the two sexes and their desires. What the diary calls the 'grand historical picture' will appear further on; but first, let us turn to the question suggested by outlines and memoirs and Vita as Orlando, which is the initial offered by *Orlando*'s own subtitle.

[12] Nigel Nicolson, *Portrait of a Marriage* (London: Weidenfeld and Nicolson, 1973), 201.
[13] Squier, 'Tradition and Revision', 168.

Introduction

Orlando is not exactly a fake biography, of a purely fictitious subject; but nor is it much like a biographical *roman-à-clef*, in which the subject would secretly stand for some real-life personage. For it is as though all the doors had been left on the latch, or in some cases wide open, so that the reader, far from having to struggle with the lock, can be in no doubt as to who is being represented or intended in its hero(ine). From the outset, as we have seen, Orlando and Vita Sackville-West are identified, and the published version is openly dedicated to her. Not only that: the photographs, included in the first edition and reproduced here, are all of Vita or members of her family. *Orlando* is wearing its sources and inspiration on its sleeve: it is straightaway a tease to the conventions which ought to be keeping fiction and real lives officially separate. There is Vita herself, in the photographs, on the dedication page, for all the world to see and read: the fiction links it to a real person. Yet at the same time, the photographs show the 'real' Vita posing, taking on parts from her own life and her ancestors', so that real life itself is shown to be made up of imaginary identifications. All family album photographs have this quality: they are both a factual record—how it was, really, then—and also poses, a self-conscious construction of an image, both at the time of taking and in the mode of preservation and display. But Vita Sackville-West was something else as well.

Vita was the perfect subject for the exploration of multiple roles which the text of *Orlando* takes up. In effect, she lived her life as a conscious dramatic exhibition of this type of mobility. As writer, traveller, aristocrat, lesbian, mother, diplomat's wife (to name some), she was seen by Woolf as someone who shifted between far more roles than she did herself. The sheer number of possible designations already pushes her in the direction of the fantastical multiplicity of identities which Woolf so adeptly exploited in *Orlando*. Her own background and present-day existence were extraordinary enough to suggest this: it was almost as though she had been granted a licence to do what others could only read or dream about.

Vita was the latest in the line of noble Sackvilles whose history she had lovingly written in *Knole and the Sackvilles* (1922), on which Woolf drew extensively for her background to *Orlando*. She took upon herself the conserving role of historian, and prided herself on the continuity and illustriousness of her ancestry. Since the sixteenth century, when one of them was granted the estate by Elizabeth I, the Sackvilles had consistently been men of national importance. They made up a long run of statesmen, ambassadors, and minor men of letters, and it is not difficult to imagine how Vita, herself the wife of a twentieth-century ambassador, Harold Nicolson, and a prolific seeker after literary fame, should both have found points of correspondence in this history and—for the two are no doubt inseparable—been prompted in the choices of her own life by the models provided by her extraordinary array of forebears.

Parallel to this exalted English heritage was something quite different, whose sensational qualities immediately add the zest of high romance to what might otherwise constitute a relatively tedious line of successes and successions. Vita's grandfather, himself an ambassador, had been involved for years with an internationally famous Spanish dancer called Pepita, allegedly of gypsy origin (Vita was to write her story in the thirties). He had several children with her, including Vita's mother, Victoria. Having been brought up in relative obscurity in the south of France, and then taken for a short while to England to be introduced to her hitherto unknown noble relatives, Victoria found herself at the age of 19 whisked across the Atlantic to act as a society hostess for her father, who at this point was ambassador to the United States. According to the legend, she refused whole dance-floors of eligible suitors and then returned to England a few years later where she promptly fell for and married none other than her cousin, the heir apparent to Knole and the Sackvilles' title. Of this union Vita Sackville-West was the offspring. She was thus born of a dubiously double Sackville pairing compounded of fantastically disparate elements: her father's side was straightforwardly Sackville, while her mother's parents were Sackville plus a whole spread of highly romantic elements: the gypsy, the artist, the woman celebrity. In one way, Victoria literally repeated her mother's story, identifying herself with the foreign Pepita—Victoria had lived abroad and was illegitimate—and allying herself to a Sackville named, like her own father, Lionel. In 1910, this match provoked a much-publicized court case to decide the inheritance of Knole, and the complexities of the relationships already indicate what extraordinary material it was, both for sensationalization in the press and, later, for the fascination it might offer to a self-professed serious novelist in search of a wild biographical story.

Vita's own adoption of different identities, oscillating between the respectable and the Bohemian, the English and the cosmopolitan, as well as between different sexual roles, as wife and as lesbian lover, acts out in exaggerated form a similar pattern to her mother's repetition of *her* mother's story. Virginia Woolf's background, on the other hand, was prosaic by comparison with this. Her father, Leslie Stephen, was the principal editor of the unfailingly respectful *Dictionary of National Biography*, which comes in explicitly for a mocking remark or two in the pages of *Orlando* and stands in Woolf's representation for the epitome of lumbering Victorian seriousness and hypocrisy. If Vita—whose name means life—was literally the embodiment of what biography (etymologically 'life-writing') puts into books, then Virginia in a sense was the daughter of life already monumentalized on the shelf. To kick up her heels and be off was to run away from the formalities of her father's model of biography and make 'life' into the spectacle of Vita rather than the tome of an exemplary dead man.

In *Jacob's Room* (1922), Woolf's hero is set the essay question 'Does history consist in the biographies of great men?'. Woolf's implied answer is a strong negative. *Jacob's Room* is itself concerned with exploring the relations between biography and narrative and the development of masculinity, and in this respect *Orlando* is a kind of ironic sequel to the earlier novel, taking apart the components of masculine biographical identity in a rather different, but directly related way. The formal dissections of *Jacob's Room*, its implicit debunking of the ideals of Victorian biography, derive from a preoccupation Woolf shared with many of her literary friends. She later tried her hand at a serious biography of her own (on Roger Fry), and in addition to *Orlando* wrote another joke biography (*Flush*, the story of Elizabeth Barrett Browning's dog). Throughout her life she read and wrote about what she called 'the lives of the obscure' and especially (the two often overlapped) about the lives of women.

The biographical interest addressed the way of writing as much as the question of whose lives were worth writing. What form could come closest to capturing the elusive

Introduction

something she called 'life?' Which people's lives should be
written, by whom, and with what interest or aim? Her
essay on 'The Art of Biography' deals with the shift away
from what she dismissed as the too selective and reverential
modes of the nineteenth-century kind of biography.[14]
Lytton Strachey is singled out as one of a new generation
now experimenting with other ways of writing biography:
as so often in Woolf, innovation is associated with a
repudiation of something Victorian, a category itself associated with her parents' values. Strachey's *Eminent Victorians* had been a bestseller from the time of its publication
in 1918. The title is mildly ironic, since the book is partly
a tarnishing, or at least a modification, of the formerly
invulnerable images of nineteenth-century figureheads like
Cardinal Manning and Florence Nightingale.

Woolf liked much less Strachey's later *Elizabeth and
Essex*, which came out in the same year as *Orlando* (1928),
and which she saw as having gone too far in its turn away
from substantiated fact, in the absence of knowledge about
a distant period. At the beginning of an earlier essay, 'The
New Biography', close in time to *Orlando*, she had set up
the difficulty of the genre of biography as being one of
trying to find a *modus vivendi*, or rather a *modus scribendi*,
that might do justice to both the 'granite' and the 'rainbow', the solid fact and the less tangible individuality of a
life. *Elizabeth and Essex* had departed too far into the
realm of speculative fantasy, and she was not least dis-
pleased by its concentration on the (only supposed) love
affair between the queen and her courtier. In *Orlando*,

[14] 'The Art of Biography' (1939), rpr. Virginia Woolf, *The Crowded
Dance of Modern Life*, ed. Rachel Bowlby (Harmondsworth: Penguin,
1993).

Woolf was deliberately letting herself off this particular biographical hook—'limitation' is the word she uses—by taking a subject without any restrictions at all. And this was also, perhaps, her vision of Vita, with whom she had been passionately in love, as the pure rainbow, living a life unbound by any of the constraints of real-life granite.

One aspect which emerges sharply from the documents surrounding Vita Sackville-West's non-*Orlando* life is the difference in the sheer breadth of 'real-life' experiences between the two women. 'Virginia''s interest in 'Vita' often reads like that of the innocent, unworldly girl fascinated with the woman who had and did it all—the things which Woolf could 'only' write about. She saw it this way herself—as in this extract from a letter to Vita visiting her husband Harold Nicolson in 1927:

Now you are nearly at Teheran I make out, motoring across mountains; stopping at some shed I daresay for lunch, sandwiches, wine. You are very excited, all in a whirl, like a flock of birds flying across; Harold will be pacing up and down his room. I think of this journey so that I could write a book about not being a Passenger to Teheran [the title of the book Vita had written about her journey there the previous year]: but its silly to tell you my version, as perhaps you have your own.[15]

Woolf 'makes out' what intriguing things Vita may be doing; she has her version, and it does not seem to matter whether this is quite the same as hers ('*perhaps* you have your own'). But this leads to two other considerations. The first is that it is impossible, for either Virginia Woolf or V. Sackville-West (the name under which she published) to keep distinct the life and its writing. In both cases, their

[15] *The Letters of Virginia Woolf*, ed. Nigel Nicolson and Joanne Trautmann, 6 vols. (London: Hogarth Press, 1975–84), iii. 326.

lives were partly made up of writing, and writing was an attempt (in very different ways for each) to 'put a construction' on something that only thereby became the life she had lived or was living.

In a biography that is simply and aptly entitled *Vita*, Victoria Glendenning brings out this aspect very well. In effect, she gently chides Nigel Nicolson for taking his parents' declarations of marital happiness at face value in the account he gives of Vita and Harold in *Portrait of a Marriage*. Glendenning does not counter with the notion that they were not happy after all, but rather wishes to stress that their endless letter-writing was itself a means of inventing or constructing a mutual happiness which in their case depended quite directly on an exchange of written words:

The expression of love can be self-conscious and self-regarding even when it is heartfelt. In his letters to Vita, as she in hers, Harold made a closed circle of emotion and 'literature'. The words made bearable the emotion; the emotion fuelled the words. Harold was an obsessional and gifted recorder. Sometimes, for such people, an act or an emotion is being put into words even as it is being experienced. This accounts for the impression of theatricality and deliberateness that a sustained reading of the letters may produce.[16]

The writing does not simply come after, record, or fail to do justice to the life, or parts of it, that have already been lived. The same is true for Vita's many representations of her own and her parents' lives, and the history of her family, in both fictional and non-fictional form, and it is

---

[16] Victoria Glendenning, *Vita: The Life of V. Sackville-West* (London: Weidenfeld and Nicolson, 1983), 159.

evident too in the letters she and Virginia write to one another during the composition of *Orlando*.

The second point about the complexity of the relations between living and writing concerns not so much Vita and Virginia themselves, but the way that they have come to figure for their readers. During the 1970s and 1980s, a great deal of material—'primary' sources such as the letters and Woolf's diaries, and 'secondary' work in the form of biographies—has become available in published form, to both scholars and other readers. In 1990 there was a four-part dramatization of *Portrait of a Marriage* on British television. These stories have a fascination now which involves the selection of and emphasis on elements which would not have been so obvious, or not so acceptable for publication, at the time of their writing or doing. Vita's lesbian relationships become part of a widespread interest in the early part of this century as a time of sexual experimentation, in its practices and in its theories; and 'Bloomsbury' books of all sorts have been steady sellers and frequently bestsellers for many years now. These personalities are fascinating and fantastical characters for readers and viewers today, and their 'actual' lives—the documentary stuff of which 'factual' biographies are constructed—function in a similar way to the fictional fantasy of *Orlando*. The extraordinary lives cannot be neatly divided between reality and imagination, fact and fantasy.

Portrait of a Marriage, in which Nigel Nicolson published with explanatory chapters his mother's memoir of her affair with Violet Trefusis and other material about his parents' relationship, is an interesting example of the double aspect of these texts. When it came out in 1973, the book was taken up as a timely contribution to the post-1960s debate about 'open' marriage, with the Nicolsons

appearing to be an exemplary non-possessive, companion-
able couple, each allowing the other the freedom of different relationships. At the same time, there was all the
fascination of an inside scoop on a secret chapter of an
extraordinary life. Vita's narrative, which is the book's
primary exhibit, is itself written in this hybrid way: she
makes a gesture towards its scientific interest at the start,
and then gets on with telling a riveting and melodramatic
tale of desperate passions. At the same time, *Portrait of a
Marriage* itself can be read as a son's homage to his parents,
particularly to his mother, and his elaboration of a beautiful
story to frame the evidence of their lives.

These two, related aspects—the exemplary-didactic
('story for our times') and the projective (identifying
oneself, as biographer or reader, with another's story) can
be seen to operate together over and over again in the
publication and reception of biographies. It is both ironic
and fitting that the persons who lie behind, if not blatantly
in front of, the façade of *Orlando*, that superb dissection
of every kind of biographical and autobiographical myth-
making, should themselves have become fair game—both
targets for theories and beautiful Bloomsbury icons—in
the historical fantasies of the later part of the twentieth
century.

Orlando's narrator—not that we should necessarily take
him or her at his word—explicitly makes a connection
between biography and history. This passage occurs after
Orlando's change of sex, when she is enjoying 'society' life
as a London lady in the eighteenth century:

To give a truthful account of London society at that or indeed
any other time, is beyond the powers of the biographer or the
historian. Only those who have little need of the truth, and no

respect for it—the poets and the novelists—can be trusted to do it, for this is one of the cases where the truth does not exist. (p. 184)

The coy inconsistency here, with the narrator both denying that there is a truth of London society and appointing 'the poets and novelists' to render it, is perhaps less interesting than the general implication that biography and history share a disqualification for dealing with the more intangible, 'rainbow'-like aspects of life, whether individual or collective.

Nothing that Orlando's biographer says has to be taken at face value, still less as an expression of Woolf's values. But there is a play here between truth, whether biographical or historical or of some other kind, and the forms of its representation, which is indicative of one of *Orlando*'s seriously joking preoccupations. In moving so deftly and so rapidly from one age to the following (Orlando is a youth in the reign of Elizabeth I, and ends up as a woman of 36 in the 'Present Moment', precisely marked at the year of the book's publication, 1928), Woolf is able to tease out some of the assumptions about the nature of historical change and—inseparably—how it can be narrated by the historian who, as we have seen, is supposed to be on the side of respect for truth as opposed to literature's cavalier attitude to it.

And since the 'London society' passage puts us somewhere in the eighteenth century, this is perhaps the moment to point out that *Orlando*'s narrative mode, freely transporting its hero(ine) between periods and places and literary styles, owes much to Daniel Defoe and Laurence Sterne, two writers whom Woolf implicitly acknowledged as precursors of her own anti-realist stance (she wrote essays about both). In the first mention in her diary of the novel that would be *Orlando*, she says, 'I might write a Defoe narrative for fun'.[17] And in many ways the book can be seen as a loving rewrite of *Tristram Shandy*, sharing its mockery of scholarly practices and narrative conventions, and turning around the temporal twist—Tristram takes hundreds of pages even to get to the point of being born— by featuring a biographical subject who moves effortlessly through a life that lasts hundreds of years. There is also the not insignificant shift in the sexual stories: Tristram's nameless injury to his young male person at the casement window is a curtailment which goes together with his failure to develop according to a heroic model, but Orlando's parallel feminization adds, if anything, to her powers by giving her even more opportunities for experience and angles of vision.

The narrator seems positively to take pleasure in Orlando's temporal mobility, ending and beginning chapters with loud summaries of the contrasts between the age just gone and the one into which s/he is entering. Here is one example, the opening of Chapter V:

The great cloud which hung, not only over London, but over the whole of the British Isles on the first day of the nineteenth century stayed, or rather, did not stay, for it was buffeted about constantly by blustering gales, long enough to have extraordinary consequences upon those who lived beneath its shadow. A change seemed to have come over the climate of England. Rain fell frequently, but only in fitful gusts, which were no sooner over than they began again. The sun shone, of course, but it was so girt about with clouds and the air was so saturated with water, that its beams were discoloured and purples, oranges, and reds of

[17] *Diary*, iii. 131.

a dull sort took the place of the more positive landscapes of the eighteenth century. (p. 217)

Here, parodically, we are given the moment of historical change as precisely that of the chronological turnover from one century to the next, and its direct linking to a parallel change in the weather. The usual priorities have been reversed, so that now clock and climate, at once the most man-made and the most natural of phenomena, seem to conspire in an odd partnership to determine every other kind of change. This then draws attention to the way in which historical narratives do often covertly rely on quite arbitrary temporal and atmospheric markers, with the weather transmuted to a general metaphor. In recent history, for example, we are quite accustomed to seeing the 'swinging' sixties, the 'grey' recession seventies, and the 'me-generation' eighties as three separate periods with distinct 'climates' of activity and thought.

But in the second paragraph of this chapter, *Orlando*'s narrator seems to move into a slightly different mode:

Thus, stealthily and imperceptibly, none marking the exact day or hour of the change, the constitution of England was altered and nobody knew it. Everywhere the effects were felt. The hardy country gentleman, who had sat down gladly to a meal of ale and beef in a room designed, perhaps by the brothers Adam, with classic dignity, now felt chilly. Rugs appeared; beards were grown; trousers were fastened tight under the instep. The chill which he felt in his legs the country gentleman soon transferred to his house; furniture was muffled; walls and tables were covered; nothing was left bare. (p. 143)

Now the change has become not immediate, determined by the date, but gradual, something which in retrospect can definitely be seen to have occurred, but has come about unforeseen, 'stealthily and imperceptibly'. At this point, then, it is as though the narrator is acknowledging the necessity of the periodic markers, inexact and arbitrary though they may be. At the same time, the pre-existence of symbolic divisions, between centuries and between decades, for instance, itself has an effect on the way we conceptualize what is going on around us: the 1990s come towards us as though demanding to be given a personality, and already connoted with the burden or opportunity of being the last decade of the twentieth century, and the centenary of the *fin-de-siècle* age of decadence.

The passage then departs into characterization by appearances and the environment of daily life: the food, the interiors, the faces, the clothes. Here, too, the narrator is both mocking a certain kind of reduction of cultural history to visual tableaux and also suggesting that these details of ordinary living are precisely the things that make the differences between one time or one culture and another in the way that we imagine them. From another angle, the question of how to 'show' a given period— Woolf's 'grand historical picture'—is pointed up by the focus in this novel on lists. Most memorably, she gives the inventory of what Orlando buys to refurbish her mansion some time in the seventeenth century (p. 105). This is first a parody of documentary exactitude (as if the evidence could 'speak for itself', without needing to be interpreted), but it is also a pointing up of the way in which 'facts' never do yield a meaningful 'portrait' of the age or place or person: they have to be given a context before they will make any sense. Or, to put this the other way round, only within particular contexts would they be picked out as meaningful facts in the first place, and that necessarily makes them open to question, to a different framing.

Introduction

The representation of historical differences was a problem that fascinated Woolf throughout her life. Even though
Orlando is in fact the only one of her novels not set wholly
in the present or close to it (*The Years* begins in the late
nineteenth century), she regularly dramatizes the way in
which history, or past generations, figure for her characters; and she tends to see the understanding of a person's
identity in the present, both as an individual and as part of
a group, as tied to their sense of a relation (or lack of
relation) to the past. Woolf's own perspective derives from
the nineteenth-century literary interest in the idea of
history as a matter of imaginative reconstructions rather
than factual record; Walter Pater's evocations of classical
Greece are exemplary here, and were undoubtedly significant for Woolf. *Between the Acts* (1941), the last novel, is a
bleaker, less playful exploration of some of the same
questions as *Orlando*'s' featuring as it does a village pageant
of the ages of English history, performed right on the brink
of the Second World War. As with the 'fact and fantasy' of
biography, 'history' too is seen to be compounded irrecon-
cilably of an urge towards a hypothetically final truth—
what really happened, how it really was—and an acknow-
ledgement that our interest in other ages, like our interest
in other people, is to some extent dependent on what we
wish or fear in the past or our pasts.

Orlando proceeds even further, however, into the damp
and murky depths of how different ages are distinguished
from one another. A little further on into the general account of the nineteenth century, there is this, beginning with
a pseudo-return to the theory of climatic determination:

The damp struck within. Men felt the chill in their hearts; the
damp in their minds. In a desperate effort to snuggle their feelings

into some sort of warmth one subterfuge was tried after another. Love, birth, and death were all swaddled in a variety of fine phrases. The sexes drew further and further apart. No open conversation was tolerated. ... Thus the British Empire came into existence; and thus—for there is no stopping damp; it gets into the inkpot as it gets into the woodwork—sentences swelled, adjectives multiplied, lyrics became epics, and little trifles that had been essays a column long were now encyclopaedias in ten or twenty volumes. (p. 219)

The joke here is that while this purports to be a passage deriding the Victorians' repressively euphemistic compulsions—'no open conversation was tolerated'—it is itself a virtuoso exercise in the versatility of metaphors, as the 'damp' shifts deviously around between entities that do not belong in the same physical or linguistic spaces—weather, hearts, feelings, minds. 'Love, birth, and death' are then apparently represented as things-in-themselves, whose sufferings from the ubiquitous damp will need to be rectified; but then the next clause, by tucking them up with a purely linguistic material, 'a variety of fine phrases', muddles up the distinction between reality and figures of speech once again.

This brings us to one more way in which *Orlando* points up a problem and a joke about the representation of history and biography. For here Woolf is taking matters very directly and unequivocally (plenty of fine phrases, but they proclaim themselves as such) into the indissoluble connections between the resources of language and the ways that the world is perceived. Throughout *Orlando*, we run into literary figures. Orlando him/herself, writing a poem for most of her life and her biography, is the prime example; and her name itself recalls a whole line of literary heroes— from the medieval *Chanson de Roland* (the French version

[xxxiii]

of the name), through Ariosto's epic *Orlando Furioso*, to Shakespeare's *As You Like It*, in which Orlando cross-dresses as a woman.

But the novel also includes a large cast of poets and essayists, the 'great men' of literary history turning up with unfailing regularity in every age. In one sense this is another way of caricaturing the portrayal of historical periods by means of a few leading characters of literary and political note set against a general cultural background or 'backcloth'—in a literalization of this effect, Orlando returning up the Thames to England to take part in the early eighteenth century has Addison, Dryden, and Pope in a coffee-house indicated to her by the captain. It is at this point that *Orlando*'s pseudo-editor makes one of his— there is no doubt that it is a his—few interventions, fussily informing the reader that this is a historically impossible trio: 'The Captain must have been mistaken, as a reference to any textbook of literature will show; but the mistake was a kindly one, and so we let it stand' (p. 160). And indeed, in our view of the eighteenth century, Addison just *is* there sitting in a coffee-house and engaging in the famous conviviality of the period, just as the clichéd image would lead us to expect. But in another sense, *Orlando*'s frequent references to changes in language, and especially literary language, also suggest a serious point about the linguistic lenses through which we see our own age and others. Any bygone usage will carry a connotation of archaism and quaintness which it did not have at the time when it was current, so that access to the past 'as it was', even through the words in which it represented itself, is by definition impossible.

Orlando also plays around with the relations between new cultural objects and their effects on language and thinking. Telegraph poles and telegraph offices appear in the novel a number of times (latterly, when Orlando keeps sending enigmatic messages about toy boats to her husband somewhere round Cape Horn), the first—in the novel's chronological terms—*avant la lettre*, or rather with the word preceding the thing:

Now her toes tingled; now her marrow. She had the queerest sensation about the thigh bones. Her hairs seemed to erect themselves. Her arms sang and twanged as the telegraph wires would be singing and twanging in twenty years or so. But all this agitation seemed at length to concentrate in her hands. (pp. 228–9)

By absurdly using a metaphor taken from something not yet invented, Woolf draws attention to the way that technical and other forms of innovation cannot simply be separated from the structures of thought and syntax which they both draw on and develop. A recent example would be the language of computers, which has rapidly made its mark upon everyday thought and speech. Woolf's own diaries are packed with direct and indirect explorations of the interface between modern things and modern thinking: in both a practical and a literary sense, she was interested in analysing everything to do with changes in an environment that was itself made up indissociably of both words and their objects.

Orlando undermines the belief in a developmental historical or personal narrative, in which everything can be seen to lead up to a finely conclusive present; and the novel also, as we have seen, constantly pushes on the reader's attention the fact that it is only (but also proudly) a thing of words and their histories, making up one questionable view of its story by means of narrative techniques that are of the same kind as those deployed by fictions which declare themselves as such.

Sexes change and sexuality changes with such unbounded and joyous momentum in *Orlando* that it would be easy (and perhaps more fun) to miss the serious point that the novel is suggesting a crucial link between these phenomena and those connected with more general and public forms of history and identity. Here the telegraph wires passage is as good a place to begin as any, since it is peculiar for reasons apart from the historical-linguistic reversal. In this passage, the nineteenth-century Orlando goes on to succumb to what she feels as an irrepressible urge for a wedding ring (which, in another reversal of the normal temporal sequence, she then proceeds to procure and wear as an item of apparel before a husband conveniently shows up as the proper accessory to go with it). The eroticism of the passage is curiously at odds with the general stance of this section, which will soon go on to make a disgruntled contrast between the casual sex of the eighteenth century ('one would meet a boy trifling with a girl under a hawthorn hedge frequently enough') and the stodgy ties of the nineteenth ('Couples trudged and plodded in the middle of the road indissolubly linked together', p. 231).

Orlando's switch of sex from man to woman is only the most blatant among the novel's many cases of sexual indeterminacy—as with the peculiar Archduke who reveals herself a disguised Archduchess, or with Orlando and her eventual husband identifying one another cross-sexually (' "You're a woman, Shel!" . . . "You're a man, Orlando!" ', p. 240). These are highlighted throughout in relation to what seems to be indicated as some basic arbitrariness about any assignment of one or the other sex to someone.

Introduction

It is from the very first sentence: 'He—for there could be no doubt of his sex, though the fashion of the time did something to disguise it—was in the act of slicing at the head of a Moor which swung from the rafters.' (p. 13) Here the denial of the doubt is just what lets in the doubt, by saying what it says needs no saying. And the deviousness of this move seems to be echoed by the immediate mention of disguise, as though sex were going to turn out to be a matter of tricks and cover-ups, of looking like what you are not, or what you may not be after all. And the peculiarity is reinforced by the lack of logic in the statement on close inspection. If it is the 'fashion' of the time, it ought to make the sex recognizable rather than not (we are not told that Orlando was dressed as a woman). It is the eph-emerality associated with fashion which acts as a decoy from the other inconsistency, and this is the first heralding of what will be the narrator's own doubling of his or her hero or heroine's many ruses and masquerades. Later, when Orlando the woman engages in multiple shifts—for instance when she dresses up as a man and then reveals herself a woman so as to take part in female conversations from which men are excluded—the narrator, who up till then has seemed male or declared himself sexless ('neutral') seems somehow to have had access to the scene.

This sexual indeterminacy also straightaway raises the question of the biographer's own historical place. In this first sentence, is he in the same century as Orlando here, or the same century as his hypothetical readers who need to have their distance from the Elizabethan period footnoted by an allusion to 'the fashion of the time'? Orlando's historical as well as sexual mobility, followed by that of his or her pursuing biographer, will become an occasion—many occasions—for the narrator to show up assumptions that are normally made about the shared social knowledge of writers and readers. For yet one more possible interpretation of this sentence—and the book starts as it will go on, by provoking the reader with its uncertainties—would suggest that at some times fashion disguises the sex more than at others. Which would leave us back just where we started, since it would then be necessary to decide which kind of a period this was, and whether the sex could be assumed to be disguised or not (if it always was, then it would be no disguise at all, since the sign, however different from what it indicated, would be clearly readable).

The lawsuit Orlando faces to determine her right to inherit the estate when she returns to England as a woman posits this uncertainty from the other direction. Whereas the example above, and other discussions in the novel, focus on a visual indeterminacy (is it a he or a she? and are the clothes disguising it or revealing it?), the lawsuit stresses that, in the absence of any obvious classification, it has to be fixed, by fiat, in a way that implicitly has no particular reference to any reality:

The chief charges against her were (1) that she was dead, and therefore could not hold any property whatsoever; (2) that she was a woman, which amounts to much the same thing; (3) that she was an English Duke who had married one Rosina Pepita, a dancer; and had by her three sons ... thus it was in a highly ambiguous condition, uncertain whether she was alive or dead, man or woman, Duke or nonentity, that she posted down to her country seat, where, pending the legal judgement, she had the Law's permission to reside in a state of incognito or incognita, as the case might turn out to be. (p. 161)

In order for Orlando to continue with her life, she has to be granted an agreed identity, and in this sense to have a sex—one sex or the other and only one—is (literally) vital: if you are not unequivocally male or female, you cannot be accorded the other attributes of a person—starting, as the passage demonstrates by a *reductio ad absurdum*, with life itself ('alive or dead', one or the other, to be determined), and extending to aspects of status. 'Incognito or incognita, as the case might turn out to be' reveals once more the either/or structure of these distinctions—always in terms of a need to choose between one of two mutually exclusive characteristics—and also suggests the way in which the sexual division seeps into the very framework of language as the legal and the grammatical 'cases' come to overlap. There is no using language, or being represented in it, without initially being 'he or she', just as (or unjust as) an implicitly 'legal judgement'—normally less marked or disputed than for Orlando—about the assignment of a sex is a prerequisite for any socially recognizable identity.

It is worth pointing out here how directly Woolf is drawing for this episode on Vita Sackville-West's own history. The 1910 trial to determine the inheritance of Knole, her family seat, involved every aspect of the *Orlando* case except the gender dispute, though supplying instead the added spice of a quasi-incestuous marriage (Vita's mother Victoria having married her first cousin, and both being Sackvilles). The name 'Pepita' really was the name of Victoria's mother, a Spanish dancer who had a number of children with Lionel Sackville-West, an ambassador. Bizarrely, the case turned out to be a matter of proving Victoria's illegitimacy (her brother was trying to prove that their parents had been married after all) in order that Vita's father, though not descended in a direct line, should become the legitimate heir. The *Orlando* case does not involve the question of legitimacy and paternity that was central to the Sackville-West case, but the parallels between the two show how completely, in the determination of paternity and in the determination of sex, something taken for natural becomes in practice a matter of social decision, revealed as such only when it is openly in dispute. The real-life case is an even more perfect illustration than the fictional one of the arbitrariness of paternity and legitimacy, as questions for legal judgement; and *Orlando* extends the same principle to the distinction of sex, even closer to the bone.

The juxtaposition of the two categories of sex (male or female?) and status (noble or nonentity?) can further be related to Orlando's story immediately after her (apparently arbitrary and unmotivated) change of sex while he is ambassador in Constantinople. For one thing—and again without explanation—the change follows soft on the heels of Orlando's elevation to a rank of honour, a ceremony which is abruptly ended by the beginnings of a local revolution. And then, after her feminine awakening, Orlando is taken off to live among gypsies.

The gypsies are represented as a community unconcerned with the categories which preoccupy Orlando's future judges. They are not interested in the ownership of property; they are unimpressed by Orlando's alleged nobility, when their own families have a far longer continuous history than his, but not in terms of the competitive prowess which has distinguished and rewarded the English nobleman's family; lastly, and perhaps most intriguingly of all, they do not make any apparent (visible) distinction between two sexes, a point that is made only when Orlando, about to embark for the voyage back to England, for the first time dresses herself as a woman, in the event as an English lady:

[xl]

Introduction

It is a strange fact, but a true one, that up to th
scarcely given her sex a thought. Perhaps the
which she had hitherto worn had done something
thoughts; and the gipsy women, except in one or two
particulars, differ very little from the gipsy men. (p. 147)

The collapse or abandonment of social and proprietorial
interests is thus pointedly aligned both to the change from
male to female and to the diminishing of the importance of
sexual differences.

It is significant here too that Orlando's scarcely giving
her sex a thought is an attitude held up as an ideal by
Woolf for the creative writer in *A Room of One's Own*,
which is from the same period as *Orlando*. There she
declares, notoriously, that 'It is fatal for anyone who writes
to think of their sex'.[18] In this passage from *Orlando*, it
would seem that not thinking of one's sex goes together
with not thinking of ownership, conquest, status, and all
the other preoccupations which Woolf associates—in *A
Room of One's Own* and elsewhere—with what she calls a
'patriarchy'. (And in this light, the use of the word
'distract' here is a distracting, though possibly ironic,
restoration of the perspective of the 'civilized' world of
sexual and other distinctions which the passage is ostensi-
bly questioning.)

From this context, however, it would seem to be important that Orlando is only able to attain the ideal of not
thinking of her sex, or being distracted from that concern,
at precisely the point at which she has just become a
woman. Once bound back for the hierarchies and legalities
of England, she can only be the kind of woman that is

[18] Woolf, *A Room of One's Own* (1928; rpt. Harmondsworth: Penguin, 1967), 102.

pposed to fit with the type of man fostered in a culture of legitimacies and Christian–Western superiorities ('slicing at the head of a Moor', as the very first sentence of the novel concisely characterized Orlando's playful education).

This in turn might be connected to the following admission or examination by the biographer towards the end, when Orlando has not only finally published her poem but been awarded (as Vita Sackville-West was for *The Land*) a prestigious literary prize:

> But (here another self came skipping over the top of her mind like the beam from a lighthouse). Fame! (She laughed.) Fame! Seven editions. A prize. Photographs in the evening papers (here she alluded to the 'Oak Tree' and 'The Burdett Coutts' Memorial Prize which she had won; and we must snatch space to remark how discomposing it is for her biographer that this culmination to which the whole book moved, this peroration with which the book was to end, should be dashed from us on a laugh casually like this; but the truth is that when we write of a woman, everything is out of place—culminations and perorations; the accent never falls where it does with a man). (pp. 297–8)

In *Orlando*, it seems that a multiplicity of selves—both simultaneously, especially in 1928, and via the changes of identity throughout her long biography—has something characteristically feminine about it, marking a difference from the (here implicitly masculine) biographer who wants everything to be in its place, with predictable ends and conclusions in language, narratives, and behaviour. In this respect, *Orlando* draws out a distinctly feminine inflection of the modernist interest in the poses and masks of literary selves shared by such figures as Wyndham Lewis, Ezra Pound, and W. B. Yeats. Yet in the passage above, Orlando's eccentric laughter does not contradict a pleasure in being granted the recognition of an official prize.

Introduction

There are direct echoes, once again, of Vita's intriguing mobility, in both geographical and personal senses: she had in fact been to Constantinople both as the wife of the British ambassador and to enjoy what she called 'roughing it' on camping expeditions, both the great lady and the granddaughter of the dancer descended from gypsies. Here too, Woolf's identification with this performance of double identities can be seen. Touchingly, when she was working in 1926 on the introduction to an anthology of photographs taken by her great-aunt, Julia Margaret Cameron, Virginia sent Vita a picture of a coronet she had found, hoping thereby to confirm that her relative had, like Vita, a romantically hybrid background: 'I want to prove her base and noble—it fits in with all her oddities.'[19]

So Woolf is not straightforwardly critical of the masculine privileges and traditions in this novel, nor does she seem, here or elsewhere, to be recommending a return to, or a revolution in favour of, something imagined as a less 'civilized' form of life. What *Orlando* does seem to suggest is that it might be easier from the place of someone identified as a woman to imagine that values and views and selves are not necessarily, or even desirably, 'composed' in the way that the biographer would have it. It is as a woman, wondering why she is dutifully pouring out tea for Alexander Pope in the eighteenth century, that Orlando is led to give herself the distance of inverted commas in reflecting on historical and collective, as well as personal and sexual identities: 'What's an "age", indeed? What are "we"?' (p. 196).

In one passage, this is put in terms of speculations about a 'vacillation' from one sex to the other that is true for

[19] *Letters*, iii. 280.

everyone, not just for Orlando. This 'mixture in her of man and woman, one being uppermost and then the other' (p. 181) is the structure which has been linked to Woolf's conception of androgyny, outlined in a different way from the other quotation about the fatality of thinking of your sex as the writer's ideal in *A Room of One's Own*. Woolf was writing at a time when there was great interest in and investigation of the phenomena and determinations of sexuality and sexual identities. Instead of it being taken for granted, or rather for natural, that men and women were simply different, with whatever consequences followed from the specific form of the assumption (from the merely physical to those that encompassed the whole of emotional and intellectual life as well), now the very origins of masculinity and femininity and the forms of sexual interest that might accompany them were being perceived in some quarters as being in need of explanation.

One illustration of this, from the same year as *Orlando*, is the much more overtly lesbian novel by Radclyffe Hall, *The Well of Loneliness* (it was successfully prosecuted for obscenity, which shows that the new explorations were not calmly welcomed or accepted). Following Havelock Ellis's influential writings, Hall retains quite traditional masculine and feminine identifications for the female couple she describes, her aim being to make homosexuality into one more natural identity, albeit an unusual one, given from birth in the same way that she assumes heterosexuality to be. For Freud, the conditions are rather different in that both attraction to the other sex and attraction to the same sex require explanation (neither is more natural), as do the taking up of a masculine or a feminine identity, which will not necessarily correspond to the physical sex.

Ironically, Freud's psychoanalytic story of the development of heterosexual femininity parallels Orlando's in that it involves a passage through an initial period identical with boyhood before this is lost with the turn towards what will become femininity. Femininity for Orlando is the point of opening up—she gains something and loses nothing—from which places and identities come to be more mobile, and this outcome could be inferred from Freud's account; he states for instance that 'in the course of some women's lives there is a repeated alternation between periods in which masculinity or femininity gains the upper hand'.[20] But the 'normal', heterosexual femininity which is socially prescribed is reached by so arduous a series of renunciations of other identifications that he is led to conclude instead that, far from being open-ended, it is a place from which exits will not easily occur:

A man of about thirty strikes us as a youthful, somewhat unformed individual, whom we expect to make powerful use of the possibilities for development opened up to him by analysis. A woman of the same age, however, often frightens us by her psychical rigidity and unchangeability. Her libido has taken up final positions and seems incapable of exchanging them for others.[21]

In *Orlando*, on the other hand, where social limitations barely intrude upon the hero(ine's) movements (she does have to pour out tea for Alexander Pope, but does not stay for long in that setting), the change of sex at the same age is the start of a wider life in which she will enjoy the best of both worlds, both or multiple kinds of identity:

[20] Freud, 'Femininity' (1933), *New Introductory Lectures on Psycho-Analysis*, Pelican Freud Library (Harmondsworth: Penguin, 1973), 165.
[21] Ibid. 169.

She had, it seems, no difficulty in sustaining the different parts, for her sex changed far more frequently than those who have worn only one set of clothing can conceive; nor can there be any doubt that she reaped a twofold harvest by this device; the pleasures of life were increased and its experiences multiplied. For the probity of breeches she exchanged the seductiveness of petticoats and enjoyed the love of both sexes equally. (p. 211)

Once again the clothing focus—*Orlando*'s wonderfully perverse hemline history—literalizes the stress on sexual identity as more of a teasing disguise—a 'device' or play of dressing up and consciously taking on parts. Even Thomas Carlyle's *Sartor Resartus* (1839), which also purports to believe that apparel is all, starts to look a little dowdy when set next to the flamboyant masquerading of *Orlando*. It is as though Woolf were wilfully turning on its head the austere restrictions of the either/or demand that a person identify themselves as one sex or the other, or that matters of sex should have the stern formality of a serious case, whether legal, grammatical, or medical. 'Probity'—the respectable, the proven, the correct—is not just modified but reversed into the shifting sexuality of its gay abandonment, where nothing is 'only one' or only once: 'frequently', 'different parts', 'twofold', 'multiplied', 'both'.

All this seems an almost immeasurable distance away from the restraints upon women that Woolf analyses in *A Room of One's Own* and elsewhere, and from the difficulties of being a normal woman that Freud's tougher line evokes. But this, I think, is the point of *Orlando*: it is a 'what if', a serious fantasy which imagines what femininity (or, for that matter, another masculinity) might be in quite different conditions—if anything were possible. It is not a programme (Woolf deplored literature that was political in this practical sense), but nor is it just a laugh.

Orlando herself, as we have seen, demonstrates in the novel how a feminine laugh might be 'discomposing' to the certainties of a biographer who wants to know where he is, and where she is. And this laugh is as seductive for her readers as Orlando's layers of petticoats for her admirers, or as Vita Sackville-West for her reader Virginia Woolf. These pleasures of changing might themselves figure as invitations to different identities, for *Orlando*'s readers. One of the new traits identified as succeeding her change of sex is Orlando's interest in mirrors (p. 150); and it seems only fitting that Vita should have immediately written on first looking into *Orlando*, '[Y]ou have invented a new form of Narcissism'.[22] Of course, Vita had more reasons than most readers to see herself in the mirror of Orlando; but the comment is a happy recognition of *Orlando*'s jubilant transference of the sense of its exhilarating power to discompose and recompose, to put identities on and off at will.

A love letter *and* a serious work of criticism, not one at the expense of the other, or the second superior to the first: *Orlando*'s 'what if' is a playful and serious proposal that pleasures might be increased if these two categories, like other such pairs, were no longer seen as mutually exclusive. Or as Woolf put it herself:

Well but Orlando was the result of a perfectly definite, indeed overmastering impulse. I want fun. I want fantasy. I want (& this was serious) to give things their caricature value. And still the mood hangs about me. I want to write a story, say of Newnham or the womans movement, in the same vein.[23]

[22] *Letters of Vita Sackville-West to Virginia Woolf*, 289.
[23] *Diary*, iii. 175.

NOTE ON THE TEXT
AND ILLUSTRATIONS

THIS text follows the first edition of *Orlando*, published in 1928 by the Hogarth Press in London. The manuscript of *Orlando* is at Knole in Kent, the Sackville-West home; there is a copy of it on microfilm in the Bodleian Library, Oxford. The notes to this edition point out significant differences between published text and manuscript, and readers who wish to know more are referred to Madeline Moore's invaluable edition and commentary (see 'Select Bibliography', below).

This edition makes minor adjustments to hyphenation, word division ('tomorrow', 'tonight' 'someone', etc.), 'ize' for 'ise', the dropping of the full point after 'Mr' and 'Mrs', and the use of single rather than double quotes, in order to be consistent, and to follow current standard usage.

'The Russian Princess as a Child' is a photograph of Vanessa Bell's daughter Angelica. 'Orlando on her return to England', after Lely, was taken by Vanessa Bell, 'Orlando at the present time' by Leonard Woolf. Both of these are photographs of Vita Sackville-West. The 'historical' illustrations are photographs of portraits at Knole.

In the first edition plates 2 to 8 appeared opposite the text which now falls on pages 48, 110, 118, 151, 237, 254, and 306.

SELECT BIBLIOGRAPHY

BIBLIOGRAPHY

KIRKPATRICK, B. J., *A Bibliography of Virginia Woolf* (2nd edn.; Oxford: University Press, 1980).

BIOGRAPHY

BELL, QUENTIN, *Virginia Woolf: A Biography* (2 vols.; London: Hogarth Press, 1972).

POOLE, ROGER, *The Unknown Virginia Woolf* (Cambridge: University Press, 1978).

ROSE, PHYLLIS, *Woman of Letters: A Life of Virginia Woolf* (New York: Oxford University Press, 1978).

WOOLF, LEONARD, *An Autobiography* (2 vols.; Oxford: University Press, 1980).

EDITIONS

The Diary of Virginia Woolf, ed. Anne Olivier Bell, assisted by Andrew McNeillie (5 vols.; London: Hogarth Press, 1977–84).

The Letters of Virginia Woolf, ed. Nigel Nicolson and Joanne Trautmann (6 vols.; London: Hogarth Press, 1975–84).

GENERAL CRITICISM

BENNETT, JOAN, *Virginia Woolf: Her Art as a Novelist* (Cambridge University Press, 1945, 1964).

BOWLBY, RACHEL, *Virginia Woolf: Feminist Destinations* (Oxford: Blackwell, 1988).

BREWSTER, DOROTHY, *Virginia Woolf* (London: Allen and Unwin, 1963).

DI BATTISTA, MARIA, *Virginia Woolf's Major Novels* (New Haven, Conn., and London: Yale University Press, 1980).

FLEISHMAN, AVROM, *Virginia Woolf: A Critical Reading* (Baltimore, Johns Hopkins University Press, 1977).

Select Bibliography

FREEDMAN, RALPH, *Virginia Woolf: Revaluation and Continuity* (Berkeley: University of California Press, 1980).

GUIGET, JEAN, *Virginia Woolf and her Works*, trans. Jean Stewart (London: Hogarth Press, 1965).

LEASKA, MITCHELL A., *The Novels of Virginia Woolf* (New York: John Jay Press, 1977).

LEE, HERMIONE, *The Novels of Virginia Woolf* (London: Methuen, 1977).

MAJUMDAR, ROBIN, and MCLAURIN, ALLEN (eds.), *Virginia Woolf: The Critical Heritage* (London, Routledge and Kegan Paul, 1975).

MARCUS, JANE (ed.), *New Feminist Essays on Virginia Woolf* (London: Macmillan, 1981).

MARDER, HERBERT, *Feminism and Art: A Study of Virginia Woolf* (New Haven, Conn., and London: Yale University Press, 1968).

MCLAURIN, ALLEN, *Virginia Woolf: The Echoes Enslaved* (Cambridge: University Press, 1973).

MINOW-PINKNEY, MAKIKO, *Virginia Woolf and the Problem of the Subject* (Brighton: Harvester, 1987).

MOODY, A. D., *Virginia Woolf* (Edinburgh: Oliver and Boyd, 1963).

THAKUR, N. C., *The Symbolism of Virginia Woolf* (London: Oxford University Press, 1965).

WARNER, ERIC (ed.) *Virginia Woolf: A Centenary Perspective* (London: Macmillan, 1984).

ZWERDLING, ALEX, *Virginia Woolf and the Real World* (Berkeley: University of California Press, 1986).

On *Orlando*

ABEL, ELIZABETH, *Virginia Woolf and the Fictions of Psychoanalysis* (Berkeley: University of California Press, 1989).

BALDANZA, FRANK O., '*Orlando* and the Sackvilles', *PMLA* 70, no. 1 (Mar. 1955), 274–9.

BROWN, CAROLYN, 'Feminist Literary Strategies in the Postmodern Condition', in Helen Carr (ed.), *From My Guy to Sci-Fi:*

[1]

Select Bibliography

Genre and Women's Writing in the Postmodern World (London: Pandora Press, 1989), 112–34.

DE SALVO, LOUISE A., and LEASKA, MITCHELL A. (eds.), *The Letters of Vita Sackville-West to Virginia Woolf* (New York: William Morrow and Company, Inc., 1985).

FOX, ALICE, *Virginia Woolf and the English Renaissance* (Oxford: Clarendon Press, 1990).

GLENDENNING, VICTORIA, *Vita: The Life of V. Sackville-West* (London: Weidenfeld & Nicolson, 1983).

KNOPP, SHERRON E., ' "If I Saw You Would You Kiss Me?": Sapphism and the Subversiveness of Virginia Woolf's *Orlando*', *PMLA* 103, no. 1 (Jan. 1988), 24–33.

LITTLE, JUDY, '(En)gendering Laughter: Woolf's *Orlando* as Contraband in the Age of Joyce', *Women's Studies*, 15, nos. 1–3 (1988), 179–91.

LOVE, JEAN O., '*Orlando* and its Genesis: Venturing and Experimenting in Art, Love, and Sex', in Ralph Freedman (ed.), *Virginia Woolf: Revaluation and Continuity* (Berkeley: University of California Press, 1980), 189–218.

MOORE, MADELINE, '*Orlando*: An Imaginative Answer', in *The Short Season Between Two Silences: The Mystical and the Political in Virginia Woolf* (Boston: George Allen and Unwin, 1984).

——'*Orlando*: An Edition of the Manuscript', in *Twentieth-Century Literature*, 25, nos. 3–4 (Fall/Winter 1979), 303–45.

NICOLSON, NIGEL, *Portrait of a Marriage* (London: Weidenfeld & Nicolson, 1973).

SACKVILLE-WEST, V., *Knole and the Sackvilles* (1922; rpt. Sevenoaks: Ernest Benn, 1965).

SQUIER, SUSAN, 'Tradition and Revision in Woolf's *Orlando*: Defoe and "The Jessamy Brides" ', *Women's Studies*, 12, no. 2 (1986), 167–77.

WILSON, J. J., 'Why is *Orlando* Difficult?', in Jane Marcus (ed.), *New Feminist Essays on Virginia Woolf* (London: Macmillan, 1981), 170–84.

A CHRONOLOGY OF VIRGINIA WOOLF

Life	*Historical and Cultural Background*
1882 (25 Jan.) Adeline Virginia Stephen (VW) born at 22 Hyde Park Gate, London.	Deaths of Darwin, Trollope, D. G. Rossetti; Joyce born; Stravinsky born; Married Women's Property Act; Society for Psychical Research founded.
1895 (5 May) Death of mother, Julia Stephen; VW's first breakdown occurs soon afterwards.	Death of T. H. Huxley; X-rays discovered; invention of the cinematograph; wireless telegraphy invented; arrest, trials, and conviction of Oscar Wilde. Wilde, *The Importance of Being Earnest* and *An Ideal Husband* Wells, *The Time Machine*
1896 (Nov.) Travels in France with sister Vanessa.	Death of William Morris; *Daily Mail* started. Hardy, *Jude the Obscure* Housman, *A Shropshire Lad*
1897 (10 April) Marriage of half-sister Stella; (19 July) death of Stella; (Nov.) VW learning Greek and History at King's College, London.	Queen Victoria's Diamond Jubilee; Tate Gallery opens. Stoker, *Dracula* James, *What Maisie Knew*
1898	Deaths of Gladstone and Lewis Carroll; radium and plutonium discovered. Wells, *The War of the Worlds*
1899 (30 Oct.) VW's brother Thoby goes up to Trinity College, Cambridge, where he forms friendships with Lytton Strachey, Leonard Woolf, Clive Bell, and others of the future Bloomsbury Group (VW's younger brother Adrian follows him to Trinity in 1902).	Boer War begins. Births of Bowen and Coward. Symons, *The Symbolist Movement in Literature* James, *The Awkward Age* Freud, *The Interpretation of Dreams*
1900	Deaths of Nietzsche, Wilde, and Ruskin; *Daily Express* started; Planck announces quantum theory; Boxer Rising. Conrad, *Lord Jim*

1901		Death of Queen Victoria; accession of Edward VII; first wireless communication between Europe and USA; 'World's Classics' series begun. Kipling, *Kim*
1902	VW starts private lessons in Greek with Janet Case.	End of Boer War; British Academy founded; *Encyclopaedia Britannica* (10th edn.); *TLS* started. Bennett, *Anna of the Five Towns* James, *The Wings of the Dove*
1903		Deaths of Gissing and Spencer; *Daily Mirror* started; Wright brothers make their first aeroplane flight; Emmeline Pankhurst founds Women's Social and Political Union. Butler, *The Way of All Flesh* James, *The Ambassadors* Moore, *Principia Ethica*
1904	(22 Feb.) Death of father, Sir Leslie Stephen. In spring, VW travels to Italy with Vanessa and friend Violet Dickinson. (10 May) VW has second nervous breakdown and is ill for three months. Moves to 46 Gordon Square. (14 Dec.) VW's first publication appears.	Deaths of Christina Rossetti and Chekhov; Russo-Japanese War; *Entente Cordiale* between Britain and France. Chesterton, *The Napoleon of Notting Hill* Conrad, *Nostromo* James, *The Golden Bowl*
1905	(March, April) Travels in Portugal and Spain. Writes reviews and teaches once a week at Morley College, London.	Einstein, *Special Theory of Relativity*; Sartre born. Shaw, *Major Barbara* and *Man and Superman* Wells, *Kipps* Forster, *Where Angels Fear to Tread*
1906	(Sept. and Oct.) Travels in Greece. (20 Nov.) Death of Thoby Stephen.	Death of Ibsen; Beckett born; Liberal Government elected; Campbell-Bannerman Prime Minister; launch of HMS *Dreadnought*.
1907	(7 Feb.) Marriage of Vanessa to Clive Bell. VW moves with Adrian to 29 Fitzroy Square. At work on her first novel, 'Melymbrosia' (working title for *The Voyage Out*).	Auden born; Anglo-Russian Entente. Synge, *The Playboy of the Western World* Conrad, *The Secret Agent* Forster, *The Longest Journey*

1908	(Sept.) Visits Italy with the Bells.	Asquith Prime Minister; Old Age Pensions Act; Elgar's First Symphony. Bennett, *The Old Wives' Tale* Forster, *A Room with a View* Chesterton, *The Man Who Was Thursday*
1909	(17 Feb.) Lytton Strachey proposes marriage. (30 March) First meets Lady Ottoline Morrell. (April) Visits Florence. (Aug.) Visits Bayreuth and Dresden.	Death of Meredith; 'People's Budget'; English Channel flown by Blériot. Wells, *Tono-Bungay* Masterman, *The Condition of England* Marinetti, *Futurist Manifesto*
1910	(Jan.) Works for women's suffrage. (June–Aug.) Spends time in a nursing home at Twickenham.	Deaths of Edward VII, Tolstoy, and Florence Nightingale; accession of George V; *Encyclopaedia Britannica* (11th edn.); Roger Fry's Post-Impressionist Exhibition. Bennett, *Clayhanger* Forster, *Howards End* Yeats, *The Green Helmet* Wells, *The History of Mr Polly*
1911	(April) Travels to Turkey, where Vanessa is ill. (Nov.) Moves to 38 Brunswick Square, sharing house with Adrian, John Maynard Keynes, Duncan Grant, and Leonard Woolf.	National Insurance Act; Suffragette riots. Conrad, *Under Western Eyes* Wells, *The New Machiavelli* Lawrence, *The White Peacock*
1912	Rents Asheham House. (Feb.) Spends some days in Twickenham nursing home. (10 Aug.) Marriage to Leonard Woolf. Honeymoon in Provence, Spain, and Italy. (Oct.) Moves to 13 Clifford's Inn, London.	Second Post-Impressionist Exhibition; Suffragettes active; strikes by dockers, coal-miners, and transport workers; Irish Home Rule Bill rejected by Lords; sinking of SS *Titanic*; death of Scott in the Antarctic; *Daily Herald* started. English translations of Chekhov and Dostoevsky begin to appear.
1913	(March) MS of *The Voyage Out* delivered to publisher. Unwell most of summer. (9 Sept.) Suicide attempt. Remains under care of nurses and husband for rest of year.	*New Statesman* started; Suffragettes active. Lawrence, *Sons and Lovers*

1914	(16 Feb.) Last nurse leaves. Moves to Richmond, Surrey.	Irish Home Rule Bill passed by Parliament; First World War begins (4 Aug.); Dylan Thomas born. Lewis, *Blast* Joyce, *Dubliners* Yeats, *Responsibilities* Hardy, *Satires of Circumstance* Bell, *Art*
1915	Purchase of Hogarth House, Richmond. (26 March) *The Voyage Out* published. (April, May) Bout of violent madness; under care of nurses until November.	Death of Rupert Brooke; Einstein, *General Theory of Relativity*; Second Battle of Ypres; Dardanelles Campaign; sinking of SS *Lusitania*; air attacks on London. Ford, *The Good Soldier* Lawrence, *The Rainbow* Brooke, *1914 and Other Poems* Richardson, *Pointed Roofs*
1916	(17 Oct.) Lectures to Richmond branch of the Women's Co-operative Guild. Regular work for *TLS*.	Death of James; Lloyd George Prime Minister; First Battle of the Somme; Battle of Verdun; Gallipoli Campaign; Easter Rising in Dublin. Joyce, *Portrait of the Artist as a Young Man*
1917	(July) Hogarth Press commences publication with 'The Mark on the Wall' and a story by Leonard Woolf. VW begins work on *Night and Day*.	Death of Edward Thomas. Third Battle of Ypres (Passchendaele); T. E. Lawrence's campaigns in Arabia; USA enters the War; Revolution in Russia (Feb., Oct.); Balfour Declaration. Eliot, *Prufrock and Other Observations*
1918	Writes reviews and *Night and Day*; also sets type for the Hogarth Press. (15 Nov.) First meets T. S. Eliot.	Death of Owen; Second Battle of the Somme; final German offensive collapses; Armistice with Germany (11 Nov.); Franchise Act grants vote to women over 30; influenza pandemic kills millions. Lewis, *Tarr* Hopkins, *Poems* Strachey, *Eminent Victorians*
1919	(1 July) Purchase of Monk's House, Rodmell, Sussex. (20 Oct.) *Night and Day* published.	Treaty of Versailles; Alcock and Brown fly the Atlantic; National Socialists founded in Germany. Sinclair, *Mary Olivier* Shaw, *Heartbreak House*
1920	Works on journalism and *Jacob's Room*.	League of Nations established. Pound, *Hugh Selwyn Mauberley* Lawrence, *Women in Love* Eliot, *The Sacred Wood* Fry, *Vision and Design*

1921	(7 or 8 April) *Monday or Tuesday* published. Ill for summer months. (4 Nov.) Finishes *Jacob's Room*.	Irish Free State founded. Huxley, *Crome Yellow*
1922	(Jan. to May) Ill. (14 Dec.) First meets Vita Sackville-West. (24 Oct.) *Jacob's Room* published.	Bonar Law Prime Minister; Mussolini forms Fascist Government in Italy; death of Proust; *Encyclopaedia Britannica* (12th edn.); *Criterion* founded; BBC founded; Irish Free State proclaimed. Eliot, *The Waste Land* Galsworthy, *The Forsyte Saga* Joyce, *Ulysses* Mansfield, *The Garden Party* Wittgenstein, *Tractatus Logico-Philosophicus*
1923	(March, April) Visits Spain. Works on 'The Hours', the first version of *Mrs Dalloway*.	Baldwin Prime Minister; BBC radio begins broadcasting (Nov.); death of K. Mansfield.
1924	Purchase of lease on 52 Tavistock Square, Bloomsbury. Gives lecture that becomes 'Mr Bennett and Mrs Brown'. (8 Oct.) Finishes *Mrs Dalloway*.	First (minority) Labour Government; Ramsay MacDonald Prime Minister; deaths of Lenin, Kafka, and Conrad. Ford, *Some Do Not* Forster, *A Passage to India* O'Casey, *Juno and the Paycock* Coward, *The Vortex*
1925	(23 April) *The Common Reader* published. (14 May) *Mrs Dalloway* published. Ill during summer.	Gerhardie, *The Polyglots* Ford, *No More Parades* Huxley, *Those Barren Leaves* Whitehead, *Science and the Modern World*
1926	(Jan.) Unwell with German measles. Writes *To the Lighthouse*.	General Strike (3–12 May); *Encyclopaedia Britannica* (13th edn.); first television demonstration. Ford, *A Man Could Stand Up* Tawney, *Religion and the Rise of Capitalism*
1927	(March, April) Travels in France and Italy. (5 May) *To the Lighthouse* published. (5 Oct.) Begins *Orlando*.	Lindbergh flies solo across the Atlantic; first 'talkie' films.
1928	(11 Oct.) *Orlando* published. Delivers lectures at Cambridge on which she bases *A Room of One's Own*.	Death of Hardy; votes for women over 21. Yeats, *The Tower* Lawrence, *Lady Chatterley's Lover* Waugh, *Decline and Fall* Sherriff, *Journey's End* Ford, *Last Post* Huxley, *Point Counter Point* Bell, *Civilization*

1929	(Jan.) Travels to Berlin. (24 Oct.) *A Room of One's Own* published.	2nd Labour Government, MacDonald Prime Minister; collapse of New York Stock Exchange; start of world economic depression. Graves, *Goodbye to All That* Aldington, *Death of a Hero* Green, *Living*
1930	(20 Feb.) First meets Ethel Smyth; (29 May) Finishes first version of *The Waves*.	Mass unemployment; television starts in USA; deaths of Lawrence and Conan Doyle. Auden, *Poems* Eliot, *Ash Wednesday* Waugh, *Vile Bodies* Coward, *Private Lives* Lewis, *Apes of God*
1931	(April) Car tour through France. (8 Oct.) *The Waves* published. Writes *Flush*.	Formation of National Government; abandonment of Gold Standard; death of Bennett; Japan invades China.
1932	(21 Jan.) Death of Lytton Strachey. (13 Oct.) *The Common Reader*, 2nd series, published. Begins *The Years*, at this point called 'The Pargiters'.	Roosevelt becomes President of USA; hunger marches start in Britain; *Scrutiny* starts. Huxley, *Brave New World*
1933	(May) Car tour of France and Italy. (5 Oct.) *Flush* published.	Deaths of Galsworthy and George Moore; Hitler becomes Chancellor of Germany. Orwell, *Down and Out in Paris and London* Wells, *The Shape of Things to Come*
1934	Works on *The Years*. (9 Sept.) Death of Roger Fry.	Waugh, *A Handful of Dust* Graves, *I, Claudius* Beckett, *More Pricks than Kicks* Toynbee, *A Study of History*
1935	Rewrites *The Years*. (May) Car tour of Holland, Germany, and Italy.	George V's Silver Jubilee; Baldwin Prime Minister of National Government; Germany re-arms; Italian invasion of Abyssinia (Ethiopia). Isherwood, *Mr Norris Changes Trains* T. S. Eliot, *Murder in the Cathedral*
1936	(May–Oct.) Ill. Finishes *The Years*. Begins *Three Guineas*.	Death of George V; accession of Edward VIII; abdication crisis; accession of George VI; Civil War breaks out in Spain; first of the Moscow show trials; Germany re-occupies the Rhineland; BBC television begins (2 Nov); deaths of Chesterton, Kipling, and Houseman. Orwell, *Keep the Aspidistra Flying*

1937   (15 March) *The Years* published. Begins *Roger Fry: A Biography*. (18 July) Death in Spanish Civil War of Julian Bell, son of Vanessa.

Chamberlain Prime Minister; destruction of Guernica; death of Barrie.
Orwell, *The Road to Wigan Pier*

1938   (2 June) *Three Guineas* published. Works on *Roger Fry*, and begins to envisage *Between the Acts*.

German *Anschluss* with Austria; Munich agreement; dismemberment of Czechoslovakia; first jet engine.
Beckett, *Murphy*
Bowen, *The Death of the Heart*
Greene, *Brighton Rock*

1939   VW moves to 37 Mecklenburgh Square, but lives mostly at Monk's House. Works on *Between the Acts*. Meets Freud in London.

End of Civil War in Spain; Russo-German pact; Germany invades Poland (Sept.); Britain and France declare war on Germany (3 Sept.); deaths of Freud, Yeats, and Ford.
Joyce, *Finnegans Wake*
Isherwood, *Goodbye to Berlin*

1940   (25 July) *Roger Fry* published. (10 Sept.) Mecklenburgh Square house bombed. (18 Oct.) Witnesses the ruins of 52 Tavistock Square, destroyed by bombs. (23 Nov.) Finishes *Between the Acts*.

Germany invades north-west Europe; fall of France; evacuation of British troops from Dunkirk; Battle of Britain; beginning of 'the Blitz'; National Government under Churchill.

1941   (26 Feb.) Revises *Between the Acts*. Becomes ill. (28 March) Drowns herself in River Ouse, near Monk's House. (July) *Between the Acts* published.

Germany invades USSR; Japanese destroy US Fleet at Pearl Harbor; USA enters war; death of Joyce.

Orlando

A BIOGRAPHY

TO

V. SACKVILLE WEST

Preface*

MANY friends have helped me in writing this book. Some are dead and so illustrious that I scarcely dare name them, yet no one can read or write without being perpetually in the debt of Defoe, Sir Thomas Browne, Sterne, Sir Walter Scott, Lord Macaulay, Emily Brontë, De Quincey, and Walter Pater,*—to name the first that come to mind. Others are alive, and though perhaps as illustrious in their own way, are less formidable for that very reason. I am specially indebted to Mr C. P. Sanger, without whose knowledge of the law of real property this book could never have been written. Mr Sydney-Turner's wide and peculiar erudition has saved me, I hope, some lamentable blunders. I have had the advantage—how great I alone can estimate—of Mr Arthur Waley's knowledge of Chinese. Madame Lopokova (Mrs J. M. Keynes) has been at hand to correct my Russian. To the unrivalled sympathy and imagination of Mr Roger Fry I owe whatever understanding of the art of painting I may possess. I have, I hope, profited in another department by the singularly penetrating, if severe, criticism of my nephew Mr Julian Bell. Miss M. K. Snowdon's indefatigable researches in the archives of Harrogate and Cheltenham were none the less arduous for being vain. Other friends have helped me in ways too various to specify. I must content myself with naming Mr Angus Davidson; Mrs Cartwright; Miss Janet Case; Lord Berners (whose knowledge of Elizabethan music has proved invaluable); Mr Francis Birrell; my brother, Dr Adrian Stephen; Mr F. L. Lucas; Mr and Mrs Desmond Maccarthy; that most inspiriting of critics, my brother-in-law, Mr Clive Bell; Mr G. H. Rylands; Lady Colefax; Miss Nellie Boxall; Mr J. M. Keynes; Mr Hugh Walpole; Miss Violet Dickinson; the Hon. Edward Sackville West; Mr and Mrs St John Hutchinson; Mr Duncan Grant; Mr and Mrs Stephen Tomlin; Mr and Lady Ottoline Morrell; my mother-in-law, Mrs Sydney Woolf; Mr Osbert Sitwell; Madame Jacques Raverat; Colonel Cory Bell; Miss Valerie Taylor; Mr J. T. Sheppard; Mr and Mrs T. S. Eliot; Miss Ethel Sands; Miss Nan Hudson; my nephew Mr Quentin Bell (an old and valued collaborator in fiction); Mr Raymond Mortimer; Lady Gerald Wellesley; Mr Lytton Strachey; the Viscountess Cecil; Miss Hope Mirrlees; Mr E. M. Forster; the Hon. Harold Nicolson; and my sister, Vanessa Bell—but the list threatens to grow too long and is already far too distinguished. For while it rouses in me memories of the pleasantest kind it will inevitably wake expectations in the reader which the book itself can only disappoint. Therefore I will conclude by thanking the officials of the British Museum and Record Office for their wonted courtesy; my niece Miss Angelica Bell, for a service which none but she could have rendered; and my husband for the patience with which he has invariably helped my researches and for the profound historical knowledge to which these pages owe whatever degree of accuracy they may attain. Finally, I would thank, had I not lost his name and address, a gentleman in America, who has generously and gratuitously corrected the punctuation, the botany, the entomology, the geography, and the chronology of previous works of mine and will, I hope, not spare his services on the present occasion.

Contents

Illustrations

CHAPTER I

HE—for there could be no doubt of his sex, though the fashion of the time did something to disguise it—was in the act of slicing at the head of a Moor* which swung from the rafters. It was the colour of an old football, and more or less the shape of one, save for the sunken cheeks and a strand or two of coarse, dry hair, like the hair on a cocoanut. Orlando's father, or perhaps his grandfather, had struck it from the shoulders of a vast Pagan who had started up under the moon in the barbarian fields of Africa; and now it swung, gently, perpetually, in the breeze which never ceased blowing through the attic rooms of the gigantic house of the lord who had slain him.

Orlando's fathers had ridden in fields of asphodel, and stony fields, and fields watered by strange rivers, and they had struck many heads of many colours off many shoulders, and brought them back to hang from the rafters. So too would Orlando, he vowed. But since he was sixteen only, and too young to ride with them in Africa or France, he would steal away from his mother and the peacocks in the garden and go to his attic room and there lunge and plunge and slice the air with his blade. Sometimes he cut the cord so that the skull bumped on the floor and he had to string it up again, fastening it with some chivalry* almost out of reach so that his enemy grinned at him through shrunk, black lips triumphantly. The skull swung to and fro, for the house, at the top of which he lived, was so vast that there seemed trapped in it the wind itself, blowing this way, blowing that way, winter and summer. The green arras with the hunters on it moved perpetually. His fathers had been noble since they had been at all. They came out of the northern mists wearing coronets on their heads. Were not the bars of darkness in the room, and the yellow pools which chequered the floor, made by the sun falling through the stained glass of a vast coat of arms in the window? Orlando stood now in the midst of the yellow body of an heraldic leopard. When he put his hand on the window-sill to push the window open, it was instantly coloured red, blue, and yellow like a butterfly's wing. Thus, those who like symbols, and have a turn for the deciphering of them, might observe that though the shapely legs, the handsome body, and the well-set shoulders were all of them decorated with various tints of heraldic light, Orlando's face, as he threw the window open, was lit solely by the sun itself. A more candid, sullen face it would be impossible to find. Happy the mother who bears, happier still the biographer* who records the life of such a one! Never need she vex herself, nor he invoke the help of novelist or poet. From deed to deed, from glory to glory, from office to office he must go, his scribe following after, till they reach whatever seat it may be that is the height of their desire. Orlando, to look at, was cut out precisely for some such career. The red of the cheeks was covered with peach down; the down on the lips was only a little thicker than the down on the cheeks. The lips themselves were short and slightly drawn back over teeth of an exquisite and almond whiteness. Nothing disturbed the arrowy nose in its short, tense flight; the hair was dark, the ears small, and fitted closely to the head. But, alas, that these catalogues of youthful beauty cannot end without mentioning forehead and eyes. Alas, that people are seldom born devoid of all three; for directly we glance at Orlando standing by the window, we must admit that he had eyes like drenched violets, so large that the water seemed to have brimmed in them and widened them; and a brow like the swelling of a marble dome pressed between the two blank medallions which were his temples.* Directly we glance at eyes and forehead, thus do we rhapsodize. Directly we glance* at eyes and forehead, we have to admit a thousand disagreeables which it is the aim of every good biographer to ignore. Sights disturbed him, like that of his mother, a very beautiful lady in green walking out to feed the peacocks with Twitchett, her maid, behind her: sights exalted him—the birds and the trees; and made him in love with death—the evening sky, the homing rooks; and so, mounting up the spiral stairway into his brain—which was a roomy one—all these sights, and the garden sounds too, the hammer beating, the wood chopping, began that riot and confusion of the passions and emotions which every good biographer detests. But to continue—Orlando slowly drew in his head, sat down at the table, and, with the half-conscious air of one doing what they do every day of their lives at this hour, took out a writing book labelled 'Æthelbert: A Tragedy in Five Acts',* and dipped an old stained goose quill in the ink.

Soon he had covered ten pages and more with poetry. He was fluent, evidently, but he was abstract. Vice, Crime, Misery were the personages of his drama; there were Kings and Queens of impossible territories; horrid plots confounded them; noble sentiments suffused them; there was never a word said as he himself would have said it, but all was turned with a fluency and sweetness which, considering his age—he was not yet seventeen—and that the sixteenth century had still some years of its course to run, were remarkable enough. At last, however, he came to a halt. He was describing, as all young poets are for ever describing, nature, and in order to match the shade of green precisely he looked (and here he showed more audacity than most) at the thing itself, which happened to be a laurel bush growing beneath the window. After that, of course, he could write no more. Green in nature is one thing, green in literature another. Nature and letters seem to have a natural antipathy; bring them together and they tear each other to pieces. The shade of green Orlando now saw spoilt his rhyme and split his metre. Moreover, nature has tricks of her own. Once look out of a window at bees among flowers, at a yawning dog, at the sun setting, once think 'how many more suns shall I see set', etc. etc. (the thought is too well known to be worth writing out) and one drops the pen, takes one's cloak, strides out of the room, and catches one's foot on a painted chest as one does so. For Orlando was a trifle clumsy.*

He was careful to avoid meeting anyone. There was Stubbs,* the gardener, coming along the path. He hid behind a tree till he had passed. He let himself out at a little gate in the garden wall. He skirted all stables, kennels, breweries, carpenters' shops, washhouses, places where they make tallow candles, kill oxen, forge horse-shoes, stitch jerkins—for the house was a town ringing with men at work at their various crafts—and gained the ferny path leading uphill through the park unseen. There is perhaps a kinship among qualities; one draws another along with it; and the biographer should here call attention to the fact that this clumsiness is often mated with a love of solitude. Having stumbled over a chest, Orlando naturally loved solitary places, vast views, and to feel himself for ever and ever and ever alone.

So, after a long silence, 'I am alone', he breathed at last, opening his lips for the first time in this record. He had walked very quickly uphill through ferns and hawthorn bushes, startling deer and wild birds, to a place crowned by a single oak tree.* It was very high, so high indeed that nineteen English counties could be seen beneath; and on clear days thirty or perhaps forty, if the weather was very fine. Sometimes one could see the English Channel,* wave reiterating upon wave. Rivers could be seen and pleasure boats gliding on them; and galleons setting out to sea; and armadas with puffs of smoke from which came the dull thud of cannon firing; and forts on the coast; and castles among the meadows; and here a watch tower; and there a fortress; and again some vast mansion like that of Orlando's father, massed like a town in the valley circled by walls. To the east there were the spires of London and the smoke of the city; and perhaps on the very sky line, when the wind was in the right quarter, the craggy top and serrated edges of Snowdon herself showed mountainous* among the clouds. For a moment Orlando stood counting, gazing, recognizing. That was his father's house; that his uncle's. His aunt owned those three great turrets among the trees there. The heath was theirs and the forest; the pheasant and the deer, the fox, the badger, and the butterfly.

He sighed profoundly, and flung himself—there was a passion in his movements which deserves the word—on the earth at the foot of the oak tree. He loved, beneath all this summer transiency, to feel the earth's spine beneath him; for such he took the hard root of the oak tree to be; or, for image followed image, it was the back of a great horse that he was riding; or the deck of a tumbling ship—it was anything indeed, so long as it was hard, for he felt the need of something which he could attach his floating heart to; the heart that tugged at his side; the heart that seemed filled with spiced and amorous gales every evening about this time when he walked out. To the oak tree he tied it* and as he lay there, gradually the flutter in and about him stilled itself; the little leaves hung, the deer stopped; the pale summer clouds stayed; his limbs grew heavy on the ground; and he lay so still that by degrees the deer stepped nearer and the rooks wheeled round him and the swallows dipped and circled and the dragon-flies shot past, as if all the fertility and amorous activity of a summer's evening were woven web-like about his body.

After an hour or so—the sun was rapidly sinking, the white clouds had turned red, the hills were violet, the woods purple, the valleys black—a trumpet sounded. Orlando leapt to his feet. The shrill sound came from the valley. It came from a dark spot down there; a spot compact and mapped out; a maze; a town, yet girt about with walls; it came from the heart of his own great house in the valley, which, dark before, even as he looked and the single trumpet duplicated and reduplicated itself with other shriller sounds, lost its darkness and became pierced with lights. Some were small hurrying lights, as if servants

[19]

dashed along corridors to answer summonses: others were high and lustrous lights, as if they burnt in empty banqueting-halls made ready to receive guests who had not come; and others dipped and waved and sank and rose, as if held in the hands of troops of serving men, bending, kneeling, rising, receiving, guarding, and escorting with all dignity indoors a great Princess alighting from her chariot. Coaches turned and wheeled in the courtyard. Horses tossed their plumes. The Queen had come.

Orlando looked no more. He dashed downhill. He let himself in at a wicket gate. He tore up the winding staircase. He reached his room. He tossed his stockings to one side of the room, his jerkin to the other. He dipped his head. He scoured his hands. He pared his finger nails. With no more than six inches of looking-glass and a pair of old candles to help him, he had thrust on crimson breeches, lace collar, waistcoat of taffeta, and shoes with rosettes on them as big as double dahlias in less than ten minutes by the stable clock. He was ready. He was flushed. He was excited. But he was terribly late.

By short cuts known to him, he made his way now through the vast congeries of rooms and staircases to the banqueting-hall, five acres distant on the other side of the house. But half-way there, in the back quarters where the servants lived, he stopped. The door of Mrs Stewkley's sitting-room stood open— she was gone, doubtless, with all her keys to wait

upon her mistress. But there, sitting at the servants'
dinner table* with a tankard beside him and paper in
front of him, sat a rather fat, shabby man, whose ruff
was a thought dirty, and whose clothes were of
hodden brown.* He held a pen in his hand, but he
was not writing. He seemed in the act of rolling some
thought up and down, to and fro in his mind till it
gathered shape or momentum to his liking. His eyes,
globed and clouded like some green stone of curious
texture, were fixed. He did not see Orlando. For all
his hurry, Orlando stopped dead. Was this a poet?
Was he writing poetry? 'Tell me', he wanted to say,
'everything in the whole world'—for he had the
wildest, most absurd, extravagant ideas about poets
and poetry—but how speak to a man who does not
see you? who sees ogres, satyrs, perhaps the depths
of the sea instead? So Orlando stood gazing while
the man turned his pen in his fingers, this way and
that way; and gazed and mused; and then, very
quickly, wrote half-a-dozen lines and looked up.
Whereupon Orlando, overcome with shyness, darted
off and reached the banqueting-hall only just in time
to sink upon his knees and, hanging his head in
confusion, to offer a bowl of rose water to the great
Queen herself.

Such was his shyness that he saw no more of her
than her ringed hands in water; but it was enough. It
was a memorable hand; a thin hand with long fingers
always curling as if round orb or sceptre; a nervous,

crabbed, sickly hand; a commanding hand too; a hand that had only to raise itself for a head to fall; a hand, he guessed, attached to an old body that smelt like a cupboard in which furs are kept in camphor; which body was yet caparisoned in all sorts of brocades and gems; and held itself very upright though perhaps in pain from sciatica; and never flinched though strung together by a thousand fears; and the Queen's eyes were light yellow. All this he felt as the great rings flashed in the water and then something pressed his hair—which, perhaps, accounts for his seeing nothing more likely to be of use to a historian. And in truth, his mind was such a welter of opposites—of the night and the blazing candles, of the shabby poet and the great Queen, of silent fields and the clatter of serving men—that he could see nothing; or only a hand.

By the same showing, the Queen herself can have seen only a head. But if it is possible from a hand to deduce a body, informed with all the attributes of a great Queen, her crabbedness, courage, frailty, and terror, surely a head can be as fertile, looked down upon from a chair of state by a lady whose eyes were always, if the waxworks at the Abbey* are to be trusted, wide open. The long, curled hair, the dark head bent so reverently, so innocently before her, implied a pair of the finest legs* that a young noble-man has ever stood upright upon; and violet eyes; and a heart of gold; and loyalty and manly charm—

all qualities which the old woman loved the more the more they failed her. For she was growing old and worn and bent before her time. The sound of cannon was always in her ears. She saw always the glistening poison drop and the long stiletto.* As she sat at table she listened; she heard the guns in the Channel;* she dreaded—was that a curse, was that a whisper? Innocence, simplicity, were all the more dear to her for the dark background she set them against. And it was that same night, so tradition has it,* when Orlando was sound asleep, that she made over formally, putting her hand and seal finally to the parchment, the gift of the great monastic house that had been the Archbishop's and then the King's to Orlando's father.

Orlando slept all night in ignorance. He had been kissed by a queen without knowing it. And perhaps, for women's hearts are intricate, it was his ignorance and the start he gave when her lips touched him that kept the memory of her young cousin (for they had blood in common) green in her mind. At any rate, two years of this quiet country life had not passed, and Orlando had written no more perhaps than twenty tragedies and a dozen histories and a score of sonnets when a message came that he was to attend the Queen at Whitehall.

'Here', she said, watching him advance down the long gallery towards her, 'comes my innocent!' (There was a serenity about him always which had the look of innocence when, technically, the word was no longer applicable.)

'Come!' she said. She was sitting bolt upright beside the fire. And she held him a foot's pace from her and looked him up and down. Was she matching her speculations the other night with the truth now visible? Did she find her guesses justified? Eyes, mouth, nose, breast, hips, hands—she ran them over; her lips twitched visibly as she looked; but when she saw his legs she laughed out loud. He was the very image of a noble gentleman. But inwardly? She flashed her yellow hawk's eyes upon him as if she would pierce his soul. The young man withstood her gaze blushing only a damask rose as became him. Strength, grace, romance, folly, poetry, youth—she read him like a page. Instantly she plucked a ring from her finger (the joint was swollen rather) and as she fitted it to his, named him her Treasurer and Steward; next hung about him chains of office; and bidding him bend his knee, tied round it at the slenderest part the jewelled order of the Garter. Nothing after that was denied him. When she drove in state he rode at her carriage door. She sent him to Scotland on a sad embassy to the unhappy Queen.* He was about to sail for the Polish wars when she recalled him. For how could she bear to think of that tender flesh torn and that curly head rolled in the dust? She kept him with her. At the height of her triumph when the guns were booming at the Tower and the air was thick enough with gunpowder to make one sneeze and the huzzas of the people rang beneath the windows, she pulled him down among the cushions where her women had laid her (she was so worn and old) and made him bury his face in that astonishing composition—she had not changed her dress for a month—which smelt for all the world, he thought, recalling his boyish memory, like some old cabinet at home where his mother's furs were stored. He rose, half suffocated from the embrace. 'This', she breathed, 'is my victory!'—even as a rocket roared up and dyed her cheeks scarlet.

For the old woman loved him. And the Queen, who knew a man when she saw one, though not, it is said, in the usual way, plotted for him a splendid ambitious career. Lands were given him, houses assigned him. He was to be the son of her old age; the limb of her infirmity; the oak tree on which she leant her degradation. She croaked out these promises and strange domineering tendernesses (they were at Richmond now) sitting bolt upright in her stiff brocades by the fire which, however high they piled it, never kept her warm.

Meanwhile, the long winter months drew on. Every tree in the Park was lined with frost. The river ran sluggishly. One day when the snow was on the ground and the dark panelled rooms were full of shadows and the stags were barking in the Park, she saw in the mirror, which she kept for fear of spies always by her, through the door, which she kept for fear of murderers always open, a boy—could it be Orlando?—kissing a girl—who in the Devil's name was the brazen hussy? Snatching at her golden-hilted sword she struck violently at the mirror. The glass crashed; people came running; she was lifted and set in her chair again; but she was stricken after that and groaned much, as her days wore to an end, of man's treachery.

It was Orlando's fault perhaps; yet, after all, are we to blame Orlando? The age was the Elizabethan; their morals were not ours; nor their poets; nor their climate; nor their vegetables even. Everything was different. The weather itself, the heat and cold of summer and winter, was, we may believe, of another temper altogether. The brilliant amorous day was divided as sheerly from the night as land from water. Sunsets were redder and more intense; dawns were whiter and more auroral. Of our crepuscular half-lights and lingering twilights they knew nothing. The rain fell vehemently, or not at all. The sun blazed or there was darkness. Translating this to the spiritual regions as their wont is, the poets sang beautifully how roses fade and petals fall. The moment is brief they sang; the moment is over; one long night is then to be slept by all. As for using the artifices of the greenhouse or conservatory to prolong or preserve these fresh pinks and roses, that was not their way. The withered intricacies and ambiguities of our more gradual and doubtful age were unknown to them. Violence was all. The flower bloomed and faded. The sun rose and sank. The lover loved and went. And what the poets said in rhyme, the young translated into practice. Girls were roses, and their seasons were short as the flowers'. Plucked they must be before nightfall; for the day was brief and the day was all. Thus, if Orlando followed the leading of the climate, of the poets, of the age itself, and plucked his flower in the window-seat even with the snow on the ground and the Queen vigilant in the corridor, we can scarcely bring ourselves to blame him. He was young; he was boyish; he did but as nature bade him do. As for the girl, we know no more than Queen Elizabeth herself did what her name was. It may have been Doris, Chloris, Delia, or Diana, for he made rhymes to them all in turn; equally, she may have been a court lady, or some serving maid. For Orlando's taste was broad; he was no lover of garden flowers only; the wild and the weeds even had always a fascination for him.

Here, indeed, we lay bare rudely, as a biographer may, a curious trait in him, to be accounted for, perhaps, by the fact that a certain grandmother of his had worn a smock and carried milkpails. Some grains of the Kentish or Sussex earth were mixed with the thin, fine fluid which came to him from Normandy. He held that the mixture of brown earth and blue blood was a good one. Certain it is that he had always a liking for low company, especially for that of lettered people whose wits so often keep them under, as if there were the sympathy of blood between them. At this season of his life, when his head brimmed with rhymes and he never went to bed without striking off some conceit, the cheek of an innkeeper's daughter seemed fresher and the wit of a gamekeeper's niece seemed quicker than those of the ladies at Court. Hence, he began going frequently to Wapping Old Stairs and the beer gardens at night, wrapped in a grey cloak to hide the star at his neck and the garter at his knee. There, with a mug before him, among the sanded alleys and bowling greens and all the simple architecture of such places, he listened to sailors' stories of hardship and horror and cruelty on the Spanish main; how some had lost their toes, others their noses—for the spoken story was never so rounded or so finely coloured as the written. Especially he loved to hear them volley forth their songs of the Azores, while the parrakeets, which they had brought from those parts, pecked at the rings in their ears, tapped with their hard acquisitive beaks at the rubies on their fingers, and swore as vilely as their masters. The women were scarcely less bold in their speech and less free in their manner than the birds. They perched on his knee, flung their arms round his neck and, guessing that something out of the common lay hid beneath his duffle cloak, were quite as eager to come at the truth of the matter as Orlando himself.

Nor was opportunity lacking. The river was astir

early and late with barges, wherries, and craft of all description. Every day sailed to sea some fine ship bound for the Indies; now and again another blackened and ragged with hairy unknown men on board crept painfully to anchor. No one missed a boy or girl if they dallied a little on the water after sunset; or raised an eyebrow if gossip had seen them sleeping soundly among the treasure sacks safe in each other's arms. Such indeed was the adventure that befel Orlando, Sukey, and the Earl of Cumberland. The day was hot; their loves had been active; they had fallen asleep among the rubies. Late that night the Earl, whose fortunes were much bound up in the Spanish ventures, came to check the booty alone with a lantern. He flashed the light on a barrel. He started back with an oath. Twined about the cask two spirits lay sleeping. Superstitious by nature, and his conscience laden with many a crime, the Earl took the couple—they were wrapped in a red cloak, and Sukey's bosom was almost as white as the eternal snows of Orlando's poetry—for a phantom sprung from the graves of drowned sailors to upbraid him. He crossed himself. He vowed repentance. The row of alms houses still standing in the Sheen Road is the visible fruit of that moment's panic. Twelve poor old women of the parish today drink tea and tonight bless his Lordship for a roof above their heads; so that illicit love in a treasure ship—but we omit the moral.

Soon, however, Orlando grew tired, not only of

the discomfort of this way of life, and of the crabbed streets of the neighbourhood, but of the primitive manner of the people. For it has to be remembered that crime and poverty had none of the attraction for the Elizabethans that they have for us. They had none of our modern shame of book learning; none of our belief that to be born the son of a butcher is a blessing and to be unable to read a virtue; no fancy that what we call 'life' and 'reality' are somehow connected with ignorance and brutality; nor, indeed, any equivalent for these two words at all. It was not to seek 'life' that Orlando went among them; not in quest of 'reality' that he left them. But when he had heard a score of times how Jakes had lost his nose and Sukey her honour—and they told the stories admirably, it must be admitted—he began to be a little weary of the repetition, for a nose can only be cut off in one way and maidenhood lost in another—or so it seemed to him—whereas the arts and the sciences had a diversity about them which stirred his curiosity profoundly. So, always keeping them in happy memory, he left off frequenting the beer gardens and the skittle alleys, hung his grey cloak in his wardrobe, let his star shine at his neck and his garter twinkle at his knee, and appeared once more at the Court of King James.* He was young, he was rich, he was handsome. No one could have been received with greater acclamation than he was.

It is certain indeed that many ladies were ready to

show him their favours. The names of three at least were freely coupled with his in marriage—Clorinda,* Favilla, Euphrosyne—so he called them in his sonnets.

To take them in order; Clorinda was a sweet-mannered gentle lady enough;—indeed Orlando was greatly taken with her for six months and a half, but she had white eyelashes and could not bear the sight of blood. A hare brought up roasted at her father's table turned her faint. She was much under the influence of the Priests too, and stinted her underlinen in order to give to the poor. She took it on her to reform Orlando of his sins, which sickened him, so that he drew back from the marriage, and did not much regret it when she died soon after of the small-pox.

Favilla, who comes next, was of a different sort altogether. She was the daughter of a poor Somerset-shire gentleman: who, by sheer assiduity and the use of her eyes had worked her way up at court, where her address in horsemanship, her fine instep, and her grace in dancing won the admiration of all. Once, however, she was so ill-advised as to whip a spaniel that had torn one of her silk stockings (and it must be said in justice that Favilla had few stockings and those for the most part of drugget*) within an inch of its life beneath Orlando's window. Orlando, who was a passionate lover of animals, now noticed that her teeth were crooked, and the two front turned inward, which, he said, is a sure sign of a perverse and cruel disposition in women, and so broke the engagement that very night for ever.

The third, Euphrosyne, was by far the most serious of his flames. She was by birth one of the Irish Desmonds and had therefore a family tree of her own as old and deeply rooted as Orlando's itself. She was fair, florid, and a trifle phlegmatic. She spoke Italian well, had a perfect set of teeth in the upper jaw, though those on the lower were slightly discoloured. She was never without a whippet or spaniel at her knee; fed them with white bread from her own plate; sang sweetly to the virginals; and was never dressed before mid-day owing to the extreme care she took of her person. In short, she would have made a perfect wife for such a nobleman as Orlando, and matters had gone so far that the lawyers on both sides were busy with covenants, jointures, settlements, messuages, tenements, and whatever is needed before one great fortune can mate with another when, with the suddenness and severity that then marked the English climate, came the Great Frost.*

The Great Frost was, historians tell us, the most severe that has ever visited these islands. Birds froze in mid-air and fell like stones to the ground. At Norwich a young countrywoman started to cross the road in her usual robust health and was seen by the onlookers to turn visibly to powder and be blown in a puff of dust over the roofs as the icy blast struck her at the street corner. The mortality among sheep and cattle was enormous. Corpses froze and could not be drawn from the sheets. It was no uncommon sight to come upon a whole herd of swine frozen immovable upon the road. The fields were full of shepherds, ploughmen, teams of horses, and little bird-scaring boys all struck stark in the act of the moment, one with his hand to his nose, another with the bottle to his lips, a third with a stone raised to throw at the ravens who sat, as if stuffed, upon the hedge within a yard of him. The severity of the frost was so extraordinary that a kind of petrifaction sometimes ensued; and it was commonly supposed that the great increase of rocks in some parts of Derbyshire was due to no eruption, for there was none, but to the solidification of unfortunate wayfarers who had been turned literally to stone where they stood. The Church could give little help in the matter, and though some landowners had these relics blessed, the most part preferred to use them either as landmarks, scratching-posts for sheep, or, when the form of the stone allowed, drinking troughs for cattle, which purposes they serve, admirably for the most part, to this day.

But while the country people suffered the extremity of want, and the trade of the country was at a standstill, London enjoyed a carnival of the utmost brilliancy. The Court was at Greenwich, and the new King seized the opportunity that his coronation gave him to curry favour with the citizens. He directed that the river, which was frozen to a depth of twenty feet and more for six or seven miles* on either side, should be swept, decorated and given all the semblance of a park or pleasure ground, with arbours, mazes, alleys, drinking booths, etc., at his expense. For himself and the courtiers, he reserved a certain space immediately opposite the Palace gates; which, railed off from the public only by a silken rope, became at once the centre of the most brilliant society in England. Great statesmen, in their beards and ruffs, despatched affairs of state under the crimson awning of the Royal Pagoda. Soldiers planned the conquest of the Moor and the downfall of the Turk in striped arbours surmounted by plumes of ostrich feathers. Admirals strode up and down the narrow pathways, glass in hand, sweeping the horizon and telling stories of the north-west passage and the Spanish Armada.* Lovers dallied upon divans spread with sables. Frozen roses fell in showers when the Queen and her ladies walked abroad. Coloured balloons hovered motionless in the air. Here and there burnt vast bonfires of cedar and oak wood, lavishly salted, so that the flames were of green, orange, and purple fire. But however fiercely they burnt, the heat was not enough to melt the ice which, though of singular transparency, was yet of the hardness of steel. So clear indeed was it that there could be seen, congealed at a depth of several feet, here a porpoise, there a flounder. Shoals of eels lay motionless in a trance, but whether their state was one of death or merely of suspended animation which the warmth would revive puzzled the philosophers. Near London Bridge, where the river had frozen to a depth of some twenty fathoms, a wrecked wherry boat was plainly visible, lying on the bed of the river where it had sunk last autumn, overladen with apples. The old bumboat woman, who was carrying her fruit to market on the Surrey side, sat there in her plaids and farthingales with her lap full of apples, for all the world as if she were about to serve a customer, though a certain blueness about the lips hinted the truth. 'Twas a sight King James specially liked to look upon, and he would bring a troupe of courtiers to gaze with him. In short, nothing could exceed the brilliancy and gaiety of the scene by day. But it was at night that the carnival was at its merriest. For the frost continued unbroken; the nights were of perfect stillness; the moon and stars blazed with the hard fixity of diamonds, and to the fine music of flute and trumpet the courtiers danced.

Orlando, it is true, was none of those who tread lightly the corantoe and lavolta;* he was clumsy and a little absent-minded. He much preferred the plain dances of his own country, which he danced as a child to these fantastic foreign measures. He had indeed just brought his feet together about six in the evening of the seventh of January at the finish of some such quadrille or minuet when he beheld, coming from the pavilion of the Muscovite Embassy, a figure, which, whether boy's or woman's, for the loose tunic and trousers of the Russian fashion served to disguise the sex, filled him with the highest curiosity. The person, whatever the name or sex, was about middle height, very slenderly fashioned, and dressed entirely in oyster-coloured velvet, trimmed with some unfamiliar greenish-coloured fur. But these details were obscured by the extraordinary seductiveness which issued from the whole person. Images, metaphors of the most extreme and extravagant twined and twisted in his mind. He called her a melon, a pineapple, an olive tree, an emerald, and a fox in the snow all in the space of three seconds—he did not know whether he had heard her, tasted her, seen her, or all three together. (For though we must pause not a moment in the narrative we may here hastily note that all his images at this time were simple in the extreme to match his senses and were mostly taken from things he had liked the taste of as a boy. But if his senses were simple they were at the same time extremely strong. To pause therefore and seek the reasons of things is out of the question.) ... A melon, an emerald, a fox in the snow—so he raved, so he stared. When the boy, for alas, a boy it must be—no woman could skate with such speed and vigour—swept almost on tiptoe past him, Orlando was ready to tear his hair with vexation that the person was of his own sex, and thus all embraces were out of the question.

But the skater came closer. Legs, hands, carriage, were a boy's, but no boy ever had a mouth like that; no boy had those breasts; no boy had eyes which looked as if they had been fished from the bottom of the sea. Finally, coming to a stop and sweeping a curtsey with the utmost grace to the King, who was shuffling past on the arm of some Lord-in-waiting, the unknown skater came to a standstill. She was not a handsbreadth off. She was a woman. Orlando stared; trembled; turned hot; turned cold; longed to hurl himself through the summer air; to crush acorns beneath his feet; to toss his arms with the beech trees and the oaks. As it was, he drew his lips up over his small white teeth; opened them perhaps half an inch as if to bite; shut them as if he had bitten. The Lady Euphrosyne hung upon his arm.

The stranger's name,* he found, was the Princess Marousha Stanilovska Dagmar Natasha lliana Romanovitch, and she had come in the train of the Muscovite Ambassador, who was her uncle perhaps, or perhaps her father, to attend the coronation. Very little was known of the Muscovites. In their great beards and furred hats they sat almost silent; drinking some black liquid which they spat out now and then upon the ice. None spoke English, and French with which some at least were familiar was then little spoken at the English Court.

It was through this accident that Orlando and the Princess became acquainted. They were seated opposite each other at the great table spread under a huge awning for the entertainment of the notables. The Princess was placed between two young Lords, one Lord Francis Vere and the other the young Earl of Moray. It was laughable to see the predicament she soon had them in, for though both were fine lads in their way, the babe unborn had as much knowledge of the French tongue as they had. When at the beginning of dinner the Princess turned to the Earl and said, with a grace which ravished his heart, 'Je crois avoir fait la connaissance d'un gentilhomme qui vous était apparenté en Pologne l'été dernier', or 'La beauté des dames de la cour d'Angleterre me met dans le ravissement. On ne peut voir une dame plus gracieuse que votre reine, ni une coiffure plus belle que la sienne,'* both Lord Francis and the Earl showed the highest embarrassment. The one helped her largely to horse-radish sauce, the other whistled to his dog and made him beg for a marrow bone. At this the Princess could no longer contain her laughter, and Orlando, catching her eyes across the boars' heads and stuffed peacocks, laughed too. He laughed, but the laugh on his lips froze in wonder. Whom had he loved, what had he loved, he asked himself in a tumult of emotion, until now? An old woman, he answered, all skin and bone. Red-cheeked trulls too many to mention. A puling nun. A hard-bitten cruel-mouthed adventuress. A nodding mass of lace and ceremony. Love had meant to him nothing but sawdust and cinders. The joys he had had of it tasted insipid in the extreme. He marvelled how he could have gone through with it without yawning. For as he looked the thickness of his blood melted; the ice turned to wine in his veins; he heard the waters flowing and the birds singing; spring broke over the hard wintry landscape; his manhood woke; he grasped a sword in his hand; he charged a more daring foe than Pole or Moor; he dived in deep water; he saw the flower of danger growing in a crevice; he stretched his hand—in fact he was rattling off one of his most impassioned sonnets when the Princess addressed him, 'Would you have the goodness to pass the salt?'

He blushed deeply.

'With all the pleasure in the world, Madame,' he replied, speaking French with a perfect accent.* For, heaven be praised, he spoke the tongue as his own; his mother's maid had taught him. Yet perhaps it would have been better for him had he never learnt that tongue; never answered that voice; never followed the light of those eyes . . .

The Princess continued. Who were those bumpkins, she asked him, who sat beside her with the manners of stablemen? What was the nauseating mixture they had poured on her plate? Did the dogs eat at the same table with the men in England? Was that figure of fun at the end of the table with her hair rigged up like a Maypole (comme une grande perche

[39]

mal fagotée)* really the Queen? And did the King always slobber like that? And which of those popinjays was George Villiers? Though these questions rather discomposed Orlando at first, they were put with such archness and drollery that he could not help but laugh; and he saw from the blank faces of the company that nobody understood a word, he answered her as freely as she asked him, speaking, as she did, in perfect French.

Thus began an intimacy between the two which soon became the scandal of the Court.

Soon it was observed Orlando paid the Muscovite far more attention than mere civility demanded. He was seldom far from her side, and their conversation, though unintelligible to the rest, was carried on with such animation, provoked such blushes and laughter, that the dullest could guess the subject. Moreover, the change in Orlando himself was extraordinary. Nobody had ever seen him so animated. In one night he had thrown off his boyish clumsiness; he was changed from a sulky stripling, who could not enter a ladies' room without sweeping half the ornaments from the table, to a nobleman, full of grace and manly courtesy. To see him hand the Muscovite (as she was called) to her sledge, or offer her his hand for the dance, or catch the spotted kerchief which she had let drop, or discharge any other of those manifold duties which the supreme lady exacts and the lover hastens to anticipate was a sight to kindle the dull eyes of age, and to make the quick pulse of youth beat faster. Yet over it all hung a cloud. The old men shrugged their shoulders. The young tittered between their fingers. All knew that Orlando was betrothed to another. The Lady Margaret O'Brien O'Dare O'Reilly Tyrconnel (for that was the proper name of Euphrosyne of the Sonnets) wore Orlando's splendid sapphire on the second finger of her left hand. It was she who had the supreme right to his attentions. Yet she might drop all the handkerchiefs in her wardrobe (of which she had many scores) upon the ice and Orlando never stooped to pick them up. She might wait twenty minutes for him to hand her to her sledge, and in the end have to be content with the services of her Blackamoor. When she skated, which she did rather clumsily, no one was at her elbow to encourage her, and, if she fell, which she did rather heavily, no one raised her to her feet and dusted the snow from her petticoats. Although she was naturally phlegmatic, slow to take offence, and more reluctant than most people to believe that a mere foreigner could oust her from Orlando's affections, still even the Lady Margaret herself was brought at last to suspect that something was brewing against her peace of mind.

Indeed, as the days passed, Orlando took less and less care to hide his feelings. Making some excuse or other, he would leave the company as soon as they had dined, or steal away from the skaters, who were forming sets for a quadrille. Next moment it would be seen that the Muscovite was missing too. But what most outraged the Court, and stung it in its tenderest part, which is its vanity, was that the couple was often seen to slip under the silken rope, which railed off the Royal enclosure from the public part of the river and to disappear among the crowd of common people. For suddenly the Princess would stamp her foot and cry, 'Take me away. I detest your English mob,' by which she meant the English Court itself. She could stand it no longer. It was full of prying old women, she said, who stared in one's face, and of bumptious young men who trod on one's toes. They smelt bad. Their dogs ran between her legs. It was like being in a cage. In Russia they had rivers ten miles broad on which one could gallop six horses abreast all day long without meeting a soul. Besides, she wanted to see the Tower, the Beefeaters, the Heads on Temple Bar, and the jewellers' shops in the city. Thus, it came about that Orlando took her into the city, showed her the Beefeaters and the rebels' heads, and bought her whatever took her fancy in the Royal Exchange. But this was not enough. Each increasingly desired the other's company in privacy all day long where there were none to marvel or to stare. Instead of taking the road to London, therefore, they turned the other way about and were soon beyond the crowd among the frozen reaches of the Thames where, save for sea birds and some old country woman hacking at the ice in a vain attempt to draw a pailful of water or gathering what sticks or dead leaves she could find for firing, not a living soul ever came their way. The poor kept closely to their cottages, and the better sort, who could afford it, crowded for warmth and merriment to the city.

Hence, Orlando and Sasha, as he called her for short, and because it was the name of a white Russian fox* he had had as a boy—a creature soft as snow, but with teeth of steel, which bit him so savagely that his father had it killed*—hence, they had the river to themselves. Hot with skating and with love they would throw themselves down in some solitary reach,* where the yellow osiers fringed the bank, and wrapped in a great fur cloak Orlando would take her in his arms, and know, for the first time, he murmured, the delights of love. Then, when the ecstasy was over and they lay lulled in a swoon on the ice, he would tell her of his other loves, and how, compared with her, they had been of wood, of sackcloth, and of cinders. And laughing at his vehemence, she would turn once more in his arms and give him, for love's sake, one more embrace. And then they would marvel that the ice did not melt with their heat, and pity the poor old woman who had no such natural means of thawing it, but must hack at it with a chopper of cold steel. And then, wrapped in their sables, they would talk of everything under the sun; of sights and travels; of Moor and Pagan; of this man's beard and that woman's skin; of a rat that fed from her hand at table;

of the arras that moved always in the hall at home; of a face; of a feather. Nothing was too small for such converse, nothing was too great.

Then, suddenly Orlando would fall into one of his moods of melancholy; the sight of the old woman hobbling over the ice might be the cause of it, or nothing; and would fling himself face downwards on the ice and look into the frozen waters and think of death. For the philosopher is right* who says that nothing thicker than a knife's blade separates happiness from melancholy; and he goes on to opine that one is twin fellow to the other; and draws from this the conclusion that all extremes of feeling are allied to madness; and so bids us take refuge in the true Church (in his view the Anabaptist), which is the only harbour, port, anchorage, etc., he said, for those tossed on this sea.

'All ends in death,' Orlando would say, sitting upright, his face clouded with gloom. (For that was the way his mind worked now, in violent see-saws from life to death, stopping at nothing in between, so that the biographer must not stop either, but must fly as fast as he can and so keep pace with the unthinking passionate foolish actions and sudden extravagant words in which, it is impossible to deny, Orlando at this time of his life indulged.)

'All ends in death,' Orlando would say, sitting upright on the ice. But Sasha who after all had no English blood in her but was from Russia where the

sunsets are longer, the dawns less sudden, and sentences often left unfinished from doubt as to how
best to end them—Sasha stared at him, perhaps
sneered at him, for he must have seemed a child to
her, and said nothing. But at length the ice grew cold
beneath them, which she disliked, so pulling him to
his feet again, she talked so enchantingly, so wittily,
so wisely (but unfortunately always in French, which
notoriously loses its flavour in translation) that he
forgot the frozen waters or night coming or the old
woman or whatever it was, and would try to tell
her—plunging and splashing among a thousand
images which had gone as stale as the women who
inspired them—what she was like. Snow, cream,
marble, cherries, alabaster, golden wire? None of
these. She was like a fox, or an olive tree; like the
waves of the sea when you look down upon them
from a height; like an emerald; like the sun on a green
hill which is yet clouded—like nothing he had seen
or known in England. Ransack the language as he
might, words failed him. He wanted another landscape, and another tongue. English was too frank, too
candid, too honeyed a speech for Sasha. For in all she
said, however open she seemed and voluptuous, there
was something hidden; in all she did, however daring,
there was something concealed. So the green flame
seems hidden in the emerald, or the sun prisoned in a
hill. The clearness was only outward; within was a
wandering flame. It came; it went; she never shone

with the steady beam of an Englishwoman—here, however, remembering the Lady Margaret and her petticoats, Orlando ran wild in his transports and swept her over the ice, faster, faster, vowing that he would chase the flame, dive for the gem, and so on and so on, the words coming on the pants of his breath with the passion of a poet whose poetry is half pressed out of him by pain.

But Sasha was silent. When Orlando had done telling her that she was a fox, an olive tree, or a green hill-top, and had given her the whole history of his family; how their house was one of the most ancient in Britain; how they had come from Rome with the Caesars and had the right to walk down the Corso (which is the chief street in Rome) under a tasselled palanquin,* which he said is a privilege reserved only for those of imperial blood (for there was an orgulous credulity about him which was pleasant enough), he would pause and ask her, Where was her own house? What was her father? Had she brothers? Why was she here alone with her uncle? Then, somehow, though she answered readily enough, an awkwardness would come between them. He suspected at first that her rank was not as high as she would like; or that she was ashamed of the savage ways of her people, for he had heard that the women in Muscovy wear beards and the men are covered with fur from the waist down; that both sexes are smeared with tallow to keep the cold out, tear meat with their fingers and live in huts where an English noble would scruple to keep his cattle; so that he forbore to press her. But on reflection, he concluded that her silence could not be for that reason; she herself was entirely free from hair on the chin; she dressed in velvet and pearls, and her manners were certainly not those of a woman bred in a cattle-shed.

What, then, did she hide from him? The doubt underlying the tremendous force of his feelings was like a quicksand beneath a monument which shifts suddenly and makes the whole pile shake. The agony would seize him suddenly. Then he would blaze out in such wrath that she did not know how to quiet him. Perhaps she did not want to quiet him; perhaps his rages pleased her and she provoked them purposely—such is the curious obliquity of the Muscovitish temperament.

To continue the story—skating farther than their wont that day they reached that part of the river where the ships had anchored and been frozen in midstream. Among them was the ship of the Muscovite Embassy flying its double-headed black eagle from the main mast, which was hung with many-coloured icicles several yards in length. Sasha had left some of her clothing on board, and supposing the ship to be empty they climbed on deck and went in search of it. Remembering certain passages in his own past, Orlando would not have marvelled had some good citizens sought this refuge before them; and so it turned out. They had not ventured far when a fine young man started up from some business of his own behind a coil of rope and saying, apparently, for he spoke Russian, that he was one of the crew and would help the Princess to find what she wanted, lit a lump of candle and disappeared with her into the lower parts of the ship.

Time went by, and Orlando, wrapped in his own dreams, thought only of the pleasures of life; of his jewel—of her rarity; of means for making her irrevocably and indissolubly his own. Obstacles there were and hardships to overcome. She was determined to live in Russia, where there were frozen rivers and wild horses and men, she said, who gashed each other's throats open. It is true that a landscape of pine and snow, habits of lust and slaughter, did not entice him. Nor was he anxious to cease his pleasant country ways of sport and tree-planting;* relinquish his office; ruin his career; shoot the reindeer instead of the rabbit; drink vodka instead of canary, and slip a knife up his sleeve—for what purpose, he knew not. Still, all this and more than all this he would do for her sake. As for his marriage with the Lady Margaret, fixed though it was for this day sennight,* the thing was so palpably absurd that he scarcely gave it a thought. Her kinsmen would abuse him for deserting a great lady; his friends would deride him for ruining the finest career in the world for a Cossack woman and a waste of snow—it weighed not a straw in the balance compared with Sasha herself. On the first dark night they would fly. They would take ship to Russia. So he pondered; so he plotted as he walked up and down the deck.

He was recalled, turning westward, by the sight of the sun, slung like an orange on the cross of St Paul's. It was blood-red and sinking rapidly. It must be almost evening. Sasha had been gone this hour and more. Seized instantly with those dark forebodings which shadowed even his most confident thoughts of her, he plunged the way he had seen them go into the hold of the ship; and, after stumbling among chests and barrels in the darkness, was made aware by a faint glimmer in a corner that they were seated there. For one second, he had a vision of them; saw Sasha seated on the sailor's knee; saw her bend towards him; saw them embrace before the light was blotted out in a red cloud by his rage. He blazed into such a howl of anguish that the whole ship echoed. Sasha threw herself between them, or the sailor would have been stifled before he could draw his cutlass. Then a deadly sickness came over Orlando, and they had to lay him on the floor and give him brandy to drink before he revived. And then, when he had recovered and was sat upon a heap of sacking on deck, Sasha hung over him, passing before his dizzied eyes softly, sinuously, like the fox that had bit him, now cajoling, now denouncing, so that he came to doubt what he had seen. Had not the candle guttered; had not the shadows moved? The box was heavy, she said; the man was helping her to move it. Orlando believed her one moment—for who can be sure that his rage has not painted what he most dreads to find?—the next was the more violent with anger at her deceit. Then Sasha herself turned white; stamped her foot on deck, said she would go that night, and called upon her Gods to destroy her, if she, a Romanovitch, had lain in the arms of a common seaman. Indeed, looking at them together (which he could hardly bring himself to do) Orlando was outraged by the foulness of his imagination that could have painted so frail a creature in the paw of that hairy sea brute. The man was huge; stood six feet four in his stockings, wore common wire rings in his ears; and looked like a dray horse upon which some wren or robin has perched in its flight. So he yielded; believed her; and asked her pardon. Yet when they were going down the ship's side, lovingly again, Sasha paused with her hand on the ladder, and called back to this tawny wide-cheeked monster a volley of Russian greetings, jests, or endearments, not a word of which Orlando could understand. But there was something in her tone (it might be the fault of the Russian consonants) that reminded Orlando of a scene some nights since, when he had come upon her in secret gnawing a candle-end in a corner, which she had picked from the floor. True, it was pink; it was gilt; and it was from the King's table; but it was tallow, and she gnawed it.

[50]

Was there not, he thought, handing her on to the ice, something rank in her,* something coarse flavoured, something peasant born? And he fancied her at forty grown unwieldy though she was now slim as a reed, and lethargic though she was now blithe as a lark. But again as they skated towards London such suspicions melted in his breast, and he felt as if he had been hooked by a great fish through the nose and rushed through the waters unwillingly, yet with his own consent.

It was an evening of astonishing beauty. As the sun sank, all the domes, spires, turrets, and pinnacles of London rose in inky blackness against the furious red sunset clouds. Here was the fretted cross at Charing; there the dome of St Paul's; there the massy square of the Tower buildings; there like a grove of trees stripped of all leaves save a knob at the end were the heads on the pikes at Temple Bar. Now the Abbey windows were lit up and burnt like a heavenly, many-coloured shield (in Orlando's fancy); now all the west seemed a golden window with troops of angels (in Orlando's fancy again) passing up and down the heavenly stairs perpetually. All the time they seemed to be skating in fathomless depths of air, so blue the ice had become; and so glassy smooth was it that they sped quicker and quicker to the city with the white gulls circling about them, and cutting in the air with their wings the very same sweeps that they cut on the ice with their skates.

Sasha, as if to reassure him, was tenderer than usual and even more delightful. Seldom would she talk about her past life, but now she told him how, in winter in Russia, she would listen to the wolves howling across the steppes, and thrice, to show him, she barked like a wolf. Upon which he told her of the stags in the snow at home, and how they would stray into the great hall* for warmth and be fed by an old man with porridge from a bucket. And then she praised him—for his love of beasts; for his gallantry; for his legs. Ravished with her praises and shamed to think how he had maligned her by fancying her on the knees of a common sailor and grown fat and lethargic at forty, he told her that he could find no words to praise her; yet instantly bethought him how she was like the spring and green grass and rushing waters, and seizing her more tightly than ever, he swung her with him half across the river so that the gulls and the cormorants swung too. And halting at length, out of breath, she said, panting slightly, that he was like a million-candled Christmas tree (such as they have in Russia) hung with yellow globes; incandescent; enough to light a whole street by; (so one might translate it) for what with his glowing cheeks, his dark curls, his black and crimson cloak, he looked as if he were burning with his own radiance, from a lamp lit within.

All the colour, save the red of Orlando's cheeks, soon faded. Night came on. As the orange light of sunset vanished it was succeeded by an astonishing white glare from the torches, bonfires, flaming cressets,* and other devices by which the river was lit up and the strangest transformation took place. Various churches and noblemen's palaces, whose fronts were of white stone showed in streaks and patches as if floating on the air. Of St Paul's, in particular, nothing was left but a gilt cross. The Abbey appeared like the grey skeleton of a leaf. Everything suffered emaciation and transformation. As they approached the carnival, they heard a deep note like that struck on a tuning-fork which boomed louder and louder until it became an uproar. Every now and then a great shout followed a rocket into the air. Gradually they could discern little figures breaking off from the vast crowd and spinning hither and thither like gnats on the surface of a river. Above and around this brilliant circle like a bowl of darkness pressed the deep black of a winter's night. And then into this darkness there began to rise with pauses, which kept the expectation alert and the mouth open, flowering rockets; crescents; serpents; a crown. At one moment the woods and distant hills showed green as on a summer's day; the next all was winter and blackness again.

By this time Orlando and the Princess were close to the Royal enclosure and found their way barred by a great crowd of the common people, who were pressing as near to the silken rope as they dared. Loth to end their privacy and encounter the sharp eyes that

were on the watch for them, the couple lingered
there, shouldered by apprentices; tailors; fishwives;
horse dealers; cony catchers;* starving scholars;
maid-servants in their whimples; orange girls;
ostlers;* sober citizens; bawdy tapsters; and a crowd
of little ragamuffins such as always haunt the outskirts
of a crowd, screaming and scrambling among people's
feet—all the riff-raff of the London streets indeed
was there, jesting and jostling, here casting dice,
telling fortunes, shoving, tickling, pinching; here
uproarious, there glum; some of them with mouths
gaping a yard wide; others as little reverent as daws
on a house-top—all as variously rigged out as their
purse or stations allowed; here in fur and broadcloth;
there in tatters with their feet kept from the ice only
by a dishclout* bound about them. The main press of
people, it appeared, stood opposite a booth or stage
something like our Punch and Judy show upon which
some kind of theatrical performance was going forward. A black man was waving his arms and vocifer-
ating. There was a woman in white laid upon a bed.
Rough though the staging was, the actors running up
and down a pair of steps and sometimes tripping, and
the crowd stamping their feet and whistling, or when
they were bored, tossing a piece of orange peel on to
the ice which a dog would scramble for, still the
astonishing, sinuous melody of the words stirred
Orlando like music. Spoken with extreme speed and
a daring agility of tongue which reminded him of the

sailors singing in the beer gardens at Wapping, the words even without meaning were as wine to him. But now and again a single phrase would come to him over the ice which was as if torn from the depths of his heart. The frenzy of the Moor seemed to him his own frenzy, and when the Moor suffocated the woman in her bed it was Sasha he killed with his own hands.

At last the play was ended. All had grown dark. The tears streamed down his face. Looking up into the sky there was nothing but blackness there too. Ruin and death, he thought, cover all. The life of man ends in the grave. Worms devour us.

> Methinks it should be now a huge eclipse
> Of sun and moon, and that the affrighted globe
> Should yawn——*

Even as he said this a star of some pallor rose in his memory. The night was dark; it was pitch dark; but it was such a night as this that they had waited for; it was on such a night as this that they had planned to fly. He remembered everything. The time had come. With a burst of passion he snatched Sasha to him, and hissed in her ear 'Jour de ma vie!'* It was their signal. At midnight they would meet at an inn near Blackfriars. Horses waited there. Everything was in readiness for their flight. So they parted, she to her tent, he to his. It still wanted an hour of the time.

Long before midnight Orlando was in waiting. The

night was of so inky a blackness that a man was on you before he could be seen, which was all to the good, but it was also of the most solemn stillness so that a horse's hoof, or a child's cry, could be heard at a distance of half a mile. Many a time did Orlando, pacing the little courtyard, hold his heart at the sound of some nag's steady footfall on the cobbles, or at the rustle of a woman's dress. But the traveller was only some merchant, making home belated; or some woman of the quarter whose errand was nothing so innocent. They passed, and the street was quieter than before. Then those lights which burnt downstairs in the small, huddled quarters where the poor of the city lived moved up to the sleeping-rooms, and then, one by one, were extinguished. The street lanterns in these purlieus were few at most; and the negligence of the night watchman often suffered them to expire long before dawn. The darkness then became even deeper than before. Orlando looked to the wicks of his lantern, saw to the saddle girths; primed his pistols; examined his holsters; and did all these things a dozen times at least till he could find nothing more needing his attention. Though it still lacked some twenty minutes to midnight, he could not bring himself to go indoors to the inn parlour, where the hostess was still serving sack and the cheaper sort of canary wine to a few seafaring men, who would sit there trolling their ditties, and telling their stories of Drake, Hawkins, and Grenville, till they toppled off the benches and rolled asleep on the sanded floor. The darkness was more compassionate to his swollen and violent heart. He listened to every footfall; speculated on every sound. Each drunken shout and each wail from some poor wretch laid in the straw or in other distress cut his heart to the quick, as if it boded ill omen to his venture. Yet, he had no fear for Sasha. Her courage made nothing of the adventure. She would come alone, in her cloak and trousers, booted like a man. Light as her footfall was, it would hardly be heard, even in this silence.

So he waited in the darkness. Suddenly he was struck in the face by a blow, soft, yet heavy, on the side of his cheek. So strung with expectation was he, that he started and put his hand to his sword. The blow was repeated a dozen times on forehead and cheek. The dry frost had lasted so long that it took him a minute to realize that these were raindrops falling; the blows were the blows of the rain. At first, they fell slowly, deliberately, one by one. But soon the six drops became sixty; then six hundred; then ran themselves together in a steady spout of water. It was as if the hard and consolidated sky poured itself forth in one profuse fountain. In the space of five minutes Orlando was soaked to the skin.

Hastily putting the horses under cover,* he sought shelter beneath the lintel of the door whence he could still observe the courtyard. The air was thicker now than ever, and such a steaming and droning rose from

[57]

the downpour that no footfall of man or beast could be heard above it. The roads, pitted as they were with great holes, would be under water and perhaps impassable. But of what effect this would have upon their flight he scarcely thought. All his senses were bent upon gazing along the cobbled pathway—gleaming in the light of the lantern—for Sasha's coming. Sometimes, in the darkness, he seemed to see her wrapped about with rain strokes. But the phantom vanished. Suddenly, with an awful and ominous voice, a voice full of horror and alarm which raised every hair of anguish in Orlando's soul, St Paul's struck the first stroke of midnight. Four times more it struck remorselessly. With the superstition of a lover, Orlando had made out that it was on the sixth stroke that she would come. But the sixth stroke echoed away, and the seventh came and the eighth, and to his apprehensive mind they seemed notes first heralding and then proclaiming death and disaster. When the twelfth struck he knew that his doom was sealed. It was useless for the rational part of him to reason; she might be late; she might be prevented; she might have missed her way. The passionate and feeling heart of Orlando knew the truth. Other clocks struck, jangling one after another. The whole world seemed to ring with the news of her deceit and his derision. The old suspicions subterraneously at work in him rushed forth from concealment openly. He was bitten by a swarm of snakes, each more poisonous than the last. He stood in the doorway in the tremendous rain without moving. As the minutes passed, he sagged a little at the knees. The downpour rushed on. In the thick of it, great guns seemed to boom. Huge noises as of the tearing and rending of oak trees could be heard. There were also wild cries and terrible inhuman groanings. But Orlando stood there immovable till Paul's clock struck two, and then, crying aloud with an awful irony, and all his teeth showing, 'Jour de ma vie!' he dashed the lantern to the ground, mounted his horse and galloped he knew not where.

Some blind instinct, for he was past reasoning, must have driven him to take the river bank in the direction of the sea. For when the dawn broke, which it did with unusual suddenness, the sky turning a pale yellow and the rain almost ceasing, he found himself on the banks of the Thames off Wapping. Now a sight of the most extraordinary nature met his eyes. Where, for three months and more, there had been solid ice of such thickness that it seemed permanent as stone, and a whole gay city had been stood on its pavement, was now a race of turbulent yellow waters. The river had gained its freedom in the night. It was as if a sulphur spring (to which view many philosophers inclined) had risen from the volcanic regions beneath and burst the ice asunder with such vehemence that it swept the huge and massy fragments furiously apart. The mere look of the water was enough to turn one giddy. All was riot and confusion. The river was strewn with icebergs. Some of these were as broad as a bowling green and as high as a house; others no bigger than a man's hat, but most fantastically twisted. Now would come down a whole convoy of ice blocks sinking everything that stood in their way. Now, eddying and swirling like a tortured serpent, the river would seem to be hurtling itself between the fragments and tossing them from bank to bank, so that they could be heard smashing against the piers and pillars. But what was the most awful and inspiring of terror was the sight of the human creatures who had been trapped in the night and now paced their twisting and precarious islands in the utmost agony of spirit. Whether they jumped into the flood or stayed on the ice their doom was certain. Sometimes quite a cluster of these poor creatures would come down together, some on their knees, others suckling their babies. One old man seemed to be reading aloud from a holy book. At other times, and his fate perhaps was the most dreadful, a solitary wretch would stride his narrow tenement alone. As they swept out to sea, some could be heard crying vainly for help, making wild promises to amend their ways, confessing their sins and vowing altars and wealth if God would hear their prayers. Others were so dazed with terror that they sat immovable and silent looking steadfastly before them. One crew of young watermen or post-boys, to judge by their liveries, roared and shouted the lewdest tavern songs, as if in bravado, and were dashed against a tree and sunk with blasphemies on their lips. An old noble- man—for such his furred gown and golden chain proclaimed him—went down not far from where Orlando stood, calling vengeance upon the Irish rebels,* who, he cried with his last breath, had plotted this devilry. Many perished clasping some silver pot or other treasure to their breasts; and at least a score of poor wretches were drowned by their own cupid- ity, hurling themselves from the bank into the flood rather than let a gold goblet escape them, or see before their eyes the disappearance of some furred gown. For furniture, valuables, possessions of all sorts were carried away on the icebergs. Among other strange sights was to be seen a cat suckling its young; a table laid sumptuously for a supper of twenty; a couple in bed; together with an extraordinary number of cooking utensils.

Dazed and astounded, Orlando could do nothing for some time but watch the appalling race of waters as it hurled itself past him. At last, seeming to recollect himself, he clapped spurs to his horse and galloped hard along the river bank in the direction of the sea. Rounding a bend of the river, he came opposite that reach where, not two days ago, the ships of the Ambassadors had seemed immovably frozen. Hastily, he made count of them all: the French; the Spanish; the Austrian; the Turk. All still floated, though the French had broken loose from her moorings, and the Turkish vessel had taken a great rent in her side and was fast filling with water. But the Russian ship was nowhere to be seen. For one moment Orlando thought it must have foundered; but, raising himself in his stirrups and shading his eyes, which had the sight of a hawk's, he could just make out the shape of a ship on the horizon. The black eagles were flying from the mast-head. The ship of the Muscovite Embassy was standing out to sea.

Flinging himself from his horse, he made, in his rage, as if he would breast the flood. Standing knee-deep in water he hurled at the faithless woman all the insults that have ever been the lot of her sex. Faithless, mutable, fickle, he called her; devil, adulteress, deceiver; and the swirling waters took his words, and tossed at his feet a broken pot and a little straw.

CHAPTER II

THE biographer is now faced with a difficulty which
it is better perhaps to confess than to gloss over. Up
to this point in telling the story of Orlando's life,
documents, both private and historical, have made it
possible to fulfil the first duty of a biographer, which
is to plod, without looking to right or left, in the
indelible footprints of truth; unenticed by flowers;
regardless of shade; on and on methodically till we
fall plump into the grave and write *finis* on the
tombstone above our heads. But now we come to an
episode which lies right across our path, so that there
is no ignoring it. Yet it is dark, mysterious, and
undocumented; so that there is no explaining it.
Volumes might be written in interpretation of it;
whole religious systems founded upon the significa-
tion of it. Our simple duty is to state the facts as far
as they are known, and so let the reader make of them
what he may.

In the summer of that disastrous winter which saw
the frost, the flood, the deaths of many thousands,
and the complete downfall of Orlando's hopes—for
he was exiled from Court; in deep disgrace with the
most powerful nobles of his time; the Irish house of
Desmond was justly enraged; the King had already
trouble enough with the Irish not to relish this further
addition—in that summer Orlando retired to his great

house in the country and there lived in complete solitude. One June morning—it was Saturday the 18th—he failed to rise at his usual hour, and when his groom went to call him he was found fast asleep. Nor could he be awakened. He lay as if in a trance, without perceptible breathing; and though dogs were set to bark under his window; cymbals, drums, bones beaten perpetually in his room; a gorse bush put under his pillow; and mustard plasters applied to his feet, still he did not wake, take food, or show any sign of life for seven whole days. On the seventh day he woke at his usual time (a quarter before eight, precisely) and turned the whole posse of caterwauling wives and village soothsayers out of his room; which was natural enough; but what was strange was that he showed no consciousness of any such trance, but dressed himself and sent for his horse as if he had woken from a single night's slumber. Yet some change, it was suspected, must have taken place in the chambers of his brain, for though he was perfectly rational and seemed graver and more sedate in his ways than before, he appeared to have an imperfect recollection of his past life. He would listen when people spoke of the great frost or the skating or the carnival, but he never gave any sign, except by passing his hand across his brow as if to wipe away some cloud, of having witnessed them himself. When the events of the past six months were discussed, he seemed not so much distressed as puzzled, as if he were troubled by confused memories of some time long gone or were trying to recall stories told him by another. It was observed that if Russia was mentioned or Princesses or ships, he would fall into a gloom of an uneasy kind and get up and look out of the window or call one of the dogs to him, or take a knife and carve a piece of cedar wood. But the doctors were hardly wiser then than they are now,* and after prescribing rest and exercise, starvation and nourishment, society and solitude, that he should lie in bed all day and ride forty miles between lunch and dinner, together with the usual sedatives and irritants, diversified, as the fancy took them, with possets of newt's slobber on rising, and draughts of peacock's gall on going to bed, they left him to himself, and gave it as their opinion that he had been asleep for a week.

But if sleep it was, of what nature, we can scarcely refrain from asking, are such sleeps as these? Are they remedial measures—trances in which the most galling memories, events that seem likely to cripple life for ever, are brushed with a dark wing which rubs their harshness off and gilds them, even the ugliest and basest, with a lustre, an incandescence? Has the finger of death to be laid on the tumult of life from time to time lest it rend us asunder? Are we so made that we have to take death in small doses daily or we could not go on with the business of living? And then what strange powers are these that penetrate our most secret ways and change our most treasured possessions without our willing it? Had Orlando, worn out by the extremity of his suffering, died for a week, and then come to life again? And if so, of what nature is death and of what nature life? Having waited well over half an hour for an answer to these questions, and none coming, let us get on with the story.

Now Orlando gave himself up to a life of extreme solitude. His disgrace at Court and the violence of his grief were partly the reason of it, but as he made no effort to defend himself and seldom invited anyone to visit him (though he had many friends who would willingly have done so) it appeared as if to be alone in the great house of his fathers suited his temper. Solitude was his choice. How he spent his time, nobody quite knew. The servants, of whom he kept a full retinue, though much of their business was to dust empty rooms and to smooth the coverlets of beds that were never slept in, watched, in the dark of the evening, as they sat over their cakes and ale, a light passing along the galleries, through the banqueting-halls, up the staircase, into the bedrooms, and knew that their master was perambulating the house alone. None dared follow him, for the house was haunted by a great variety of ghosts, and the extent of it made it easy to lose one's way and either fall down some hidden staircase or open a door which, should the wind blow it to, would shut upon one for ever—accidents of no uncommon occurrence, as the frequent discovery of the skeletons of men and animals in attitudes of great agony made evident. Then the light would be lost altogether, and Mrs Grimsditch, the housekeeper, would say to Mr Dupper,* the chaplain, how she hoped his Lordship had not met with some bad accident. Mr Dupper would opine that his Lordship was on his knees, no doubt, among the tombs of his ancestors in the Chapel, which was in the Billiard Table Court, half a mile away on the south side. For he had sins on his conscience, Mr Dupper was afraid; upon which Mrs Grimsditch would retort, rather sharply, that so had most of us; and Mrs Stewkley and Mrs Field and old Nurse Carpenter would all raise their voices in his Lordship's praise; and the grooms and the stewards would swear that it was a thousand pities to see so fine a nobleman moping about the house when he might be hunting the fox or chasing the deer; and even the little laundry maids and scullery maids, the Judys and the Faiths, who were handing round the tankards and cakes, would pipe up their testimony to his Lordship's gallantry; for never was there a kinder gentleman, or one more free with those little pieces of silver which serve to buy a knot of ribbon or put a posy in one's hair; until even the Blackamoor whom they called Grace Robinson by way of making a Christian woman of her, understood what they were at, and agreed that his Lordship was a handsome, pleasant, darling gentleman in the only way she could, that is to say by showing all her teeth at once in a broad grin. In short, all his serving men and women held him in high respect, and cursed the foreign Princess (but they called her by a coarser name than that) who had brought him to this pass.

But though it was probably cowardice, or love of hot ale, that led Mr Dupper to imagine his Lordship safe among the tombs so that he need not go in search of him, it may well have been that Mr Dupper was right. Orlando now took a strange delight in thoughts of death and decay, and, after pacing the long galleries and ballrooms with a taper in his hand, looking at picture after picture as if he sought the likeness of somebody whom he could not find, would mount into the family pew and sit for hours watching the banners stir and the moonlight waver with a bat or death's head moth to keep him company. Even this was not enough for him, but he must descend into the crypt where his ancestors lay,* coffin piled upon coffin, for ten generations together. The place was so seldom visited that the rats made free with the lead work, and now a thigh bone would catch at his cloak as he passed, or he would crack the skull of some old Sir Malise as it rolled beneath his foot. It was a ghastly sepulchre; dug deep beneath the foundations of the house as if the first Lord of the family, who had come from France with the Conqueror, had wished to testify how all pomp is built upon corruption; how the skeleton lies beneath the flesh; how we that dance and sing above must lie below; how the crimson velvet turns to dust; how the ring (here Orlando, stooping his lantern, would pick up a gold circle lacking a stone, that had rolled into a corner) loses its ruby and the eye which was so lustrous shines no more. 'Nothing remains of all these Princes', Orlando would say, indulging in some pardonable exaggeration of their rank, 'except one digit,' and he would take a skeleton hand in his and bend the joints this way and that. 'Whose hand was it?' he went on to ask. 'The right or the left? The hand of man or woman, of age or youth? Had it urged the war horse, or plied the needle? Had it plucked the rose, or grasped cold steel? Had it——' but here either his invention failed him or, what is more likely, provided him with so many instances of what a hand can do that he shrank, as his wont was, from the cardinal labour of composition, which is excision, and he put it with the other bones, thinking how there was a writer called Thomas Browne,* a Doctor of Norwich, whose writing upon such subjects took his fancy amazingly.

So, taking his lantern and seeing that the bones were in order, for though romantic, he was singularly methodical* and detested nothing so much as a ball of string on the floor, let alone the skull of an ancestor, he returned to that curious, moody pacing down the galleries, looking for something among the pictures, which was interrupted at length by a veritable spasm of sobbing, at the sight of a Dutch snow scene by an unknown artist. Then it seemed to him that life was not worth living any more. Forgetting the bones of his ancestors and how life is founded on a grave, he stood there shaken with sobs, all for the desire of a woman in Russian trousers, with slanting eyes, a pouting mouth and pearls about her neck. She had gone. She had left him. He was never to see her again. And so he sobbed. And so he found his way back to his own rooms; and Mrs Grimsditch, seeing the light in the window, put the tankard from her lips and said Praise be to God, his Lordship was safe in his room again; for she had been thinking all this while that he was foully murdered.*

Orlando now drew his chair up to the table; opened the works of Sir Thomas Browne and proceeded to investigate the delicate articulation of one of the doctor's longest and most marvellously contorted cogitations.

For though these are not matters on which a biographer can profitably enlarge it is plain enough to those who have done a reader's part in making up from bare hints dropped here and there the whole boundary and circumference of a living person; can hear in what we only whisper a living voice; can see, often when we say nothing about it, exactly what he looked like; know without a word to guide them precisely what he thought—and it is for readers such as these that we write—it is plain then to such a reader that Orlando was strangely compounded of many humours—of melancholy, of indolence, of passion, of love of solitude, to say nothing of all those contortions and subtleties of temper which were indicated on the first page, when he slashed at a dead nigger's head; cut it down; hung it chivalrously out of his reach again and then betook himself to the window-seat with a book. The taste for books was an early one. As a child he was sometimes found at midnight by a page still reading. They took his taper away, and he bred glow-worms to serve his purpose. They took the glow-worms away, and he almost burnt the house down with a tinder. To put it in a nutshell, leaving the novelist to smooth out the crumpled silk and all its implications, he was a nobleman afflicted with a love of literature. Many people of his time, still more of his rank, escaped the infection and were thus free to run or ride or make love at their own sweet will. But some were early infected by a germ said to be bred of the pollen of the asphodel* and to be blown out of Greece and Italy, which was of so deadly a nature that it would shake the hand as it was raised to strike, and cloud the eye as it sought its prey, and make the tongue stammer as it declared its love. It was the fatal nature of this disease to substitute a phantom for reality, so that Orlando, to whom fortune had given every gift—plate, linen, houses, men-servants, carpets, beds in profusion—had only to open a book for the whole vast accumulation to turn to mist. The nine acres of stone which were his house vanished; one hundred and fifty indoor servants disappeared; his eighty riding horses became invisible; it would take too long to count the carpets, sofas, trappings, china, plate, cruets, chafing dishes and other movables often of beaten gold, which evaporated like so much sea mist under the miasma. So it was, and Orlando would sit by himself, reading, a naked man.

The disease gained rapidly upon him now in his solitude. He would read often six hours into the night; and when they came to him for orders about the slaughtering of cattle or the harvesting of wheat, he would push away his folio and look as if he did not understand what was said to him. This was bad enough and wrung the hearts of Hall, the falconer, of Giles, the groom, of Mrs Grimsditch, the house-keeper, of Mr Dupper, the chaplain. A fine gentleman like that, they said, had no need of books. Let him leave books, they said, to the palsied or the dying. But worse was to come. For once the disease of reading has laid upon the system it weakens it so that it falls an easy prey to that other scourge which dwells in the inkpot and festers in the quill. The wretch takes to writing. And while this is bad enough in a poor man, whose only property is a chair and a table set beneath a leaky roof—for he has not much to lose, after all—the plight of a rich man, who has houses and cattle, maid-servants, asses and linen, and yet writes books, is pitiable in the extreme. The flavour of it all goes out of him; he is riddled by hot irons; gnawed by vermin. He would give every penny he has (such is the malignity of the germ) to write one little book and become famous; yet all the gold in Peru will not buy him the treasure of a well-turned line. So he falls into consumption and sickness, blows his brains out, turns his face to the wall. It matters not in what attitude they find him. He has passed through the gates of Death and known the flames of Hell.

Happily, Orlando was of a strong constitution and the disease (for reasons presently to be given) never broke him down as it has broken many of his peers. But he was deeply smitten with it, as the sequel shows. For when he had read for an hour or so in Sir Thomas Browne, and the bark of the stag and the call of the night watchman showed that it was the dead of night and all safe asleep, he crossed the room, took a silver key from his pocket and unlocked the doors of a great inlaid cabinet* which stood in the corner. Within were some fifty drawers of cedar wood and upon each was a paper neatly written in Orlando's hand. He paused, as if hesitating which to open. One was inscribed 'The Death of Ajax', another 'The Birth of Pyramus', another 'Iphigenia in Aulis', another 'The Death of Hippolytus', another 'Meleager', another 'The Return of Odysseus',—in fact there was scarcely a single drawer that lacked the name of some mythological personage at a crisis of his career. In each drawer lay a document of considerable size all written over in Orlando's hand. The truth was that Orlando had been afflicted thus for many years. Never had any boy begged apples as Orlando begged paper; nor sweetmeats as he begged ink. Stealing away from talk and games, he had hidden himself behind curtains, in priest's holes, or in the cupboard behind his mother's bedroom* which had a great hole in the floor and smelt horribly of starling's dung, with an inkhorn in one hand, a pen in another, and on his knee a roll of paper. Thus had been written,* before he was turned twenty-five, some forty-seven plays, histories, romances, poems; some in prose, some in verse; some in French, some in Italian; all romantic, and all long. One he had had printed* by John Ball of the Feathers and Coronet opposite St Paul's Cross, Cheapside; but though the sight of it gave him extreme delight, he had never dared show it even to his mother, since to write, much more to publish, was, he knew, for a nobleman an inexpiable disgrace.

Now, however, that it was the dead of night and he was alone, he chose from this repository one thick document called 'Xenophila a Tragedy' or some such title, and one thin one, called simply 'The Oak Tree' (this was the only monosyllabic title among the lot), and then he approached the inkhorn, fingered the quill, and made other such passes as those addicted to this vice begin their rites with. But he paused.

As this pause was of extreme significance in his history, more so, indeed, than many acts which bring men to their knees and make rivers run with blood, it behoves us to ask why he paused; and to reply, after due reflection, that it was for some such reason as this. Nature, who has played so many queer tricks upon us, making us so unequally of clay and diamonds, of rainbow and granite,* and stuffed them into a case, often of the most incongruous, for the poet has a butcher's face and the butcher a poet's; nature, who delights in muddle and mystery, so that even now (the first of November 1927)* we know not why we go upstairs, or why we come down again, our most daily movements are like the passage of a ship on an unknown sea, and the sailors at the mast-head ask, pointing their glasses to the horizon; Is there land or is there none? to which, if we are prophets, we make answer 'Yes'; if we are truthful we say 'No'; nature, who has so much to answer for besides the perhaps unwieldy length of this sentence, has further complicated her task and added to our confusion by providing not only a perfect rag-bag of odds and ends within us—a piece of a policeman's trousers lying cheek by jowl with Queen Alexandra's wedding veil—but has contrived that the whole assortment shall be lightly stitched together by a single thread. Memory is the seamstress, and a capricious one at that. Memory runs her needle in and out, up and down, hither and thither. We know not what comes next, or what follows after. Thus, the most ordinary movement in the world, such as sitting down at a table and pulling the inkstand towards one, may agitate a thousand odd, disconnected fragments, now bright, now dim, hanging and bobbing and dipping and flaunting, like the underlinen of a family of fourteen on a line in a gale of wind. Instead of being a single, downright, bluff piece of work of which no man need feel ashamed, our commonest deeds are set about with a fluttering and flickering of wings, a rising and falling of lights. Thus it was that Orlando, dipping his pen in the ink, saw the mocking face of the lost Princess and asked himself a million questions instantly which were as arrows dipped in gall. Where was she; and why had she left him? Was the Ambassador her uncle or her lover? Had they plotted? Was she forced? Was she married? Was she dead?—all of which so drove their venom into him that, as if to vent his agony somewhere, he plunged his quill so deep into the inkhorn that the ink spirted over the table, which act, explain it how one may (and no explanation perhaps is possible—Memory is inexplicable), at once substituted for the face of the Princess a face of a very different sort. But whose was it, he asked himself? And he had to wait, perhaps half a minute, looking at the new picture which lay on top of the old, as one lantern slide is half seen through the next, before he could say to himself, 'This is the face of that rather fat, shabby man who sat in

Twitchett's room ever so many years ago when old
Queen Bess came here to dine; and I saw him,'
Orlando continued, catching at another of those little
coloured rags, 'sitting at the table, as I peeped in on
my way downstairs, and he had the most amazing
eyes,' said Orlando, 'that ever were, but who the
devil was he?' Orlando asked, for here Memory added
to the forehead and eyes, first, a coarse, grease-stained
ruffle, then a brown doublet, and finally a pair of
thick boots such as citizens wear in Cheapside. 'Not
a Nobleman; not one of us,' said Orlando (which he
would not have said aloud, for he was the most
courteous of gentlemen; but it shows what an effect
noble birth has upon the mind and incidentally how
difficult it is for a nobleman to be a writer), 'a poet, I
dare say.' By all the laws, Memory, having disturbed
him sufficiently, should now have blotted the whole
thing out completely, or have fetched up something
so idiotic and out of keeping—like a dog chasing a
cat or an old woman blowing her nose into a red
cotton handkerchief—that, in despair of keeping pace
with her vagaries, Orlando should have struck his pen
in earnest against his paper. (For we can, if we have
the resolution, turn the hussy, Memory, and all her
ragtag and bobtail out of the house.) But Orlando
paused. Memory still held before him the image of a
shabby man with big, bright eyes. Still he looked, still
he paused. It is these pauses that are our undoing. It
is then that sedition enters the fortress and our troops

[77]

rise in insurrection. Once before he had paused, and love with its horrid rout, its shawms,* its cymbals, and its heads with gory locks torn from the shoulders had burst in. From love he had suffered the tortures of the damned. Now, again, he paused, and into the breach thus made, leapt Ambition, the harridan, and Poetry, the witch, and Desire of Fame, the strumpet; all joined hands and made of his heart their dancing ground. Standing upright in the solitude of his room, he vowed that he would be the first poet of his race and bring immortal lustre upon his name. He said (reciting the names and exploits of his ancestors) that Sir Boris had fought and killed the Paynim; Sir Gawain, the Turk; Sir Miles, the Pole; Sir Andrew, the Frank; Sir Richard, the Austrian; Sir Jordan, the Frenchman; and Sir Herbert, the Spaniard. But of all that killing and campaigning, that drinking and love-making, that spending and hunting and riding and eating, what remained? A skull; a finger. Whereas, he said, turning to the page of Sir Thomas Browne, which lay open upon the table—and again he paused. Like an incantation rising from all parts of the room, from the night wind and the moonlight, rolled the divine melody of those words which, lest they should outstare this page, we will leave where they lie entombed, not dead, embalmed rather, so fresh is their colour, so sound their breathing—and Orlando, comparing that achievement with those of his ancestors, cried out that they and their deeds were dust and ashes, but this man and his words were immortal.

He soon perceived, however, that the battles which Sir Miles and the rest had waged against armed knights to win a kingdom, were not half so arduous as this which he now undertook to win immortality against the English language. Anyone moderately familiar with the rigours of composition will not need to be told the story in detail; how he wrote and it seemed good; read and it seemed vile; corrected and tore up; cut out; put in; was in ecstasy; in despair; had his good nights and bad mornings; snatched at ideas and lost them; saw his book plain before him and it vanished; acted his people's parts as he ate; mouthed them as he walked; now cried; now laughed; vacillated between this style and that; now preferred the heroic and pompous; next the plain and simple; now the vales of Tempe;* then the fields of Kent or Cornwall; and could not decide whether he was the divinest genius or the greatest fool in the world.

It was to settle this last question that he decided after many months of such feverish labour, to break the solitude of years and communicate with the outer world. He had a friend in London, one Giles Isham,* of Norfolk, who, though of gentle birth, was acquainted with writers and could doubtless put him in touch with some member of that blessed, indeed sacred, fraternity. For, to Orlando in the state he was now in, there was a glory about a man who had written a book and had it printed, which outshone all the glories of blood and state. To his imagination it seemed as if even the bodies of those instinct with such divine thoughts must be transfigured. They must have aureoles for hair, incense for breath, and roses must grow between their lips—which was certainly not true either of himself or Mr Dupper. He could think of no greater happiness than to be allowed to sit behind a curtain and hear them talk. Even the imagination of that bold and various discourse made the memory of what he and his courtier friends used to talk about—a dog, a horse, a woman, a game of cards—seem brutish in the extreme. He bethought him with pride that he had always been called a scholar, and sneered at for his love of solitude and books. He had never been apt at pretty phrases. He would stand stock still, blush, and stride like a grenadier in a ladies' drawing-room. He had twice fallen, in sheer abstraction, from his horse. He had broken Lady Winchilsea's fan* once while making a rhyme. Eagerly recalling these and other instances of his unfitness for the life of society, an ineffable hope, that all the turbulence of his youth, his clumsiness, his blushes, his long walks, and his love of the country proved that he himself belonged to the sacred race rather than to the noble—was by birth a writer, rather than an aristocrat—possessed him. For the first time since the night of the great flood he was happy.

He now commissioned Mr Isham of Norfolk to deliver to Mr Nicholas Greene* of Clifford's Inn a document which set forth Orlando's admiration for his works (for Nick Greene was a very famous writer at that time) and his desire to make his acquaintance; which he scarcely dared ask; for he had nothing to offer in return; but if Mr Nicholas Greene would condescend to visit him, a coach and four would be at the corner of Fetter Lane at whatever hour Mr Greene chose to appoint, and bring him safely to Orlando's house. One may fill up the phrases which then followed; and figure Orlando's delight when, in no long time, Mr Greene signified his acceptance of the Noble Lord's invitation; took his place in the coach and was set down in the hall to the south of the main building punctually at seven o'clock on Monday, April the twenty-first.

Many Kings, Queens, and Ambassadors had been received there; Judges had stood there in their ermine. The loveliest ladies of the land had come there; and the sternest warriors. Banners hung there which had been at Flodden and at Agincourt.* There were displayed the painted coats of arms with their lions and their leopards and their coronets. There were the long tables where the gold and silver plate was stood; and there the vast fireplaces of wrought Italian marble where nightly a whole oak tree, with its million leaves and its nests of rook and wren, was burnt to ashes. Nicholas Greene, the poet stood there now, plainly dressed in his slouched hat and black doublet, carrying in one hand a small bag.

That Orlando as he hastened to greet him was slightly disappointed was inevitable. The poet was not above middle height; was of a mean figure; was lean and stooped somewhat, and, stumbling over the mastiff on entering, the dog bit him. Moreover, Orlando for all his knowledge of mankind was puzzled where to place him. There was something about him which belonged neither to servant, squire, or noble. The head with its rounded forehead and beaked nose was fine, but the chin receded. The eyes were brilliant, but the lips hung loose and slobbered. It was the expression of the face as a whole, however, that was disquieting. There was none of that stately composure which makes the faces of the nobility so pleasing to look at; nor had it anything of the dignified servility of a well-trained domestic's face; it was a face seamed, puckered, and drawn together. Poet though he was, it seemed as if he were more used to scold than to flatter; to quarrel than to coo; to scramble than to ride; to struggle than to rest; to hate than to love. This, too, was shown by the quickness of his movements; and by something fiery and suspicious in his glance. Orlando was somewhat taken aback. But they went to dinner.

Here, Orlando, who usually took such things for granted, was, for the first time, unaccountably ashamed of the number of his servants and of the splendour of his table. Stranger still, he bethought him with pride—for the thought was generally distasteful—of that great grandmother Moll who had milked the cows. He was about somehow to allude to this humble woman and her milk-pails, when the poet forestalled him by saying that it was odd, seeing how common the name of Greene was, that the family had come over with the Conqueror and was of the highest nobility in France. Unfortunately, they had come down in the world and done little more than leave their name to the royal borough of Greenwich. Further talk of the same sort, about lost castles, coats of arms, cousins who were baronets in the north, intermarriage with noble families in the west, how some Greens spelt the name with an e at the end, and others without, lasted till the venison was on the table. Then Orlando contrived to say something of Grandmother Moll and her cows, and had eased his heart a little of its burden by the time the wild-fowl were before them. But it was not until the Malmsey* was passing freely that Orlando dared mention what he could not help thinking a more important matter than the Greens or the cows; that is to say the sacred subject of poetry. At the first mention of the word, the poet's eyes flashed fire; he dropped the fine gentleman airs he had worn; thumped his glass on the table, and launched into one of the longest, most intricate, most passionate, and bitterest stories that Orlando had ever heard, save from the lips of a jilted

woman, about a play of his; another poet; and a
critic. Of the nature of poetry itself, Orlando only
gathered that it was harder to sell than prose, and
though the lines were shorter took longer in the
writing. So the talk went on with ramifications
interminable, until Orlando ventured to hint that he
had himself been so rash as to write—but here the
poet leapt from his chair. A mouse had squeaked in
the wainscot, he said. The truth was, he explained,
that his nerves were in a state where a mouse's squeak
upset them for a fortnight. Doubtless the house was
full of vermin, but Orlando had not heard them. The
poet then gave Orlando the full story of his health for
the past ten years or so. It had been so bad that one
could only marvel that he still lived. He had had the
palsy, the gout, the ague, the dropsy, and the three
sorts of fever in succession; added to which he had an
enlarged heart, a great spleen, and a diseased liver.
But, above all, he had, he told Orlando, sensations in
his spine which defied description. There was one
knob about the third from the top which burnt like
fire; another about second from the bottom which
was cold as ice. Sometimes he woke with a brain like
lead; at others it was as if a thousand wax tapers were
alight and people were throwing fireworks inside
him. He could feel a rose leaf through his mattress,
he said; and knew his way almost about London by
the feel of the cobbles. Altogether he was a piece of
machinery so finely made and curiously put together

(here he raised his hand as if unconsciously, and indeed it was of the finest shape imaginable) that it confounded him to think that he had only sold five hundred copies of his poem, but that of course was largely due to the conspiracy against him. All he could say, he concluded, banging his fist upon the table, was that the art of poetry was dead in England.

How that could be with Shakespeare, Marlowe, Ben Jonson, Browne, Donne, all now writing or just having written, Orlando, reeling off the names of his favourite heroes, could not think.

Greene laughed sardonically. Shakespeare, he admitted, had written some scenes that were well enough; but he had taken them chiefly from Marlowe. Marlowe was a likely boy, but what could you say of a lad who died before he was thirty? As for Browne, he was for writing poetry in prose, and people soon got tired of such conceits as that. Donne was a mountebank who wrapped up his lack of meaning in hard words. The gulls were taken in; but the style would be out of fashion twelve months hence. As for Ben Jonson—Ben Jonson was a friend of his and he never spoke ill of his friends.

No, he concluded, the great age of literature is past; the great age of literature was the Greek; the Elizabethan age was inferior in every respect to the Greek. In such ages men cherished a divine ambition which he might call La Gloire (he pronounced it Glawr, so that Orlando did not at first catch his meaning). Now all young writers were in the pay of the booksellers and poured out any trash that would sell. Shakespeare was the chief offender in this way and Shakespeare was already paying the penalty. Their own age, he said, was marked by precious conceits and wild experiments—neither of which the Greeks would have tolerated for a moment. Much though it hurt him to say it—for he loved literature as he loved his life—he could see no good in the present and had no hope of the future. Here he poured himself out another glass of wine.

Orlando was shocked by these doctrines; yet could not help observing that the critic himself seemed by no means downcast. On the contrary, the more he denounced his own time, the more complacent he became. He could remember, he said, a night at the Cock Tavern in Fleet Street when Kit Marlowe was there and some others. Kit was in high feather, rather drunk, which he easily became, and in a mood to say silly things. He could see him now, brandishing his glass at the company and hiccoughing out, 'Stap my vitals, Bill' (this was to Shakespeare), 'there's a great wave coming and you're on the top of it,' by which he meant, Greene explained, that they were trembling on the verge of a great age in English literature, and that Shakespeare was to be a poet of some importance. Happily for himself, he was killed two nights later in a drunken brawl, and so did not live to see how this prediction turned out. 'Poor foolish fellow,' said

Greene, 'to go and say a thing like that. A great age, forsooth—the Elizabethan a great age!

'So, my dear Lord,' he continued, settling himself comfortably in his chair and rubbing the wine-glass between his fingers, 'we must make the best of it, cherish the past and honour those writers—there are still a few left of 'em—who take antiquity for their model and write, not for pay but for Glawr.' (Orlando could have wished him a better accent.) 'Glawr', said Greene, 'is the spur of noble minds. Had I a pension of three hundred pounds a year paid quarterly, I would live for Glawr alone. I would lie in bed every morning reading Cicero. I would imitate his style so that you couldn't tell the difference between us. That's what I call fine writing,' said Greene; 'that's what I call Glawr. But it's necessary to have a pension to do it.'

By this time Orlando had abandoned all hope of discussing his own work with the poet; but this mattered the less as the talk now got upon the lives and characters of Shakespeare, Ben Jonson, and the rest, all of whom Greene had known intimately and about whom he had a thousand anecdotes of the most amusing kind to tell. Orlando had never laughed so much in his life. These, then, were his gods! Half were drunken and all were amorous. Most of them quarrelled with their wives; not one of them was above a lie or an intrigue of the most paltry kind. Their poetry was scribbled down on the backs of washing bills held to the heads of printer's devils at the street door. Thus Hamlet went to press; thus Lear; thus Othello. No wonder, as Greene said, that these plays show the faults they do. The rest of the time was spent in carousings and junketings in taverns and in beer gardens, when things were said that passed belief for wit, and things were done that made the utmost frolic of the courtiers seem pale in comparison. All this Greene told with a spirit that roused Orlando to the highest pitch of delight. He had a power of mimicry that brought the dead to life, and could say the finest things of books provided they were written three hundred years ago.*

So time passed, and Orlando felt for his guest a strange mixture of liking and contempt, of admiration and pity, as well as something too indefinite to be called by any one name, but had something of fear in it and something of fascination. He talked incessantly about himself, yet was such good company that one could listen to the story of his ague for ever. Then he was so witty; then he was so irreverent; then he made so free with the names of God and Woman; then he was so full of queer crafts and had such strange lore in his head; could make salad in three hundred different ways; knew all that could be known of the mixing of wines; played half-a-dozen musical instruments, and was the first person, and perhaps the last, to toast cheese in the great Italian fireplace. That he did not know a geranium from a carnation, an oak

from a birch tree, a mastiff from a greyhound, a teg*
from a ewe, wheat from barley, plough land from
fallow; was ignorant of the rotation of the crops;
thought oranges grew underground and turnips on
trees; preferred any townscape to any landscape;—all
this and much more amazed Orlando, who had never
met anybody of his kind before. Even the maids, who
despised him, tittered at his jokes, and the men-
servants, who loathed him, hung about to hear his
stories. Indeed, the house had never been so lively as
now that he was there—all of which gave Orlando a
great deal to think about, and caused him to compare
this way of life with the old. He recalled the sort of
talk he had been used to about the King of Spain's
apoplexy or the mating of a bitch; he bethought him
how the day passed between the stables and the
dressing closet; he remembered how the Lords snored
over their wine and hated anybody who woke them
up. He bethought him how active and valiant they
were in body; how slothful and timid in mind.
Worried by these thoughts, and unable to strike a
proper balance, he came to the conclusion that he had
admitted to his house a plaguey spirit of unrest that
would never suffer him to sleep sound again.

At the same moment, Nick Greene came to precisely the opposite conclusion. Lying in bed of a
morning on the softest pillows between the smoothest
sheets and looking out of his oriel window upon turf
which for centuries had known neither dandelion nor

dock weed, he thought that unless he could somehow make his escape, he should be smothered alive. Getting up and hearing the pigeons coo, dressing and hearing the fountains fall, he thought that unless he could hear the drays roar upon the cobbles of Fleet Street, he would never write another line. If this goes on much longer, he thought, hearing the footman mend the fire and spread the table with silver dishes next door, I shall fall asleep and (here he gave a prodigious yawn) sleeping die.

So he sought Orlando in his room, and explained that he had not been able to sleep a wink all night because of the silence. (Indeed, the house was surrounded by a park fifteen miles in circumference and a wall ten feet high.) Silence, he said, was of all things the most oppressive to his nerves. He would end his visit, by Orlando's leave, that very morning. Orlando felt some relief at this, yet also a great reluctance to let him go. The house, he thought, would seem very dull without him. On parting (for he had never yet liked to mention the subject), he had the temerity to press his play upon the Death of Hercules upon the poet and ask his opinion of it. The poet took it; muttered something about Glawr and Cicero, which Orlando cut short by promising to pay the pension quarterly; whereupon Greene, with many protestations of affection, jumped into the coach and was gone.

The great hall had never seemed so large, so splendid, or so empty as the chariot rolled away. Orlando knew that he would never have the heart to make toasted cheese in the Italian fireplace again. He would never have the wit to crack jokes about Italian pictures; never have the skill to mix punch as it should be mixed; a thousand good quips and cranks would be lost to him. Yet what a relief to be out of the sound of that querulous voice, what a luxury to be alone once more, so he could not help reflecting, as he unloosed the mastiff which had been tied up these six weeks because it never saw the poet without biting him.

Nick Greene was set down at the corner of Fetter Lane that same afternoon, and found things going on much as he had left them. Mrs Greene, that is to say, was giving birth to a baby in one room; Tom Fletcher was drinking gin in another. Books were tumbled all about the floor; dinner—such as it was—was set on a dressing-table where the children had been making mud pies. But this, Greene felt, was the atmosphere for writing; here he could write, and write he did. The subject was made for him. A noble Lord at home. A visit to a Nobleman in the country—his new poem was to have some such title as that. Seizing the pen with which his little boy was tickling the cat's ears, and dipping it in the egg-cup which served for inkpot, Greene dashed off a very spirited satire there and then. It was so done to a turn that no one could doubt that the young Lord who was roasted was

Orlando; his most private sayings and doings, his enthusiasms and follies, down to the very colour of his hair and the foreign way he had of rolling his r's, were there to the life. And if there had been any doubt about it, Greene clinched the matter by introducing, with scarcely any disguise, passages from that aristocratic tragedy, the Death of Hercules, which he found as he expected, wordy and bombastic in the extreme.

The pamphlet, which ran at once into several editions, and paid the expenses of Mrs Greene's tenth lying-in, was soon sent by friends who take care of such matters to Orlando himself. When he had read it, which he did with deadly composure from start to finish, he rang for the footman; delivered the document to him at the end of a pair of tongs; bade him drop it in the filthiest heart of the foulest midden* on the estate. Then, when the man was turning to go he stopped him, 'Take the swiftest horse in the stable,' he said, 'ride for dear life to Harwich. There embark upon a ship which you will find bound for Norway. Buy for me from the King's own kennels the finest elk-hounds of the Royal strain, male and female. Bring them back without delay. For', he murmured, scarcely above his breath as he turned to his books, 'I have done with men.'

The footman, who was perfectly trained in his duties, bowed and disappeared. He fulfilled his task so efficiently that he was back that day three weeks,

leading in his hand a leash of the finest elk-hounds,*
one of whom, a female, gave birth that very night*
under the dinner-table to a litter of eight fine puppies.
Orlando had them brought to his bedchamber.

'For', he said, 'I have done with men.'

Nevertheless, he paid the pension quarterly.

Thus, at the age of thirty, or thereabouts, this young
Nobleman had not only had every experience that life
has to offer, but had seen the worthlessness of them
all. Love and ambition, women and poets were all
equally vain. Literature was a farce. The night after
reading Greene's Visit to a Nobleman in the Country,
he burnt in a great conflagration fifty-seven poetical
works, only retaining 'The Oak Tree', which was his
boyish dream and very short. Two things alone
remained to him in which he now put any trust: dogs
and nature; an elk-hound and a rose bush. The world,
in all its variety, life in all its complexity, had shrunk
to that. Dogs and a bush were the whole of it. So
feeling quit of a vast mountain of illusion, and very
naked in consequence, he called his hounds to him
and strode through the Park.

So long had he been secluded, writing and reading,
that he had half forgotten the amenities of nature,
which in June can be great. When he reached that
high mound whence on fine days half of England
with a slice of Wales and Scotland thrown in can be
seen, he flung himself under his favourite oak tree

and felt that if he need never speak to another man or woman so long as he lived; if his dogs did not develop the faculty of speech; if he never met a poet or a Princess again, he might make out what years remained to him in tolerable content.

Here he came then, day after day, week after week, month after month, year after year. He saw the beech trees turn golden and the young ferns unfurl; he saw the moon sickle and then circular; he saw—but probably the reader can imagine the passage which should follow and how every tree and plant in the neighbourhood is described first green, then golden; how moons rise and suns set; how spring follows winter and autumn summer; how night succeeds day and day night; how there is first a storm and then fine weather; how things remain much as they are for two or three hundred years or so, except for a little dust and a few cobwebs which one old woman can sweep up in half an hour; a conclusion which, one cannot help feeling, might have been reached more quickly by the simple statement that 'Time passed' (here the exact amount could be indicated in brackets) and nothing whatever happened.*

But Time, unfortunately, though it makes animals and vegetables bloom and fade with amazing punctuality, has no such simple effect upon the mind of man. The mind of man, moreover, works with equal strangeness upon the body of time. An hour, once it lodges in the queer element of the human spirit, may be stretched to fifty or a hundred times its clock length; on the other hand, an hour may be accurately represented on the timepiece of the mind by one second. This extraordinary discrepancy between time on the clock and time in the mind is less known than it should be and deserves fuller investigation. But the biographer, whose interests are, as we have said, highly restricted, must confine himself to one simple statement: when a man has reached the age of thirty, as Orlando now had, time when he is thinking becomes inordinately long; time when he is doing becomes inordinately short. Thus Orlando gave his orders and did the business of his vast estates in a flash; but directly he was alone on the mound under the oak tree, the seconds began to round and fill until it seemed as if they would never fall. They filled themselves, moreover, with the strangest variety of objects. For not only did he find himself confronted by problems which have puzzled the wisest of men, such as What is love? What friendship? What truth? but directly he came to think about them, his whole past, which seemed to him of extreme length and variety, rushed into the falling second, swelled it a dozen times its natural size, coloured it a thousand tints, and filled it with all the odds and ends in the universe.

In such thinking (or by whatever name it should be called) he spent months and years of his life. It would be no exaggeration to say that he would go out after breakfast a man of thirty and come home to dinner a man of fifty-five at least. Some weeks added a century to his age, others no more than three seconds at most. Altogether, the task of estimating the length of human life (of the animals' we presume not to speak) is beyond our capacity, for directly we say that it is ages long, we are reminded that it is briefer than the fall of a rose leaf to the ground. Of the two forces which alternately, and what is more confusing still, at the same moment, dominate our unfortunate numb-skulls—brevity and diuturnity—Orlando was some-times under the influence of the elephant-footed deity, then of the gnat-winged fly. Life seemed to him of prodigious length. Yet even so, it went like a flash. But even when it stretched longest and the moments swelled biggest and he seemed to wander alone in deserts of vast eternity,* there was no time for the smoothing out and deciphering of those thickly scored parchments which thirty years among men and women had rolled tight in his heart and brain. Long before he had done thinking about Love (the oak tree had put forth its leaves and shaken them to the ground a dozen times in the process) Ambition would jostle it off the field, to be replaced by Friendship or Literature. And as the first question had not been settled—What is Love?—back it would come at the least provocation or none, and hustle Books or Met-aphors or What one lives for into the margin, there to wait till they saw their chance to rush into the field again. What made the process still longer was that it was profusely illustrated, not only with pictures, as that of old Queen Elizabeth, laid on her tapestry couch in rose-coloured brocade with an ivory snuff-box in her hand and a gold-hilted sword by her side, but with scents—she was strongly perfumed—and with sounds; the stags were barking in Richmond Park that winter's day. And so, the thought of love would be all ambered over with snow and winter; with log fires burning; with Russian women, gold swords, and the bark of stags; with old King James' slobbering and fireworks and sacks of treasure in the holds of Elizabethan sailing ships. Every single thing, once he tried to dislodge it from its place in his mind, he found thus cumbered with other matter like the lump of glass which, after a year at the bottom of the sea, is grown about with bones and dragon-flies, and coins and the tresses of drowned women.

'Another metaphor by Jupiter!' he would exclaim as he said this (which will show the disorderly and circuitous way in which his mind worked and explain why the oak tree flowered and faded so often before he came to any conclusion about Love). 'And what's the point of it?' he would ask himself. 'Why not say simply in so many words——' and then he would try to think for half an hour,—or was it two years and a half?—how to say simply in so many words what love is. 'A figure like that is manifestly untruthful,' he argued, 'for no dragon-fly, unless under very exceptional circumstances, could live at the bottom of the sea. And if literature is not the Bride and Bedfellow of Truth, what is she? Confound it all,' he cried, 'why say Bedfellow when one's already said Bride? Why not simply say what one means and leave it?'

So then he tried saying the grass is green and the sky is blue and so to propitiate the austere spirit of poetry whom still, though at a great distance, he could not help reverencing. 'The sky is blue,' he said, 'the grass is green.' Looking up, he saw that, on the contrary, the sky is like the veils which a thousand Madonnas have let fall from their hair; and the grass fleets* and darkens like a flight of girls fleeing the embraces of hairy satyrs* from enchanted woods. 'Upon my word,' he said (for he had fallen into the bad habit of speaking aloud), 'I don't see that one's more true than another. Both are utterly false.' And he despaired of being able to solve the problem of what poetry is and what truth is and fell into a deep dejection.

And here we may profit by a pause in his soliloquy to reflect how odd it was to see Orlando stretched there on his elbow on a June day and to reflect that this fine fellow with all his faculties about him and a healthy body, witness cheeks and limbs—a man who never thought twice about heading a charge or fighting a duel*—should be so subject to the lethargy of thought, and rendered so susceptible by it, that when it came to a question of poetry, or his own competence in it, he was as shy as a little girl behind her mother's cottage door. In our belief, Greene's ridicule of his tragedy hurt him as much as the Princess' ridicule of his love. But to return——

Orlando went on thinking. He kept looking at the grass and at the sky and trying to bethink him what a true poet, who has his verses published in London, would say about them. Memory meanwhile (whose habits have already been described) kept steady before his eyes the face of Nicholas Greene, as if that sardonic loose-lipped man, treacherous as he had proved himself, were the Muse in person, and it was to him that Orlando must do homage. So Orlando, that summer morning, offered him a variety of phrases, some plain, others figured, and Nick Greene kept shaking his head and sneering and muttering something about Glawr and Cicero and the death of poetry in our time. At length, starting to his feet (it was now winter and very cold) Orlando swore one of the most remarkable oaths of his lifetime, for it bound him to a servitude than which none is stricter. 'I'll be blasted', he said, 'if I ever write another word, or try to write another word to please Nick Greene or the Muse. Bad, good, or indifferent, I'll write, from this day forward, to please myself'; and here he made as if he were tearing a whole budget* of papers across and tossing them in the face of that sneering loose-lipped man. Upon which, as a cur ducks if you stoop to shy a stone at him, Memory ducked her effigy of

Nick Greene out of sight, and substituted for it—
nothing whatever.

But Orlando, all the same, went on thinking. He
had indeed much to think of. For when he tore the
parchment across, he tore, in one rending, the scrolloping,* emblazoned scroll which he had made out in
his own favour in the solitude of his room appointing
himself, as the King appoints Ambassadors, the first
poet of his race, the first writer of his age, conferring
eternal immortality upon his soul and granting his
body a grave among laurels and the intangible banners
of a people's reverence perpetually. Eloquent as this
all was, he now tore it up and threw it in the dustbin.
'Fame', he said, 'is like' (and since there was no Nick
Greene to stop him, he went on to revel in images of
which we will choose only one or two of the quietest)
'a braided coat which hampers the limbs; a jacket of
silver which curbs the heart; a painted shield which
covers a scarecrow,' etc. etc. The pith of his phrases
was that while fame impedes and constricts, obscurity
wraps about a man like a mist; obscurity is dark,
ample, and free; obscurity lets the mind take its way
unimpeded. Over the obscure man is poured the merci-
ful suffusion of darkness. None knows where he goes
or comes. He may seek the truth and speak it; he alone
is free; he alone is truthful; he alone is at peace. And
so he sank into a quiet mood, under the oak tree, the
hardness of whose roots, exposed above the ground,
seemed to him rather comfortable than otherwise.

Sunk for a long time in profound thoughts as to the value of obscurity, and the delight of having no name, but being like a wave which returns to the deep body of the sea; thinking how obscurity rids the mind of the irk of envy and spite; how it sets running in the veins the free waters of generosity and magnanimity; and allows giving and taking without thanks offered or praise given; which must have been the way of all great poets, he supposed (though his knowledge of Greek was not enough to bear him out), for, he thought, Shakespeare must have written like that, and the church builders built like that, anonymously, needing no thanking or naming, but only their work in the daytime and a little ale perhaps at night—'What an admirable life this is,' he thought, stretching his limbs out under the oak tree. 'And why not enjoy it this very moment?' The thought struck him like a bullet. Ambition dropped like a plummet. Rid of the heartburn of rejected love, and of vanity rebuked, and all the other stings and pricks which the nettle-bed of life had burnt upon him when ambitious of fame, but could no longer inflict upon one careless of glory, he opened his eyes, which had been wide open all the time, but had seen only thoughts, and saw, lying in the hollow beneath him, his house.

There it lay* in the early sunshine of spring. It looked a town rather than a house, but a town built, not hither and thither, as this man wished or that, but circumspectly, by a single architect with one idea in his head. Courts and buildings, grey, red, plum colour, lay orderly and symmetrical; the courts were some of them oblong and some square; in this was a fountain; in that a statue; the buildings were some of them low, some pointed; here was a chapel, there a belfry; spaces of the greenest grass lay in between and clumps of cedar trees and beds of bright flowers; all were clasped—yet so well set out was it that it seemed that every part had room to spread itself fittingly—by the roll of a massive wall; while smoke from innumerable chimneys curled perpetually into the air. This vast, yet ordered building, which could house a thousand men and perhaps two thousand horses, was built, Orlando thought, by workmen whose names are unknown. Here have lived, for more centuries than I can count, the obscure generations of my own obscure family. Not one of these Richards, Johns, Annes, Elizabeths has left a token of himself behind him, yet all, working together with their spades and their needles, their love-making and their child-bearing, have left this.

Never had the house looked more noble and humane.

Why, then, had he wished to raise himself above them? For it seemed vain and arrogant in the extreme to try to better that anonymous work of creation; the labours of those vanished hands. Better was it to go unknown and leave behind you an arch, a potting shed, a wall where peaches ripen, than to burn like a meteor and leave no dust. For after all, he said, kindling as he looked at the great house on the greensward below, the unknown lords and ladies who lived there never forgot to set aside something for those who come after; for the roof that will leak; for the tree that will fall. There was always a warm corner for the old shepherd in the kitchen; always food for the hungry; always their goblets were polished, though they lay sick, and their windows were lit though they lay dying. Lords though they were, they were content to go down into obscurity with the molecatcher and the stone-mason. Obscure noblemen, forgotten builders—thus he apostrophized them with a warmth that entirely gainsaid such critics as called him cold, indifferent, slothful (the truth being that a quality often lies just on the other side of the wall from where we seek it)—thus he apostrophized his house and race in terms of the most moving eloquence; but when it came to the peroration—and what is eloquence that lacks a peroration?—he fumbled. He would have liked to have ended with a flourish to the effect that he would follow in their footsteps and add another stone to their building. Since, however, the building already covered nine acres, to add even a single stone seemed superfluous. Could one mention furniture in a peroration? Could one speak of chairs and tables and mats to lie beside people's beds? For whatever the peroration wanted, that was what the house stood in need of. Leaving his speech unfinished for the moment, he strode downhill again resolved henceforward to devote himself to the furnishing of the mansion. The news—that she was to attend him instantly—brought tears to the eyes of good old Mrs Grimsditch, now grown somewhat old. Together they perambulated the house.

The towel horse in the King's bedroom ('and that was King Jamie, my Lord,' she said, hinting that it was many a day since a King had slept under their roof; but the odious Parliament days* were over and there was now a Crown in England again) lacked a leg; there were no stands to the ewers in the little closet leading into the waiting room of the Duchess's page; Mr Greene had made a stain on the carpet with his nasty pipe smoking, which she and Judy, for all their scrubbing, had never been able to wash out. Indeed, when Orlando came to reckon up the matter of furnishing with rosewood chairs and cedar-wood cabinets, with silver basins, china bowls, and Persian carpets, everyone of the three hundred and sixty-five bedrooms* which the house contained, he saw that it would be no light one; and if some thousands of pounds of his estate remained over, these would do little more than hang a few galleries with tapestry, set the dining hall with fine, carved chairs and provide mirrors of solid silver and chairs of the same metal (for which he had an inordinate passion) for the furnishing of the royal bedchambers.

He now set to work in earnest, as we can prove beyond a doubt if we look at his ledgers. Let us glance at an inventory of what he bought at this time, with the expenses totted up in the margin—but these we omit.

'To fifty pairs of Spanish blankets, ditto curtains of crimson and white taffeta; the valence to them of white satin embroidered with crimson and white silk. . . .

'To seventy yellow satin chairs and sixty stools, suitable with their buckram covers to them all. . . .

'To sixty seven walnut tree tables. . . .

'To seventeen dozen boxes containing each dozen five dozen of Venice glasses. . . .

'To one hundred and two mats, each thirty yards long. . . .

'To ninety seven cushions of crimson damask laid with silver parchment lace and footstools of cloth of tissue and chairs suitable. . . .

'To fifty branches for a dozen lights apiece. . . .'

Already—it is an effect lists have upon us—we are beginning to yawn. But if we stop, it is only that the catalogue is tedious, not that it is finished. There are ninety-nine pages more of it and the total sum disbursed ran into many thousands—that is to say millions of our money. And if his day was spent like this, at night again, Lord Orlando might be found reckoning out what it would cost to level a million molehills, if the men were paid tenpence an hour; and again, how many hundredweight of nails at 5½d. a gill were needed to repair the fence round the park, which was fifteen miles in circumference. And so on and so on.

The tale, we say, is tedious, for one cupboard is much like another, and one molehill not much different from a million. Some pleasant journeys it cost him; and some fine adventures. As, for instance, when he set a whole city of blind women near Bruges to stitch hangings for a silver canopied bed; and the story of his adventure with a Moor in Venice of whom he bought (but only at the sword's point) his lacquered cabinet, might, in other hands, prove worth the telling. Nor did the work lack variety; for here would come, drawn by teams from Sussex, great trees, to be sawn across and laid along the gallery for flooring; and then a chest from Persia, stuffed with wool and sawdust, from which, at last, he would take a single plate, or one topaz ring.

At length, however, there was no room in the galleries for another table; no room on the tables for another cabinet; no room in the cabinet for another rose-bowl; no room in the bowl for another handful of potpourri; there was no room for anything anywhere; in short the house was furnished. In the garden snowdrops, crocuses, hyacinths, magnolias, roses, lilies, asters, the dahlia in all its varieties, pear trees and apple trees and cherry trees and mulberry trees, with an enormous quantity of rare and flowering shrubs, of trees evergreen and perennial, grew so thick on each other's roots that there was no plot of earth without its bloom, and no stretch of sward without its shade. In addition, he had imported wild fowl with gay plumage; and two Malay bears, the surliness of whose manners concealed, he was certain, trusty hearts.

All now was ready; and when it was evening and the innumerable silver sconces* were lit and the light airs which for ever moved about the galleries stirred the blue and green arras,* so that it looked as if the huntsmen were riding and Daphne flying;* when the silver shone and lacquer glowed and wood kindled; when the carved chairs held their arms out and dolphins swam upon the walls with mermaids on their backs; when all this and much more than all this was complete and to his liking, Orlando walked through the house with his elk-hounds following and felt content. He had matter now, he thought, to fill out his peroration. Perhaps it would be well to begin the speech all over again. Yet, as he paraded the galleries he felt that still something was lacking. Chairs and tables, however richly gilt and carved, sofas, resting on lions' paws with swans' necks curving under them, beds even of the softest swansdown are not by themselves enough. People sitting in them, people lying in them improve them amazingly. Accordingly Orlando now began a series of very splendid entertainments to the nobility and gentry of the neighbourhood. The three hundred and sixty-five bedrooms were full for a month at a time. Guests jostled each other on the fifty-two staircases. Three hundred servants bustled about the pantries. Banquets took place almost nightly. Thus, in a very few years, Orlando had worn the nap off his velvet, and spent the half of his fortune; but he had earned the good opinion of his neighbours, held a score of offices in the county, and was annually presented with perhaps a dozen volumes dedicated to his Lordship in rather fulsome terms by grateful poets. For though he was careful not to consort with writers at that time and kept himself always aloof from ladies of foreign blood, still, he was excessively generous both to women and to poets, and both adored him.

But when the feasting was at its height and his guests were at their revels, he was apt to take himself off to his private room alone. There when the door was shut, and he was certain of privacy, he would have out an old writing book, stitched together with silk stolen from his mother's workbox, and labelled in a round schoolboy hand,* 'The Oak Tree, A Poem'. In this he would write till midnight chimed and long after. But as he scratched out as many lines as he wrote in, the sum of them was often, at the end of the year, rather less than at the beginning, and it looked as if in the process of writing the poem would be completely unwritten. For it is for the historian of letters to remark that he had changed his style amazingly. His floridity was chastened; his abundance curbed; the age of prose was congealing those warm fountains. The very landscape outside was less stuck about with garlands and the briars themselves were less thorned and intricate. Perhaps the senses were a little duller and honey and cream less seductive to the palate. Also that the streets were better drained and the houses better lit had its effect upon the style, it cannot be doubted.

One day he was adding a line or two with enormous labour to 'The Oak Tree, A Poem', when a shadow crossed the tail of his eye. It was no shadow, he soon saw, but the figure of a very tall lady in riding hood and mantle crossing the quadrangle on which his room looked out. As this was the most private of the courts, and the lady was a stranger to him, Orlando marvelled how she had got there. Three days later the same apparition appeared again; and on Wednesday noon appeared once more. This time, Orlando was determined to follow her, nor apparently was she afraid to be found, for she slackened her steps as he came up and looked him full in the face. Any other woman thus caught in a Lord's private grounds would have been afraid; any other woman with that face, head-dress, and aspect would have thrown her mantilla across her shoulders to hide it. For this lady resembled nothing so much as a hare; a hare startled, but obdurate; a hare whose timidity is overcome by an immense and foolish audacity; a hare that sits upright and glowers at its pursuer with great, bulging eyes; with ears erect but quivering, with nose pointed, but twitching. This hare, moreover, was six feet high and wore a headdress into the bargain of some antiquated kind which made her look still taller. Thus confronted, she stared at Orlando with a stare in which timidity and audacity were most strangely combined.

First, she asked him, with a proper, but somewhat clumsy curtsey, to forgive her her intrusion. Then, rising to her full height again, which must have been something over six feet two, she went on to say—but with such a cackle of nervous laughter, so much tee-heeing and haw-hawing that Orlando thought she must have escaped from a lunatic asylum—that she was the Archduchess Harriet* Griselda of Finster-Aarhorn and Scand-op-Boom in the Roumanian territory. She desired above all things to make his acquaintance, she said. She had taken lodging over a baker's shop at the Park Gates. She had seen his picture and it was the image of a sister of hers who was—here she guffawed—long since dead. She was visiting the English court. The Queen was her Cousin. The King was a very good fellow but seldom went to bed sober. Here she tee-heed and haw-hawed again. In short, there was nothing for it but to ask her in and give her a glass of wine.

Indoors, her manners regained the hauteur natural to a Roumanian Archduchess; and had she not shown a knowledge of wines rare in a lady, and made some observations upon firearms and the customs of sportsmen in her country, which were sensible enough, the talk would have lacked spontaneity. Jumping to her feet at last, she announced that she would call the following day, swept another prodigious curtsey and departed. The following day, Orlando rode out. The next, he turned his back; on the third he drew his curtain. On the fourth it rained, and as he could not keep a lady in the wet, nor was altogether averse to company, he invited her in and asked her opinion whether a suit of armour, which belonged to an ancestor of his, was the work of Jacobi or of Topp. He inclined to Topp. She held another opinion—it matters very little which. But it is of some importance to the course of our story that, in illustrating her argument, which had to do with the working of the tie pieces, the Archduchess Harriet took the golden shin case and fitted it to Orlando's leg.

That he had a pair of the shapeliest legs that any Nobleman has ever stood upright upon has already been said.

Perhaps something in the way she fastened the ankle buckle; or her stooping posture; or Orlando's long seclusion; or the natural sympathy which is between the sexes; or the Burgundy; or the fire—any of these causes may have been to blame; for certainly blame there is on one side or another, when a Nobleman of Orlando's breeding, entertaining a lady in his house, and she his elder by many years, with a face a yard long and staring eyes, dressed somewhat ridiculously too, in a mantle and riding cloak though the season was warm—blame there is when such a Nobleman is

[111]

so suddenly and violently overcome by passion of some sort that he has to leave the room.

But what sort of passion, it may well be asked, could this be? And the answer is double faced as Love herself. For Love—but leaving Love out of the argument for a moment, the actual event was this:

When the Archduchess Harriet Griselda stooped to fasten the buckle, Orlando heard, suddenly and unaccountably, far off the beating of Love's wings. The distant stir of that soft plumage roused in him a thousand memories of rushing waters, of loveliness in the snow and faithlessness in the flood; and the sound came nearer; and he blushed and trembled; and he was moved as he had thought never to be moved again; and he was ready to raise his hands and let the bird of beauty alight upon his shoulders, when—horror!—a creaking sound like that the crows make tumbling over the trees began to reverberate; the air seemed dark with coarse black wings; voices croaked; bits of straw, twigs, and feathers dropped; and there pitched down upon his shoulders the heaviest and foulest of the birds; which is the vulture. Thus he rushed from the room and sent the footman to see the Archduchess Harriet to her carriage.

For Love, to which we may now return, has two faces; one white, the other black; two bodies; one smooth, the other hairy. It has two hands, two feet, two nails, two, indeed, of every member and each one is the exact opposite of the other. Yet, so strictly are they joined together that you cannot separate them. In this case, Orlando's love began her flight towards him with her white face turned, and her smooth and lovely body outwards. Nearer and nearer she came wafting before her airs of pure delight. All of a sudden (at the sight of the Archduchess presumably) she wheeled about, turned the other way round; showed herself black, hairy, brutish; and it was Lust the vulture, not Love, the Bird of Paradise, that flopped, foully and disgustingly, upon his shoulders. Hence he ran; hence he fetched the footman.

But the harpy is not so easily banished as all that. Not only did the Archduchess continue to lodge at the Baker's, but Orlando was haunted every day and night by phantoms of the foulest kind. Vainly, it seemed, had he furnished his house with silver and hung the walls with arras, when at any moment a dung-bedraggled fowl could settle upon his writing table. There she was, flopping about among the chairs; he saw her waddling ungracefully across the galleries. Now, she perched, top heavy upon a fire screen. When he chased her out, back she came and pecked at the glass till she broke it.

Thus realizing that his home was uninhabitable, and that steps must be taken to end the matter instantly, he did what any other young man would have done in his place, and asked King Charles* to send him as Ambassador Extraordinary to Constantinople.* The King was walking in Whitehall. Nell Gwyn was on his arm. She was pelting him with hazel nuts. 'Twas a thousand pities, that amorous lady sighed, that such a pair of legs should leave the country.

Howbeit, the Fates were hard; she could do no more than toss one kiss over her shoulder before Orlando sailed.

CHAPTER III

It is, indeed, highly unfortunate, and much to be regretted that at this stage of Orlando's career, when he played a most important part in the public life of his country, we have least information to go upon. We know that he discharged his duties to admiration—witness his Bath and his Dukedom. We know that he had a finger in some of the most delicate negotiations between King Charles and the Turks—to that, treaties in the vault of the Record Office bear testimony. But the revolution which broke out during his period of office, and the fire which followed, have so damaged or destroyed all those papers from which any trustworthy record could be drawn, that what we can give is lamentably incomplete. Often the paper was scorched a deep brown in the middle of the most important sentence. Just when we thought to elucidate a secret that has puzzled historians for a hundred years, there was a hole in the manuscript big enough to put your finger through. We have done our best to piece out a meagre summary from the charred fragments that remain; but often it has been necessary to speculate, to surmise, and even to use the imagination.

Orlando's day was passed, it would seem, somewhat in this fashion. About seven, he would rise, wrap himself in a long Turkish cloak, light a cheroot, and lean his elbows on the parapet. Thus he would stand, gazing at the city beneath him, apparently entranced. At this hour the mist would lie so thick that the domes of Santa Sofia and the rest would seem to be afloat; gradually the mist would uncover them; the bubbles would be seen to be firmly fixed; there would be the river; there the Galata Bridge; there the green-turbaned pilgrims without eyes or noses, begging alms; there the pariah dogs picking up offal; there the shawled women; there the innumerable donkeys; there men on horses carrying long poles. Soon, the whole town would be astir with the cracking of whips, the beating of gongs, cryings to prayer, lashing of mules, and rattle of brass-bound wheels, while sour odours, made from bread fermenting and incense, and spice, rose even to the heights of Pera itself and seemed the very breath of the strident multi-coloured and barbaric population.

Nothing, he reflected, gazing at the view which was now sparkling in the sun, could well be less like the counties of Surrey and Kent or the towns of London and Tunbridge Wells. To the right and left rose in bald and stony prominence the inhospitable Asian mountains, to which the arid castle of a robber chief or two might hang; but parsonage there was none, nor manor house, nor cottage, nor oak, elm, violet, ivy, or wild eglantine. There were no hedges for ferns to grow on, and no fields for sheep to graze. The houses were white as egg-shells and as bald. That he, who was English root and fibre, should yet exult to the depths of his heart in this wild panorama,* and gaze and gaze at those passes and far heights planning journeys there alone on foot where only the goat and shepherd had gone before; should feel a passion of affection for the bright, unseasonable flowers, love the unkempt, pariah dogs beyond even his elk-hounds at home, and snuff the acrid, sharp smell of the streets eagerly into his nostrils, surprised him. He wondered if, in the season of the Crusades, one of his ancestors had taken up with a Circassian peasant woman; thought it possible; fancied a certain darkness in his complexion; and, going indoors again, withdrew to his bath.

An hour later, properly scented, curled, and anointed, he would receive visits from secretaries and other high officials carrying, one after another, red boxes which yielded only to his own golden key. Within were papers of the highest importance, of which only fragments, here a flourish, there a seal firmly attached to a piece of burnt silk, now remain. Of their contents then, we cannot speak, but can only testify that Orlando was kept busy, what with his wax and seals, his various coloured ribbons which had to be diversely attached, his engrossing of titles and making of flourishes round capital letters, till luncheon came—a splendid meal of perhaps thirty courses.

After luncheon, lackeys announced that his coach and six was at the door, and he went, preceded by purple Janissaries* running on foot and waving great ostrich feather fans above their heads, to call upon the other ambassadors and dignitaries of state. The ceremony was always the same. On reaching the courtyard, the Janissaries struck with their fans upon the main portal, which immediately flew open revealing a large chamber, splendidly furnished. Here were seated two figures, generally of the opposite sexes. Profound bows and curtseys were exchanged. In the first room, it was permissible only to mention the weather. Having said that it was fine or wet, hot or cold, the Ambassador then passed on to the next chamber, where again, two figures rose to greet him. Here it was only permissible to compare Constantinople as a place of residence with London; and the Ambassador naturally said that he preferred Constantinople, and his hosts naturally said, though they had not seen it, that they preferred London. In the next chamber, King Charles's and the Sultan's healths had to be discussed at some length. In the next were discussed the Ambassador's health and that of his host's wife, but more briefly. In the next the Ambassador complimented his host upon his furniture, and the host complimented the Ambassador upon his dress. In the next, sweet meats were offered, the host deploring their badness, the Ambassador extolling their goodness. The ceremony ended at length with the smoking of a hookah and the drinking of a glass of coffee; but though the motions of smoking and drinking were gone through punctiliously there was neither tobacco in the pipe nor coffee in the glass, as, had either smoke or drink been real, the human frame would have sunk beneath the surfeit. For, no sooner had the Ambassador despatched one such visit, than another had to be undertaken. The same ceremonies were gone through* in precisely the same order six or seven times over at the houses of the other great officials, so that it was often late at night before the Ambassador reached home. Though Orlando performed these tasks to admiration and never denied that they are, perhaps, the most important part of a diplomatist's duties, he was undoubtedly fatigued by them, and often depressed to such a pitch of gloom that he preferred to take his dinner alone with his dogs. To them, indeed, he might be heard talking in his own tongue. And sometimes, it is said, he would pass out of his own gates late at night so disguised that the sentries did not know him. Then he would mingle with the crowd on the Galata Bridge; or stroll through the bazaars; or throw aside his shoes and join the worshippers in the Mosques. Once, when it was given out that he was ill of a fever, shepherds, bringing their goats to market, reported that they had met an English Lord on the mountain top and heard him praying to his God. This was thought to be Orlando himself, and his prayer was, no doubt, a poem said aloud, for it was known that he still carried about with him, in the bosom of his cloak, a much scored manuscript; and servants, listening at the door, heard the Ambassador chanting something in an odd, sing-song voice when he was alone.

It is with fragments such as these that we must do our best to make up a picture of Orlando's life and character at this time. There exist, even to this day, rumours, legends, anecdotes of a floating and unauthenticated kind about Orlando's life in Constantinople —(we have quoted but a few of them) which go to prove that he possessed, now that he was in the prime of life, the power to stir the fancy and rivet the eye which will keep a memory green long after all that more durable qualities can do to preserve it is forgotten. The power is a mysterious one compounded of beauty, birth, and some rarer gift, which we may call glamour and have done with it. 'A million candles', as Sasha had said, burnt in him without his being at the trouble of lighting a single one. He moved like a stag, without any need to think about his legs. He spoke in his ordinary voice and echo beat a silver gong. Hence rumours gathered round him. He became the adored of many women and some men. It was not necessary that they should speak to him or even that they should see him; they conjured up before them especially when the scenery was romantic, or the sun was setting, the figure of a noble gentleman in silk stockings. Upon the poor and uneducated, he had the same power as upon the rich. Shepherds, gipsies, donkey drivers, still sing songs about the English Lord 'who dropped his emeralds in the well', which undoubtedly refer to Orlando, who once, it seems, tore his jewels from him in a moment of rage or intoxication and flung them in a fountain; whence they were fished by a page boy. But this romantic power, it is well known, is often associated with a nature of extreme reserve. Orlando seems to have made no friends. As far as is known, he formed no attachments. A certain great lady came all the way from England in order to be near him, and pestered him with her attentions, but he continued to discharge his duties so indefatigably that he had not been Ambassador at the Horn for more than two years and a half before King Charles signified his intention of raising him to the highest rank in the peerage. The envious said that this was Nell Gwyn's tribute to the memory of a leg. But, as she had seen him once only, and was then busily engaged in pelting her royal master with nutshells, it is likely that it was his merits that won him his Dukedom,* not his calves.

Here we must pause, for we have reached a moment of great significance in his career. For the conferring of the Dukedom was the occasion of a very famous, and indeed, much disputed incident, which we must now describe, picking our way among burnt papers and little bits of tape as best we may. It was at the end of the great fast of Ramadan that the Order of the Bath and the patent of nobility arrived in a frigate

[121]

commanded by Sir Adrian Scrope; and Orlando made this the occasion for an entertainment more splendid than any that has been known before or since in Constantinople. The night was fine; the crowd immense, and the windows of the Embassy brilliantly illuminated. Again, details are lacking, for the fire had its way with all such records, and has left only tantalizing fragments which leave the most important points obscure. From the diary of John Fenner Brigge, however, an English naval officer, who was among the guests, we gather that people of all nationalities 'were packed like herrings in a barrel' in the courtyard. The crowd pressed so unpleasantly close that Brigge soon climbed into a Judas tree, the better to observe the proceedings. The rumour had got about among the natives (and here is additional proof of Orlando's mysterious power over the imagination) that some kind of miracle was to be performed. 'Thus,' writes Brigge (but his manuscript is full of burns and holes, some sentences being quite illegible), 'when the rockets began to soar into the air, there was considerable uneasiness among us lest the native population should be seized . . . fraught with unpleasant consequences to all . . . English ladies in the company, I own that my hand went to my cutlass. Happily,' he continues in his somewhat long-winded style, 'these fears seemed, for the moment, groundless and, observing the demeanour of the natives . . . I came to the conclusion that this demonstration of our skill in the art of pyrotechny was valuable, if only because it impressed upon them . . . the superiority of the British, . . . Indeed, the sight was one of indescribable magnificence. I found myself alternately praising the Lord that he had permitted . . . and wishing that my poor, dear mother . . . By the Ambassador's orders, the long windows, which are so imposing a feature of Eastern architecture, for though ignorant in many ways . . . were thrown wide; and within, we could see a tableau vivant or theatrical display in which English ladies and gentlemen . . . represented a masque the work of one . . . The words were inaudible, but the sight of so many of our countrymen and women, dressed with the highest elegance and distinction . . . moved me to emotions of which I am certainly not ashamed, though unable . . . I was intent upon observing the astonishing conduct of Lady —— which was of a nature to fasten the eyes of all upon her, and to bring discredit upon her sex and country, when'—unfortunately a branch of the Judas tree broke, Lieutenant Brigge fell to the ground, and the rest of the entry records only his gratitude to Providence (who plays a very large part in the diary) and the exact nature of his injuries.

Happily, Miss Penelope Hartopp, daughter of the General of that name, saw the scene from inside and carries on the tale in a letter, much defaced too, which ultimately reached a female friend at Tunbridge Wells.* Miss Penelope was no less lavish in her enthusiasm than the gallant officer. 'Ravishing,' she exclaims ten times on one page, 'wondrous . . . utterly beyond description . . . gold plate . . . candelabras . . . negroes in plush breeches . . . pyramids of ice . . . fountains of negus* . . . jellies made to represent His Majesty's ships . . . swans made to represent water lilies . . . birds in golden cages . . . gentlemen in slashed crimson velvet . . . Ladies' headdresses *at least* six foot high . . . musical boxes . . . Mr Peregrine said I looked *quite* lovely which I only repeat to you, my dearest, because I know . . . Oh! how I longed for you all! . . . surpassing anything we have seen at the Pantiles . . . oceans to drink . . . some gentlemen overcome . . . Lady Betty ravishing . . . Poor Lady Bonham made the unfortunate mistake of sitting down without a chair beneath her . . . Gentlemen all very gallant . . . wished a thousand times for you and dearest Betsy . . . But the sight of all others, the cynosure of all eyes . . . as all admitted, for none could be so vile as to deny it, was the Ambassador himself. Such a leg! Such a countenance!! Such princely manners!!! To see him come into the room! To see him go out again! And something *interesting* in the expression, which makes one feel, one scarcely knows why, that he has *suffered*! They say a lady was the cause of it. The heartless monster!!! How can one of our *reputed tender sex* have had the effrontery!!! He is unmarried, and half the ladies in the place are wild for love of him . . . A thousand, thousand kisses to Tom, Gerry, Peter, and dearest Mew' [presumably her cat].

From the Gazette of the time, we gather that 'as the clock struck twelve, the Ambassador appeared on the centre Balcony which was hung with priceless rugs. Six Turks of the Imperial Body Guard, each over six foot in height, held torches to his right and left. Rockets rose into the air at his appearance, and a great shout went up from the people, which the Ambassador acknowledged, bowing deeply, and speaking a few words of thanks in the Turkish language, which it was one of his accomplishments to speak with fluency. Next, Sir Adrian Scrope, in the full dress of a British Admiral, advanced; the Ambassador knelt on one knee; the Admiral placed the Collar of the Most Noble Order of the Bath round his neck, then pinned the Star to his breast; after which another gentleman of the diplomatic corps advancing in a stately manner placed on his shoulders the ducal robes, and handed him on a crimson cushion, the ducal coronet.'

At length, with a gesture of extraordinary majesty and grace, first bowing profoundly, then raising himself proudly erect, Orlando took the golden circlet of strawberry leaves and placed it, with a gesture which none that saw it ever forgot, upon his brows. It was at this point that the first disturbance began. Either the people had expected a miracle—some say a shower of gold was prophesied to fall from the

skies—which did not happen, or this was the signal
chosen for the attack to begin; nobody seems to
know; but as the coronet settled on Orlando's brows
a great uproar rose. Bells began ringing; the harsh
cries of the prophets were heard above the shouts of
the people; many Turks fell flat to the ground and
touched the earth with their foreheads. A door burst
open. The natives pressed into the banqueting rooms.
Women shrieked. A certain lady, who was said to be
dying for love of Orlando, seized a candelabra and
dashed it to the ground. What might not have happened, had it not been for the presence of Sir Adrian
Scrope and a squad of British blue-jackets, nobody
can say. But the Admiral ordered the bugles to be
sounded; a hundred blue-jackets* stood instantly at
attention; the disorder was quelled, and quiet, at least
for the time being, fell upon the scene.

So far, we are on the firm, if rather narrow, ground
of ascertained truth. But nobody has ever known
exactly what took place later that night. The testimony of the sentries and others seems, however, to
prove that the Embassy was empty of company, and
shut up for the night in the usual way by two A.M.
The Ambassador was seen to go to his room, still
wearing the insignia of his rank, and shut the door.
Some say he locked it, which was against his custom.
Others maintain that they heard music of a rustic
kind, such as shepherds play, later that night in the
courtyard under the Ambassador's window. A

washer-woman, who was kept awake by toothache, said that she saw a man's figure, wrapped in a cloak or dressing gown, come out upon the balcony. Then, she said, a woman, much muffled, but apparently of the peasant class, was drawn up by means of a rope which the man let down to her on to the balcony. There, the washer-woman said, they embraced passionately 'like lovers', and went into the room together, drawing the curtains so that no more could be seen.*

Next morning, the Duke, as we must now call him, was found by his secretaries sunk in profound slumber amid bed clothes that were much tumbled. The room was in some disorder, his coronet having rolled on the floor, and his cloak and garter being flung all of a heap on a chair. The table was littered with papers. No suspicion was felt at first, as the fatigues of the night had been great. But when afternoon came and he still slept, a doctor was summoned. He applied remedies which had been used on the previous occasion, plasters, nettles, emetics, etc., but without success. Orlando slept on. His secretaries then thought it their duty to examine the papers on the table. Many were scribbled over with poetry, in which frequent mention was made of an oak tree. There were also various state papers and others of a private nature concerning the management of his estates in England. But at length they came upon a document of far greater significance. It was nothing less, indeed, than a deed of marriage, drawn up, signed, and witnessed between his Lordship, Orlando, Knight of the Garter, etc., etc., etc., and Rosina Pepita,* a dancer, father unknown, but reputed a gipsy, mother also unknown but reputed a seller of old iron in the market-place over against the Galata Bridge. The secretaries looked at each other in dismay. And still Orlando slept. Morning and evening they watched him, but, save that his breathing was regular and his cheeks still flushed their habitual deep rose, he gave no sign of life. Whatever science or ingenuity could do to waken him they did. But still he slept.

On the seventh day of his trance (Thursday, May the 10th) the first shot was fired of that terrible and bloody insurrection of which Lieutenant Brigge had detected the first symptoms. The Turks rose against the Sultan, set fire to the town, and put every foreigner they could find, either to the sword or to the bastinado.* A few English managed to escape; but, as might have been expected, the gentlemen of the British Embassy preferred to die in defence of their red boxes, or, in extreme cases, to swallow bunches of keys rather than let them fall into the hands of the Infidel. The rioters broke into Orlando's room, but seeing him stretched to all appearances dead they left him untouched, and only robbed him of his coronet and the robes of the Garter.

And now again obscurity descends, and would indeed that it were deeper! Would, we almost have it in our hearts to exclaim, that it were so deep that we could see nothing whatever through its opacity! Would that we might here take the pen and write Finis to our work! Would that we might spare the reader what is to come and say to him in so many words, Orlando died and was buried. But here, alas, Truth, Candour, and Honesty, the austere Gods who keep watch and ward by the inkpot of the biographer, cry No! Putting their silver trumpets to their lips they demand in one blast, Truth! And again they cry Truth! and sounding yet a third time in concert they peal forth, The Truth and nothing but the Truth!

At which—Heaven be praised! for it affords us a breathing space—the doors gently open, as if a breath of the gentlest and holiest zephyr had wafted them apart, and three figures enter. First, comes our Lady of Purity; whose brows are bound with fillets of the whitest lamb's wool; whose hair is as an avalanche of the driven snow; and in whose hand reposes the white quill of a virgin goose. Following her, but with a statelier step, comes our Lady of Chastity; on whose brow is set like a turret of burning but unwasting fire a diadem of icicles; her eyes are pure stars, and her fingers, if they touch you, freeze you to the bone. Close behind her, sheltering indeed in the shadow of her more stately sisters, comes our Lady of Modesty, frailest and fairest of the three; whose face is only shown as the young moon shows when it is thin and sickle shaped and half hidden among clouds. Each

[129]

advances towards the centre of the room where Orlando still lies sleeping; and with gestures at once appealing and commanding, *Our Lady of Purity* speaks first:

'I am the guardian of the sleeping fawn; the snow is dear to me; and the moon rising; and the silver sea. With my robes I cover the speckled hen's eggs and the brindled* sea shell; I cover vice and poverty. On all things frail or dark or doubtful, my veil descends. Wherefore, speak not, reveal not. Spare, O spare!'

Here the trumpets peal forth.

'Purity Avaunt! Begone Purity!'

Then *Our Lady of Chastity* speaks:

'I am she whose touch freezes and whose glance turns to stone. I have stayed the star in its dancing, and the wave as it falls. The highest Alps are my dwelling place; and when I walk, the lightnings flash in my hair; where my eyes fall, they kill. Rather than let Orlando wake, I will freeze him to the bone. Spare, O spare!'

Here the trumpets peal forth.

'Chastity Avaunt! Begone Chastity!'

Then *Our Lady of Modesty* speaks, so low that one can hardly hear:

'I am she that men call Modesty. Virgin I am and ever shall be. Not for me the fruitful fields and the fertile vineyard. Increase is odious to me; and when the apples burgeon or the flocks breed, I run, I run; I

let my mantle fall. My hair covers my eyes. I do not
see. Spare, O spare!'

Again the trumpets peal forth:

'Modesty Avaunt! Begone Modesty!'

With gestures of grief and lamentation the three
sisters now join hands and dance slowly, tossing their
veils and singing as they go:

'Truth come not out from your horrid den. Hide
deeper, fearful Truth. For you flaunt in the brutal
gaze of the sun things that were better unknown and
undone; you unveil the shameful; the dark you make
clear, Hide! Hide! Hide!'

Here they make as if to cover Orlando with their
draperies. The trumpets, meanwhile, still blare forth,

'The Truth and nothing but the Truth.'

At this the Sisters try to cast their veils over the
mouths of the trumpets so as to muffle them, but in
vain, for now all the trumpets blare forth together,

'Horrid Sisters, go!'*

The sisters become distracted and wail in unison,
still circling and flinging their veils up and down.

'It has not always been so! But men want us no
longer; the women detest us. We go; we go. I (*Purity
says this*) to the hen roost. I (*Chastity says this*) to the
still unravished* heights of Surrey.* I (*Modesty says
this*) to any cosy nook where there are ivy and
curtains in plenty.'

'For there, not here (all speak together joining
hands and making gestures of farewell and despair

towards the bed where Orlando lies sleeping) dwell still in nest and boudoir, office and lawcourt those who love us; those who honour us, virgins and city men; lawyers and doctors; those who prohibit; those who deny; those who reverence without knowing why; those who praise without understanding; the still very numerous (Heaven be praised) tribe of the respectable; who prefer to see not; desire to know not; love the darkness; those still worship us, and with reason; for we have given them Wealth, Prosperity, Comfort, Ease. To them we go, you we leave. Come, Sisters, come! This is no place for us here.'

They retire in haste, waving their draperies over their heads, as if to shut out something that they dare not look upon and close the door behind them.

We are, therefore, now left entirely alone in the room with the sleeping Orlando and the trumpeters. The trumpeters, ranging themselves side by side in order, blow one terrific blast:—

'THE TRUTH!'

at which Orlando woke.

He stretched himself. He rose. He stood upright in complete nakedness before us, and while the trumpets pealed Truth! Truth! Truth! we have no choice left but confess—he was a woman.

*　　*　　*　　*　　*

The sound of the trumpets died away and Orlando stood stark naked. No human being, since the world began, has ever looked more ravishing. His form combined in one the strength of a man and a woman's grace. As he stood there, the silver trumpets prolonged their note, as if reluctant to leave the lovely sight which their blast had called forth—and Chastity, Purity, and Modesty, inspired, no doubt, by Curiosity, peeped in at the door and threw a garment like a towel at the naked form which, unfortunately, fell short by several inches. Orlando looked himself up and down in a long looking-glass, without showing any signs of discomposure, and went, presumably, to his bath.

We may take advantage of this pause in the narrative to make certain statements. Orlando had become a woman—there is no denying it. But in every other respect, Orlando remained precisely as he had been. The change of sex, though it altered their future, did nothing whatever to alter their identity. Their faces remained, as their portraits prove, practically the same. His memory—but in future we must, for convention's sake, say 'her' for 'his', and 'she' for 'he'—her memory then, went back through all the events of her past life without encountering any obstacle. Some slight haziness there may have been, as if a few dark drops had fallen into the clear pool of memory; certain things had become a little dimmed; but that was all. The change seemed to have been accomplished painlessly and completely and in such a way that Orlando herself showed no surprise at it. Many people, taking this into account, and holding that such a change of sex is against nature, have been at great pains to prove (1) that Orlando had always been a woman, (2) that Orlando is at this moment a man. Let biologists and psychologists determine. It is enough for us to state the simple fact; Orlando was a man till the age of thirty;* when he became a woman and has remained so ever since.

But let other pens treat of sex and sexuality;* we quit such odious subjects as soon as we can. Orlando had now washed, and dressed herself in those Turkish coats and trousers which can be worn indifferently by either sex; and was forced to consider her position. That it was precarious and embarrassing in the extreme must be the first thought of every reader who has followed her story with sympathy. Young, noble, beautiful, she had woken to find herself in a position than which we can conceive none more delicate for a young lady of rank. We should not have blamed her had she rung the bell, screamed, or fainted. But Orlando showed no such signs of perturbation. All her actions were deliberate in the extreme, and might indeed have been thought to show tokens of pre-meditation. First, she carefully examined the papers on the table; took such as seemed to be written in poetry, and secreted them in her bosom; next she called her Seleuchi hound,* which had never left her bed all these days, though half famished with hunger, fed and combed him; then stuck a pair of pistols in her belt; finally wound about her person several

1. ORLANDO AS A BOY
The original frontispiece to the Hogarth edition of 1928

2. THE RUSSIAN PRINCESS AS A CHILD

3. THE ARCHDUCHESS HARRIET

4. ORLANDO AS AMBASSADOR

5. ORLANDO ON HER RETURN TO ENGLAND

6. ORLANDO ABOUT THE YEAR 1840

7. MARMADUKE BONTHROP SHELMERDINE, ESQUIRE

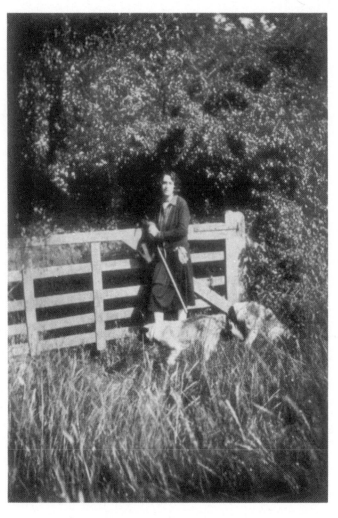

8. ORLANDO AT THE PRESENT TIME

strings of emeralds and pearls of the finest orient*
which had formed part of her Ambassadorial wardrobe. This done, she leant out of the window, gave
one low whistle, and descended the shattered and
bloodstained staircase, now strewn with the litter of
waste-paper baskets, treaties, despatches, seals, sealing wax, etc., and so entered the courtyard. There, in
the shadow of a giant fig tree, waited an old gipsy on
a donkey. He led another by the bridle. Orlando
swung her leg over it; and thus, attended by a lean
dog, riding a donkey, in company of a gipsy, the
Ambassador of Great Britain at the Court of the
Sultan left Constantinople.

They rode for several days and nights and met with
a variety of adventures, some at the hands of men,
some at the hands of nature, in all of which Orlando
acquitted herself with courage. Within a week they
reached the high ground outside Broussa,* which was
then the chief camping ground of the gipsy tribe to
which Orlando had allied herself. Often she had
looked at those mountains from her balcony at the
Embassy; often had longed to be there; and to find
oneself where one has longed to be always, to a
reflective mind, gives food for thought. For some
time, however, she was too well pleased with the
change to spoil it by thinking. The pleasure of having
no documents to seal or sign, no flourishes to make,
no calls to pay, was enough. The gipsies followed the
grass; when it was grazed down, on they moved

again. She washed in streams if she washed at all; no boxes, red, blue, or green, were presented to her; there was not a key, let alone a golden key, in the whole camp; as for 'visiting', the word was unknown. She milked the goats; she collected brushwood; she stole a hen's egg now and then, but always put a coin or a pearl in place of it; she herded cattle; she stripped vines; she trod the grape; she filled the goat-skin and drank from it; and when she remembered how, at about this time of day, she should have been making the motions of drinking and smoking over an empty coffee-cup and a pipe which lacked tobacco, she laughed aloud, cut herself another hunch* of bread, and begged for a puff from old Rustum's pipe, filled though it was with cow dung.

The gipsies, with whom it is obvious that she must have been in secret communication before the revolution, seem to have looked upon her as one of themselves (which is always the highest compliment a people can pay), and her dark hair and dark complexion bore out the belief that she was, by birth, one of them and had been snatched by an English Duke from a nut tree when she was a baby and taken to that barbarous land where people live in houses because they are too feeble and diseased to stand the open air. Thus, though in many ways inferior to them, they were willing to help her to become more like them; taught her their arts of cheese-making and basket-weaving, their science of stealing and bird-snaring, and were even prepared to consider letting her marry among them.

But Orlando had contracted in England some of the customs or diseases (whatever you choose to consider them) which cannot, it seems, be expelled. One evening, when they were all sitting round the camp fire and the sunset was blazing over the Thessalian hills, Orlando exclaimed:

'How good to eat!'

(The gipsies have no word for 'beautiful'. This is the nearest.)

All the young men and women burst out laughing uproariously. The sky good to eat, indeed! The elders, however, who had seen more of foreigners than they had, became suspicious. They noticed that Orlando often sat for whole hours doing nothing whatever, except look here and then there; they would come upon her on some hill-top staring straight in front of her, no matter whether the goats were grazing or straying. They began to suspect that she had other beliefs than their own, and the older men and women thought it probable that she had fallen into the clutches of the vilest and cruellest among all the Gods, which is Nature. Nor were they far wrong. The English disease, a love of Nature, was inborn in her, and here, where Nature was so much larger and more powerful than in England, she fell into its hands as she had never done before. The malady is too well known, and has been, alas, too often described to

need describing afresh, save very briefly. There were
mountains; there were valleys; there were streams.
She climbed the mountains; roamed the valleys; sat
on the banks of the streams. She likened the hills to
ramparts, to the breasts of doves, and the flanks of
kine. She compared the flowers to enamel and the
turf to Turkey rugs worn thin. Trees were withered
hags, and sheep were grey boulders. Everything, in
fact, was something else. She found the tarn on the
mountain-top and almost threw herself in to seek the
wisdom she thought lay hid there; and when, from
the mountain-top, she beheld far off, across the Sea
of Marmara, the plains of Greece, and made out (her
eyes were admirable) the Acropolis with a white
streak or two, which must, she thought, be the
Parthenon, her soul expanded with her eyeballs, and
she prayed that she might share the majesty of the
hills, know the serenity of the plains, etc, etc., as all
such believers do. Then, looking down, the red
hyacinth, the purple iris wrought her to cry out in
ecstasy at the goodness, the beauty of nature; raising
her eyes again, she beheld the eagle soaring, and
imagined its raptures and made them her own.
Returning home, she saluted each star, each peak, and
each watch-fire as if they signalled to her alone; and
at last, when she flung herself upon her mat in the
gipsies' tent, she could not help bursting out again,
How good to eat! How good to eat! (For it is a
curious fact that though human beings have such

imperfect means of communication, that they can only say 'good to eat' when they mean 'beautiful' and the other way about, they will yet endure ridicule and misunderstanding rather than keep any experience to themselves.) All the young gipsies laughed. But Rustum el Sadi, the old man who had brought Orlando out of Constantinople on his donkey, sat silent. He had a nose like a scimitar; his cheeks were furrowed as if from the age-long descent of iron hail; he was brown and keen-eyed, and as he sat tugging at his hookah he observed Orlando narrowly. He had the deepest suspicion that her God was Nature. One day he found her in tears. Interpreting this to mean that her God had punished her, he told her that he was not surprised. He showed her the fingers of his left hand, withered by the frost; he showed her his right foot, crushed where a rock had fallen. This, he said, was what her God did to men. When she said, 'But so beautiful', using the English word, he shook his head; and when she repeated it he was angry. He saw that she did not believe what he believed, and that was enough, wise and ancient as he was, to enrage him.

This difference of opinion disturbed Orlando, who had been perfectly happy until now. She began to think, was Nature beautiful or cruel; and then she asked herself what this beauty was; whether it was in things themselves, or only in herself; so she went on to the nature of reality, which led her to truth, which in its turn led to Love, Friendship, Poetry (as in the days on the high mound at home); which meditations, since she could impart no word of them, made her long, as she had never longed before, for pen and ink.

'Oh! if only I could write!' she cried (for she had the odd conceit of those who write that words written are shared). She had no ink; and but little paper. But she made ink from berries and wine; and finding a few margins and blank spaces in the manuscript of 'The Oak Tree', managed, by writing a kind of shorthand, to describe the scenery in a long, blank version poem, and to carry on a dialogue with herself about this Beauty and Truth concisely enough. This kept her extremely happy for hours on end. But the gipsies became suspicious. First, they noticed that she was less adept than before at milking and cheese-making; next, she often hesitated before replying; and once a gipsy boy who had been asleep, woke in a terror feeling her eyes upon him. Sometimes this constraint would be felt by the whole tribe, number-ing some dozens of grown men and women. It sprang from the sense they had (and their senses are very sharp and much in advance of their vocabulary) that whatever they were doing crumbled like ashes in their hands. An old woman making a basket, a boy skin-ning a sheep, would be singing or crooning content-edly at their work, when Orlando would come into the camp, fling herself down by the fire and gaze into the flames. She need not even look at them, and yet they felt, here is someone who doubts; (we make a rough-and-ready translation from the gipsy language) here is someone who does not do the thing for the sake of doing; nor looks for looking's sake; here is someone who believes neither in sheep-skin nor basket; but sees (here they looked apprehensively about the tent) something else. Then a vague but most unpleasant feeling would begin to work in the boy and in the old woman. They broke their withys; they cut their fingers. A great rage filled them. They wished Orlando would leave the tent and never come near them again. Yet she was of a cheerful and willing disposition, they owned; and one of her pearls was enough to buy the finest herd of goats in Broussa.

Slowly, she began to feel that there was some difference between her and the gipsies which made her hesitate sometimes to marry and settle down among them for ever. At first she tried to account for it by saying that she came of an ancient and civilized race, whereas these gipsies were an ignorant people, not much better than savages. One night when they were questioning her about England she could not help with some pride describing the house where she was born, how it had 365 bedrooms and had been in the possession of her family for four or five hundred years. Her ancestors were earls, or even dukes, she added. At this she noticed again that the gipsies were uneasy; but not angry as before when she had praised the beauty of nature. Now they were courteous, but concerned as people of fine breeding are when a stranger has been made to reveal his low birth or poverty. Rustum followed her out of the tent alone and said that she need not mind if her father were a Duke, and possessed all the bedrooms and furniture that she described. They would none of them think the worse of her for that. Then she was seized with a shame that she had never felt before. It was clear that Rustum and the other gipsies thought a descent of four or five hundred years only* the meanest possible. Their own families went back at least two or three thousand years. To the gipsy whose ancestors had built the Pyramids centuries before Christ was born, the genealogy of Howards and Plantagenets* was no better and no worse than that of the Smiths and the Joneses; both were negligible. Moreover, where the shepherd boy had a lineage of such antiquity, there was nothing specially memorable or desirable in ancient birth; vagabonds and beggars all shared it. And then, though he was too courteous to speak openly, it was clear that the gipsy thought that there was no more vulgar ambition than to possess bedrooms by the hundred (they were on top of a hill as they spoke; it was night; the mountains rose around them) when the whole earth is ours. Looked at from the gipsy point of view, a Duke, Orlando understood, was nothing but a profiteer or robber who snatched land and money from people who rated these things of little worth, and could think of nothing better to

do than to build three hundred and sixty-five bedrooms when one was enough, and none was even
better than one. She could not deny that her ancestors
had accumulated field after field; house after house;
honour after honour; yet had none of them been
saints or heroes, or great benefactors of the human
race. Nor could she counter the argument (Rustum
was too much of a gentleman to press it, but she
understood) that any man who did now what her
ancestors had done three or four hundred years ago
would be denounced—and by her own family most
loudly—for a vulgar upstart, an adventurer, a *nou-
veau riche*.

She sought to answer such arguments by the familiar if oblique method of finding the gipsy life itself
rude and barbarous; and so, in a short time, much
bad blood was bred between them. Indeed, such
differences of opinion are enough to cause bloodshed
and revolution. Towns have been sacked for less, and
a million martyrs have suffered at the stake rather
than yield an inch upon any of the points here
debated. No passion is stronger in the breast of man
than the desire to make others believe as he believes.
Nothing so cuts at the root of his happiness and fills
him with rage as the sense that another rates low what
he prizes high. Whigs and Tories, Liberal party and
Labour party*—for what do they battle except their
own prestige? It is not love of truth but desire to
prevail that sets quarter against quarter and makes

parish desire the downfall of parish. Each seeks peace of mind and subserviency rather than the triumph of truth and the exaltation of virtue—but these moralities belong, and should be left to the historian, since they are as dull as ditch water.

'Four hundred and seventy-six bedrooms* mean nothing to them,' sighed Orlando.

'She prefers a sunset to a flock of goats,' said the gipsies.

What was to be done, Orlando could not think. To leave the gipsies and become once more an Ambassador seemed to her intolerable. But it was equally impossible to remain for ever where there was neither ink nor writing paper, neither reverence for the Talbots nor respect for a multiplicity of bedrooms. So she was thinking, one fine morning on the slopes of Mount Athos, when minding her goats. And then Nature, in whom she trusted, either played her a trick or worked a miracle—again, opinions differ too much for it to be possible to say which. Orlando was gazing rather disconsolately at the steep hill-side in front of her. It was now midsummer, and if we must compare the landscape to anything, it would have been to a dry bone; to a sheep's skeleton; to a gigantic skull picked white by a thousand vultures. The heat was intense, and the little fig tree under which Orlando lay only served to print patterns of fig-leaves upon her light burnous.*

Suddenly a shadow, though there was nothing to

cast a shadow, appeared on the bald mountain-side opposite. It deepened quickly and soon a green hollow showed where there had been barren rock before. As she looked, the hollow deepened and widened, and a great park-like space opened in the flank of the hill. Within, she could see an undulating and grassy lawn; she could see oak trees dotted here and there; she could see the thrushes hopping among the branches. She could see the deer stepping delicately from shade to shade, and could even hear the hum of insects and the gentle sighs and shivers of a summer's day in England. After she had gazed entranced for some time, snow began falling; soon the whole landscape was covered and marked with violet shades instead of yellow sunlight. Now she saw heavy carts coming along the roads, laden with tree trunks, which they were taking, she knew, to be sawn for firewood; and then appeared the roofs and belfries and towers and courtyards of her own home. The snow was falling steadily, and she could now hear the slither and flop which it made as it slid down the roof and fell to the ground. The smoke went up from a thousand chimneys. All was so clear and minute that she could see a daw pecking for worms in the snow. Then, gradually, the violet shadows deepened and closed over the carts and the lawns and the great house itself. All was swallowed up. Now there was nothing left of the grassy hollow, and instead of the green lawns was only the blazing hill-side which a thousand vultures seemed to have picked bare. At this, she burst into a passion of tears, and striding back to the gipsies' camp, told them that she must sail for England the very next day.

It was happy for her that she did so. Already the young men had plotted her death. Honour, they said, demanded it, for she did not think as they did. Yet they would have been sorry to cut her throat; and welcomed the news of her departure. An English merchant ship, as luck would have it, was already under sail in the harbour about to return to England; and Orlando, by breaking off another pearl from her necklace, not only paid her passage but had some bank-notes left over in her wallet. These she would have liked to present to the gipsies. But they despised wealth she knew; and she had to content herself with embraces, which on her part were sincere.

CHAPTER IV

WITH some of the guineas left from the sale of the tenth pearl on her string, Orlando bought herself a complete outfit of such clothes as women then wore, and it was in the dress of a young Englishwoman of rank that she now sat on the deck of the *Enamoured Lady*. It is a strange fact, but a true one, that up to this moment she had scarcely given her sex a thought. Perhaps the Turkish trousers which she had hitherto worn had done something to distract her thoughts; and the gipsy women, except in one or two important particulars, differ very little from the gipsy men. At any rate, it was not until she felt the coil of skirts about her legs and the Captain offered, with the greatest politeness, to have an awning spread for her on deck, that she realized with a start the penalties and the privileges of her position. But that start was not of the kind that might have been expected.

It was not caused, that is to say, simply and solely by the thought of her chastity and how she could preserve it. In normal circumstances a lovely young woman alone would have thought of nothing else; the whole edifice of female government is based on that foundation stone; chastity is their jewel, their centre-piece, which they run mad to protect, and die when ravished of. But if one has been a man for thirty years or so, and an Ambassador into the bargain, if one has held a Queen in one's arms and one or two other ladies, if report be true, of less exalted rank, if one has married a Rosina Pepita, and so on, one does not perhaps give such a very great start about that. Orlando's start was of a very complicated kind, and not to be summed up in a trice. Nobody, indeed, ever accused her of being one of those quick wits who run to the end of things in a minute. It took her the entire length of the voyage to moralize out the meaning of her start, and so, at her own pace, we will follow her.

'Lord,' she thought, when she had recovered from her start, stretching herself out at length under her awning, 'this is a pleasant, lazy way of life, to be sure. But', she thought, giving her legs a kick, 'these skirts are plaguey things to have about one's heels. Yet the stuff (flowered paduasoy*) is the loveliest in the world. Never have I seen my own skin (here she laid her hand on her knee) look to such advantage as now. Could I, however, leap overboard and swim in clothes like these? No! Therefore, I should have to trust to the protection of a blue-jacket. Do I object to that? Now do I?' she wondered, here encountering the first knot in the smooth skein of her argument.

Dinner came before she had untied it, and then it was the Captain himself—Captain Nicholas Benedict Bartolus, a sea-captain of distinguished aspect, who did it for her as he helped her to a slice of corned beef.

'A little of the fat, Ma'am?' he asked. 'Let me cut

you just the tiniest little slice the size of your finger nail.' At those words a delicious tremor ran through her frame. Birds sang; the torrents rushed. It recalled the feeling of indescribable pleasure with which she had first seen Sasha, hundreds of years ago. Then she had pursued, now she fled. Which is the greater ecstasy? The man's or the woman's?* And are they not perhaps the same? No, she thought, this is the most delicious (thanking the Captain but refusing), to refuse, and see him frown. Well, she would, if he wished it, have the very thinnest, smallest shiver* in the world. This was the most delicious of all, to yield and see him smile. 'For nothing', she thought, regaining her couch on deck, and continuing the argument, 'is more heavenly than to resist and to yield; to yield and to resist. Surely it throws the spirit into such a rapture as nothing else can. So that I'm not sure', she continued, 'that I won't throw myself overboard, for the mere pleasure of being rescued by a blue-jacket after all.'

(It must be remembered that she was like a child entering into possession of a pleasaunce* or toy cupboard; her arguments would not commend themselves to mature women, who have had the run of it all their lives.)

'But what used we young fellows in the cockpit of the *Marie Rose* to say about a woman who threw herself overboard for the pleasure of being rescued by a blue-jacket?' she said. 'We had a word for them.

Ah! I have it . . .' (But we must omit that word; it
was disrespectful in the extreme and passing strange
on a lady's lips.) 'Lord! Lord!' she cried again at the
conclusion of her thoughts, 'must I then begin to
respect the opinion of the other sex, however monstrous I think it? If I wear skirts, if I can't swim, if I
have to be rescued by a blue-jacket, by God!' she
cried, 'I must!' Upon which a gloom fell over her.
Candid by nature, and averse to all kinds of equivo-
cation, to tell lies bored her. It seemed to her a
roundabout way of going to work. Yet, she reflected,
the flowered paduasoy—the pleasure of being rescued
by a blue-jacket—if these were only to be obtained
by roundabout ways, roundabout one must go, she
supposed. She remembered how, as a young man, she
had insisted that women must be obedient, chaste,
scented, and exquisitely apparelled. 'Now I shall have
to pay in my own person for those desires,' she
reflected; 'for women are not (judging by my own
short experience of the sex) obedient, chaste, scented,
and exquisitely apparelled by nature. They can only
attain these graces, without which they may enjoy
none of the delights of life, by the most tedious
discipline. 'There's the hairdressing,' she thought,
'that alone will take an hour of my morning; there's
looking in the looking-glass, another hour; there's
staying* and lacing; there's washing and powdering;
there's changing from silk to lace and from lace to
paduasoy; there's being chaste year in year out. . . .'

Here she tossed her foot impatiently, and showed an inch or two of calf. A sailor on the mast, who happened to look down at the moment, started so violently that he missed his footing and only saved himself by the skin of his teeth. 'If the sight of my ankles means death to an honest fellow who, no doubt, has a wife and family to support, I must, in all humanity, keep them covered,' Orlando thought. Yet her legs were among her chiefest beauties. And she fell to thinking what an odd pass we have come to when all a woman's beauty has to be kept covered lest a sailor may fall from a mast-head. 'A pox on them!' she said, realizing for the first time what, in other circumstances, she would have been taught as a child, that is to say, the sacred responsibilities of womanhood.

'And that's the last oath I shall ever be able to swear,' she thought, 'once I set foot on English soil. And I shall never be able to crack a man over the head, or tell him he lies in his teeth, or draw my sword and run him through the body, or sit among my peers, or wear a coronet, or walk in procession, or sentence a man to death, or lead an army, or prance down Whitehall on a charger, or wear seventy-two different medals on my breast. All I can do, once I set foot on English soil, is to pour out tea and ask my lords how they like it. D'you take sugar?* D'you take cream?' And mincing out the words, she was horrified to perceive how low an opinion she was forming of the other sex, the manly, to which it had once been her pride to belong. 'To fall from a mast-head', she thought, 'because you see a woman's ankles; to dress up like a Guy Fawkes* and parade the streets, so that women may praise you; to deny a woman teaching lest she may laugh at you; to be the slave of the frailest chit in petticoats, and yet to go about as if you were the Lords of creation.—Heavens!' she thought, 'what fools they make of us—what fools we are!' And here it would seem from some ambiguity in her terms that she was censuring both sexes equally, as if she belonged to neither; and indeed, for the time being, she seemed to vacillate; she was man; she was woman; she knew the secrets, shared the weaknesses of each. It was a most bewildering and whirligig state of mind to be in. The comforts of ignorance seemed utterly denied her. She was a feather blown on the gale. Thus it is no great wonder, as she pitted one sex against the other, and found each alternately full of the most deplorable infirmities, and was not sure to which she belonged—it was no great wonder that she was about to cry out that she would return to Turkey and become a gipsy again when the anchor fell with a great splash into the sea; the sails came tumbling on deck, and she perceived (so sunk had she been in thought that she had seen nothing for several days) that the ship was anchored off the coast of Italy. The Captain at once sent to ask the honour of her company ashore with him in the long-boat.

When she returned the next morning, she stretched herself on her couch under the awning and arranged her draperies with the greatest decorum about her ankles.

'Ignorant and poor as we are compared with the other sex,' she thought, continuing the sentence which she had left unfinished the other day, 'armoured with every weapon as they are, while they debar us even from a knowledge of the alphabet' (and from these opening words it is plain that something had happened during the night to give her a push towards the female sex, for she was speaking more as a woman speaks than as a man, yet with a sort of content after all), 'still—they fall from the mast-head.' Here she gave a great yawn and fell asleep. When she woke, the ship was sailing before a fair breeze so near the shore that towns on the cliffs' edge seemed only kept from slipping into the water by the interposition of some great rock or the twisted roots of some ancient olive tree. The scent of oranges wafted from a million trees, heavy with the fruit, reached her on deck. A score of blue dolphins, twisting their tails, leapt high now and again into the air. Stretching her arms out (arms, she had learnt already, have no such fatal effects as legs), she thanked Heaven that she was not prancing down Whitehall on a war-horse, nor even sentencing a man to death. 'Better is it', she thought, 'to be clothed with poverty and ignorance, which are the dark garments of the female sex; better to leave the rule and discipline of the world to others; better be quit of martial ambition, the love of power, and all the other manly desires if so one can more fully enjoy the most exalted raptures known to the human spirit, which are', she said aloud, as her habit was when deeply moved, 'contemplation, solitude, love.'

'Praise God that I'm a woman!' she cried, and was about to run into the extreme folly—than which none is more distressing in woman or man either—of being proud of her sex, when she paused over the singular word, which, for all we can do to put it in its place, has crept in at the end of the last sentence: Love. 'Love,' said Orlando. Instantly—such is its impetuosity—love took a human shape—such is its pride. For where other thoughts are content to remain abstract, nothing will satisfy this one but to put on flesh and blood, mantilla* and petticoats, hose and jerkin. And as all Orlando's loves had been women, now, through the culpable laggardry of the human frame to adapt itself to convention, though she herself was a woman, it was still a woman she loved; and if the consciousness of being of the same sex had any effect at all, it was to quicken and deepen those feelings which she had had as a man. For now a thousand hints and mysteries became plain to her that were then dark. Now, the obscurity, which divides the sexes and lets linger innumerable impurities in its gloom, was removed, and if there is anything in what the poet says about truth and beauty, this affection gained in beauty what it lost in falsity. At last, she cried, she knew Sasha as she was, and in the ardour of this discovery, and in the pursuit of all those treasures which were now revealed, she was so rapt and enchanted that it was as if a cannon ball had exploded at her ear when a man's voice said, 'Permit me, Madam,' a man's hand raised her to her feet; and the fingers of a man with a three-masted sailing ship tattooed on the middle finger pointed to the horizon.

'The cliffs of England, Ma'am,' said the Captain, and he raised the hand which had pointed at the sky to the salute. Orlando now gave a second start, even more violent than the first.

'Christ Jesus!' she cried.

Happily, the sight of her native land after long absence excused both start and exclamation, or she would have been hard put to it to explain to Captain Bartolus the raging and conflicting emotions which now boiled within her. How tell him that she, who now trembled on his arm, had been a Duke and an Ambassador? How explain to him that she, who had been lapped like a lily in folds of paduasoy, had hacked heads off, and lain with loose women among treasure sacks in the holds of pirate ships on summer nights when the tulips were abloom and the bees buzzing off Wapping Old Stairs? Not even to herself could she explain the giant start she gave, as the resolute right hand of the sea-captain indicated the cliffs of the British Islands.

'To refuse and to yield,' she murmured, 'how delightful; to pursue and conquer, how august; to perceive and to reason, how sublime.' Not one of these words so coupled together seemed to her wrong; nevertheless, as the chalky cliffs loomed nearer, she felt culpable; dishonoured; unchaste, which, for one who had never given the matter a thought, was strange. Closer and closer they drew, till the samphire* gatherers, hanging half-way down the cliff, were plain to the naked eye. And watching them, she felt, scampering up and down within her, like some derisive ghost who in another instant will pick up her skirts and flaunt out of sight, Sasha the lost, Sasha the memory, whose reality she had proved just now so surprisingly—Sasha, she felt, mopping and mowing* and making all sorts of disrespectful gestures towards the cliffs and the samphire gatherers; and when the sailors began chanting, 'So good-bye and adieu to you, Ladies of Spain', the words echoed in Orlando's sad heart, and she felt that however much landing there meant comfort, meant opulence, meant consequence and state (for she would doubtless pick up some noble Prince and reign, his consort, over half Yorkshire*), still, if it meant conventionality, meant slavery, meant deceit, meant denying her love, fettering her limbs, pursing her lips, and restraining her tongue, then she would turn about with the ship and set sail once more for the gipsies.

Among the hurry of these thoughts, however, there

now rose, like a dome of smooth, white marble, something which, whether fact or fancy, was so impressive to her fevered imagination that she settled upon it as one has seen a swarm of vibrant dragon-flies alight, with apparent satisfaction, upon the glass bell which shelters some tender vegetable. The form of it, by the hazard of fancy, recalled that earliest, most persistent memory—the man with the big fore-head in Twitchett's sitting-room, the man who sat writing, or rather looking, but certainly not at her, for he never seemed to see her poised there in all her finery, lovely boy though she must have been, she could not deny it—and whenever she thought of him, the thought spread round it, like the risen moon on turbulent waters, a sheet of silver calm. Now her hand went to her bosom (the other was still in the Captain's keeping), where the pages of her poem were hidden safe. It might have been a talisman that she kept there. The distraction of sex, which hers was, and what it meant, subsided; she thought now only of the glory of poetry, and the great lines of Marlowe, Shakespeare, Ben Jonson, Milton began booming and reverberating, as if a golden clapper beat against a golden bell in the cathedral tower which was her mind. The truth was that the image of the marble dome which her eyes had first discovered so faintly that it suggested a poet's forehead and thus started a flock of irrelevant ideas, was no figment, but a reality; and as the ship advanced down the Thames before a favouring gale, the image with all its associations gave place to the truth, and revealed itself as nothing more and nothing less than the dome of a vast cathedral rising among a fretwork of white spires.

'St Paul's,' said Captain Bartolus, who stood by her side. 'The Tower of London,' he continued. 'Greenwich Hospital, erected in memory of Queen Mary by her husband, his late majesty, William the Third. Westminster Abbey. The Houses of Parliament.' As he spoke, each of these famous buildings rose to view. It was a fine September morning. A myriad of little watercraft plied from bank to bank. Rarely has a gayer, or more interesting, spectacle presented itself to the gaze of a returned traveller. Orlando hung over the prow, absorbed in wonder. Her eyes had been used too long to savages and nature not to be entranced by these urban glories. That, then, was the dome of St Paul's which Mr Wren had built* during her absence. Near by, a shock of golden hair burst from a pillar—Captain Bartolus was at her side to inform her that that was the Monument; there had been a plague and a fire* during her absence, he said. Do what she could to restrain them, the tears came to her eyes, until, remembering that it is becoming in a woman to weep, she let them flow. Here, she thought, had been the great carnival. Here, where the waves slapped briskly, had stood the Royal Pavilion. Here she had first met Sasha. About here (she looked down into the sparkling waters) one had been used to see the frozen bumboat woman with her apples on her lap. All that splendour and corruption was gone. Gone, too, was the dark night, the monstrous downpour, the violent surges of the flood. Here, where yellow icebergs had raced circling with a crew of terror-stricken wretches on top, a covey of swans floated, orgulous, undulant, superb. London itself had completely changed since she had last seen it. Then, she remembered, it had been a huddle of little black, beetle-browed houses. The heads of rebels had grinned on pikes at Temple Bar. The cobbled pavements had reeked of garbage and ordure. Now, as the ship sailed past Wapping, she caught glimpses of broad and orderly thoroughfares. Stately coaches drawn by teams of well-fed horses stood at the doors of houses whose bow windows, whose plate glass, whose polished knockers, testified to the wealth and modest dignity of the dwellers within. Ladies in flowered silk (she put the Captain's glass to her eye) walked on raised footpaths. Citizens in broidered coats took snuff at street corners under lamp-posts. She caught sight of a variety of painted signs swinging in the breeze and could form a rapid notion from what was painted on them of the tobacco, of the stuff, of the silk, of the gold, of the silver ware, of the gloves, of the perfumes, and of a thousand other articles which were sold within. Nor could she do more as the ship sailed to its anchorage by London Bridge than glance at coffee-house windows where, on balconies, since the weather was fine, a great number of decent citizens sat at ease, with china dishes in front of them, clay pipes by their sides, while one among them read from a news sheet, and was frequently interrupted by the laughter or the comments of the others. Were these taverns, were these wits, were these poets? she asked of Captain Bartolus, who obligingly informed her that even now—if she turned her head a little to the left and looked along the line of his first finger—so—they were passing the Cocoa Tree, where,—yes, there he was—one might see Mr Addison taking his coffee; the other two gentlemen—'there, Ma'am, a little to the right of the lamp-post, one of 'em humped, t'other much the same as you or me'—were Mr Dryden and Mr Pope.[1] 'Sad dogs,' said the Captain, by which he meant that they were Papists,* 'but men of parts, none the less,' he added, hurrying aft to superintend the arrangements for landing.

'Addison, Dryden, Pope,' Orlando repeated as if the words were an incantation. For one moment she saw the high mountains above Broussa, the next, she had set her foot upon her native shore.

But now Orlando was to learn how little the most tempestuous flutter of excitement avails against the

---

[1] The Captain must have been mistaken, as a reference to any textbook of literature will show; but the mistake was a kindly one, and so we let it stand.*

iron countenance of the law; how harder than the stones of London Bridge it is, and than the lips of a cannon more severe. No sooner had she returned to her home in Blackfriars* than she was made aware by a succession of Bow Street runners and other grave emissaries from the Law Courts that she was a party to three major suits which had been preferred against her during her absence, as well as innumerable minor litigations, some arising out of, others depending on them. The chief charges against her were (1) that she was dead, and therefore could not hold any property whatsoever; (2) that she was a woman, which amounts to much the same thing; (3) that she was an English Duke who had married one Rosina Pepita, a dancer; and had had by her three sons, which sons now declaring that their father was deceased, claimed that all his property descended to them. Such grave charges as these would, of course, take time and money to dispose of. All her estates were put in Chancery and her titles pronounced in abeyance while the suits were under litigation. Thus it was in a highly ambiguous condition, uncertain whether she was alive or dead, man or woman, Duke or nonentity, that she posted down to her country seat, where, pending the legal judgement, she had the Law's permission to reside in a state of incognito or incognita, as the case might turn out to be.

It was a fine evening in December when she arrived and the snow was falling and the violet shadows were

slanting much as she had seen them from the hill-top
at Broussa. The great house lay more like a town than
a house, brown and blue, rose and purple in the snow,
with all its chimneys smoking busily as if inspired
with a life of their own. She could not restrain a cry
as she saw it there tranquil and massive, couched
upon the meadows. As the yellow coach entered the
park and came bowling along the drive between the
trees, the red deer raised their heads as if expectantly,
and it was observed that instead of showing the
timidity natural to their kind, they followed the coach
and stood about the courtyard when it drew up. Some
tossed their antlers, others pawed the ground as the
step was let down and Orlando alighted. One, it is
said, actually knelt in the snow before her. She had
not time to reach her hand towards the knocker
before both wings of the great door were flung open,
and there, with lights and torches held above their
heads, were Mrs Grimsditch, Mr Dupper, and a
whole retinue of servants come to greet her. But the
orderly procession was interrupted first by the impetuosity of Canute,* the elk-hound, who threw
himself with such ardour upon his mistress that he
almost knocked her to the ground; next, by the
agitation of Mrs Grimsditch, who, making as if to
curtsey, was overcome with emotion and could do
no more than gasp Milord! Milady! Milady! Milord!
until Orlando comforted her with a hearty kiss upon
both her cheeks. After that, Mr Dupper began to

read from a parchment, but the dogs barking, the huntsmen winding their horns, and the stags, who had come into the courtyard in the confusion, baying the moon, not much progress was made, and the company dispersed within after crowding about their Mistress, and testifying in every way to their great joy at her return.

No one showed an instant's suspicion that Orlando was not the Orlando they had known. If any doubt there was in the human mind the action of the deer and the dogs would have been enough to dispel it, for the dumb creatures, as is well known, are far better judges both of identity and character than we are. Moreover, said Mrs Grimsditch, over her dish of china tea, to Mr Dupper that night, if her Lord was a Lady now, she had never seen a lovelier one, nor was there a penny piece to choose between them; one was as well-favoured as the other; they were as like as two peaches on one branch; which, said Mrs Grimsditch, becoming confidential, she had always had her suspicions (here she nodded her head very mysteriously), which it was no surprise to her (here she nodded her head very knowingly), and for her part, a very great comfort; for what with the towels wanting mending and the curtains in the chaplain's parlour being moth-eaten round the fringes, it was time they had a Mistress among them.

'And some little masters and mistresses to come after her,' Mr Dupper added, being privileged by virtue of his holy office to speak his mind on such delicate matters as these.

So, while the old servants gossiped in the servants' hall, Orlando took a silver candle in her hand and roamed once more through the halls, the galleries, the courts, the bedrooms; saw loom down at her again the dark visage of this Lord Keeper, that Lord Chamberlain, among her ancestors; sat now in this chair of state, now reclined on that canopy of delight; observed the arras, how it swayed; watched the huntsmen riding and Daphne flying; bathed her hand, as she had loved to do as a child, in the yellow pool of light which the moonlight made falling through the heraldic Leopard in the window; slid along the polished planks of the gallery, the other side of which was rough timber; touched this silk, that satin; fancied the carved dolphins swam; brushed her hair with King James' silver brush; buried her face in the pot-pourri, which was made as the Conqueror had taught them many hundred years ago and from the same roses; looked at the garden and imagined the sleeping crocuses, the dormant dahlias; saw the frail nymphs gleaming white in the snow and the great yew hedges, thick as a house, black behind them; saw the orangeries and the giant medlars;—all this she saw, and each sight and sound, rudely as we write it down, filled her heart with such a lust and balm of joy, that at length, tired out, she entered the Chapel and sank into the old red armchair in which her ancestors used to hear service. There she lit a cheroot ('twas a habit she had brought back from the East) and opened the Prayer Book.

It was a little book bound in velvet, stitched with gold, which had been held by Mary Queen of Scots* on the scaffold, and the eye of faith could detect a brownish stain, said to be made of a drop of the Royal blood. But what pious thoughts it roused in Orlando, what evil passions it soothed asleep, who dare say, seeing that of all communions this with the deity is the most inscrutable? Novelist, poet, historian all falter with their hand on that door; nor does the believer himself enlighten us, for is he more ready to die than other people, or more eager to share his goods? Does he not keep as many maids and carriage horses as the rest? and yet with it all, holds a faith he says which should make goods a vanity and death desirable. In the Queen's prayer-book, along with the blood-stain, was also a lock of hair and a crumb of pastry; Orlando now added to these keepsakes a flake of tobacco, and so, reading and smoking, was moved by the humane jumble of them all—the hair, the pastry, the blood-stain, the tobacco—to such a mood of contemplation as gave her a reverent air suitable in the circumstances, though she had, it is said, no traffic with the usual God. Nothing, however, can be more arrogant, though nothing is commoner than to assume that of Gods there is only one, and of religions none but the speaker's. Orlando, it seemed, had a faith of her own. With all the religious ardour in the world, she now reflected upon her sins and the imperfections that had crept into her spiritual state. The letter S, she reflected, is the serpent in the poet's Eden. Do what she would there were still too many of these sinful reptiles in the first stanzas of 'The Oak Tree'. But 'S' was nothing, in her opinion, compared with the termination 'ing'. The present participle is the Devil himself, she thought (now that we are in the place for believing in Devils). To evade such temptations is the first duty of the poet, she concluded, for as the ear is the antechamber to the soul, poetry can adulterate and destroy more surely than lust or gunpowder. The poet's, then, is the highest office of all, she continued. His words reach where others fall short. A silly song of Shakespeare's has done more for the poor and the wicked than all the preachers and philanthropists in the world. No time, no devotion, can be too great, therefore, which makes the vehicle of our message less distorting. We must shape our words till they are the thinnest integument for our thoughts. Thoughts are divine, etc. Thus it is obvious that she was back in the confines of her own religion which time had only strengthened in her absence, and was rapidly acquiring the intolerance of belief.

'I am growing up,' she thought, taking her taper at last. 'I am losing some illusions,' she said, shutting Queen Mary's book, 'perhaps to acquire others,' and she descended among the tombs where the bones of her ancestors lay.

But even the bones of her ancestors, Sir Miles, Sir Gervase, and the rest, had lost something of their sanctity since Rustum el Sadi had waved his hand that night in the Asian mountains. Somehow the fact that only three or four hundred years ago these skeletons had been men with their way to make in the world like any modern upstart, and that they had made it by acquiring houses and offices, garters and ribbands, as any other upstart does, while poets, perhaps, and men of great mind and breeding had preferred the quietude of the country, for which choice they paid the penalty by extreme poverty, and now hawked broadsheets in the Strand, or herded sheep in the fields, filled her with remorse. She thought of the Egyptian pyramids and what bones lie beneath them as she stood in the crypt; and the vast, empty hills which lie above the Sea of Marmara seemed, for the moment, a finer dwelling-place than this many-roomed mansion in which no bed lacked its quilt and no silver dish its silver cover.

'I am growing up,' she thought, taking her taper. 'I am losing my illusions, perhaps to acquire new ones,' and she paced down the long gallery to her bedroom. It was a disagreeable process, and a troublesome. But it was interesting, amazingly, she thought, stretching her legs out to her log fire (for no sailor was present), and she reviewed, as if it were an avenue of great edifices, the progress of her own self along her own past.

How she had loved sound when she was a boy, and thought the volley of tumultuous syllables from the lips the finest of all poetry. Then—it was the effect of Sasha and her disillusionment perhaps—into this high frenzy was let fall some black drop, which turned her rhapsody into sluggishness. Slowly there had opened within her something intricate and many-chambered, which one must take a torch to explore, in prose not verse; and she remembered how passionately she had studied that doctor at Norwich, Browne, whose book was at her hand there. She had formed here in solitude after her affair with Greene, or tried to form, for Heaven knows these growths are agelong in coming, a spirit capable of resistance. 'I will write', she had said, 'what I enjoy writing'; and so had scratched out twenty-six volumes. Yet still, for all her travels and adventures and profound thinkings and turnings this way and that, she was only in process of fabrication. What the future might bring, Heaven only knew. Change was incessant, and change perhaps would never cease. High battlements of thought,* habits that had seemed durable as stone, went down like shadows at the touch of another mind and left a naked sky and fresh stars twinkling in it. Here she went to the window, and in spite of the cold could not help unlatching it. She leant out into the damp night air. She heard a fox bark in the woods, and the clutter of a pheasant trailing through the branches. She heard the snow slither and flop from the roof to the ground. 'By my life,' she exclaimed, 'this is a thousand times better than Turkey. Rustum,' she cried, as if she were arguing with the gipsy (and in this new power of bearing an argument in mind and continuing it with someone who was not there to contradict she showed again the development of her soul), 'you were wrong. This is better than Turkey. Hair, pastry, tobacco—of what odds and ends are we compounded,' she said (thinking of Queen Mary's prayer-book). 'What a phantasmagoria the mind is and meeting-place of dissemblables! At one moment we deplore our birth and state and aspire to an ascetic exaltation; the next we are overcome by the smell of some old garden path and weep to hear the thrushes sing.' And so bewildered as usual by the multitude of things which call for explanation and imprint their message without leaving any hint as to their meaning, she threw her cheroot out of the window and went to bed.

Next morning, in pursuance of these thoughts, she had out her pen and paper, and started afresh upon 'The Oak Tree', for to have ink and paper in plenty when one has made do with berries and margins is a delight not to be conceived. Thus she was now striking out a phrase in the depths of despair, now in the heights of ecstasy writing one in, when a shadow darkened the page. She hastily hid her manuscript.

As her window gave on to the most central of the courts, as she had given orders that she would see no one, as she knew no one and was herself legally unknown, she was first surprised at the shadow, then indignant at it, then (when she looked up and saw what caused it) overcome with merriment. For it was a familiar shadow, a grotesque shadow, the shadow of no less a personage than the Archduchess Harriet Griselda of Finster-Aarhorn and Scand-op-Boom in the Roumanian territory. She was loping across the court in her old black riding-habit and mantle as before. Not a hair of her head was changed. This then was the woman who had chased her from England! This was the eyrie of that obscene vulture—this the fatal fowl herself! At the thought that she had fled all the way to Turkey to avoid her seductions (now become excessively flat), Orlando laughed aloud. There was something inexpressibly comic in the sight. She resembled, as Orlando had thought before, nothing so much as a monstrous hare. She had the staring eyes, the lank cheeks, the high headdress of that animal. She stopped now, much as a hare sits erect in the corn when thinking itself unobserved, and stared at Orlando, who stared back at her from the window. After they had stared like this for a certain time, there was nothing for it but to ask her in, and soon the two ladies were exchanging compliments while the Archduchess struck the snow from her mantle.

'A plague on women,' said Orlando to herself, going to the cupboard to fetch a glass of wine, 'they never leave one a moment's peace. A more ferreting, inquisiting, busybodying set of people don't exist. It was to escape this Maypole that I left England, and now'—here she turned to present the Archduchess with the salver, and behold—in her place stood a tall gentleman in black. A heap of clothes lay in the fender. She was alone with a man.

Recalled thus suddenly to a consciousness of her sex which she had completely forgotten, and of his, which was now remote enough to be equally upsetting, Orlando felt seized with faintness.

'La!' she cried, putting her hand to her side, 'how you frighten me!'

'Gentle creature,' cried the Archduchess, falling on one knee and at the same time pressing a cordial to Orlando's lips, 'forgive me for the deceit I have practised on you!'

Orlando sipped the wine and the Archduke knelt and kissed her hand.

In short, they acted the parts of man and woman for ten minutes with great vigour and then fell into natural discourse. The Archduchess (but she must in future be known as the Archduke) told his story—that he was a man and always had been one; that he had seen a portrait of Orlando and fallen hopelessly in love with him; that to compass his ends, he had dressed as a woman and lodged at the Baker's shop;

that he was desolated when he fled to Turkey; that he had heard of her change and hastened to offer his services (here he teed and heed intolerably). For to him, said the Archduke Harry, she was and would ever be the Pink, the Pearl, the Perfection of her sex. The three p's would have been more persuasive if they had not been interspersed with tee-hees and haw-haws of the strangest kind. 'If this is love,' said Orlando to herself, looking at the Archduke on the other side of the fender, and now from the woman's point of view, 'there is something highly ridiculous about it.'

Falling on his knees,* the Archduke Harry made the most passionate declaration of his suit. He told her that he had something like twenty million ducats in a strong box at his castle. He had more acres than any nobleman in England. The shooting was excellent: he could promise her a mixed bag of ptarmigan and grouse such as no English moor, or Scotch either, could rival. True, the pheasants had suffered from the gape* in his absence, and the does had slipped their young, but that could be put right, and would be with her help when they lived in Roumania together.

As he spoke, enormous tears formed in his rather prominent eyes and ran down the sandy tracts of his long and lanky cheeks.

That men cry as frequently and as unreasonably as women, Orlando knew from her own experience as a man, but she was beginning to be aware that women should be shocked when men display emotion in their presence, and so, shocked she was.

The Archduke apologized. He commanded himself sufficiently to say that he would leave her now, but would return on the following day for his answer.

That was a Tuesday. He came on Wednesday; he came on Thursday; he came on Friday; and he came on Saturday. It is true that each visit began, continued, or concluded with a declaration of love, but in between there was much room for silence. They sat on either side of the fireplace and sometimes the Archduke knocked over the fire-irons and Orlando picked them up again. Then the Archduke would bethink him how he had shot an elk in Sweden, and Orlando would ask, was it a very big elk, and the Archduke would say that it was not as big as the reindeer which he had shot in Norway; and Orlando would ask, had he ever shot a tiger, and the Archduke would say he had shot an albatross, and Orlando would say (half hiding her yawn) was an albatross as big as an elephant, and the Archduke would say— something very sensible, no doubt, but Orlando heard it not, for she was looking at her writing-table, out of the window, at the door. Upon which the Archduke would say, 'I adore you', at the very same moment that Orlando said 'Look, it's beginning to rain', at which they were both much embarrassed, and blushed scarlet, and could neither of them think what to say next. Indeed, Orlando was at her wits' end what to talk about and had she not bethought her of a game called Fly Loo,* at which great sums of money can be lost with very little expense of spirit, she would have had to marry him, she supposed; for how else to get rid of him she knew not. By this device, however, and it was a simple one, needing only three lumps of sugar and a sufficiency of flies, the embarrassment of conversation was overcome and the necessity of marriage avoided. For now, the Archduke would bet her five hundred pounds to a tester that a fly would settle on this lump and not on that. Thus, they would have occupation for a whole morning watching the flies (who were naturally sluggish at this season and often spent an hour or so circling round the ceiling) until at length some fine blue-bottle made his choice and the match was won. Many hundreds of pounds changed hands between them at this game, which the Archduke, who was a born gambler, swore was every bit as good as horse racing, and vowed he could play at for ever. But Orlando soon began to weary.

'What's the good of being a fine young woman in the prime of life', she asked, 'if I have to pass all my mornings watching blue-bottles with an Archduke?'

She began to detest the sight of sugar; flies made her dizzy. Some way out of the difficulty there must be, she supposed, but she was still awkward in the arts of her sex, and as she could no longer knock a man over the head or run him through the body with

a rapier, she could think of no better method than
this. She caught a blue-bottle, gently pressed the life
out of it (it was half dead already, or her kindness for
the dumb creatures would not have permitted it) and
secured it by a drop of gum arabic to a lump of sugar.
While the Archduke was gazing at the ceiling, she
deftly substituted this lump for the one she had laid
her money on, and crying 'Loo Loo!' declared that
she had won her bet. Her reckoning was that the
Archduke, with all his knowledge of sport and horse-
racing, would detect the fraud and, as to cheat at Loo
is the most heinous of crimes, and men have been
banished from the society of mankind to that of apes
in the tropics for ever because of it, she calculated
that he would be manly enough to refuse to have
anything further to do with her. But she misjudged
the simplicity of the amiable nobleman. He was no
nice judge of flies. A dead fly looked to him much
the same as a living one. She played the trick twenty
times on him and he paid her over £17,250 (which is
about £40,885:6:8* of our own money) before
Orlando cheated so grossly that even he could be
deceived no longer. When he realized the truth at last,
a painful scene ensued. The Archduke rose to his full
height. He coloured scarlet. Tears rolled down his
cheeks one by one. That she had won a fortune from
him was nothing—she was welcome to it; that she
had deceived him was something—it hurt him to
think her capable of it; but that she had cheated at

[175]

Loo was everything. To love a woman who cheated at play was, he said, impossible. Here he broke down completely. Happily, he said, recovering slightly, there were no witnesses. She was, after all, only a woman, he said. In short, he was preparing in the chivalry of his heart to forgive her and had bent to ask her pardon for the violence of his language, when she cut the matter short, as he stooped his proud head, by dropping a small toad between his skin and his shirt.

In justice to her, it must be said that she would infinitely have preferred a rapier. Toads are clammy things to conceal about one's person a whole morning. But if rapiers are forbidden, one must have recourse to toads. Moreover toads and laughter between them sometimes do what cold steel cannot. She laughed. The Archduke blushed. She laughed. The Archduke cursed. She laughed. The Archduke slammed the door.

'Heaven be praised!' cried Orlando still laughing. She heard the sound of chariot wheels driven at a furious pace down the courtyard. She heard them rattle along the road. Fainter and fainter the sound became. Now it faded away altogether.

'I am alone,' said Orlando, aloud since there was no one to hear.

That silence is more profound after noise still wants the confirmation of science. But that loneliness is more apparent directly after one has been made love to, many women would take their oath. As the sound of the Archduke's chariot wheels died away, Orlando felt drawing further from her and further from her an Archduke (she did not mind that), a fortune (she did not mind that), a title (she did not mind that), the safety and circumstance of married life (she did not mind that), but life she heard going from her, and a lover. 'Life and a lover,' she murmured; and going to her writing-table she dipped her pen in the ink and wrote:

'Life and a lover'—a line which did not scan and made no sense with what went before—something about the proper way of dipping sheep to avoid the scab. Reading it over she blushed and repeated,

'Life and a lover.' Then laying her pen aside she went into her bedroom, stood in front of her mirror, and arranged her pearls about her neck. Then since pearls do not show to advantage against a morning gown of sprigged cotton, she changed to a dove grey taffeta; thence to one of peach bloom; thence to a wine-coloured brocade. Perhaps a dash of powder was needed, and if her hair were disposed—so—about her brow, it might become her. Then she slipped her feet into pointed slippers, and drew an emerald ring upon her finger. 'Now,' she said when all was ready and lit the silver sconces on either side of the mirror. What woman would not have kindled to see what Orlando saw then burning in the snow—for all about the looking-glass were snowy lawns, and she was like a fire, a burning bush, and the candle flames about her head were silver leaves; or again, the glass was green water, and she a mermaid, slung with pearls, a siren* in a cave, singing so that oarsmen leant from their boats and fell down, down to embrace her; so dark, so bright, so hard, so soft, was she,* so astonishingly seductive that it was a thousand pities that there was no one there to put it in plain English, and say outright, 'Damn it, Madam, you are loveliness incarnate,' which was the truth. Even Orlando (who had no conceit of her person) knew it, for she smiled the involuntary smile which women smile when their own beauty, which seems not their own, forms like a drop falling or a fountain rising and confronts them all of a sudden in the glass—this smile she smiled and then she listened for a moment and heard only the leaves blowing and the sparrows twittering, and then she sighed, 'Life, a lover,' and then she turned on her heel with extraordinary rapidity; whipped her pearls from her neck, stripped the satins from her back, stood erect in the neat black silk knickerbockers of an ordinary nobleman, and rang the bell. When the servant came, she told him to order a coach and six to be in readiness instantly. She was summoned by urgent affairs to London. Within an hour of the Archduke's departure, off she drove.

And as she drove, we may seize the opportunity, since the landscape was of a simple English kind which needs no description, to draw the reader's attention more particularly than we could at the moment to one or two remarks which have slipped in here and there in the course of the narrative. For example, it may have been observed that Orlando hid her manuscripts when interrupted. Next, that she looked long and intently in the glass; and now, as she drove to London, one might notice her starting and suppressing a cry when the horses galloped faster than she liked. Her modesty as to her writing, her vanity as to her person, her fears for her safety all seems to hint that what was said a short time ago about there being no change in Orlando the man and Orlando the woman, was ceasing to be altogether true. She was becoming a little more modest, as women are, of her brains, and a little more vain, as women are, of her person. Certain susceptibilities were asserting themselves, and others were diminishing. The change of clothes had, some philosophers will say, much to do with it. Vain trifles as they seem, clothes have, they say, more important offices than merely to keep us warm. They change our view of the world and the world's view of us. For example, when Captain Bartolus saw Orlando's skirt, he had an awning stretched for her immediately, pressed her to take another slice of beef, and invited her to go ashore with him in the long-boat. These compliments would certainly not have been paid her had her skirts, instead of flowing, been cut tight to her legs in the fashion of breeches. And when we are paid compliments, it behoves us to make some return. Orlando curtseyed; she complied; she flattered the good man's humours as she would not have done had his neat breeches been a woman's skirts, and his braided coat a woman's satin bodice. Thus, there is much to support the view that it is clothes that wear us and not we them; we may make them take the mould of arm or breast, but they mould our hearts, our brains, our tongues to their liking. So, having now worn skirts for a considerable time, a certain change was visible in Orlando, which is to be found if the reader will look at plate 5, even in her face. If we compare the picture of Orlando as a man with that of Orlando as a woman we shall see that though both are undoubtedly one and the same person, there are certain changes. The man has his hand free to seize his sword, the woman must use hers to keep the satins from slipping from her shoulders. The man looks the world full in the face, as if it were made for his uses and fashioned to his liking. The woman takes a sidelong glance at it, full of subtlety, even of suspicion. Had they both worn the same clothes, it is possible that their outlook might have been the same.

That is the view of some philosophers and wise ones, but on the whole, we incline to another. The difference between the sexes is, happily, one of great profundity. Clothes are but a symbol of something hid deep beneath. It was a change in Orlando herself that dictated her choice of a woman's dress and of a woman's sex. And perhaps in this she was only expressing rather more openly than usual—openness indeed was the soul of her nature—something that happens to most people without being thus plainly expressed. For here again, we come to a dilemma. Different though the sexes are, they intermix. In every human being a vacillation from one sex to the other takes place, and often it is only the clothes that keep the male or female likeness, while underneath the sex is the very opposite of what it is above. Of the complications and confusions which thus result everyone has had experience; but here we leave the general question and note only the odd effect it had in the particular case of Orlando herself.

For it was this mixture in her of man and woman, one being uppermost and then the other, that often gave her conduct an unexpected turn. The curious of her own sex would argue, for example, if Orlando was a woman, how did she never take more than ten minutes to dress? And were not her clothes chosen rather at random, and sometimes worn rather shabby? And then they would say, still, she has none of the formality of a man, or a man's love of power. She is excessively tender-hearted. She could not endure to see a donkey beaten or a kitten drowned. Yet again, they noted, she detested household matters, was up at dawn and out among the fields in summer before the sun had risen. No farmer knew more about the crops than she did. She could drink with the best and liked games of hazard. She rode well and drove six horses at a gallop over London Bridge. Yet again, though bold and active as a man, it was remarked that the sight of another in danger brought on the most womanly palpitations. She would burst into tears on slight provocation. She was unversed in geography, found mathematics intolerable, and held some caprices which are more common among women than men, as for instance that to travel south is to travel downhill.* Whether, then, Orlando was most man or woman, it is difficult to say and cannot now be decided. For her coach was now rattling on the cobbles. She had reached her home in the city. The steps were being let down; the iron gates were being opened. She was entering her father's house at Blackfriars, which though fashion was fast deserting that end of the town, was still a pleasant, roomy mansion, with gardens running down to the river, and a pleasant grove of nut trees to walk in.

Here she took up her lodging and began instantly to look about her for what she had come in search of—that is to say, life and a lover. About the first there might be some doubt; the second she found without the least difficulty two days after her arrival. It was a Tuesday that she came to town. On Thursday she went for a walk in the Mall, as was then the habit of persons of quality. She had not made more than a

turn or two of the avenue before she was observed by
a little knot of vulgar people who go there to spy
upon their betters. As she came past them, a common
woman carrying a child at her breast stepped forward,
peered familiarly into Orlando's face, and cried out,
'Lawk upon us, if it ain't the Lady Orlando!' Her
companions came crowding round, and Orlando
found herself in a moment the centre of a mob of
staring citizens and tradesmen's wives, all eager to
gaze upon the heroine of the celebrated lawsuit.*
Such was the interest that the case excited in the
minds of the common people. She might, indeed,
have found herself gravely discommoded by the pressure of the crowd—she had forgotten that ladies are
not supposed to walk in public places alone—had not
a tall gentleman at once stepped forward and offered
her the protection of his arm. It was the Archduke.
She was overcome with distress and yet with some
amusement at the sight. Not only had this magnani-
mous nobleman forgiven her, but in order to show
that he took her levity with the toad in good part, he
had procured a jewel made in the shape of that reptile
which he pressed upon her with a repetition of his
suit as he handed her to her coach.

What with the crowd, what with the Duke, what
with the jewel, she drove home in the vilest temper
imaginable. Was it impossible then to go for a walk
without being half-suffocated, presented with a toad
set in emeralds, and asked in marriage by an Arch-

duke? She took a kinder view of the case next day when she found on her breakfast table half a dozen billets* from some of the greatest ladies in the land—Lady Suffolk, Lady Salisbury, Lady Chesterfield, Lady Tavistock, and others who reminded her in the politest manner of old alliances between their families and her own, and desired the honour of her acquaintance. Next day, which was a Saturday, many of these great ladies waited on her in person. On Tuesday, about noon, their footmen brought cards of invitation to various routs,* dinners, and assemblies in the near future; so that Orlando was launched without delay, and with some splash and foam at that, upon the waters of London society.

To give a truthful account of London society at that or indeed at any other time, is beyond the powers of the biographer or the historian. Only those who have little need of the truth, and no respect for it—the poets and the novelists—can be trusted to do it, for this is one of the cases where the truth does not exist. Nothing exists. The whole thing is a miasma—a mirage. To make our meaning plain—Orlando would come home from one of these routs at three or four in the morning with cheeks like a Christmas tree and eyes like stars. She would untie a lace, pace the room a score of times, untie another lace, stop, and pace the room again. Often the sun would be blazing over Southwark chimneys before she could persuade herself to get into bed, and there she would lie,

pitching and tossing, laughing and sighing for an hour
or longer, before she slept at last. And what was all
this stir about? Society. And what had society said or
done to throw a reasonable lady into such an excitement? In plain language, nothing. Rack her memory
as she would, next day Orlando could never remember a single word to magnify into the name something. Lord O. had been gallant. Lord A. polite. The
Marquis of C. charming. Mr M. amusing. But when
she tried to recollect in what their gallantry, politeness, charm, or wit had consisted, she was bound to
suppose her memory at fault, for she could not name
a thing. It was the same always. Nothing remained
over the next day, yet the excitement of the moment
was intense. Thus we are forced to conclude that
society is one of those brews such as skilled house-
keepers serve hot about Christmas time, whose flavour depends upon the proper mixing and stirring of
a dozen different ingredients. Take one out, and it is
in itself insipid. Take away Lord O., Lord A., Lord
C., or Mr M., and separately each is nothing. Stir
them all together and they combine to give off the
most intoxicating of flavours, the most seductive of
scents. Yet this intoxication, this seductiveness,
entirely evade our analysis. At one and the same time,
therefore, society is everything and society is nothing.
Society is the most powerful concoction in the world
and society has no existence whatsoever. Such monsters the poets and the novelists alone can deal with;

with such something-nothings their works are stuffed out to prodigious size; and to them with the best will in the world we are content to leave it.

Following the example of our predecessors, therefore, we will only say that society in the reign of Queen Anne was of unparalleled brilliance. To have the entry there was the aim of every well-bred person. The graces were supreme. Fathers instructed their sons, mothers their daughters. No education was complete for either sex which did not include the science of deportment, the art of bowing and curtseying, the management of the sword and the fan, the care of the teeth, the conduct of the leg, the flexibility of the knee, the proper methods of entering and leaving the room, with a thousand etceteras, such as will immediately suggest themselves to anybody who has himself been in society. Since Orlando had won the praise of Queen Elizabeth for the way she handed a bowl of rose water as a boy, it must be supposed that she was sufficiently expert to pass muster. Yet it is true that there was an absentmindedness about her which sometimes made her clumsy; she was apt to think of poetry when she should have been thinking of taffeta; her walk was a little too much of a stride for a woman, perhaps, and her gestures, being abrupt, might endanger a cup of tea on occasion.

Whether this slight disability was enough to counterbalance the splendour of her bearing, or whether she inherited a drop too much of that black humour

which ran in the veins of all her race, certain it is that
she had not been in the world more than a score of
times before she might have been heard to ask herself,
had there been anybody but her spaniel Pippin* to
hear her, 'What the devil is the matter with me?' The
occasion was Tuesday, the 16th of June 1712; she had
just returned from a great ball at Arlington House;
the dawn was in the sky, and she was pulling off her
stockings. 'I don't care if I never meet another soul as
long as I live,' cried Orlando, bursting into tears.
Lovers she had in plenty, but life, which is, after all,
of some importance in its way, escaped her. 'Is this',
she asked—but there was none to answer, 'is this',
she finished her sentence all the same, 'what people
call life?' The spaniel raised her forepaw in token of
sympathy. The spaniel licked Orlando with her
tongue. Orlando stroked the spaniel with her hand.
Orlando kissed the spaniel with her lips. In short,
there was the truest sympathy between them that can
be between a dog and its mistress, and yet it cannot
be denied that the dumbness of animals is a great
impediment to the refinements of intercourse. They
wag their tails; they bow the front part of the body
and elevate the hind; they roll, they jump, they paw,
they whine, they bark, they slobber, they have all
sorts of ceremonies and artifices of their own, but the
whole thing is of no avail, since speak they cannot.
Such was her quarrel, she thought, setting the dog
gently on to the floor, with the great people at

Arlington House. They, too, wag their tails, bow, roll, jump, paw, and slobber, but talk they cannot. 'All these months that I've been out in the world', said Orlando, pitching one stocking across the room, 'I've heard nothing but what Pippin might have said. I'm cold. I'm happy. I'm hungry. I've caught a mouse. I've buried a bone. Please kiss my nose.' And it was not enough.

How, in so short a time, she had passed from intoxication to disgust we will only seek to explain by supposing that this mysterious composition which we call society, is nothing absolutely good or bad in itself, but has a spirit in it, volatile but potent, which either makes you drunk when you think it, as Orlando thought it, delightful, or gives you a head-ache when you think it, as Orlando thought it, repulsive. That the faculty of speech has much to do with it either way, we take leave to doubt. Often a dumb hour is the most ravishing of all; brilliant wit can be tedious beyond description. But to the poets we leave it, and so on with our story.

Orlando threw the second stocking after the first and went to bed dismally enough, determined that she would forswear society for ever. But again as it turned out, she was too hasty in coming to her conclusions. For the very next morning she woke to find, among the usual cards of invitation upon her table, one from a certain great Lady, the Countess of R. Having determined overnight that she would never go into society again, we can only explain Orlando's behaviour—she sent a messenger hot-foot to R—— House to say that she would attend her Ladyship with all the pleasure in the world—by the fact that she was still suffering from the effect of three honeyed words dropped into her ear on the deck of the *Enamoured Lady* by Captain Nicholas Benedict Bartolus as they sailed down the Thames. Addison, Dryden, Pope, he had said, pointing to the Cocoa Tree, and Addison, Dryden, Pope had chimed in her head like an incantation ever since. Who can credit such folly? but so it was. All her experience with Nick Greene had taught her nothing. Such names still exercised over her the most powerful fascination. Something, perhaps, we must believe in, and as Orlando, we have said, had no belief in the usual divinities she bestowed her credulity upon great men—yet with a distinction. Admirals, soldiers, statesmen, moved her not at all. But the very thought of a great writer stirred her to such a pitch of belief that she almost believed him to be invisible. Her instinct was a sound one. One can only believe entirely, perhaps, in what one cannot see. The little glimpse she had of these great men from the deck of the ship was of the nature of a vision. That the cup was china, or the gazette paper, she doubted. When Lord O. said one day that he had dined with Dryden the night before, she flatly disbelieved him. Now, the Lady R.'s reception room had the reputation of being the antechamber to the presence room of genius; it was the place where men and women met to swing censers and chant hymns to the bust of genius in a niche in the wall. Sometimes the God himself vouchsafed his presence for a moment. Intellect alone admitted the suppliant, and nothing (so the report ran) was said inside that was not witty.

It was thus with great trepidation that Orlando entered the room. She found a company already assembled in a semicircle round the fire. Lady R., an oldish lady, of dark complexion, with a black lace mantilla on her head, was seated in a great arm-chair in the centre. Thus being somewhat deaf, she could control the conversation on both sides of her. On both sides of her sat men and women of the highest distinction. Every man, it was said, had been a Prime Minister and every woman, it was whispered, had been the mistress of a king. Certain it is that all were brilliant, and all were famous. Orlando took her seat with a deep reverence in silence. . . . After three hours, she curtseyed profoundly and left.

But what, the reader may ask with some exasperation, happened in between? In three hours, such a company must have said the wittiest, the profoundest, the most interesting things in the world. So it would seem indeed. But the fact appears to be that they said nothing. It is a curious characteristic which they share with all the most brilliant societies that the world has seen. Old Madame du Deffand and her friends talked for fifty years without stopping. And of it all, what remains? Perhaps three witty sayings. So that we are at liberty to suppose either that nothing was said, or that nothing witty was said, or that the fraction of three witty sayings lasted eighteen thousand two hundred and fifty nights, which does not leave a liberal allowance of wit for any one of them.

The truth would seem to be—if we dare use such a word in such a connection—that all these groups of people lie under an enchantment. The hostess is our modern Sibyl.* She is a witch who lays her guests under a spell. In this house they think themselves happy; in that witty; in a third profound. It is all an illusion (which is nothing against it, for illusions are the most valuable and necessary of all things, and she who can create one is among the world's greatest benefactors), but as it is notorious that illusions are shattered by conflict with reality, so no real happiness, no real wit, no real profundity are tolerated where the illusion prevails. This serves to explain why Madame du Deffand said no more than three witty things in the course of fifty years. Had she said more, her circle would have been destroyed. The witticism, as it left her lips, bowled over the current conversation as a cannon ball lays low the violets and the daisies. When she made her famous 'mot de Saint Denis' the very grass was singed. Disillusionment and desolation followed. Not a word was uttered. 'Spare us another such, for Heaven's sake, Madame!' her friends cried with one accord. And she obeyed. For almost seventeen years she said nothing memorable and all went well. The beautiful counterpane of illusion lay unbroken on her circle as it lay unbroken on the circle of Lady R. The guests thought that they were happy, thought that they were witty, thought that they were profound, and, as they thought this, other people thought it still more strongly; and so it got about that nothing was more delightful than one of Lady R.'s assemblies; everyone envied those who were admitted; those who were admitted envied themselves because other people envied them; and so there seemed no end to it—except that which we have now to relate.

For about the third time Orlando went there a certain incident occurred. She was still under the illusion that she was listening to the most brilliant epigrams in the world, though, as a matter of fact, old General C. was only saying, at some length, how the gout had left his left leg and gone to his right, while Mr L. interrupted when any proper name was mentioned, 'R.? Oh! I know Billy R. as well as I know myself. S.? My dearest friend. T.? Stayed with him a fortnight in Yorkshire'—which, such is the force of illusion, sounded like the wittiest repartee, the most searching comment upon human life, and kept the company in a roar; when the door opened and a little gentleman entered whose name Orlando did not catch. Soon a curiously disagreeable sensation came over her. To judge from their faces, the rest began to feel it as well. One gentleman said there was a draught. The Marchioness of C. feared a cat must be under the sofa. It was as if their eyes were being slowly opened after a pleasant dream and nothing met them but a cheap wash-stand and a dirty counterpane. It was as if the fumes of some delicious wine were slowly leaving them. Still the General talked and still Mr L. remembered. But it became more and more apparent how red the General's neck was, how bald Mr L.'s head was. As for what they said—nothing more tedious and trivial could be imagined. Everybody fidgeted and those who had fans yawned behind them. At last Lady R. rapped with hers upon the arm of her great chair. Both gentlemen stopped talking.

Then the little gentleman said,

He said next,

He said finally,[1]

Here, it cannot be denied, was true wit, true wisdom, true profundity. The company was thrown into complete dismay. One such saying was bad enough; but three, one after another, on the same evening! No society could survive it.

'Mr Pope,' said old Lady R. in a voice trembling with sarcastic fury, 'you are pleased to be witty.' Mr Pope flushed red. Nobody spoke a word. They sat in dead silence some twenty minutes. Then, one by one,

---

[1] These sayings are too well known to require repetition, and besides, they are all to be found in his published works.

they rose and slunk from the room. That they would ever come back after such an experience was doubtful. Link-boys* could be heard calling their coaches all down South Audley Street. Doors were slammed and carriages drove off. Orlando found herself near Mr Pope on the staircase. His lean and misshapen frame was shaken by a variety of emotions. Darts of malice, rage, triumph, wit, and terror (he was shaking like a leaf) shot from his eyes. He looked like some squat reptile set with a burning topaz in its forehead. At the same time, the strangest tempest of emotion seized now upon the luckless Orlando. A disillusionment so complete as that inflicted not an hour ago leaves the mind rocking from side to side. Everything appears ten times more bare and stark than before. It is a moment fraught with the highest danger for the human spirit. Women turn nuns and men priests in such moments. In such moments, rich men sign away their wealth; and happy men cut their throats with carving knives. Orlando would have done all willingly, but there was a rasher thing still for her to do, and this she did. She invited Mr Pope to come home with her.

For if it is rash to walk into a lion's den unarmed, rash to navigate the Atlantic in a rowing boat, rash to stand on one foot on the top of St Paul's, it is still more rash to go home alone with a poet. A poet is Atlantic and lion in one. While one drowns us the other gnaws us. If we survive the teeth, we succumb to the waves. A man who can destroy illusions is both beast and flood. Illusions are to the soul what atmosphere is to the earth. Roll up that tender air and the plant dies, the colour fades. The earth we walk on is a parched cinder. It is marl we tread and fiery cobbles scorch our feet. By the truth we are undone. Life is a dream. 'Tis waking that kills us. He who robs us of our dreams robs us of our life—(and so on for six pages if you will, but the style is tedious and may well be dropped).

On this showing, however, Orlando should have been a heap of cinders by the time the chariot drew up at her house in Blackfriars. That she was still flesh and blood, though certainly exhausted, is entirely due to a fact to which we drew attention earlier in the narrative. The less we see the more we believe. Now the streets that lie between Mayfair and Blackfriars were at that time very imperfectly lit. True, the lighting was a great improvement upon that of the Elizabethan age. Then the benighted traveller had to trust to the stars or the red flame of some night watchman to save him from the gravel pits at Park Lane or the oak woods where swine rootled in the Tottenham Court Road. But even so it wanted much of our modern efficiency. Lamp-posts lit with oil-lamps occurred every two hundred yards or so, but between lay a considerable stretch of pitch darkness. Thus for ten minutes Orlando and Mr Pope would be in blackness; and then for about half a minute

again in the light. A very strange state of mind was
thus bred in Orlando. As the light faded, she began
to feel steal over her the most delicious balm. 'This is
indeed a very great honour for a young woman to be
driving with Mr Pope,' she began to think, looking at
the outline of his nose. 'I am the most blessed of my
sex. Half an inch from me—indeed, I feel the knot of
his knee ribbons pressing against my thigh—is the
greatest wit in Her Majesty's dominions. Future ages
will think of us with curiosity and envy me with
fury.' Here came the lamp-post again. 'What a foolish
wretch I am!' she thought. 'There is no such thing as
fame and glory. Ages to come will never cast a
thought on me or on Mr Pope either. What's an
"age", indeed? What are "we"?' and their progress
through Berkeley Square seemed the groping of two
blind ants, momentarily thrown together without
interest or concern in common, across a blackened
desert. She shivered. But here again was darkness.
Her illusion revived. 'How noble his brow is,' she
thought (mistaking a hump on a cushion for Mr
Pope's forehead in the darkness). 'What a weight of
genius lives in it! What wit, wisdom, and truth—
what a wealth of all those jewels, indeed, for which
people are ready to barter their lives! Yours is the
only light that burns for ever. But for you the human
pilgrimage would be performed in utter darkness';
(here the coach gave a great lurch as it fell into a rut
in Park Lane) 'without genius we should be upset and

undone. Most august, most lucid of beams,'—thus she was apostrophizing the hump on the cushion when they drove beneath one of the street lamps in Berkeley Square and she realized her mistake. Mr Pope had a forehead no bigger than another man's. 'Wretched man,' she thought, 'how you have deceived me! I took that hump for your forehead. When one sees you plain, how ignoble, how despicable you are! Deformed and weakly, there is nothing to venerate in you, much to pity, most to despise.'

Again they were in darkness and her anger became modified directly she could see nothing but the poet's knees.

'But it is I that am a wretch,' she reflected, once they were in complete obscurity again, 'for base as you may be, am I not still baser? It is you who nourish and protect me, you who scare the wild beast, frighten the savage, make me clothes of the silk-worm's wool, and carpets of the sheep's. If I want to worship, have you not provided me with an image of yourself and set it in the sky? Are not evidences of your care everywhere? How humble, how grateful, how docile, should I not be, therefore? Let it be all my joy to serve, honour, and obey you.'

Here they reached the big lamp-post at the corner of what is now Piccadilly Circus. The light blazed in her eyes, and she saw, besides some degraded crea-tures of her own sex, two wretched pigmies on a stark desert land. Both were naked, solitary, and defenceless. The one was powerless to help the other. Each had enough to do to look after itself. Looking Mr Pope full in the face, 'It is equally vain', she thought, 'for you to think you can protect me, or for me to think I can worship you. The light of truth beats upon us without shadow, and the light of truth is damnably unbecoming to us both.'

All this time, of course, they went on talking agreeably, as people of birth and education use, about the Queen's temper and the Prime Minister's gout, while the coach went from light to darkness down the Haymarket, along the Strand, up Fleet Street, and reached, at length, her house in Blackfriars. For some time the dark spaces between the lamps had been becoming brighter and the lamps themselves less bright—that is to say, the sun was rising, and it was in the equable but confused light of a summer's morning in which everything is seen but nothing is seen distinctly that they alighted, Mr Pope handing Orlando from her carriage and Orlando curtseying Mr Pope to precede her into her mansion with the most scrupulous attention to the rites of the Graces.

From the foregoing passage, however, it must not be supposed that genius (but the disease is now stamped out in the British Isles, the late Lord Tennyson, it is said, being the last person to suffer from it) is constantly alight, for then we should see everything plain and perhaps should be scorched to death in the process. Rather it resembles the lighthouse in its working, which sends one ray and then no more for a time; save that genius is much more capricious in its manifestations and may flash six or seven beams in quick succession (as Mr Pope did that night) and then lapse into darkness for a year or for ever. To steer by its beams is therefore impossible, and when the dark spell is on them men of genius are, it is said, much like other people.

It was happy for Orlando, though at first disappointing, that this should be so, for she now began to live much in the company of men of genius. Nor were they so different from the rest of us as one might have supposed. Addison, Pope, Swift, proved, she found, to be fond of tea. They liked arbours. They collected little bits of coloured glass. They adored grottos. Rank was not distasteful to them. Praise was delightful. They wore plum-coloured suits one day and grey another. Mr Swift had a fine malacca cane. Mr Addison scented his handkerchiefs. Mr Pope suffered with his head. A piece of gossip did not come amiss. Nor were they without their jealousies. (We are jotting down a few reflections that came to Orlando higgledy-piggledy.) At first, she was annoyed with herself for noticing such trifles, and kept a book in which to write down their memorable sayings, but the page remained empty. All the same, her spirits revived, and she took to tearing up her cards of invitation to great parties; kept her evenings free; began to look forward to Mr Pope's visit, to Mr

Addison's, to Mr Swift's and so on and so on. If the reader will here refer to the *Rape of the Lock*, to the *Spectator*, to *Gulliver's Travels*, he will understand precisely what these mysterious words may mean. Indeed, biographers and critics might save themselves all their labours if readers would only take this advice. For when we read:

> Whether the Nymph shall break Diana's Law,
> Or some frail China Jar receive a Flaw,
> Or stain her Honour, or her new Brocade,
> Forget her Pray'rs or miss a Masquerade,
> Or lose her Heart, or Necklace, at a Ball.*

—we know as if we heard him how Mr Pope's tongue flickered like a lizard's, how his eyes flashed, how his hand trembled, how he loved, how he lied, how he suffered. In short, every secret of a writer's soul, every experience of his life, every quality of his mind is written large in his works, yet we require critics to explain the one and biographers to expound the other. That time hangs heavy on people's hands is the only explanation of the monstrous growth.

So, now that we have read a page or two of the *Rape of the Lock*, we know exactly why Orlando was so much amused and so much frightened and so very bright-cheeked and bright-eyed that afternoon.

Mrs Nelly then knocked at the door to say that Mr Addison waited on her Ladyship. At this, Mr Pope got up with a wry smile, made his congee,* and limped off. In came Mr Addison. Let us, as he takes his seat, read the following passage from the *Spectator*:*

'I consider woman as a beautiful, romantic animal, that may be adorned with furs and feathers, pearls and diamonds, ores and silks. The lynx shall cast its skin at her feet to make her a tippet, the peacock, parrot and swan shall pay contributions to her muff; the sea shall be searched for shells, and the rocks for gems, and every part of nature furnish out its share towards the embellishment of a creature that is the most consummate work of it. All this, I shall indulge them in, but as for the petticoat I have been speaking of, I neither can, nor will allow it.'

We hold that gentleman, cocked hat and all, in the hollow of our hands. Look once more into the crystal. Is he not clear to the very wrinkle in his stocking? Does not every ripple and curve of his wit lie exposed before us, and his benignity and his timidity and his urbanity and the fact that he would marry a Countess and die very respectably in the end? All is clear. And when Mr Addison has said his say, there is a terrific rap at the door, and Mr Swift, who had these arbitrary ways with him, walks in unannounced. One moment, where is *Gulliver's Travels*? Here it is! Let us read a passage from the voyage to the Houyhnhnms:*

'I enjoyed perfect Health of Body and Tranquillity of Mind; I did not find the Treachery or Inconstancy of a Friend, nor the Injuries of a secret or open

Enemy. I had no occasion of bribing, flattering or pimping, to procure the Favour of any great Man or of his Minion. I wanted no Fence against Fraud or Oppression; Here was neither Physician to destroy my Body, nor Lawyer to ruin my Fortune; No Informer to watch my Words, and Actions, or forge Accusations against me for Hire: Here were no Gibers, Censurers, Backbiters, Pickpockets, Highwaymen, House-breakers, Attorneys, Bawds, Buffoons, Gamesters, Politicians, Wits, splenetick tedious Talkers. . . .'

But stop, stop your iron pelt of words, lest you flay us all alive, and yourself too! Nothing can be plainer than that violent man. He is so coarse and yet so clean; so brutal, yet so kind; scorns the whole world, yet talks baby language to a girl, and will die, can we doubt it? in a madhouse.

So Orlando poured out tea for them all; and sometimes, when the weather was fine, she carried them down to the country with her, and feasted them royally in the Round Parlour,* which she had hung with their pictures all in a circle, so that Mr Pope could not say that Mr Addison came before him, or the other way about. They were very witty, too (but their wit is all in their books), and taught her the most important part of style, which is the natural run of the voice in speaking—a quality which none that has not heard it can imitate, not Greene even, with all his skill; for it is born of the air, and breaks like a wave on the furniture, and rolls and fades away, and is never to be recaptured, least of all by those who prick up their ears, half a century later, and try. They taught her this, merely by the cadence of their voices in speech; so that her style changed somewhat, and she wrote some very pleasant, witty verses and characters in prose. And so she lavished her wine on them and put bank-notes, which they took very kindly, beneath their plates at dinner, and accepted their dedications, and thought herself highly honoured by the exchange.

Thus time ran on, and Orlando could often be heard saying to herself with an emphasis which might, perhaps, make the hearer a little suspicious, 'Upon my soul, what a life this is!' (For she was still in search of that commodity.) But circumstances soon forced her to consider the matter more narrowly.

One day she was pouring out tea for Mr Pope while, as anyone can tell from the verses quoted above, he sat very bright-eyed, observant, and all crumpled up in a chair by her side.

'Lord,' she thought, as she raised the sugar tongs, 'how women in ages to come will envy me! And yet——' she paused; for Mr Pope needed her attention. And yet—let us finish her thought for her—when anybody says 'How future ages will envy me', it is safe to say that they are extremely uneasy at the present moment. Was this life quite so exciting, quite so flattering, quite so glorious as it sounds when the

memoir writer has done his work upon it? For one
thing, Orlando had a positive hatred of tea; for
another, the intellect, divine as it is, and all-worship-
ful, has a habit of lodging in the most seedy of
carcases, and often, alas, acts the cannibal among the
other faculties so that often, where the Mind is
biggest, the Heart, the Senses, Magnanimity, Charity,
Tolerance, Kindliness, and the rest of them scarcely
have room to breathe. Then the high opinion poets
have of themselves; then the low one they have of
others; then the enmities, injuries, envies, and repar-
tees in which they are constantly engaged; then the
volubility with which they impart them; then the
rapacity with which they demand sympathy for them;
all this, one may whisper, lest the wits may overhear
us, makes pouring out tea a more precarious and,
indeed, arduous occupation than is generally allowed.
Added to which (we whisper again lest the women
may overhear us), there is a little secret which men
share among them; Lord Chesterfield whispered it to
his son* with strict injunctions to secrecy, 'Women
are but children of a larger growth. . . . A man of sense
only trifles with them, plays with them, humours and
flatters them', which, since children always hear what
they are not meant to, and sometimes, even, grow up,
may have somehow leaked out, so that the whole
ceremony of pouring out tea is a curious one. A
woman knows very well that, though a wit sends her
his poems, praises her judgement, solicits her criti-

cism, and drinks her tea, this by no means signifies that he respects her opinions, admires her understanding, or will refuse, though the rapier is denied him, to run her through the body with his pen. All this, we say, whisper it as low as we can, may have leaked out by now; so that even with the cream jug suspended and the sugar tongs distended the ladies may fidget a little, look out of the window a little, yawn a little, and so let the sugar fall with a great plop as Orlando did now—into Mr Pope's tea. Never was any mortal so ready to suspect an insult or so quick to avenge one as Mr Pope. He turned to Orlando and presented her instantly with the rough draught of a certain famous line in the 'Characters of Women'.* Much polish was afterwards bestowed on it, but even in the original it was striking enough. Orlando received it with a curtsey. Mr Pope left her with a bow. Orlando, to cool her cheeks,* for really she felt as if the little man had struck her, strolled in the nut grove at the bottom of the garden. Soon the cool breezes did their work. To her amazement she found that she was hugely relieved to find herself alone. She watched the merry boatloads rowing up the river. No doubt the sight put her in mind of one or two incidents in her past life. She sat herself down in profound meditation beneath a fine willow tree. There she sat till the stars were in the sky. Then she rose, turned, and went into the house, where she sought her bedroom and locked the door. Now she opened a cupboard in which hung still many of the clothes she had worn as a young man of fashion, and from among them she chose a black velvet suit richly trimmed with Venetian lace. It was a little out of fashion, indeed, but it fitted her to perfection and dressed in it she looked the very figure of a noble Lord. She took a turn or two before the mirror to make sure that her petticoats had not lost her the freedom of her legs, and then let herself secretly out of doors.*

It was a fine night early in April. A myriad stars mingling with the light of a sickle moon, which again was enforced by the street lamps, made a light infinitely becoming to the human countenance and to the architecture of Mr Wren. Everything appeared in its tenderest form, yet, just as it seemed on the point of dissolution, some drop of silver sharpened it to animation. Thus it was that talk should be, thought Orlando (indulging in foolish reverie); that society should be, that friendship should be, that love should be. For, Heaven knows why, just as we have lost faith in human intercourse some random collocation of barns and trees or a haystack and a waggon presents us with so perfect a symbol of what is unattainable that we begin the search again.

She entered Leicester Square as she made these observations. The buildings had an airy yet formal symmetry not theirs by day. The canopy of the sky seemed most dexterously washed in to fill up the outline of roof and chimney. A young woman who sat dejectedly with one arm drooping by her side, the other reposing in her lap, on a seat beneath a plane tree in the middle of the square seemed the very figure of grace, simplicity, and desolation. Orlando swept her hat off to her in the manner of a gallant paying his addresses to a lady of fashion in a public place. The young woman raised her head. It was of the most exquisite shapeliness. The young woman raised her eyes. Orlando saw them to be of a lustre such as is sometimes seen on teapots but rarely in a human face. Through this silver glaze the young woman looked up at him (for a man he was to her) appealing, hoping, trembling, fearing. She rose; she accepted his arm. For—need we stress the point?—she was of the tribe which nightly burnishes their wares, and sets them in order on the common counter to wait the highest bidder. She led Orlando to the room in Gerrard Street which was her lodging. To feel her hanging lightly yet like a suppliant on her arm, roused in Orlando all the feelings which become a man. She looked, she felt, she talked like one. Yet, having been so lately a woman herself, she suspected that the girl's timidity and her hesitating answers and the very fumbling with the key in the latch and the fold of her cloak and the droop of her wrist were all put on to gratify her masculinity. Upstairs they went, and the pains which the poor creature had been at to decorate her room and hide the fact that she had no other deceived Orlando not a moment. The deception roused her scorn; the truth roused her pity. One thing showing through the other bred the oddest assortment of feeling, so that she did not know whether to laugh or to cry. Meanwhile Nell, as the girl called herself, unbuttoned her gloves; carefully concealed the left-hand thumb, which wanted mending; then drew behind a screen, where, perhaps, she rouged her cheeks, arranged her clothes, fixed a new kerchief round her neck—all the time prattling as women do, to amuse her lover, though Orlando could have sworn, from the tone of her voice, that her thoughts were elsewhere. When all was ready, out she came, prepared—but here Orlando could stand it no longer. In the strangest torment of anger, merriment, and pity she flung off all disguise and admitted herself a woman.

At this, Nell burst into such a roar of laughter as might have been heard across the way.

'Well, my dear,' she said, when she had somewhat recovered, 'I'm by no means sorry to hear it. For the plain Dunstable of the matter* is' (and it was remarkable how soon, on discovering that they were of the same sex, her manner changed and she dropped her plaintive, appealing ways), 'the plain Dunstable of the matter is, that I'm not in the mood for the society of the other sex tonight. Indeed, I'm in the devil of a fix.' Whereupon, drawing up the fire and stirring a bowl of punch, she told Orlando the whole story of her life. Since it is Orlando's life that engages us at

[208]

present, we need not relate the adventures of the other lady, but it is certain that Orlando had never known the hours speed faster or more merrily, though Mistress Nell had not a particle of wit about her, and when the name of Mr Pope came up in talk asked innocently if he were connected with the perruque maker of that name in Jermyn Street. Yet, to Orlando, such is the charm of ease and the seduction of beauty, this poor girl's talk, larded though it was with the commonest expressions of the street corners, tasted like wine after the fine phrases she had been used to, and she was forced to the conclusion that there was something in the sneer of Mr Pope, in the condescension of Mr Addison, and in the secret of Lord Chesterfield which took away her relish for the society of wits, deeply though she must continue to respect their works.

These poor creatures, she ascertained, for Nell brought Prue, and Prue Kitty, and Kitty Rose, had a society of their own of which they now elected her a member. Each would tell the story of the adventures which had landed her in her present way of life. Several were the natural daughters of earls* and one was a good deal nearer than she should have been to the King's person. None was too wretched or too poor but to have some ring or handkerchief in her pocket which stood her in lieu of pedigree. So they would draw round the punch-bowl which Orlando made it her business to furnish generously, and many were the fine tales they told and many the amusing observations they made, for it cannot be denied that when women get together—but hist—they are always careful to see that the doors are shut and that not a word of it gets into print. All they desire is— but hist again—is that not a man's step on the stair? All they desire, we were about to say when the gentleman took the very words out of our mouths. Women have no desires, says this gentleman, coming into Nell's parlour; only affectations. Without desires (she has served him and he is gone) their conversation cannot be of the slightest interest to anyone. 'It is well known', says Mr S. W.,* 'that when they lack the stimulus of the other sex, women can find nothing to say to each other. When they are alone, they do not talk, they scratch.' And since they cannot talk together and scratching cannot continue without interruption and it is well known (Mr T. R. has proved it) 'that women are incapable of any feeling of affection for their own sex and hold each other in the greatest aversion', what can we suppose that women do when they seek out each other's society?

As that is not a question that can engage the attention of a sensible man, let us, who enjoy the immunity of all biographers and historians from any sex whatever, pass it over, and merely state that Orlando professed great enjoyment in the society of her own sex, and leave it to the gentlemen to prove, as they are very fond of doing, that this is impossible.

But to give an exact and particular account of Orlando's life at this time becomes more and more out of the question. As we peer and grope in the ill-lit, ill-paved, ill-ventilated courtyards that lay about Gerrard Street and Drury Lane at that time, we seem now to catch sight of her and then again to lose it. The task is made still more difficult by the fact that she found it convenient at this time to change frequently from one set of clothes to another. Thus she often occurs in contemporary memoirs as 'Lord' So-and-so, who was in fact her cousin; her bounty is ascribed to him, and it is he who is said to have written the poems that were really hers. She had, it seems, no difficulty in sustaining the different parts, for her sex changed far more frequently than those who have worn only one set of clothing can conceive; nor can there be any doubt that she reaped a twofold harvest by this device; the pleasures of life were increased and its experiences multiplied. For the probity of breeches she exchanged the seductiveness of petticoats and enjoyed the love of both sexes equally.

So then one may sketch her spending her morning in a China robe of ambiguous gender among her books; then receiving a client or two (for she had many scores of suppliants) in the same garment; then she would take a turn in the garden and clip the nut trees—for which knee-breeches were convenient; then she would change into a flowered taffeta which best suited a drive to Richmond and a proposal of marriage from some great nobleman; and so back again to town, where she would don a snuff-coloured gown like a lawyer's and visit the courts to hear how her cases were doing,—for her fortune was wasting hourly and the suits seemed no nearer consummation than they had been a hundred years ago; and so, finally, when night came, she would more often than not become a nobleman complete from head to toe and walk the streets in search of adventure.

Returning from some of these junketings—of which there were many stories told at the time, as, that she fought a duel, served on one of the King's ships as a captain, was seen to dance naked on a balcony, and fled with a certain lady to the Low Countries where the lady's husband followed them*—but of the truth or otherwise of these stories, we express no opinion—returning from whatever her occupation may have been, she made a point sometimes of passing beneath the windows of a coffee house, where she could see the wits without being seen, and thus could fancy from their gestures what wise, witty, or spiteful things they were saying without hearing a word of them; which was perhaps an advantage; and once she stood half an hour watching three shadows on the blind drinking tea together in a house in Bolt Court.

Never was any play so absorbing. She wanted to cry out, Bravo! Bravo! For, to be sure, what a fine drama it was—what a page torn from the thickest volume of human life! There was the little shadow with the pouting lips, fidgeting this way and that on his chair, uneasy, petulant, officious; there was the bent female shadow, crooking a finger in the cup to feel how deep the tea was, for she was blind; and there was the Roman-looking rolling shadow in the big armchair—he who twisted his fingers so oddly and jerked his head from side to side and swallowed down the tea in such vast gulps. Dr Johnson, Mr Boswell, and Mrs Williams,—those were the shadows' names. So absorbed was she in the sight, that she forgot to think how other ages would have envied her, though it seems probable that on this occasion they would. She was content to gaze and gaze. At length Mr Boswell rose. He saluted the old woman with tart asperity. But with what humility did he not abase himself before the great Roman shadow, who now rose to its full height and rocking somewhat as he stood there rolled out the most magnificent phrases that ever left human lips; so Orlando thought them, though she never heard a word that any of the three shadows said as they sat there drinking tea.

At length she came home one night after one of these saunterings and mounted to her bedroom. She took off her laced coat and stood there in shirt and breeches looking out of the window. There was something stirring in the air which forbade her to go

to bed. A white haze lay over the town, for it was a
frosty night in midwinter and a magnificent vista lay
all round her. She could see St Paul's, the Tower,
Westminster Abbey, with all the spires and domes of
the city churches, the smooth bulk of its banks, the
opulent and ample curves of its halls and meeting-
places. On the north rose the smooth, shorn heights
of Hampstead, and in the west the streets and squares
of Mayfair shone out in one clear radiance. Upon this
serene and orderly prospect the stars looked down,
glittering, positive, hard, from a cloudless sky. In the
extreme clearness of the atmosphere the line of every
roof, the cowl of every chimney, was perceptible;
even the cobbles in the streets showed distinct one
from another, and Orlando could not help comparing
this orderly scene with the irregular and huddled
purlieus which had been the city of London in the
reign of Queen Elizabeth. Then, she remembered, the
city, if such one could call it, lay crowded, a mere
huddle and conglomeration of houses, under her
windows at Blackfriars. The stars reflected themselves
in deep pits of stagnant water which lay in the middle
of the streets. A black shadow at the corner where
the wine shop used to stand was, as likely as not, the
corpse of a murdered man. She could remember the
cries of many a one wounded in such night brawlings,
when she was a little boy, held to the diamond-paned
window in her nurse's arms. Troops of ruffians, men
and women, unspeakably interlaced, lurched down

the streets, trolling out wild songs with jewels flashing in their ears, and knives gleaming in their fists. On such a night as this the impermeable tangle of the forests on Highgate and Hampstead would be outlined, writhing in contorted intricacy against the sky. Here and there, on one of the hills which rose above London, was a stark gallows tree, with a corpse nailed to rot or parch on its cross; for danger and insecurity, lust and violence, poetry and filth swarmed over the tortuous Elizabethan highways and buzzed and stank—Orlando could remember even now the smell of them on a hot night—in the little rooms and narrow pathways of the city. Now—she leant out of her window—all was light, order, and serenity. There was the faint rattle of a coach on the cobbles. She heard the far-away cry of the night watchman—'Just twelve o'clock on a frosty morning'. No sooner had the words left his lips than the first stroke of midnight sounded. Orlando then for the first time noticed a small cloud gathered behind the dome of St Paul's. As the strokes sounded, the cloud increased, and she saw it darken and spread with extraordinary speed. At the same time a light breeze rose and by the time the sixth stroke of midnight had struck the whole of the eastern sky was covered with an irregular moving darkness, though the sky to the west and north stayed clear as ever. Then the cloud spread north. Height upon height above the city was engulfed by it. Only Mayfair, with all its lights shining, burnt more brilliantly than ever by contrast. With the eighth stroke, some hurrying tatters of cloud sprawled over Piccadilly. They seemed to mass themselves and to advance with extraordinary rapidity towards the west end. As the ninth, tenth, and eleventh strokes struck, a huge blackness sprawled over the whole of London. With the twelfth stroke of midnight, the darkness was complete. A turbulent welter of cloud covered the city. All was darkness; all was doubt; all was confusion. The Eighteenth century was over; the Nineteenth century had begun.

CHAPTER V

THE great cloud which hung, not only over London, but over the whole of the British Isles on the first day of the nineteenth century stayed, or rather, did not stay, for it was buffeted about constantly by blustering gales, long enough to have extraordinary consequences upon those who lived beneath its shadow. A change seemed to have come over the climate of England. Rain fell frequently, but only in fitful gusts, which were no sooner over than they began again. The sun shone, of course, but it was so girt about with clouds and the air was so saturated with water, that its beams were discoloured and purples, oranges, and reds of a dull sort took the place of the more positive landscapes of the eighteenth century. Under this bruised and sullen canopy the green of the cabbages was less intense, and the white of the snow was muddied. But what was worse, damp now began to make its way into every house—damp, which is the most insidious of all enemies, for while the sun can be shut out by blinds, and the frost roasted by a hot fire, damp steals in while we sleep; damp is silent, imperceptible, ubiquitous. Damp swells the wood, furs the kettle, rusts the iron, rots the stone. So gradual is the process, that it is not until we pick up some chest of drawers, or coal scuttle, and the whole thing drops to pieces in our hands, that we suspect even that the disease is at work.

Thus, stealthily and imperceptibly, none marking the exact day or hour of the change, the constitution of England was altered and nobody knew it. Everywhere the effects were felt. The hardy country gentleman, who had sat down gladly to a meal of ale and beef in a room designed, perhaps by the brothers Adam,* with classic dignity, now felt chilly. Rugs appeared; beards were grown; trousers were fastened tight under the instep. The chill which he felt in his legs the country gentleman soon transferred to his house; furniture was muffled; walls and tables were covered; nothing was left bare. Then a change of diet became essential. The muffin was invented and the crumpet. Coffee supplanted the after-dinner port, and, as coffee led to a drawing-room in which to drink it, and a drawing-room to glass cases, and glass cases to artificial flowers, and artificial flowers to mantelpieces, and mantelpieces to pianofortes, and pianofortes to drawing-room ballads, and drawing-room ballads (skipping a stage or two) to innumerable little dogs, mats, and china ornaments, the home— which had become extremely important—was completely altered.

Outside the house—it was another effect of the damp—ivy grew in unparalleled profusion. Houses that had been of bare stone were smothered in greenery. No garden, however formal its original design, lacked a shrubbery, a wilderness, a maze. What light penetrated to the bedrooms where children were born was naturally of an obfusc* green, and what light penetrated to the drawing-rooms where grown men and women lived came through curtains of brown and purple plush. But the change did not stop at outward things. The damp struck within. Men felt the chill in their hearts; the damp in their minds. In a desperate effort to snuggle their feelings into some sort of warmth one subterfuge was tried after another. Love, birth, and death were all swaddled in a variety of fine phrases. The sexes drew further and further apart. No open conversation was tolerated. Evasions and concealments were sedulously practised on both sides. And just as the ivy and the evergreen rioted in the damp earth outside, so did the same fertility show itself within. The life of the average woman was a succession of childbirths. She married at nineteen and had fifteen or eighteen children by the time she was thirty; for twins abounded. Thus the British Empire came into existence; and thus—for there is no stopping damp; it gets into the inkpot as it gets into the woodwork—sentences swelled, adjectives multiplied, lyrics became epics, and little trifles that had been essays a column long were now encyclopaedias in ten or twenty volumes. But Eusebius Chubb shall be our witness to the effect this all had upon the mind of a sensitive man who could do nothing to stop it. There is a passage towards the end of his memoirs where he describes how, after writing thirty-five folio pages one morning 'all about nothing' he screwed the lid on his inkpot and went for a turn in his garden. Soon he found himself involved in the shrubbery. Innumerable leaves creaked and glistened above his head. He seemed to himself 'to crush the mould of a million more under his feet'. Thick smoke exuded from a damp bonfire at the end of the garden. He reflected that no fire on earth could ever hope to consume that vast vegetable encumbrance. Wherever he looked, vegetation was rampant. Cucumbers 'came scrolloping* across the grass to his feet'. Giant cauliflowers towered deck above deck till they rivalled, to his disordered imagination, the elm trees themselves. Hens laid incessantly eggs of no special tint. Then, remembering with a sigh his own fecundity and his poor wife Jane, now in the throes of her fifteenth confinement indoors, how, he asked himself, could he blame the fowls? He looked upwards into the sky. Did not heaven itself, or that great frontispiece of heaven, which is the sky, indicate the assent indeed, the instigation of the heavenly hierarchy? For there, winter or summer, year in year out, the clouds turned and tumbled, like whales, he pondered, or elephants rather; but no, there was no escaping the simile which was pressed upon him from a thousand airy acres; the whole sky itself as it spread wide above the British Isles was nothing but a vast feather bed; and the undistinguished fecundity of the garden, the bedroom and the henroost was copied there. He went indoors, wrote the passage quoted above, laid his head in a gas oven, and when they found him later he was past revival.

While this went on in every part of England, it was all very well for Orlando to mew herself in her house at Blackfriars and pretend that the climate was the same; that one could still say what one liked and wear knee-breeches or skirts as the fancy took one. Even she, at length, was forced to acknowledge that times were changed. One afternoon in the early part of the century she was driving through St James's Park in her old panelled coach when one of those sunbeams, which occasionally, though not often, managed to come to earth, struggled through, marbling the clouds with strange prismatic colours as it passed. Such a sight was sufficiently strange after the clear and uniform skies of the eighteenth century to cause her to pull the window down and look at it. The puce and flamingo clouds made her think with a pleasurable anguish, which proves that she was insensibly afflicted with the damp already, of dolphins dying in Ionian seas. But what was her surprise when, as it struck the earth, the sunbeam seemed to call forth, or to light up, a pyramid, hecatomb, or trophy (for it had something of a banquet-table air)—a conglomeration at any rate of the most heterogeneous and ill-assorted objects, piled higgledy-piggledy in a vast mound where the statue of Queen Victoria now stands! Draped about a vast cross of fretted and floriated gold were widow's weeds and bridal veils; hooked on to other excrescences were crystal palaces,* bassinettes,* military helmets, memorial wreaths, trousers, whiskers, wedding cakes, cannon, Christmas trees, telescopes, extinct monsters, globes, maps, elephants, and mathematical instruments—the whole supported like a gigantic coat of arms on the right side by a female figure clothed in flowing white; on the left by a portly gentleman wearing a frock-coat and sponge-bag trousers. The incongruity of the objects, the association of the fully clothed and the partly draped, the garishness of the different colours and their plaid-like juxtapositions afflicted Orlando with the most profound dismay. She had never, in all her life, seen anything at once so indecent, so hideous, and so monumental. It might, and indeed it must be, the effect of the sun on the water-logged air; it would vanish with the first breeze that blew; but for all that, it looked, as she drove past, as if it were destined to endure for ever. Nothing, she felt, sinking back into the corner of her coach, no wind, rain, sun, or thunder, could ever demolish that garish erection. Only the noses would mottle and the trumpets would rust; but there they would remain, pointing east, west, south, and north, eternally. She looked back as her coach swept up Constitution Hill. Yes, there it was, still beaming placidly in a light which—she pulled her watch out of her fob—was, of course, the light of twelve o'clock mid-day. None other could be so prosaic, so matter-of-fact, so impervious to any hint of dawn or sunset, so seemingly calculated to last for ever. She was determined not to look again. Already she felt the tides of her blood run sluggishly. But what was more peculiar, a blush, vivid and singular, overspread her cheeks as she passed Buckingham Palace and her eyes seemed forced by a superior power down upon her knees. Suddenly she saw with a start that she was wearing black breeches. She never ceased blushing till she had reached her country house, which, considering the time it takes four horses to trot thirty miles, will be taken, we hope, as a signal proof of her chastity.

Once there, she followed what had now become the most imperious need of her nature and wrapped herself as well as she could in a damask quilt which she snatched from her bed. She explained to the Widow Bartholomew (who had succeeded good old Grimsditch as housekeeper) that she felt chilly.

'So do we all, m'lady,' said the Widow, heaving a profound sigh. 'The walls is sweating,' she said, with a curious, lugubrious complacency, and sure enough, she had only to lay her hand on the oak panels for the finger-prints to be marked there. The ivy had grown so profusely that many windows were now sealed up. The kitchen was so dark that they could scarcely tell a kettle from a cullender. A poor black cat had been mistaken for coals and shovelled on the fire. Most of the maids were already wearing three or four red-flannel petticoats, though the month was August.

'But is it true, m'lady,' the good woman asked, hugging herself, while the golden crucifix heaved on her bosom, 'that the Queen, bless her, is wearing a what d'you call it, a——,' the good woman hesitated and blushed.

'A crinoline,' Orlando helped her out with it (for the word had reached Blackfriars). Mrs Bartholomew nodded. The tears were already running down her cheeks, but as she wept she smiled. For it was pleasant to weep. Were they not all of them weak women? wearing crinolines the better to conceal the fact; the great fact; the only fact;* but, nevertheless, the deplorable fact; which every modest woman did her best to deny until denial was impossible; the fact that she was about to bear a child? to bear fifteen or twenty children indeed, so that most of a modest woman's life was spent, after all, in denying what, on one day at least of every year, was made obvious.

'The muffins is keepin' 'ot,' said Mrs Bartholomew, mopping up her tears, 'in the liberry.'

And wrapped in a damask bed quilt, to a dish of muffins Orlando now sat down.

'The muffins is keepin' 'ot in the liberry'—Orlando minced out the horrid cockney phrase in Mrs Bartholomew's refined cockney accents as she drank—but no, she detested the mild fluid—her tea. It was in this very room, she remembered, that Queen Elizabeth had stood astride the fireplace with a flagon of beer in her hand, which she suddenly dashed on the table when Lord Burghley tactlessly used the imperative instead of the subjunctive. 'Little man, little man,'—Orlando could hear her say—'is "must" a word to be addressed to princes?' And down came the flagon on the table: there was the mark of it still.

But when Orlando leapt to her feet, as the mere thought of that great Queen commanded, the bed quilt tripped her up, and she fell back in her armchair with a curse. Tomorrow she would have to buy twenty yards or more of black bombazine,* she supposed, to make a skirt. And then (here she blushed), she would have to buy a crinoline, and then (here she blushed) a bassinette, and then another crinoline, and so on . . . The blushes came and went with the most exquisite iteration of modesty and shame imaginable. One might see the spirit of the age blowing, now hot, now cold, upon her cheeks. And if the spirit of the age blew a little unequally, the crinoline being blushed for before the husband, her ambiguous position must excuse her (even her sex was still in dispute) and the irregular life she had lived before.

At length the colour on her cheeks resumed its stability and it seemed as if the spirit of the age—if such indeed it were—lay dormant for a time. Then Orlando felt in the bosom of her shirt as if for some locket or relic of lost affection, and drew out no such

[225]

thing, but a roll of paper, sea-stained, blood-stained, travel-stained—the manuscript of her poem, 'The Oak Tree'. She had carried this about with her for so many years now, and in such hazardous circumstances, that many of the pages were stained, some were torn, while the straits she had been in for writing paper when with the gipsies, had forced her to overscore the margins and cross the lines till the manuscript looked like a piece of darning most conscientiously carried out. She turned back to the first page and read the date, 1586, written in her own boyish hand. She had been working at it for close on three hundred years now.* It was time to make an end.* Meanwhile she began turning and dipping and reading and skipping and thinking as she read, how very little she had changed all these years. She had been a gloomy boy, in love with death, as boys are; and then she had been amorous and florid; and then she had been sprightly and satirical; and sometimes she had tried prose and sometimes she had tried drama. Yet through all these changes she had remained, she reflected, fundamentally the same. She had the same brooding meditative temper, the same love of animals and nature, the same passion for the country and the seasons.

'After all,' she thought, getting up and going to the window, 'nothing has changed. The house, the garden are precisely as they were. Not a chair has been moved, not a trinket sold. There are the same walks, the same lawns, the same trees, and the same pool, which, I dare say, has the same carp in it. True, Queen Victoria is on the throne and not Queen Elizabeth, but what difference. . . .'

No sooner had the thought taken shape, than, as if to rebuke it, the door was flung wide and in marched Basket, the butler, followed by Bartholomew, the housekeeper, to clear away tea. Orlando, who had just dipped her pen in the ink, and was about to indite some reflection upon the eternity of all things, was much annoyed to be impeded by a blot, which spread and meandered round her pen. It was some infirmity of the quill, she supposed; it was split or dirty. She dipped it again. The blot increased. She tried to go on with what she was saying; no words came. Next she began to decorate the blot with wings and whiskers, till it became a round-headed monster, something between a bat and a wombat. But as for writing poetry with Basket and Bartholomew in the room, it was impossible. No sooner had she said 'Impossible' than, to her astonishment and alarm, the pen began to curve and caracole with the smoothest possible fluency. Her page was written in the neatest sloping Italian hand with the most insipid verse she had ever read in her life:

> I am myself but a vile link
>> Amid life's weary chain
> But I have spoken hallow'd words,
>> Oh, do not say in vain!

> Will the young maiden, when her tears,
>   Alone in moonlight shine,
> Tears for the absent and the loved,
>   Murmur—

she wrote without a stop as Bartholomew and Basket grunted and groaned about the room, mending the fire, picking up the muffins.

Again she dipped her pen and off it went—

> She was so changed, the soft carnation cloud
> Once mantling o'er her cheek like that which eve
> Hangs o'er the sky, glowing with roseate hue,
> Had faded into paleness, broken by
> Bright burning blushes, torches of the tomb,*

but here, by an abrupt movement she spilt the ink over the page and blotted it from human sight she hoped for ever. She was all of a quiver, all of a stew. Nothing more repulsive could be imagined than to feel the ink flowing thus in cascades of involuntary inspiration. What had happened to her? Was it the damp,* was it Bartholomew, was it Basket, what was it? she demanded. But the room was empty. No one answered her, unless the dripping of the rain in the ivy could be taken for an answer.

Meanwhile, she became conscious, as she stood at the window, of an extraordinary tingling and vibration all over her, as if she were made of a thousand wires upon which some breeze or errant fingers were playing scales. Now her toes tingled; now her marrow. She had the queerest sensations about the thigh bones. Her hairs seemed to erect themselves. Her arms sang and twanged as the telegraph wires would be singing and twanging in twenty years or so. But all this agitation seemed at length to concentrate in her hands; and then in one hand, and then in one finger of that hand, and then finally to contract itself so that it made a ring of quivering sensibility about the second finger of the left hand. And when she raised it to see what caused this agitation, she saw nothing—nothing but the vast solitary emerald which Queen Elizabeth had given her.* And was that not enough? she asked. It was of the finest water. It was worth ten thousand pounds at least. The vibration seemed, in the oddest way (but remember we are dealing with some of the darkest manifestations of the human soul) to say No, that is not enough; and, further, to assume a note of interrogation, as though it were asking, what did it mean, this hiatus, this strange oversight? till poor Orlando felt positively ashamed of the second finger of her left hand without in the least knowing why. At this moment, Bartholomew came in to ask which dress she should lay out for dinner, and Orlando, whose senses were much quickened, instantly glanced at Bartholomew's left hand, and instantly perceived what she had never noticed before—a thick ring of rather jaundiced yellow circling the third finger where her own was bare.

'Let me look at your ring, Bartholomew,' she said, stretching her hand to take it.

At this, Bartholomew made as if she had been struck in the breast by a rogue. She started back a pace or two, clenched her hand and flung it away from her with a gesture that was noble in the extreme. 'No,' she said, with resolute dignity, her Ladyship might look if she pleased, but as for taking off her wedding ring, not the Archbishop nor the Pope nor Queen Victoria on her throne could force her to do that. Her Thomas had put it on her finger twenty-five years, six months, three weeks ago; she had slept in it; worked in it; washed in it; prayed in it; and proposed to be buried in it. In fact, Orlando understood her to say, but her voice was much broken with emotion, that it was by the gleam on her wedding ring that she would be assigned her station among the angels and its lustre would be tarnished for ever if she let it out of her keeping for a second.

'Heaven help us,' said Orlando, standing at the window and watching the pigeons at their pranks, 'what a world we live in! What a world to be sure!' Its complexities amazed her. It now seemed to her that the whole world was ringed with gold. She went in to dinner. Wedding rings abounded. She went to church. Wedding rings were everywhere. She drove out. Gold, or pinchbeck,* thin, thick, plain, smooth, they glowed dully on every hand. Rings filled the jewellers' shops, not the flashing pastes and diamonds of Orlando's recollection, but simple bands without a stone in them. At the same time, she began to notice a new habit among the town people. In the old days, one would meet a boy trifling with a girl under a hawthorn hedge frequently enough. Orlando had flicked many a couple with the tip of her whip and laughed and passed on. Now, all that was changed. Couples trudged and plodded in the middle of the road indissolubly linked together. The woman's right hand was invariably passed through the man's left and her fingers were firmly gripped by his. Often it was not till the horses' noses were on them that they budged, and then, though they moved it was all in one piece, heavily, to the side of the road. Orlando could only suppose that some new discovery had been made about the race; that they were somehow stuck together, couple after couple, but who had made it, and when, she could not guess. It did not seem to be Nature. She looked at the doves and the rabbits and the elk-hounds and she could not see that Nature had changed her ways or mended them, since the time of Elizabeth at least. There was no indissoluble alliance among the brutes that she could see. Could it be Queen Victoria then, or Lord Melbourne? Was it from them that the great discovery of marriage proceeded? Yet the Queen, she pondered, was said to be fond of dogs, and Lord Melbourne, she had heard, was said to be fond of women. It was strange—it was distasteful; indeed, there was something in this indissolubility of bodies which was repugnant to her sense of decency and sanitation. Her ruminations, however, were accompanied by such a tingling and twangling of the afflicted finger that she could scarcely keep her ideas in order. They were languishing and ogling like a housemaid's fancies. They made her blush. There was nothing for it but to buy one of those ugly bands and wear it like the rest. This she did, slipping it, overcome with shame, upon her finger in the shadow of a curtain; but without avail. The tingling persisted more violently, more indignantly than ever. She did not sleep a wink that night. Next morning when she took up the pen to write, either she could think of nothing, and the pen made one large lachrymose blot after another, or it ambled off, more alarmingly still, into mellifluous fluencies about early death and corruption, which were worse than no thinking at all. For it would seem—her case proved it—that we write, not with the fingers, but with the whole person. The nerve which controls the pen winds itself about every fibre of our being, threads the heart, pierces the liver. Though the seat of her trouble seemed to be the left hand, she could feel herself poisoned through and through, and was forced at length to consider the most desperate of remedies, which was to yield completely and submissively to the spirit of the age, and take a husband.

That this was much against her natural temperament has been sufficiently made plain. When the sound of the Archduke's chariot wheels died away, the cry that rose to her lips was 'Life! A Lover!' not 'Life! A Husband!' and it was in pursuit of this aim that she had gone to town and run about the world as has been shown in the previous chapter. Such is the indomitable nature of the spirit of the age, however, that it batters down anyone who tries to make stand against it far more effectually than those who bend its own way. Orlando had inclined herself naturally to the Elizabethan spirit, to the Restoration spirit, to the spirit of the eighteenth century, and had in consequence scarcely been aware of the change from one age to the other. But the spirit of the nineteenth century was antipathetic to her in the extreme, and thus it took her and broke her, and she was aware of her defeat at its hands as she had never been before. For it is probable that the human spirit has its place in time assigned to it; some are born of this age, some of that; and now that Orlando was grown a woman, a year or two past thirty indeed, the lines of her character were fixed,* and to bend them the wrong way was intolerable.

So she stood mournfully at the drawing-room window (Bartholomew had so christened the library) dragged down by the weight of the crinoline which she had submissively adopted. It was heavier and more drab than any dress she had yet worn. None had ever so impeded her movements. No longer could she stride through the garden with her dogs, or run lightly to the high mound and fling herself beneath the oak tree. Her skirts collected damp leaves and straw. The plumed hat tossed on the breeze. The thin shoes were quickly soaked and mud-caked. Her muscles had lost their pliancy. She became nervous lest there should be robbers behind the wainscot and afraid, for the first time in her life, of ghosts in the corridors. All these things inclined her, step by step, to submit to the new discovery, whether Queen Victoria's or another's, that each man and each woman has another allotted to it for life, whom it supports, by whom it is supported, till death them do part. It would be a comfort, she felt, to lean; to sit down; yes, to lie down; never, never, never to get up again. Thus did the spirit work upon her, for all her past pride, and as she came sloping down the scale of emotion to this lowly and unaccustomed lodging-place, those twanglings and tinglings which had been so captious and so interrogative modulated into the sweetest melodies, till it seemed as if angels were plucking harp-strings with white fingers and her whole being was pervaded by a seraphic harmony.

But whom could she lean upon? She asked that question of the wild autumn winds. For it was now October, and wet as usual. Not the Archduke; he had married a very great lady* and had hunted hares in Roumania these many years now; nor Mr M.; he was become a Catholic; nor the Marquis of C.; he made sacks in Botany Bay;* nor the Lord O.; he had long been food for fishes. One way or another, all her old cronies were gone now, and the Nells and the Kits of Drury Lane, much though she favoured them, scarcely did to lean upon.

'Whom', she asked, casting her eyes upon the revolving clouds, clasping her hands as she knelt on the window-sill, and looking the very image of appealing womanhood as she did so, 'can I lean upon?' Her words formed themselves, her hands clasped themselves, involuntarily, just as her pen had written of its own accord. It was not Orlando who spoke, but the spirit of the age. But whichever it was, nobody answered it. The rooks were tumbling pell-mell among the violet clouds of autumn. The rain had stopped at last and there was an iridescence in the sky which tempted her to put on her plumed hat and her little stringed shoes and stroll out before dinner.

'Everyone is mated except myself,' she mused, as she trailed disconsolately across the courtyard. There were the rooks; Canute and Pippin* even—transitory as their alliances were, still each this evening seemed to have a partner. 'Whereas, I, who am mistress of it all,' Orlando thought, glancing as she passed at the innumerable emblazoned windows of the hall, 'am single, am mateless, am alone.'

Such thoughts had never entered her head before. Now they bore her down unescapably. Instead of thrusting the gate open, she tapped with a gloved hand for the porter to unfasten it for her. One must lean on someone, she thought, if it is only on a porter; and half wished to stay behind and help him to grill his chop on a bucket of fiery coals, but was too timid to ask it. So she strayed out into the park alone, faltering at first and apprehensive lest there might be poachers or gamekeepers or even errand-boys to marvel that a great lady should walk alone.

At every step she glanced nervously lest some male form should be hiding behind a furze bush or some savage cow be lowering its horns to toss her. But there were only the rooks flaunting in the sky. A steel-blue plume from one of them fell among the heather. She loved wild birds' feathers. She had used to collect them as a boy. She picked it up and stuck it in her hat. The air blew upon her spirit somewhat and revived it. As the rooks went whirling and wheeling above her head and feather after feather fell gleaming through the purplish air, she followed them, her long cloak floating behind her, over the moor, up the hill. She had not walked so far for years. Six feathers had she picked from the grass and drawn between her fingers and pressed to her lips to feel their smooth, glinting plumage, when she saw, gleaming on the hillside, a silver pool, mysterious as the lake into which Sir Bedivere flung the sword of Arthur.* A single feather quivered in the air and fell into the middle of it. Then, some strange ecstasy came over her. Some wild notion she had of following the birds to the rim of the world and flinging herself on the spongy turf and there drinking forgetfulness, while the rooks' hoarse laughter sounded over her. She quickened her pace; she ran; she tripped; the tough heather roots flung her to the ground. Her ankle was broken. She could not rise. But there she lay content. The scent of the bog myrtle and the meadow-sweet was in her nostrils. The rooks' hoarse laughter was in her ears. 'I have found my mate,' she murmured. 'It is the moor. I am nature's bride,' she whispered, giving herself in rapture to the cold embraces of the grass as she lay folded in her cloak in the hollow by the pool. 'Here will I lie. (A feather fell upon her brow.) I have found a greener laurel than the bay. My forehead will be cool always. These are wild birds' feathers—the owl's, the nightjar's. I shall dream wild dreams. My hands shall wear no wedding ring,' she continued, slipping it from her finger. 'The roots shall twine about them. Ah!' she sighed, pressing her head luxuriously on its spongy pillow, 'I have sought happiness through many ages and not found it; fame and missed it; love and not known it; life—and behold, death is better. I have known many men and many women,' she continued; 'none have I understood. It is better that I should lie at peace here with only the sky above me—as the gipsy told me years ago. That was in Turkey.' And she looked straight up into the marvellous golden foam into which the clouds had churned themselves, and saw next moment a track in it, and camels passing in single file through the rocky desert among clouds of red dust; and then, when the camels had passed, there were only mountains, very high and full of clefts and with pinnacles of rock, and she fancied she heard goat bells ringing in their passes, and in their folds were fields of irises and gentian. So the sky changed and her eyes slowly lowered themselves down and down till they came to the rain-darkened earth and saw the great hump of the South Downs, flowing in one wave along the coast; and where the land parted, there was the sea, the sea with ships passing; and she fancied she heard a gun far out at sea, and thought at first, 'That's the Armada,' and then thought 'No, it's Nelson', and then remembered how those wars were over and the ships were busy merchant ships; and the sails on the winding river were those of pleasure boats. She saw, too, cattle sprinkled on the dark fields, sheep and cows, and she saw the lights coming here and there in farm-house windows, and lanterns moving among the cattle as the shepherd went his rounds and the cowman; and then the lights went out and the stars rose and tangled themselves about the sky. Indeed, she was falling asleep with the wet feathers on her face and her ear pressed to the ground when she heard, deep within, some hammer on an anvil, or was it a heart beating? Tick-tock, tick-tock, so it hammered, so it beat, the anvil, or the heart in the middle of the earth; until, as she listened, she thought it changed to the trot of a horse's hoofs; one, two, three, four, she counted;

then she heard a stumble; then, as it came nearer and nearer, she could hear the crack of a twig and the suck of the wet bog in its hoofs. The horse was almost on her. She sat upright. Towering dark against the yellow-slashed sky of dawn, with the plovers rising and falling about him, she saw a man on horseback. He started. The horse stopped.

'Madam,' the man cried, leaping to the ground, 'you're hurt!'

'I'm dead, sir!' she replied.

A few minutes later, they became engaged.

The morning after, as they sat at breakfast, he told her his name. It was Marmaduke Bonthrop Shelmerdine, Esquire.

'I knew it!' she said, for there was something romantic and chivalrous, passionate, melancholy, yet determined about him which went with the wild, dark-plumed name—a name which had, in her mind, the steel-blue gleam of rooks' wings, the hoarse laughter of their caws, the snake-like twisting descent of their feathers in a silver pool, and a thousand other things which will be described presently.

'Mine is Orlando,' she said. He had guessed it. For if you see a ship in full sail coming with the sun on it proudly sweeping across the Mediterranean from the South Seas, one says at once, 'Orlando', he explained.

In fact, though their acquaintance had been so short, they had guessed, as always happens between lovers, everything of any importance about each other in two seconds at the utmost, and it now remained only to fill in such unimportant details as what they were called; where they lived; and whether they were beggars or people of substance. He had a castle in the Hebrides,* but it was ruined, he told her. Gannets feasted in the banqueting hall. He had been a soldier and a sailor, and had explored the East. He was on his way now to join his brig at Falmouth, but the wind had fallen and it was only when the gale blew from the South-west that he could put out to sea. Orlando looked hastily from the breakfast-room window at the gilt leopard on the weather vane. Mercifully its tail pointed due east and was steady as a rock. 'Oh! Shel, don't leave me!' she cried. 'I'm passionately in love with you,' she said. No sooner had the words left her mouth than an awful suspicion rushed into both their minds simultaneously.

'You're a woman, Shel!' she cried.

'You're a man, Orlando!' he cried.

Never was there such a scene of protestation and demonstration as then took place since the world began. When it was over and they were seated again she asked him, what was this talk of a South-west gale? Where was he bound for?

'For the Horn,'* he said briefly, and blushed. (For a man had to blush as a woman had, only at rather different things.) It was only by dint of great pressure on her side and the use of much intuition that she gathered that his life was spent in the most desperate and splendid of adventures—which is to voyage round Cape Horn in the teeth of a gale. Masts had been snapped off; sails torn to ribbons (she had to drag the admission from him). Sometimes the ship had sunk, and he had been left the only survivor on a raft with a biscuit.

'It's about all a fellow can do nowadays,' he said sheepishly, and helped himself to great spoonfuls of strawberry jam. The vision which she had thereupon of this boy (for he was little more) sucking peppermints, for which he had a passion, while the masts snapped and the stars reeled and he roared brief orders to cut this adrift, to heave that overboard, brought the tears to her eyes, tears, she noted, of a finer flavour than any she had cried before. 'I am a woman,' she thought, 'a real woman, at last.' She thanked Bonthrop from the bottom of her heart for having given her this rare and unexpected delight. Had she not been lame in the left foot, she would have sat upon his knee.

'Shel, my darling,' she began again, 'tell me . . .' and so they talked two hours or more, perhaps about Cape Horn, perhaps not, and really it would profit little to write down what they said, for they knew each other so well that they could say anything, which is tantamount to saying nothing, or saying such stupid, prosy things as how to cook an omelette, or where to buy the best boots in London, things which have no lustre taken from their setting, yet are positively of amazing beauty within it. For it has come about, by the wise economy of nature, that our modern spirit can almost dispense with language; the commonest expressions do, since no expressions do; hence the most ordinary conversation is often the most poetic, and the most poetic is precisely that which cannot be written down. For which reasons we leave a great blank here, which must be taken to indicate that the space is filled to repletion.

After some days more of this kind of talk,

'Orlando, my dearest,' Shel was beginning, when there was a scuffling outside, and Basket the butler entered with the information that there was a couple of Peelers* downstairs with a warrant from the Queen.

'Show 'em up,' said Shelmerdine briefly, as if on his own quarter-deck, taking up, by instinct, a stand with his hands behind him in front of the fireplace. Two officers in bottle-green uniforms with truncheons at their hips then entered the room and stood at attention. Formalities being over, they gave into Orlando's own hands, as their commission was, a legal document of some very impressive sort, judging by the blobs of sealing wax, the ribbons, the oaths, and the signatures, which were all of the highest importance.

Orlando ran her eyes through it and then, using the first finger of her right hand as pointer, read out the following facts as being most germane to the matter.

'The lawsuits are settled,'* she read out . . . 'some in my favour, as for example . . . others not. Turkish marriage annulled (I was ambassador in Constantinople, Shel,' she explained). 'Children pronounced illegitimate (they said I had three sons by Pepita, a Spanish dancer). So they don't inherit, which is all to the good. . . . Sex? Ah! what about sex? My sex', she read out with some solemnity, 'is pronounced indisputably, and beyond the shadow of a doubt (what I was telling you a moment ago, Shel?), female. The estates which are now desequestrated in perpetuity descend and are tailed and entailed upon the heirs male of my body, or in default of marriage'—but here she grew impatient with this legal verbiage, and said, 'but there won't be any default of marriage, nor of heirs either, so the rest can be taken as read.' Whereupon she appended her own signature beneath Lord Palmerston's and entered from that moment into the undisturbed possession of her titles, her house, and her estate—which was now so much shrunk, for the cost of the lawsuits had been prodigious, that, though she was infinitely noble again, she was also excessively poor.

When the result of the lawsuit was made known (and rumour flew much quicker than the telegraph which has supplanted it), the whole town was filled with rejoicings.

[Horses were put into carriages for the sole purpose of being taken out. Empty barouches and landaus were trundled up and down the High Street incessantly. Addresses were read from the Bull. Replies were made from the Stag. The town was illuminated. Gold caskets were securely sealed in glass cases. Coins were well and duly laid under stones. Hospitals were founded. Rat and Sparrow clubs were inaugurated. Turkish women by the dozen were burnt in effigy in the market-place, together with scores of peasant boys with the label 'I am a base Pretender', lolling from their mouths. The Queen's cream-coloured ponies were soon seen trotting up the avenue with a command to Orlando to dine and sleep at the Castle, that very same night. Her table, as on a previous occasion, was snowed under with invitations from the Countess of R., Lady Q., Lady Palmerston, the Marchioness of P., Mrs W. E. Gladstone, and others, beseeching the pleasure of her company, reminding her of ancient alliances between their family and her own, etc.]*—all of which is properly enclosed in square brackets, as above, for the good reason that a parenthesis it was without any importance in

Orlando's life. She skipped it, to get on with the text. For when the bonfires were blazing in the market-place, she was in the dark woods with Shelmerdine alone. So fine was the weather that the trees stretched their branches motionless above them, and if a leaf fell, it fell, spotted red and gold, so slowly that one could watch it for half an hour fluttering and falling till it came to rest at last, on Orlando's foot.

'Tell me, Mar,'* she would say (and here it must be explained, that when she called him by the first syllable of his first name, she was in a dreamy, amorous, acquiescent mood, domestic, languid a little, as if spiced logs were burning, and it was evening, yet not time to dress, and a thought wet perhaps outside, enough to make the leaves glisten, but a nightingale might be singing even so among the azaleas, two or three dogs barking at distant farms, a cock crowing—all of which the reader should imagine in her voice)—'Tell me, Mar,' she would say, 'about Cape Horn.' Then Shelmerdine would make a little model on the ground of the Cape with twigs and dead leaves and an empty snail shell or two.

'Here's the north,' he would say. 'There's the south. The wind's coming from hereabouts. Now the brig is sailing due west; we've just lowered the top-boom mizzen: and so you see—here, where this bit of grass is, she enters the current which you'll find marked—where's my map and compasses, Bo'sun? Ah! thanks, that'll do, where the snail shell is. The current catches her on the starboard side, so we must rig the jib-boom or we shall be carried to the larboard, which is where that beech leaf is,—for you must understand my dear—' and so he would go on, and she would listen to every word; interpreting them rightly, so as to see, that is to say, without his having to tell her, the phosphorescence on the waves; the icicles clanking in the shrouds; how he went to the top of the mast in a gale; there reflected on the destiny of man; came down again; had a whisky and soda; went on shore; was trapped by a black woman; repented; reasoned it out; read Pascal; determined to write philosophy; bought a monkey; debated the true end of life; decided in favour of Cape Horn, and so on. All this and a thousand other things she understood him to say, and so when she replied, Yes, negresses are seductive, aren't they? he having told her that the supply of biscuits now gave out, he was surprised and delighted to find how well she had taken his meaning.

'Are you positive you aren't a man?' he would ask anxiously, and she would echo,

'Can it be possible you're not a woman?' and then they must put it to the proof without more ado. For each was so surprised at the quickness of the other's sympathy, and it was to each such a revelation that a woman could be as tolerant and free-spoken as a man, and a man as strange and subtle as a woman, that they had to put the matter to the proof at once.

And so they would go on talking or rather, understanding, which has become the main art of speech in an age when words are growing daily so scanty in comparison with ideas that 'the biscuits ran out' has to stand for kissing a negress in the dark when one has just read Bishop Berkeley's philosophy for the tenth time. (And from this it follows that only the most profound masters of style can tell the truth, and when one meets a simple one-syllabled writer, one may conclude, without any doubt at all, that the poor man is lying.)

So they would talk; and then, when her feet were fairly covered with spotted autumn leaves, Orlando would rise and stroll away into the heart of the woods in solitude, leaving Bonthrop sitting there among the snail shells, making models of Cape Horn. 'Bonthrop,' she would say, 'I'm off,' and when she called him by his second name, 'Bonthrop', it should signify to the reader that she was in a solitary mood, felt them both as specks on a desert, was desirous only of meeting death by herself, for people die daily, die at dinner tables, or like this, out of doors in the autumn woods; and with the bonfires blazing and Lady Palmerston or Lady Derby asking her out every night to dinner, the desire for death would overcome her, and so saying 'Bonthrop', she said in effect, 'I'm dead', and pushed her way as a spirit might through the spectre-pale beech trees, and so oared herself deep into solitude as if the little flicker of noise and movement were over and she were free now to take her way—all of which the reader should hear in her voice when she said 'Bonthrop'; and should also add, the better to illumine the word, that for him too the same word signified, mystically, separation and isolation and the disembodied pacing the deck of his brig in unfathomable seas.

After some hours of death, suddenly a jay shrieked 'Shelmerdine', and stooping, she picked up one of those autumn crocuses which to some people signify that very word, and put it with the jay's feather that came tumbling blue through the beech woods, in her breast. Then she called 'Shelmerdine' and the word went shooting this way and that way through the woods and struck him where he sat, making models out of snail shells in the grass. He saw her, and heard her coming to him with the crocus and the jay's feather in her breast, and cried 'Orlando', which meant (and it must be remembered that when bright colours like blue and yellow mix themselves in our eyes, some of it rubs off on our thoughts) first the bowing and swaying of bracken as if something were breaking through; which proved to be a ship in full sail, heaving and tossing a little dreamily, rather as if she had a whole year of summer days to make her voyage in; and so the ship bears down, heaving this way, heaving that way, nobly, indolently, and rides over the crest of this wave and sinks into the hollow of that one, and so, suddenly stands over you (who are in a little cockle shell of a boat, looking up at her) with all her sails quivering, and then, behold, they drop all of a heap on deck—as Orlando dropped now into the grass beside him.

Eight or nine days had been spent thus, but on the tenth, which was the 26th of October, Orlando was lying in the bracken, while Shelmerdine recited Shelley (whose entire works he had by heart), when a leaf which had started to fall slowly enough from a tree-top whipped briskly across Orlando's foot. A second leaf followed and then a third. Orlando shivered and turned pale. It was the wind. Shelmerdine—but it would be more proper now to call him Bonthrop—leapt to his feet.

'The wind!' he cried.

Together they ran through the woods, the wind plastering them with leaves as they ran, to the great court and through it and the little courts, frightened servants leaving their brooms and their saucepans to follow after till they reached the Chapel, and there a scattering of lights was lit as fast as could be, one knocking over this bench, another snuffing out that taper. Bells were rung. People were summoned. At length there was Mr Dupper catching at the ends of his white tie and asking where was the prayer book. And they thrust Queen Mary's prayer book in his hands and he searched hastily fluttering the pages, and said, 'Marmaduke Bonthrop Shelmerdine, and Lady Orlando, kneel down'; and they knelt down, and now they were bright and now they were dark as the light and shadow came flying helter-skelter through the painted windows; and among the banging of innumerable doors and a sound like brass pots beating, the organ sounded, its growl coming loud and faint alternately, and Mr Dupper, who was grown a very old man, tried now to raise his voice above the uproar and could not be heard and then all was quiet for a moment, and one word—it might be 'the jaws of death'—rang out clear, while all the estate servants kept pressing in with rakes and whips still in their hands to listen, and some sang aloud and others prayed, and now a bird was dashed against the pane, and now there was a clap of thunder, so that no one heard the word Obey spoken or saw, except as a golden flash, the ring pass from hand to hand. All was movement and confusion. And up they rose with the organ booming and the lightning playing and the rain pouring, and the Lady Orlando, with her ring on her finger, went out into the court in her thin dress and held the swinging stirrup, for the horse was bitted and bridled and the foam was still on his flank, for her husband to mount, which he did with one bound, and the horse leapt forward and Orlando, standing there, cried out Marmaduke Bonthrop Shelmerdine! and he answered her Orlando! and the words went dashing and circling like wild hawks together among the belfries and higher and higher, further and further, faster and faster they circled, till they crashed and fell in a shower of fragments to the ground; and she went in.

CHAPTER VI

ORLANDO went indoors. It was completely still. It was very silent. There was the ink pot; there was the pen; there was the manuscript of her poem, broken off in the middle of a tribute to eternity. She had been about to say, when Basket and Bartholomew interrupted with the tea things, nothing changes. And then, in the space of three seconds and a half, everything had changed—she had broken her ankle, fallen in love, married Shelmerdine.

There was the wedding ring on her finger to prove it. It was true that she had put it there herself before she met Shelmerdine, but that had proved worse than useless. She now turned the ring round and round, with superstitious reverence, taking care lest it should slip past the joint of her finger.

'The wedding ring has to be put on the third finger of the left hand', she said, like a child cautiously repeating its lesson, 'for it to be of any use at all.'

She spoke thus, aloud and rather more pompously than was her wont, as if she wished someone whose good opinion she desired to overhear her. Indeed, she had in mind, now that she was at last able to collect her thoughts, the effect that her behaviour would have had upon the spirit of the age. She was extremely anxious to be informed whether the steps she had taken in the matter of getting engaged to Shelmerdine and marrying him met with its approval. She was certainly feeling more herself. Her finger had not tingled once, or nothing to count, since that night on the moor. Yet, she could not deny that she had her doubts. She was married, true; but if one's husband was always sailing round Cape Horn, was it marriage? If one liked him, was it marriage? If one liked other people, was it marriage? And finally, if one still wished, more than anything in the whole world, to write poetry, was it marriage? She had her doubts.

But she would put it to the test. She looked at the ring. She looked at the ink pot. Did she dare? No, she did not. But she must. No, she could not. What should she do then? Faint, if possible. But she had never felt better in her life.

'Hang it all!' she cried, with a touch of her old spirit. 'Here goes!'

And she plunged her pen neck deep in the ink. To her enormous surprise, there was no explosion. She drew the nib out. It was wet, but not dripping. She wrote. The words were a little long in coming, but come they did. Ah! but did they make sense? she wondered, a panic coming over her lest the pen might have been at some of its involuntary pranks again. She read,

> And then I came to a field where the springing grass
> Was dulled by the hanging cups of fritillaries,
> Sullen and foreign-looking, the snaky flower,
> Scarfed in dull purple, like Egyptian girls—*

As she wrote she felt some power (remember we are dealing with the most obscure manifestations of the human spirit) reading over her shoulder, and when she had written 'Egyptian girls', the power told her to stop. Grass, the power seemed to say, going back with a ruler such as governesses use to the beginning, is all right; the hanging cups of fritillaries—admirable; the snaky flower—a thought, strong from a lady's pen, perhaps, but Wordsworth, no doubt, sanctions it; but—girls? Are girls necessary? You have a husband at the Cape, you say? Ah, well, that'll do.

And so the spirit passed on.

Orlando now performed in spirit (for all this took place in spirit) a deep obeisance to the spirit of her age, such as—to compare great things with small—a traveller, conscious that he has a bundle of cigars in the corner of his suit case, makes to the customs officer who has obligingly made a scribble of white chalk on the lid. For she was extremely doubtful whether, if the spirit had examined the contents of her mind carefully, it would not have found something highly contraband for which she would have had to pay the full fine. She had only escaped by the skin of her teeth. She had just managed, by some dexterous deference to the spirit of the age, by putting on a ring and finding a man on a moor, by loving nature and being no satirist, cynic, or psychologist— any one of which goods would have been discovered at once—to pass its examination successfully. And she heaved a deep sigh of relief, as, indeed, well she might, for the transaction between a writer and the spirit of the age is one of infinite delicacy, and upon a nice arrangement between the two the whole fortune of his works depends. Orlando had so ordered it that she was in an extremely happy position; she need neither fight her age, nor submit to it; she was of it, yet remained herself. Now, therefore, she could write, and write she did. She wrote. She wrote. She wrote.

It was now November. After November, comes December. Then January, February, March, and April. After April comes May. June, July, August follow. Next is September. Then October, and so, behold, here we are back at November again, with a whole year accomplished.

This method of writing biography, though it has its merits, is a little bare, perhaps, and the reader, if we go on with it, may complain that he could recite the calendar for himself and so save his pocket whatever sum the Hogarth Press* may think proper to charge for this book. But what can the biographer do when his subject has put him in the predicament into which Orlando has now put us? Life, it has been agreed by everyone whose opinion is worth consulting, is the only fit subject for novelist or biographer; life, the same authorities have decided, has nothing whatever to do with sitting still in a chair and thinking. Thought and life are as the poles asunder. Therefore—since sitting in a chair and thinking is precisely what Orlando is doing now—there is nothing for it but to recite the calendar, tell one's beads, blow one's nose, stir the fire, look out of the window, until she has done. Orlando sat so still that you could have heard a pin drop. Would, indeed, that a pin had dropped! That would have been life of a kind. Or if a butterfly had fluttered through the window and settled on her chair, one could write about that. Or suppose she had got up and killed a wasp. Then, at once, we could out with our pens and write. For there would be blood shed, if only the blood of a wasp. Where there is blood there is life. And if killing a wasp is the merest trifle compared with killing a man, still it is a fitter subject for novelist or biographer than this mere wool-gathering; this thinking; this sitting in a chair day in, day out, with a cigarette and a sheet of paper and a pen and an ink pot. If only subjects, we might complain (for our patience is wearing thin), had more consideration for their biographers! What is more irritating than to see one's subject, on whom one has lavished so much time and trouble, slipping out of one's grasp altogether and indulging—witness her sighs and gasps, her flushing, her palings, her eyes now bright as lamps, now haggard as dawns—what is more humiliating than to see all this dumb show of emotion and excitement gone through before our eyes when we

know that what causes it—thought and imagination—are of no importance whatsoever?

But Orlando was a woman—Lord Palmerston had
just proved it. And when we are writing the life of a
woman, we may, it is agreed, waive our demand for
action, and substitute love instead. Love, the poet has
said, is woman's whole existence.* And if we look for
a moment at Orlando writing at her table, we must
admit that never was there a woman more fitted for
that calling. Surely, since she is a woman, and a
beautiful woman, and a woman in the prime of life,
she will soon give over this pretence of writing and
thinking and begin at least to think of a gamekeeper*
(and as long as she thinks of a man, nobody objects
to a woman thinking). And then she will write him a
little note (and as long as she writes little notes
nobody objects to a woman writing either) and make
an assignation for Sunday dusk and Sunday dusk will
come; and the gamekeeper will whistle under the
window—all of which is, of course, the very stuff of
life and the only possible subject for fiction. Surely
Orlando must have done one of these things? Alas,—
a thousand times, alas, Orlando did none of them.
Must it then be admitted that Orlando was one of
those monsters of iniquity who do not love? She was
kind to dogs, faithful to friends, generosity itself to a
dozen starving poets, had a passion for poetry. But
love—as the male novelists define it—and who, after
all, speak with greater authority?—has nothing what-

ever to do with kindness, fidelity, generosity, or poetry. Love is slipping off one's petticoat and— But we all know what love is. Did Orlando do that? Truth compels us to say no, she did not. If then, the subject of one's biography will neither love nor kill, but will only think and imagine, we may conclude that he or she is no better than a corpse and so leave her.

The only resource now left us is to look out of the window. There were sparrows; there were starlings; there were a number of doves, and one or two rooks, all occupied after their fashion. One finds a worm, another a snail. One flutters to a branch, another takes a little run on the turf. Then a servant crosses the courtyard, wearing a green baize apron. Presumably he is engaged on some intrigue with one of the maids in the pantry, but as no visible proof is offered us, in the courtyard, we can but hope for the best and leave it. Clouds pass, thin or thick, with some disturbance of the colour of the grass beneath. The sun-dial registers the hour in its usual cryptic way. One's mind begins tossing up a question or two, idly, vainly, about this same life. Life, it sings, or croons rather, like a kettle on a hob, Life, life, what art thou? Light or darkness, the baize apron of the under footman or the shadow of the starling on the grass?

Let us go, then,* exploring, this summer morning, when all are adoring the plum blossom and the bee. And humming and hawing, let us ask of the starling (who is a more sociable bird than the lark) what he may think on the brink of the dust-bin, whence he picks among the sticks combings of scullion's hair. What's life, we ask, leaning on the farmyard gate; Life, Life, Life! cries the bird, as if he had heard, and knew precisely, what we meant by this bothering prying habit of ours of asking questions indoors and out and peeping and picking at daisies as the way is of writers when they don't know what to say next. Then they come here, says the bird, and ask me what life is; Life, Life, Life!

We trudge on then by the moor path, to the high brow of the wine-blue purple-dark hill, and fling ourselves down there, and dream there and see there a grasshopper, carting back to his home in the hollow, a straw. And he says (if sawings like his can be given a name so sacred and tender) Life's labour, or so we interpret the whirr of his dust-choked gullet. And the ant agrees and the bees, but if we lie here long enough to ask the moths, when they come at evening, stealing among the paler heather bells, they will breathe in our ears such wild nonsense as one hears from telegraph wires in snow storms; tee hee, haw haw. Laughter, Laughter! the moths say.

Having asked then of man and of bird and the insects, for fish, men tell us, who have lived in green caves, solitary for years to hear them speak, never, never say, and so perhaps know what life is—having asked them all and grown no wiser, but only older and colder (for did we not pray once in a way to wrap up in a book something so hard, so rare, one could swear it was life's meaning?) back we must go and say straight out to the reader who waits a-tiptoe to hear what life is—alas, we don't know.

At this moment, but only just in time to save the book from extinction, Orlando pushed away her chair, stretched her arms, dropped her pen, came to the window, and exclaimed, 'Done!'

She was almost felled to the ground by the extraordinary sight which now met her eyes. There was the garden and some birds. The world was going on as usual. All the time she was writing the world had continued.

'And if I were dead, it would be just the same!' she exclaimed.

Such was the intensity of her feelings that she could even imagine that she had suffered dissolution, and perhaps some faintness actually attacked her. For a moment she stood looking at the fair, indifferent spectacle with staring eyes. At length she was revived in a singular way. The manuscript which reposed above her heart began shuffling and beating as if it were a living thing, and, what was still odder, and showed how fine a sympathy was between them, Orlando, by inclining her head, could make out what it was that it was saying. It wanted to be read. It must be read. It would die in her bosom if it were not read. For the first time in her life she turned with violence against nature. Elk-hounds and rose bushes were about her in profusion. But elk-hounds and rose bushes can none of them read. It is a lamentable oversight on the part of Providence which had never struck her before. Human beings alone are thus gifted. Human beings had become necessary. She rang the bell. She ordered the carriage to take her to London at once.

'There's just time to catch the eleven forty-five, M'Lady,' said Basket. Orlando had not yet realized the invention of the steam engine,* but such was her absorption in the sufferings of a being, who, though not herself, yet entirely depended on her, that she saw a railway train for the first time, took her seat in a railway carriage, and had the rug arranged about her knees without giving a thought to 'that stupendous invention, which had (the historians say) completely changed the face of Europe in the past twenty years' (as, indeed, happens much more frequently than historians suppose). She noticed only that it was extremely smutty; rattled horribly; and the windows stuck. Lost in thought, she was whirled up to London in something less than an hour and stood on the platform at Charing Cross, not knowing where to go.

The old house at Blackfriars, where she had spent so many pleasant days in the eighteenth century, was now sold, part to the Salvation Army, part to an umbrella factory. She had bought another in Mayfair* which was sanitary, convenient, and in the heart of the fashionable world, but was it in Mayfair that her poem would be relieved of its desire? Pray God, she thought, remembering the brightness of their ladyships' eyes and the symmetry of their lordships' legs, they haven't taken to reading there. For that would be a thousand pities. Then there was Lady R.'s. The same sort of talk would be going on there still, she had no doubt. The gout might have shifted from the General's left leg to his right, perhaps. Mr L. might have stayed ten days with R. instead of T. Then Mr Pope would come in. Oh! but Mr Pope was dead. Who were the wits now, she wondered—but that was not a question one could put to a porter, and so she moved on. Her ears were now distracted by the jingling of innumerable bells on the heads of innumerable horses. Fleets of the strangest little boxes on wheels were drawn up by the pavement. She walked out into the Strand. There the uproar was even worse. Vehicles of all sizes, drawn by blood horses and by dray horses, conveying one solitary dowager or crowded to the top by whiskered men in silk hats, were inextricably mixed. Carriages, carts, and omnibuses seemed to her eyes, so long used to the look of a plain sheet of foolscap, alarmingly at loggerheads; and to her ears, attuned to a pen scratching, the uproar of the street sounded violently and hideously cacophonous. Every inch of the pavement was crowded. Streams of people, threading in and out between their own bodies and the lurching and lum-

bering traffic with incredible agility, poured incessantly east and west. Along the edge of the pavement
stood men, holding out trays of toys, and bawled. At
corners, women sat beside great baskets of spring
flowers and bawled. Boys running in and out of the
horses' noses, holding printed sheets to their bodies,
bawled too, Disaster! Disaster! At first Orlando
supposed that she had arrived at some moment of
national crisis; but whether it was happy or tragic,
she could not tell. She looked anxiously at people's
faces. But that confused her still more. Here would
come by a man sunk in despair, muttering to himself
as if he knew some terrible sorrow. Past him would
nudge a fat, jolly-faced fellow, shouldering his way
along as if it were a festival for all the world. Indeed,
she came to the conclusion that there was neither
rhyme nor reason in any of it. Each man and each
woman was bent on his own affairs. And where was
she to go?

She walked on without thinking, up one street and
down another, by vast windows piled with handbags,
and mirrors, and dressing gowns, and flowers, and
fishing rods, and luncheon baskets; while stuff of
every hue and pattern, thickness or thinness, was
looped and festooned and ballooned across and
across. Sometimes she passed down avenues of sedate
mansions, soberly numbered 'one', 'two', 'three', and
so on right up to two or three hundred, each the copy
of the other, with two pillars and six steps and a pair

of curtains neatly drawn and family luncheons laid on tables, and a parrot looking out of one window and a man servant out of another, until her mind was dizzied with the monotony. Then she came to great open squares with black shiny, tightly buttoned statues of fat men in the middle, and war horses prancing, and columns rising and fountains falling and pigeons fluttering. So she walked and walked along pavements between houses until she felt very hungry, and something fluttering above her heart rebuked her with having forgotten all about it. It was her manuscript. 'The Oak Tree'.

She was confounded at her own neglect. She stopped dead where she stood. No coach was in sight. The street, which was wide and handsome, was singularly empty. Only one elderly gentleman was approaching. There was something vaguely familiar to her in his walk. As he came nearer, she felt certain that she had met him at some time or other. But where? Could it be that this gentleman, so neat, so portly, so prosperous, with a cane in his hand and a flower in his button-hole, with a pink, plump face, and combed white moustaches, could it be, Yes, by jove, it was!—her old, her very old friend, Nick Greene!

At the same time he looked at her; remembered her; recognized her. 'The Lady Orlando!' he cried, sweeping his silk hat almost in the dust.

'Sir Nicholas!' she exclaimed. For she was made

aware intuitively by something in his bearing that the scurrilous penny-a-liner, who had lampooned her and many another in the time of Queen Elizabeth, was now risen in the world and become certainly a Knight and doubtless a dozen other fine things into the bargain.

With another bow, he acknowledged that her conclusion was correct; he was a Knight; he was a Litt.D.; he was a Professor. He was the author of a score of volumes. He was, in short, the most influential critic of the Victorian age.

A violent tumult of emotion besieged her at meeting the man who had caused her, years ago, so much pain. Could this be the plaguy, restless fellow who had burnt holes in her carpets, and toasted cheese in the Italian fireplace and told such merry stories of Marlowe and the rest that they had seen the sun rise nine nights out of ten? He was now sprucely dressed in a grey morning suit, had a pink flower in his button-hole, and grey suede gloves to match. But even as she marvelled, he made another profound bow, and asked her whether she would honour him by lunching with him? The bow was a thought overdone perhaps, but the imitation of fine breeding was creditable. She followed him, wondering, into a superb restaurant, all red plush, white table-cloths, and silver cruets, as unlike as could be the old tavern or coffee house with its sanded floor, its wooden benches, its bowls of punch and chocolate, and its broadsheets and spittoons. He laid his gloves neatly on the table beside him. Still she could hardly believe that he was the same man. His nails were clean; where they used to be an inch long. His chin was shaved; where a black beard used to sprout. He wore gold sleeve-links; where his ragged linen used to dip in the broth. It was not, indeed, until he had ordered the wine, which he did with a care that reminded her of his taste in Malmsey long ago, that she was convinced he was the same man. 'Ah!' he said, heaving a little sigh, which was yet comfortable enough, 'ah! my dear lady, the great days of literature are over. Marlowe, Shakespeare, Ben Jonson—those were the giants. Dryden, Pope, Addison—those were the heroes. All, all are dead now. And whom have they left us? Tennyson, Browning, Carlyle!'—he threw an immense amount of scorn into his voice. 'The truth of it is,' he said, pouring himself a glass of wine, 'that all our young writers are in the pay of the booksellers. They turn out any trash that serves to pay their tailor's bills. It is an age', he said, helping himself to hors-d'œuvres, 'marked by precious conceits and wild experiments—none of which the Elizabethans would have tolerated for an instant.

'No, my dear lady,' he continued, passing with approval the turbot au gratin, which the waiter exhibited for his sanction, 'the great days are over. We live in degenerate times. We must cherish the past; honour those writers—there are still a few left of 'em—who

take antiquity for their model and write, not for pay
but——' Here Orlando almost shouted 'Glawr!'
Indeed she could have sworn that she had heard him
say the very same things three hundred years ago.
The names were different, of course, but the spirit
was the same. Nick Greene had not changed, for all
his knighthood. And yet, some change there was. For
while he ran on about taking Addison as one's model
(it had been Cicero once, she thought) and lying in
bed of a morning (which she was proud to think her
pension paid quarterly enabled him to do) rolling the
best works of the best authors round and round on
one's tongue for an hour, at least, before setting pen
to paper, so that the vulgarity of the present time and
the deplorable condition of our native tongue (he had
lived long in America,* she believed) might be puri-
fied—while he ran on in much the same way that
Greene had run on three hundred years ago, she had
time to ask herself, how was it then that he had
changed? He had grown plump; but he was a man
verging on seventy. He had grown sleek: literature
had been a prosperous pursuit evidently; but somehow the old restless, uneasy vivacity had gone. His
stories, brilliant as they were, were no longer quite so
free and easy. He mentioned, it is true, 'my dear
friend Pope' or 'my illustrious friend Addison' every
other second, but he had an air of respectability about
him which was depressing, and he preferred, it
seemed, to enlighten her about the doings and sayings

of her own blood relations rather than tell her, as he used to do, scandal about the poets.

Orlando was unaccountably disappointed. She had thought of literature all these years (her seclusion, her rank, her sex must be her excuse) as something wild as the wind, hot as fire, swift as lightning; something errant, incalculable, abrupt, and behold, literature was an elderly gentleman in a grey suit talking about duchesses. The violence of her disillusionment was such that some hook or button fastening the upper part of her dress burst open, and out upon the table fell 'The Oak Tree', a poem.

'A manuscript!' said Sir Nicholas, putting on his gold pince-nez. 'How interesting, how excessively interesting! Permit me to look at it.' And once more, after an interval of some three hundred years, Nicholas Greene took Orlando's poem and, laying it down among the coffee cups and the liqueur glasses, began to read it. But now his verdict was very different from what it had been then. It reminded him, he said as he turned over the pages, of Addison's *Cato*.* It compared favourably with Thomson's *Seasons*.* There was no trace in it, he was thankful to say, of the modern spirit. It was composed with a regard to truth, to nature, to the dictates of the human heart, which was rare indeed, in these days of unscrupulous eccentricity. It must, of course, be published instantly.

Really Orlando did not know what he meant. She

had always carried her manuscripts about with her in the bosom of her dress. The idea tickled Sir Nicholas considerably.

'But what about royalties?' he asked.

Orlando's mind flew to Buckingham Palace and some dusky potentates who happened to be staying there.

Sir Nicholas was highly diverted. He explained that he was alluding to the fact that Messrs —— (here he mentioned a well-known firm of publishers) would be delighted, if he wrote them a line, to put the book on their list. He could probably arrange for a royalty of ten per cent on all copies up to two thousand; after that it would be fifteen. As for the reviewers, he would himself write a line to Mr ——, who was the most influential; then a compliment—say a little puff of her own poems—addressed to the wife of the editor of the —— never did any harm. He would call ——. So he ran on. Orlando understood nothing of all this, and from old experience did not altogether trust his good nature, but there was nothing for it but to submit to what was evidently his wish and the fervent desire of the poem itself. So Sir Nicholas made the blood-stained packet into a neat parcel; flattened it into his breast pocket, lest it should disturb the set of his coat; and with many compliments on both sides, they parted.

Orlando walked up the street. Now that the poem was gone,—and she felt a bare place in her breast where she had been used to carry it—she had nothing to do but reflect upon whatever she liked—the extraordinary chances it might be of the human lot. Here she was in St James's Street; a married woman; with a ring on her finger; where there had been a coffee house once there was now a restaurant; it was about half past three in the afternoon; the sun was shining; there were three pigeons; a mongrel terrier dog; two hansom cabs* and a barouche landau.* What then, was Life? The thought popped into her head violently, irrelevantly (unless old Greene were somehow the cause of it). And it may be taken as a comment, adverse or favourable, as the reader chooses to consider it upon her relations with her husband (who was at the Horn), that whenever anything popped violently into her head, she went straight to the nearest telegraph office and wired to him. There was one, as it happened, close at hand. 'My God Shel', she wired; 'life literature Greene toady—' here she dropped into a cypher language* which they had invented between them so that a whole spiritual state of the utmost complexity might be conveyed in a word or two without the telegraph clerk being any wiser, and added the words 'Rattigan Glumphoboo', which summed it up precisely. For not only had the events of the morning made a deep impression on her, but it cannot have escaped the reader's attention that Orlando was growing up—which is not necessarily growing better—and 'Rattigan Glumphoboo'

described a very complicated spiritual state—which if
the reader puts all his intelligence at our service he
may discover for himself.

There could be no answer to her telegram for some
hours; indeed, it was probable, she thought, glancing
at the sky, where the upper clouds raced swiftly past,
that there was a gale at Cape Horn, so that her
husband would be at the mast-head, as likely as not,
or cutting away some tattered spar, or even alone in a
boat with a biscuit. And so, leaving the post office,
she turned to beguile herself into the next shop,
which was a shop so common in our day that it needs
no description, yet, to her eyes, strange in the
extreme; a shop where they sold books. All her life
long Orlando had known manuscripts; she had held
in her hands the rough brown sheets on which
Spenser had written in his little crabbed hand; she
had seen Shakespeare's script and Milton's. She
owned, indeed, a fair number of quartos and folios,
often with a sonnet in her praise in them and sometimes a lock of hair. But these innumerable little
volumes, bright, identical, ephemeral, for they seemed
bound in cardboard and printed on tissue paper,
surprised her infinitely. The whole works of Shakespeare cost half a crown and could be put in your
pocket. One could hardly read them, indeed, the
print was so small, but it was a marvel, none the less.
'Works'—the works of every writer she had known
or heard of and many more stretched from end to end

of the long shelves. On tables and chairs, more 'works' were piled and tumbled, and these she saw, turning a page or two, were often works about other works by Sir Nicholas and a score of others whom, in her ignorance, she supposed, since they were bound and printed, to be very great writers too. So she gave an astounding order to the bookseller to send her everything of any importance in the shop and left.

She turned into Hyde Park, which she had known of old (beneath that cleft tree, she remembered, the Duke of Hamilton fell run through the body by Lord Mohun), and her lips, which are often to blame in the matter, began framing the words of her telegram into a senseless singsong; life literature Greene toady Rattigan Glumphoboo; so that several park keepers looked at her with suspicion and were only brought to a favourable opinion of her sanity by noticing the pearl necklace which she wore. She had carried off a sheaf of papers and critical journals from the book shop, and at length, flinging herself on her elbow beneath a tree, she spread these pages round her and did her best to fathom the noble art of prose composition as these masters practised it. For still the old credulity was alive in her; even the blurred type of a weekly newspaper had some sanctity in her eyes. So she read, lying on her elbow, an article by Sir Nicholas on the collected works of a man she had once known—John Donne. But she had pitched

herself, without knowing it, not far from the Serpentine. The barking of a thousand dogs sounded in her
ears. Carriage wheels rushed ceaselessly in a circle.
Leaves sighed overhead. Now and again a braided
skirt and a pair of tight scarlet trousers crossed the
grass within a few steps of her. Once a gigantic rubber
ball bounced on the newspaper. Violets, oranges,
reds, and blues broke through the interstices of the
leaves and sparkled in the emerald on her finger. She
read a sentence and looked up at the sky; she looked
up at the sky and looked down at the newspaper.
Life? Literature? One to be made into the other? But
how monstrously difficult! For—here came by a pair
of tight scarlet trousers—how would Addison have
put that? Here came two dogs dancing on their hind
legs. How would Lamb have described that? For
reading Sir Nicholas and his friends (as she did in the
intervals of looking about her), she somehow got the
impression—here she rose and walked—they made
one feel—it was an extremely uncomfortable feeling—one must never, never say what one thought.
(She stood on the banks of the Serpentine. It was a
bronze colour; spider-thin boats were skimming from
side to side.) They made one feel, she continued, that
one must always, always write like somebody else.
(The tears formed themselves in her eyes.) For really,
she thought, pushing a little boat off with her toe, I
don't think I could (here the whole of Sir Nicholas'
article came before her as articles do, ten minutes

after they are read, with the look of his room, his head, his cat, his writing-table, and the time of the day thrown in), I don't think I could, she continued, considering the article from this point of view, sit in a study, no, it's not a study, it's a mouldy kind of drawing-room, all day long, and talk to pretty young men, and tell them little anecdotes, which they mustn't repeat, about what Tupper said about Smiles;* and then, she continued, weeping bitterly, they're all so manly; and then, I do detest Duchesses; and I don't like cake; and though I'm spiteful enough, I could never learn to be as spiteful as all that, so how can I be a critic and write the best English prose of my time? Damn it all! she exclaimed, launching a penny steamer so vigorously that the poor little boat almost sank in the bronze-coloured waves.

Now, the truth is that when one has been in a state of mind (as nurses call it)—and the tears still stood in Orlando's eyes—the thing one is looking at becomes, not itself, but another thing, which is bigger and much more important and yet remains the same thing. If one looks at the Serpentine in this state of mind, the waves soon become just as big as the waves on the Atlantic; the toy boats become indistinguishable from ocean liners. So Orlando mistook the toy boat for her husband's brig; and the wave she had made with her toe for a mountain of water off Cape Horn; and as she watched the toy boat climb the ripple, she thought she saw Bonthrop's ship climb up and up a glassy wall; up and up it went, and a white crest with a thousand deaths in it arched over it; and through the thousand deaths it went and disappeared—'It's sunk!'* she cried out in an agony—and then, behold, there it was again sailing along safe and sound among the ducks on the other side of the Atlantic.

'Ecstasy!' she cried. 'Ecstasy! Where's the post office?' she wondered. 'For I must wire at once to Shel and tell him . . .' And repeating 'A toy boat on the Serpentine', and 'Ecstasy', alternately, for the thoughts were interchangeable and meant exactly the same thing, she hurried towards Park Lane.

'A toy boat, a toy boat, a toy boat,' she repeated, thus enforcing upon herself the fact that it is not articles by Nick Greene on John Donne nor eight-hour bills nor covenants nor factory acts* that matter; it's something useless, sudden, violent; something that costs a life; red, blue, purple; a spirit; a splash; like those hyacinths (she was passing a fine bed of them); free from taint, dependence, soilure of humanity or care for one's kind; something rash, ridiculous, like my hyacinth, husband I mean, Bonthrop: that's what it is—a toy boat on the Serpentine, ecstasy—it's ecstasy that matters. Thus she spoke aloud, waiting for the carriages to pass at Stanhope Gate, for the consequence of not living with one's husband, except when the wind is sunk, is that one talks nonsense aloud in Park Lane. It would no doubt have been different had she lived all the year round with him as

Queen Victoria recommended. As it was the thought of him would come upon her in a flash. She found it absolutely necessary to speak to him instantly. She did not care in the least what nonsense it might make, or what dislocation it might inflict on the narrative. Nick Greene's article had plunged her in the depths of despair; the toy boat had raised her to the heights of joy. So she repeated: 'Ecstasy, ecstasy', as she stood waiting to cross.

But the traffic was heavy that spring afternoon, and kept her standing there, repeating, ecstasy, ecstasy, or a toy boat on the Serpentine, while the wealth and power of England sat, as if sculptured, in hat and cloak, in four-in-hand,* victoria* and barouche landau. It was as if a golden river had coagulated and massed itself in golden blocks across Park Lane. The ladies held card-cases between their fingers; the gentlemen balanced gold-mounted canes between their knees. She stood there gazing, admiring, awe-struck. One thought only disturbed her, a thought familiar to all who behold great elephants, or whales of an incredible magnitude, and that is how do these leviathans to whom obviously stress, change, and activity are repugnant, propagate their kind? Perhaps, Orlando thought, looking at the stately, still faces, their time of propagation is over; this is the fruit; this is the consummation. What she now beheld was the triumph of an age. Portly and splendid there they sat. But now, the policeman let fall his hand; the stream became liquid; the massive conglomeration of splendid objects moved, dispersed, and disappeared into Piccadilly.

So she crossed Park Lane and went to her house in Curzon Street, where, when the meadow-sweet blew there, she could remember curlew calling and one very old man with a gun.

She could remember, she thought, stepping across the threshold of her house, how Lord Chesterfield had said—but her memory was checked. Her discreet eighteenth-century hall, where she could see Lord Chesterfield putting his hat down here and his coat down there with an elegance of deportment which it was a pleasure to watch, was now completely littered with parcels. While she had been sitting in Hyde Park the bookseller had delivered her order, and the house was crammed—there were parcels slipping down the staircase—with the whole of Victorian literature done up in grey paper and neatly tied with string. She carried as many of these packets as she could to her room, ordered footmen to bring the others, and, rapidly cutting innumerable strings, was soon surrounded by innumerable volumes.

Accustomed to the little literatures of the sixteenth, seventeenth, and eighteenth centuries, Orlando was appalled by the consequences of her order. For, of course, to the Victorians themselves Victorian literature meant not merely four great names separate and distinct but four great names sunk and embedded in a mass of Alexander Smiths, Dixons, Blacks, Milmans, Buckles, Taines, Paynes, Tuppers, Jamesons*—all vocal, clamorous, prominent, and requiring as much attention as anybody else. Orlando's reverence for print had a tough job set before it, but drawing her chair to the window to get the benefit of what light might filter between the high houses of Mayfair, she tried to come to a conclusion.

And now it is clear that there are only two ways of coming to a conclusion upon Victorian literature— one is to write it out in sixty volumes octavo, the other is to squeeze it into six lines of the length of this one. Of the two courses, economy, since time runs short, leads us to choose the second; and so we proceed. Orlando then came to the conclusion (opening half-a-dozen books) that it was very odd that there was not a single dedication to a nobleman among them; next (turning over a vast pile of memoirs) that several of these writers had family trees half as high as her own; next, that it would be impolitic in the extreme to wrap a ten-pound note round the sugar tongs* when Miss Christina Rossetti came to tea; next (here were half-a-dozen invitations to celebrate centenaries by dining) that literature since it ate all these dinners must be growing very corpulent; next (she was invited to a score of lectures on the Influence of this upon that;* the Classical revival; the Romantic survival, and other titles of the same

[277]

engaging kind) that literature since it listened to all these lectures must be growing very dry; next (here she attended a reception given by a peeress) that literature since it wore all those fur tippets must be growing very respectable; next (here she visited Carlyle's sound-proof room at Chelsea) that genius since it needed all this coddling must be growing very delicate; and so at last she reached her final conclusion, which was of the highest importance but which, as we have already much overpassed our limit of six lines, we must omit.

Orlando, having come to this conclusion, stood looking out of the window for a considerable space of time. For, when anybody comes to a conclusion it is as if they had tossed the ball over the net and must wait for the unseen antagonist to return it to them. What would be sent her next from the colourless sky above Chesterfield House, she wondered? And with her hands clasped, she stood for a considerable space of time wondering. Suddenly she started—and here we could only wish that, as on a former occasion, Purity, Chastity, and Modesty would push the door ajar and provide, at least, a breathing space in which we could think how to wrap up what now has to be told delicately, as a biographer should. But no! Having thrown their white garment at the naked Orlando and seen it fall short by several inches, these ladies had given up all intercourse with her these many years; and were now otherwise engaged. Is

nothing then, going to happen this pale March morning to mitigate, to veil, to cover, to conceal, to shroud
this undeniable event whatever it may be? For after
giving that sudden, violent start, Orlando—but
Heaven be praised, at this very moment there struck
up outside one of these frail, reedy, fluty, jerky, old-
fashioned barrel-organs which are still sometimes
played by Italian organ-grinders in back streets. Let
us accept the intervention, humble though it is, as if
it were the music of the spheres, and allow it, with all
its gasps and groans, to fill this page with sound until
the moment comes when it is impossible to deny its
coming; which the footman has seen coming and the
maid-servant; and the reader will have to see too; for
Orlando herself is clearly unable to ignore it any
longer—let the barrel-organ sound and transport us
on thought, which is no more than a little boat, when
music sounds, tossing on the waves; on thought,
which is, of all carriers, the most clumsy, the most
erratic, over the roof tops and the back gardens where
washing is hanging to—what is this place? Do you
recognize the Green and in the middle the steeple,
and the gate with a lion couchant on either side? Oh
yes, it is Kew! Well, Kew will do. So here then we
are at Kew, and I will show you today (the second of
March) under the plum tree, a grape hyacinth, and a
crocus, and a bud, too, on the almond tree; so that to
walk there is to be thinking of bulbs, hairy and red,
thrust into the earth in October; flowering now; and

[279]

to be dreaming of more than can rightly be said, and to be taking from its case a cigarette or cigar even, and to be flinging a cloak under (as the rhyme requires) an oak, and there to sit, waiting the king-fisher, which, it is said, was seen once to cross in the evening from bank to bank.

Wait! Wait! The kingfisher comes; the kingfisher comes not.

Behold, meanwhile, the factory chimneys and their smoke; behold the city clerks flashing by in their outrigger.* Behold the old lady taking her dog for a walk and the servant girl wearing her new hat for the first time not at the right angle. Behold them all. Though Heaven has mercifully decreed that the secrets of all hearts are hidden so that we are lured on for ever to suspect something, perhaps, that does not exist; still through our cigarette smoke, we see blaze up and salute the splendid fulfilment of natural desires for a hat, for a boat, for a rat in a ditch; as once one saw blazing—such silly hops and skips the mind takes when it slops like this all over the saucer and the barrel-organ plays—saw blazing a fire in a field against minarets near Constantinople.

Hail! natural desire! Hail! happiness! divine happiness! and pleasure of all sorts, flowers and wine, though one fades and the other intoxicates; and half-crown tickets out of London on Sundays, and singing in a dark chapel hymns about death, and anything, anything that interrupts and confounds the tapping of typewriters and filing of letters and forging of links and chains, binding the Empire together. Hail even the crude, red bows on shop girls' lips (as if Cupid, very clumsily, dipped his thumb in red ink and scrawled a token in passing). Hail, happiness! kingfisher flashing from bank to bank, and all fulfilment of natural desire, whether it is what the male novelist says it is; or prayer; or denial; hail! in whatever form it comes, and may there be more forms, and stranger. For dark flows the stream—would it were true, as the rhyme hints 'like a dream'—but duller and worser than that is our usual lot; without dreams, but alive, smug, fluent, habitual, under trees whose shade of an olive green drowns the blue of the wing of the vanishing bird when he darts of a sudden from bank to bank.

Hail, happiness, then, and after happiness, hail not those dreams which bloat the sharp image as spotted mirrors do the face in a country-inn parlour; dreams which splinter the whole and tear us asunder and wound us and split us apart in the night when we would sleep; but sleep, sleep, so deep that all shapes are ground to dust of infinite softness, water of dimness inscrutable, and there, folded, shrouded, like a mummy, like a moth, prone let us lie on the sand at the bottom of sleep.

But wait! but wait! we are not going, this time, visiting the blind land. Blue, like a match struck right in the ball of the innermost eye, he flys, burns, bursts the seal of sleep; the kingfisher; so that now floods back refluent like a tide, the red, thick stream of life again; bubbling, dripping; and we rise, and our eyes (for how handy a rhyme is to pass us safe over the awkward transition from death to life) fall on—(here the barrel-organ stops playing abruptly).

'It's a very fine boy, M'Lady,' said Mrs Banting, the midwife, putting her first-born child into Orlando's arms. In other words Orlando was safely delivered of a son* on Thursday, March the 20th, at three o'clock in the morning.

Once more Orlando stood at the window, but let the reader take courage; nothing of the same sort is going to happen today, which is not, by any means, the same day. No—for if we look out of the window, as Orlando was doing at the moment, we shall see that Park Lane itself has considerably changed. Indeed one might stand there ten minutes or more, as Orlando stood now, without seeing a single barouche landau. 'Look at that!' she exclaimed, some days later when an absurd truncated carriage without any horses began to glide about of its own accord. A carriage without any horses indeed! She was called away just as she said that, but came back again after a time and had another look out of the window. It was odd sort of weather nowadays. The sky itself, she could not help thinking, had changed. It was no longer so thick, so watery, so prismatic now that King Edward—see, there he was, stepping out of his neat brougham to go and visit a certain lady opposite*—had succeeded Queen Victoria. The clouds had shrunk to a thin gauze; the sky seemed made of metal, which in hot weather tarnished verdigris, copper colour or orange as metal does in a fog. It was a little alarming—this shrinkage. Everything seemed to have shrunk. Driving past Buckingham Palace last night, there was not a trace of that vast erection which she had thought everlasting; top hats, widows' weeds, trumpets, telescopes, wreaths, all had vanished and left not a stain, not a puddle even, on the pavement. But it was now—after another interval she had come back again to her favourite station in the window—now, in the evening, that the change was most remarkable. Look at the lights in the houses! At a touch, a whole room was lit; hundreds of rooms were lit; and one was precisely the same as the other. One could see everything in the little square-shaped boxes; there was no privacy; none of those lingering shadows and odd corners that there used to be; none of those women in aprons carrying wobbly lamps which they put down carefully on this table and on that. At a touch, the whole room was bright. And the sky was bright all night long; and the pavements were bright; everything was bright. She came back again at mid-day. How narrow women have grown lately! They looked like stalks of corn, straight, shining, identical. And men's faces were as bare as the palm of one's hand.

The dryness of the atmosphere brought out the colour in everything and seemed to stiffen the muscles of the cheeks. It was harder to cry now. Water was hot in two seconds. Ivy had perished or been scraped off houses. Vegetables were less fertile; families were much smaller. Curtains and covers had been frizzled up and the walls were bare so that new brilliantly coloured pictures of real things like streets, umbrellas, apples, were hung in frames, or painted upon the wood. There was something definite and distinct about the age, which reminded her of the eighteenth century, except that there was a distraction, a desperation—as she was thinking this, the immensely long tunnel in which she seemed to have been travelling for hundreds of years widened; the light poured in; her thoughts became mysteriously tightened and strung up as if a piano tuner had put his key in her back and stretched the nerves very taut; at the same time her hearing quickened; she could hear every whisper and crackle in the room so that the clock ticking on the mantelpiece beat like a hammer. And so for some seconds the light went on becoming brighter and brighter, and she saw everything more and more clearly and the clock ticked louder and louder until there was a terrific explosion right in her ear. Orlando leapt as if she had been violently struck on the head. Ten times she was struck. In fact it was ten o'clock in the morning. It was the eleventh of October. It was 1928. It was the present moment.

No one need wonder that Orlando started, pressed her hand to her heart, and turned pale. For what more terrifying revelation can there be than that it is the present moment? That we survive the shock at all is only possible because the past shelters us on one side and the future on another. But we have no time now for reflections; Orlando was terribly late already. She ran downstairs, she jumped into her motor-car, she pressed the self-starter and was off. Vast blue blocks of building rose into the air; the red cowls of chimneys were spotted irregularly across the sky; the road shone like silver-headed nails; omnibuses bore down upon her with sculptured white-faced drivers; she noticed sponges, bird-cages, boxes of green American cloth. But she did not allow these sights to sink into her mind even the fraction of an inch as she crossed the narrow plank of the present, lest she should fall into the raging torrent beneath. 'Why don't you look where you're going to? . . . Put your hand out, can't you?' —that was all she said sharply, as if the words were jerked out of her. For the streets were immensely crowded; people crossed without looking where they were going. People buzzed and hummed round the plate-glass windows within which one could see a glow of red, a blaze of yellow, as if they were bees, Orlando thought—but her thought that they were bees was violently snipped off and she saw, regaining perspective with one flick of her eye, that they were bodies.

'Why don't you look where you're going?' she snapped out.

At last, however, she drew up at Marshall & Snelgrove's* and went into the shop. Shade and scent enveloped her. The present fell from her like drops of scalding water. Light swayed up and down like thin stuffs puffed out by a summer breeze. She took a list from her bag and began reading in a curious stiff voice at first as if she were holding the words—boy's boots, bath salts, sardines—under a tap of many-coloured water. She watched them change as the light fell on them. Bath and boots became blunt, obtuse; sardines serrated itself like a saw. So she stood in the ground-floor department of Messrs Marshall & Snelgrove; looked this way and that; snuffed this smell and that and thus wasted some seconds. Then she got into the lift, for the good reason that the door stood open; and was shot smoothly upwards. The very fabric of life now, she thought as she rose, is magic. In the eighteenth century, we knew how everything was done; but here I rise through the air; I listen to voices in America; I see men flying—but how it's done, I can't even begin to wonder. So my belief in magic returns. Now the lift gave a little jerk as it stopped at the first floor; and she had a vision of innumerable coloured stuffs flaunting in a breeze from which came distinct, strange smells; and each time the lift stopped and flung its doors open, there was another slice of the world displayed with all the smells of that world clinging to it. She was reminded of the river off Wapping in the time of Elizabeth, where the treasure ships and the merchant ships used to anchor. How richly and curiously they had smelt! How well she remembered the feel of rough rubies running through her fingers when she dabbled them in a treasure sack! And then lying with Sukey—or whatever her name was—and having Cumberland's lantern flashed on them! The Cumberlands had a house in Portland Place now and she had lunched with them the other day and ventured a little joke with the old man about almshouses in the Sheen Road. He had winked. But here as the lift could go no higher, she must get out—Heaven knows into what 'department' as they called it. She stood still to consult her shopping list, but was blessed if she could see, as the list bade her, bath salts, or boy's boots anywhere about. And indeed, she was about to descend again, without buying anything, but was saved from that outrage by saying aloud automatically the last item on her list; which happened to be 'sheets for a double bed'.

'Sheets for a double bed,' she said to a man at a counter and, by a dispensation of Providence, it was sheets that the man at that particular counter happened to sell. For Grimsditch, no, Grimsditch was dead; Bartholomew, no, Bartholomew was dead; Louise then*—Louise had come to her in a great taking the other day, for she had found a hole in the bottom of the sheet in the royal bed. Many kings and queens had slept there—Elizabeth; James; Charles; George; Victoria; Edward; no wonder the sheet had a hole in it. But Louise was positive she knew who had done it. It was the Prince Consort.

'Sale bosch!' she said (for there had been another war;* this time against the Germans).

'Sheets for a double bed,' Orlando repeated dreamily, for a double bed with a silver counterpane in a room fitted in a taste which she now thought perhaps a little vulgar—all in silver; but she had furnished it when she had a passion for that metal. While the man went to get sheets for a double bed, she took out a little looking-glass and a powder puff. Women were not nearly as roundabout in their ways, she thought, powdering herself with the greatest unconcern, as they had been when she herself first turned woman and lay on the deck of the *Enamoured Lady*. She gave her nose the right tint deliberately. She never touched her cheeks. Honestly, though she was now thirty-six,* she scarcely looked a day older. She looked just as pouting, as sulky, as handsome, as rosy (like a million-candled Christmas tree, Sasha had said) as she had done that day on the ice, when the Thames was frozen and they had gone skating——

'The best Irish linen, Ma'am,' said the shopman, spreading the sheets on the counter,—and they had met an old woman picking up sticks. Here, as she was fingering the linen abstractedly, one of the swing-doors between the departments opened and let through, perhaps from the fancy-goods department, a whiff of scent, waxen, tinted as if from pink candles, and the scent curved like a shell round a figure—was it a boy's or was it a girl's?—young, slender, seductive—a girl, by God! furred, pearled, in Russian trousers; but faithless, faithless!

'Faithless!' cried Orlando (the man had gone) and all the shop seemed to pitch and toss with yellow water and far off she saw the masts of the Russian ship standing out to sea, and then, miraculously (perhaps the door opened again) the conch which the scent had made became a platform, a dais, off which stepped a fat, furred woman, marvellously well preserved, seductive, diademed, a Grand Duke's mistress; she who, leaning over the banks of the Volga, eating sandwiches, had watched men drown; and began walking down the shop towards her.

'Oh Sasha!' Orlando cried. Really, she was shocked that she should have come to this; she had grown so fat; so lethargic; and she bowed her head over the linen so that this apparition of a grey woman in fur, and a girl in Russian trousers, with all these smells of wax candles, white flowers, and old ships that it brought with it might pass behind her back unseen.

'Any napkins, towels, dusters today, Ma'am?' the shopman persisted. And it is enormously to the credit of the shopping list, which Orlando now consulted, that she was able to reply with every appearance of composure, that there was only one thing in the world she wanted and that was bath salts; which was in another department.

But descending in the lift again—so insidious is the repetition of any scene—she was again sunk far beneath the present moment; and thought when the lift bumped on the ground, that she heard a pot broken against a river bank. As for finding the right department, whatever it might be, she stood engrossed among the handbags, deaf to the suggestions of all the polite, black, combed, sprightly shop assistants, who descending as they did equally and some of them, perhaps, as proudly, even from such depths of the past as she did, chose to let down the impervious screen of the present so that today they appeared shop assistants in Marshall & Snelgrove's merely. Orlando stood there hesitating. Through the great glass doors she could see the traffic in Oxford Street. Omnibus seemed to pile itself upon omnibus and then to jerk itself apart. So the ice blocks had pitched and tossed that day on the Thames. An old nobleman in furred slippers had sat astride one of them. There he went—she could see him now—calling down maledictions upon the Irish rebels. He had sunk there, where her car stood.

'Time has passed over me,' she thought, trying to collect herself; 'this is the oncome of middle age. How strange it is! Nothing is any longer one thing. I take up a handbag and I think of an old bumboat woman frozen in the ice. Someone lights a pink candle and I see a girl in Russian trousers. When I step out of doors—as I do now,' here she stepped on to the pavement of Oxford Street, 'what is it that I taste? Little herbs. I hear goat bells. I see mountains. Turkey? India? Persia?' Her eyes filled with tears.

That Orlando had gone a little too far from the present moment will, perhaps, strike the reader who sees her now preparing to get into her motor-car with her eyes full of tears and visions of Persian mountains. And indeed, it cannot be denied that the most successful practitioners of the art of life, often unknown people by the way, somehow contrive to synchronize the sixty or seventy different times which beat simultaneously in every normal human system so that when eleven strikes, all the rest chime in unison, and the present is neither a violent disruption nor completely forgotten in the past. Of them we can justly say that they live precisely the sixty-eight or seventy-two years allotted them on the tombstone. Of the rest some we know to be dead though they walk among us; some are not yet born though they go through the forms of life; others are hundreds of years old though they call themselves thirty-six. The true length of a person's life, whatever the *Dictionary of National Biography** may say, is always a matter of dispute. For it is a difficult business—this time-keeping; nothing more quickly disorders it than contact with any of the arts; and it may have been her love of poetry that was to blame for making Orlando lose her shopping list and start home without the sardines, the bath salts, or the boots. Now as she stood with her hand on the door of her motor-car, the present again struck her on the head. Eleven times she was violently assaulted.

'Confound it all!' she cried, for it is a great shock to the nervous system, hearing a clock strike—so much so that for some time now there is nothing to be said of her save that she frowned slightly, changed her gears admirably, and cried out, as before, 'Look where you're going!' 'Don't you know your own mind?' 'Why didn't you say so then?' while the motor-car shot, swung, squeezed, and slid, for she was an expert driver,* down Regent Street, down Haymarket, down Northumberland Avenue, over Westminster Bridge, to the left, straight on, to the right, straight on again. . . .

The Old Kent Road was very crowded on Thursday, the eleventh of October 1928.* People spilt off the pavement. There were women with shopping bags. Children ran out. There were sales at drapers' shops. Streets widened and narrowed. Long vistas steadily shrunk together. Here was a market. Here a funeral. Here a procession with banners upon which was written 'Ra—Un', but what else? Meat was very red. Butchers stood at the door. Women almost had their heels sliced off. Amor Vin—that was over a porch. A woman looked out of a bedroom window, profoundly contemplative, and very still. Applejohn and Applebed, Undert—. Nothing could be seen whole or read from start to finish. What was seen begun—like two friends starting to meet each other across the street—was never seen ended. After twenty minutes the body and mind were like scraps of torn paper tumbling from a sack and, indeed, the process of motoring fast out of London so much resembles the chopping up small of identity which precedes unconsciousness and perhaps death itself that it is an open question in what sense Orlando can be said to have existed at the present moment. Indeed we should have given her over for a person entirely disassembled were it not that here, at last, one green screen was held out on the right, against which the little bits of paper fell more slowly; and then another was held out on the left so that one could see the separate scraps now turning over by themselves in the air; and then green screens were held continuously on either side, so that her mind regained the illusion of holding things within itself and she saw a cottage, a farmyard and four cows, all precisely life-size.

When this happened, Orlando heaved a sigh of relief, lit a cigarette, and puffed for a minute or two in silence. Then she called hesitatingly, as if the person she wanted might not be there, 'Orlando?' For if there are (at a venture) seventy-six different times all ticking in the mind at once, how many different people are there not—Heaven help us—all having lodgement at one time or another in the human spirit? Some say two thousand and fifty-two. So that it is the most usual thing in the world for a person to call, directly they are alone, Orlando? (if that is one's name) meaning by that, Come, come! I'm sick to death of this particular self. I want another. Hence, the astonishing changes we see in our friends. But it is not altogether plain sailing, either, for though one may say, as Orlando said (being out in the country and needing another self presumably) Orlando? still the Orlando she needs may not come; these selves of which we are built up, one on top of another, as plates are piled on a waiter's hand, have attachments elsewhere, sympathies, little constitutions and rights of their own, call them what you will (and for many of these things there is no name) so that one will only come if it is raining, another in a room with green curtains, another when Mrs Jones is not there, another if you can promise it a glass of wine—and so on; for everybody can multiply from his own experience the different terms which his different selves have made with him—and some are too wildly ridiculous to be mentioned in print at all.

So Orlando, at the turn by the barn, called 'Orlando?' with a note of interrogation in her voice and waited. Orlando did not come.

'All right then,' Orlando said, with the good humour people practise on these occasions; and tried another. For she had a great variety of selves to call upon, far more than we have been able to find room for, since a biography is considered complete if it merely accounts for six or seven selves, whereas a person may well have as many thousand. Choosing then, only those selves we have found room for, Orlando may now have called on the boy who cut the nigger's head down; the boy who strung it up again; the boy who sat on the hill; the boy who saw the poet; the boy who handed the Queen the bowl of rose water; or she may have called upon the young man who fell in love with Sasha; or upon the Courtier; or upon the Ambassador; or upon the Soldier; or upon the Traveller; or she may have wanted the woman to come to her; the Gipsy; the Fine Lady; the Hermit; the girl in love with life; the Patroness of Letters; the woman who called Mar (meaning hot baths and evening fires) or Shelmerdine (meaning crocuses in autumn woods) or Bonthrop (meaning the death we die daily) or all three together—which meant more things than we have space to write out— all were different and she may have called upon any one of them.

Perhaps; but what appeared certain (for we are now in the region of 'perhaps' and 'appears') was that the one she needed most kept aloof, for she was, to hear her talk, changing her selves as quickly as she drove— there was a new one at every corner—as happens when, for some unaccountable reason, the conscious self, which is the uppermost, and has the power to desire, wishes to be nothing but one self. This is what some people call the true self, and it is, they say, compact of all the selves we have it in us to be; commanded and locked up by the Captain self, the Key self, which amalgamates and controls them all. Orlando was certainly seeking this self as the reader can judge from overhearing her talk as she drove (and if it is rambling talk, disconnected, trivial, dull, and sometimes unintelligible, it is the reader's fault for listening to a lady talking to herself; we only copy her words as she spoke them, adding in brackets which self in our opinion is speaking, but in this we may well be wrong).

'What then? Who then?' she said. 'Thirty-six; in a motor car; a woman. Yes, but a million other things as well. A snob am I? The garter in the hall? The leopards? My ancestors? Proud of them? Yes! Greedy, luxurious, vicious? Am I? (here a new self came in). Don't care a damn if I am. Truthful? I think so. Generous? Oh, but that don't count* (here a new self came in). Lying in bed of a morning listening to the pigeons on fine linen; silver dishes; wine; maids; footmen. Spoilt? Perhaps. Too many things for nothing. Hence my books (here she mentioned fifty classical titles; which represented, so we think, the early romantic works that she tore up). Facile, glib, romantic. But (here another self came in) a duffer, a fumbler. More clumsy I couldn't be. And—and—(here she hesitated for a word and if we suggest

'Love' we may be wrong, but certainly she laughed and blushed and then cried out—) A toad set in emeralds! Harry the Archduke! Blue-bottles on the ceiling! (here another self came in). But Nell, Kit, Sasha? (she was sunk in gloom: tears actually shaped themselves and she had long given over crying). Trees, she said. (Here another self came in.) I love trees (she was passing a clump) growing there a thousand years. And barns (she passed a tumble-down barn at the edge of the road). And sheep dogs (here one came trotting across the road. She carefully avoided it). And the night. But people (here another self came in). People? (She repeated it as a question.) I don't know. Chattering, spiteful, always telling lies. (Here she turned into the High Street of her native town, which was crowded, for it was market day, with farmers, and shepherds, and old women with hens in baskets.) I like peasants. I understand crops. But (here another self came skipping over the top of her mind like the beam from a lighthouse). Fame! (She laughed.) Fame! Seven editions. A prize.* Photographs in the evening papers (here she alluded to the 'Oak Tree' and 'The Burdett Coutts' Memorial Prize which she had won; and we must snatch space to remark how discomposing it is for her biographer that this culmination to which the whole book moved, this peroration with which the book was to end, should be dashed from us on a laugh casually like this; but the truth is that when we write of a woman, everything is out of

[297]

place—culminations and perorations; the accent never falls where it does with a man). Fame! she repeated. A poet—a charlatan; both every morning as regularly as the post comes in. To dine, to meet; to meet, to dine; fame—fame! (She had here to slow down to pass through the crowd of market people. But no one noticed her. A porpoise in a fishmonger's shop* attracted far more attention than a lady who had won a prize and might, had she chosen, have worn three coronets one on top of another on her brow.) Driving very slowly she now hummed as if it were part of an old song, 'With my guineas I'll buy flowering trees, flowering trees,* flowering trees and walk among my flowering trees and tell my sons what fame is'. So she hummed, and now all her words began to sag here and there like a barbaric necklace of heavy beads. 'And walk among my flowering trees,' she sang, accenting the words strongly, 'and see the moon rise slow, the waggons go. . . .' Here she stopped short and looked ahead of her intently at the bonnet of the car in profound meditation.

'He sat at Twitchett's table', she mused, 'with a dirty ruff on. . . . Was it old Mr Baker come to measure the timber? Or was it Sh—p—re?' (for when we speak names we deeply reverence to ourselves we never speak them whole). She gazed for ten minutes ahead of her, letting the car come almost to a standstill.

'Haunted!' she cried, suddenly pressing the accelerator. 'Haunted! ever since I was a child. There flies the wild goose. It flies past the window out to sea. Up I jumped (she gripped the steering-wheel tighter) and stretched after it. But the goose flies too fast. I've seen it, here—there—there—England, Persia, Italy. Always it flies fast out to sea and always I fling after it words like nets (here she flung her hand out) which shrivel as I've seen nets shrivel drawn on deck with only sea-weed in them; and sometimes there's an inch of silver—six words—in the bottom of the net. But never the great fish who lives in the coral groves.' Here she bent her head, pondering deeply.

And it was at this moment, when she had ceased to call 'Orlando' and was deep in thoughts of something else, that the Orlando whom she had called came of its own accord; as was proved by the change that now came over her (she had passed through the lodge gates and was entering the park).

The whole of her darkened and settled, as when some foil whose addition makes the round and solidity of a surface is added to it, and the shallow becomes deep and the near distant; and all is contained as water is contained by the sides of a well. So she was now darkened, stilled, and become, with the addition of this Orlando, what is called, rightly or wrongly, a single self, a real self. And she fell silent. For it is probable that when people talk aloud, the selves (of which there may be more than two thousand) are conscious of disseverment, and are trying to communicate, but when communication is established they fall silent.

Masterfully, swiftly, she drove up the curving drive between the elms and oaks through the falling turf of the park whose fall was so gentle that had it been water it would have spread the beach with a smooth green tide. Planted here and in solemn groups were beech trees and oak trees. The deer stepped among them, one white as snow, another with its head on one side, for some wire netting had caught in its horns. All this, the trees, deer, and turf, she observed with the greatest satisfaction as if her mind had become a fluid that flowed round things and enclosed them completely. Next minute she drew up in the courtyard where, for so many hundred years she had come, on horseback or in coach and six, with men riding before or coming after; where plumes had tossed, torches flashed, and the same flowering trees that let their leaves drop now had shaken their blossoms. Now she was alone. The autumn leaves were falling. The porter opened the great gates. 'Morning, James,' she said, 'there're some things in the car. Will you bring 'em in?' words of no beauty, interest, or significance themselves, it will be conceded, but now so plumped out with meaning that they fell like ripe nuts from a tree, and proved that when the shrivelled skin of the ordinary is stuffed out with meaning it satisfies the senses amazingly. This was true indeed of every movement and action now, usual though they were; so that to see Orlando change her skirt for a pair of whipcord breeches and leather jacket, which she did in less than three minutes, was to be ravished with the beauty of movement as if Madame Lopokova were using her highest art. Then she strode into the dining-room where her old friends Dryden, Pope, Swift, Addison regarded her demurely at first as who should say Here's the prize winner! but when they reflected that two hundred guineas was in question, they nodded their heads approvingly. Two hundred guineas, they seemed to say; two hundred guineas are not to be sniffed at. She cut herself a slice of bread and ham, clapped the two together and began to eat, striding up and down the room, thus shedding her company habits in a second, without thinking. After five or six such turns, she tossed off a glass of red Spanish wine,* and, filling another which she carried in her hand, strode down the long corridor and through a dozen drawing-rooms and so began a perambulation of the house, attended by such elk-hounds and spaniels as chose to follow her.

This, too, was all in the day's routine. As soon would she come home and leave her own grandmother without a kiss as come back and leave the house unvisited. She fancied that the rooms brightened as she came in; stirred, opened their eyes as if they had been dozing in her absence. She fancied, too, that, hundreds and thousands of times as she had seen them, they never looked the same twice, as if so long a life as theirs had stored in them a myriad moods which changed with winter and summer, bright weather and dark, and her own fortunes and the people's characters who visited them. Polite, they always were to strangers, but a little weary; with her, they were entirely open and at their ease. Why not indeed? They had known each other for close on four centuries now. They had nothing to conceal. She knew their sorrows and joys. She knew what age each part of them was and its little secrets—a hidden drawer, a concealed cupboard, or some deficiency perhaps, such as a part made up, or added later. They, too, knew her in all her moods and changes. She had hidden nothing from them; had come to them as boy and woman, crying and dancing, brooding and gay. In this window-seat, she had written her first verses; in that chapel, she had been married. And she would be buried here, she reflected, kneeling on the window-sill in the long gallery and sipping her Spanish wine.* Though she could hardly fancy it, the body of the heraldic leopard would be making yellow pools on the floor the day they lowered her to lie among her ancestors. She, who believed in no immortality, could not help feeling that her soul would come and go forever with the reds on the panels and the greens on the sofa. For the room—she had strolled into the Ambassador's bedroom—shone like a shell that has lain at the bottom of the sea for centuries and has been crusted over and painted a million tints by the water; it was rose and yellow, green and sand-coloured. It was frail as a shell, as iridescent and as empty. No Ambassador would ever sleep there again. Ah, but she knew where the heart of the house still beat. Gently opening a door, she stood on the threshold so that (as she fancied) the room could not see her and watched the tapestry rising and falling on the eternal faint breeze which never failed to move it. Still the hunter rode; still Daphne flew. The heart still beat, she thought, however faintly, however far withdrawn; the frail indomitable heart of the immense building.

Now, calling her troop of dogs to her she passed down the gallery whose floor was laid with whole oak trees sawn across. Rows of chairs with all their velvets faded stood ranged against the wall holding their arms out for Elizabeth, for James, for Shakespeare it might be, for Cecil, who never came. The sight made her gloomy. She unhooked the rope that fenced them off. She sat on the Queen's chair; she opened a manuscript book lying on Lady Betty's table; she stirred her fingers in the aged rose leaves; she brushed her short hair with King James' silver brushes; she bounced up and down upon his bed (but no King would ever sleep there again, for all Louise's new sheets) and pressed her cheek against the worn silver counterpane that lay upon it. But everywhere were little lavender bags to keep the moth out and printed notices, 'Please do not touch', which, though she had put them there herself, seemed to rebuke her. The house was no longer hers entirely, she sighed. It belonged to time now; to history; was past the touch and control of the living. Never would beer be spilt here any more, she thought (she was in the bedroom that had been old Nick Greene's), or holes burnt in the carpet. Never two hundred servants come running and brawling down the corridors with warming pans and great branches for the great fireplaces. Never would ale be brewed and candles made and saddles fashioned and stone shaped in the workshops outside the house. Hammers and mallets were silent now. Chairs and beds were empty; tankards of silver and gold were locked in glass cases. The great wings of silence beat up and down the empty house.

So she sat at the end of the gallery with her dogs couched round her, in Queen Elizabeth's hard arm-chair. The gallery stretched far away to a point where the light almost failed. It was as a tunnel bored deep into the past. As her eyes peered down it, she could see people laughing and talking; the great men she had known; Dryden, Swift, and Pope; and statesmen in colloquy; and lovers dallying in the window-seats; and people eating and drinking at the long tables; and the wood smoke curling round their heads and making them sneeze and cough. Still further down, she saw sets of splendid dancers formed for the quadrille. A fluty, frail, but nevertheless stately music began to play. An organ boomed. A coffin was borne into the chapel. A marriage procession came out of it. Armed men with helmets left for the wars. They brought banners back from Flodden and Poitiers* and stuck them on the wall. The long gallery filled itself thus, and still peering further, she thought she could make out at the very end, beyond the Elizabethans and the Tudors, some one older, further, darker, a cowled figure, monastic, severe, a monk, who went with his hands clasped, and a book in them, murmuring——

Like thunder, the stable clock struck four. Never did any earthquake so demolish a whole town. The gallery and all its occupants fell to powder. Her own face, that had been dark and sombre as she gazed, was lit as by an explosion of gunpowder. In this same light everything near her showed with extreme distinctness. She saw two flies circling round and noticed the blue sheen on their bodies; she saw a knot in the wood where her foot was, and her dog's ear twitching. At the same time, she heard a bough creaking in the garden, a sheep coughing in the park, a swift screaming past the window. Her own body quivered and tingled as if suddenly stood naked in a hard frost. Yet, she kept, as she had not done when the clock struck ten in London, complete composure (for she was now one and entire, and presented, it may be, a larger surface to the shock of time). She rose, but without precipitation, called her dogs, and went firmly but with great alertness of movement down the staircase and out into the garden. Here the shadows of the plants were miraculously distinct. She noticed the separate grains of earth in the flower beds as if she had a microscope stuck to her eye. She saw the intricacy of the twigs of every tree. Each blade of grass was distinct and the marking of veins and petals. She saw Stubbs, the gardener, coming along the path, and every button on his gaiters was visible; she saw Betty and Prince, the cart horses, and never had she marked so clearly the white star on Betty's forehead, and the three long hairs that fell down below the rest on Prince's tail. Out in the quadrangle the old grey walls of the house looked like a scraped new photograph; she heard the loud speaker condensing on the terrace a dance tune that people were listening to in the red velvet opera house at Vienna. Braced and strung up by the present moment she was also strangely afraid, as if whenever the gulf of time gaped and let a second through some unknown danger might come with it. The tension was too relentless and too rigorous to be endured long without discomfort. She walked more briskly than she liked, as if her legs were moved for her, through the garden and out into the park. Here she forced herself, by a great effort, to stop by the carpenter's shop, and to stand stock-still watching Joe Stubbs fashion a cart wheel. She was standing with her eye fixed on his hand when the quarter struck. It hurtled through her like a meteor, so hot that no fingers can hold it. She saw with disgusting vividness that the thumb on Joe's right hand was without a finger nail and there was a raised saucer of pink flesh where the nail should have been. The sight was so repulsive that she felt faint for a moment, but in that moment's darkness, when her eyelids flickered, she was relieved of the pressure of the present. There was something strange in the shadow that the flicker of her eyes cast, something which (as anyone can test for himself by looking now at the sky) is always absent from the present—whence its terror, its nondescript character—something one trembles to pin through the body with a name and call beauty, for it has no body, is as a shadow without substance or quality of its own, yet has the power to change whatever it adds itself to. This shadow now, while she flickered her eye in her faintness in the carpenter's shop, stole out, and attaching itself to the innumerable sights she had been receiving, composed them into something tolerable, comprehensible. Her mind began to toss like the sea. Yes, she thought, heaving a deep sigh of relief, as she turned from the carpenter's shop to climb the hill, I can begin to live again. I am by the Serpentine, she thought, the little boat is climbing through the white arch of a thousand deaths. I am about to understand. . . .

Those were her words, spoken quite distinctly, but we cannot conceal the fact that she was now a very indifferent witness to the truth of what was before her and might easily have mistaken a sheep for a cow, or an old man called Smith for one who was called Jones and was no relation of his whatever. For the shadow of faintness which the thumb without a nail had cast had deepened now, at the back of her brain (which is the part furthest from sight), into a pool where things dwell in darkness so deep that what they are we scarcely know. She now looked down into this pool or sea in which everything is reflected—and, indeed, some say that all our most violent passions, and art and religion, are the reflections which we see in the dark hollow at the back of the head when the visible world is obscured for the time. She looked there now, long, deeply, profoundly, and immediately the ferny path up the hill along which she was walking became not entirely a path, but partly the Serpentine; the hawthorn bushes were partly ladies and gentlemen sitting with card-cases and gold-mounted canes; the sheep were partly tall Mayfair houses; everything was partly something else, as if her mind had become a forest with glades branching here and there; things came nearer, and further, and mingled and separated and made the strangest alliances and combinations in an incessant chequer of light and shade. Except when Canute, the elk-hound, chased a rabbit and so reminded her that it must be about half past four—it was indeed twenty-three minutes to six—she forgot the time.

The ferny path led, with many turns and windings,

higher and higher to the oak tree, which stood on the top. The tree had grown bigger, sturdier, and more knotted since she had known it, somewhere about the year 1588, but it was still in the prime of life. The little sharply frilled leaves were still fluttering thickly on its branches. Flinging herself on the ground, she felt the bones of the tree running out like ribs from a spine this way and that beneath her. She liked to think that she was riding the back of the world. She liked to attach herself to something hard. As she flung herself down a little square book bound in red cloth fell from the breast of her leather jacket—her poem 'The Oak Tree'. 'I should have brought a trowel,' she reflected. The earth was so shallow over the roots that it seemed doubtful if she could do as she meant and bury the book here. Besides, the dogs would dig it up. No luck ever attends these symbolical celebrations, she thought. Perhaps it would be as well then to do without them. She had a little speech on the tip of her tongue which she meant to speak over the book as she buried it. (It was a copy of the first edition, signed by author and artist.) 'I bury this as a tribute,' she was going to have said, 'a return to the land of what the land has given me,' but Lord! once one began mouthing words aloud, how silly they sounded! She was reminded of old Greene getting upon a platform the other day* comparing her with Milton (save for his blindness) and handing her a cheque for two hundred guineas. She had thought then, of the oak tree here on its hill, and what has that got to do with this, she had wondered? What has praise and fame to do with poetry? What has seven editions (the book had already gone into no less) got to do with the value of it? Was not writing poetry a secret transaction, a voice answering a voice? So that all this chatter and praise and blame and meeting people who admired one and meeting people who did not admire one was as ill suited as could be to the thing itself—a voice answering a voice. What could have been more secret, she thought, more slow, and like the intercourse of lovers, than the stammering answer she had made all these years to the old crooning song of the woods, and the farms and the brown horses standing at the gate, neck to neck, and the smithy and the kitchen and the fields, so laboriously bearing wheat, turnips, grass, and the garden blowing irises and fritillaries?

So she let her book lie unburied and dishevelled on the ground, and watched the vast view, varied like an ocean floor this evening with the sun lightening it and the shadows darkening it. There was a village with a church tower among elm trees; a grey domed manor house in a park; a spark of light burning on some glass-house; a farmyard with yellow corn stacks. The fields were marked with black tree clumps, and beyond the fields stretched long woodlands, and there was the gleam of a river, and then hills again. In the far distance Snowdon's crags broke white among the clouds; she saw the far Scottish hills and the wild tides that swirl about the Hebrides. She listened for the sound of gun-firing out at sea. No—only the wind blew. There was no war today. Drake had gone; Nelson had gone. 'And there', she thought, letting her eyes, which had been looking at these far distances, drop once more to the land beneath her, 'was my land once: that Castle between the downs was mine; and all that moor running almost to the sea was mine.' Here the landscape (it must have been some trick of the fading light) shook itself, heaped itself, let all this encumbrance of houses, castles, and woods slide off its tent-shaped sides. The bare mountains of Turkey were before her. It was blazing noon. She looked straight at the baked hill-side. Goats cropped the sandy tufts at her feet. An eagle soared above her. The raucous voice of old Rustum, the gipsy, croaked in her ears, 'What is your antiquity and your race, and your possessions compared with this? What do you need with four hundred bedrooms and silver lids on all your dishes, and housemaids dusting?'

At this moment some church clock chimed in the valley. The tent-like landscape collapsed and fell. The present showered down upon her head once more, but now that the light was fading, gentlier than before, calling into view nothing detailed, nothing small, but only misty fields, cottages with lamps in them, the slumbering bulk of a wood, and a fan-shaped light pushing the darkness before it along some lane. Whether it had struck nine, ten, or eleven, she could not say. Night had come—night that she loved of all times, night in which the reflections in the dark pool of the mind shine more clearly than by day. It was not necessary to faint now in order to look deep into the darkness where things shape themselves and to see in the pool of the mind now Shakespeare, now a girl in Russian trousers, now a toy boat on the Serpentine, and then the Atlantic itself, where it storms in great waves past Cape Horn. She looked into the darkness. There was her husband's brig, rising to the top of the wave! Up, it went, and up and up. The white arch of a thousand deaths rose before it. Oh rash, oh ridiculous man, always sailing, so uselessly, round Cape Horn in the teeth of a gale! But the brig was through the arch and out on the other side; it was safe at last!

'Ecstasy!' she cried, 'ecstasy!' And then the wind sank, the waters grew calm; and she saw the waves rippling peacefully in the moonlight.

'Marmaduke Bonthrop Shelmerdine!' she cried, standing by the oak tree.

The beautiful, glittering name fell out of the sky like a steel-blue feather. She watched it fall, turning and twisting like a slow-falling arrow that cleaves the deep air beautifully. He was coming, as he always came, in moments of dead calm; when the wave rippled and the spotted leaves fell slowly over her foot in the autumn woods; when the leopard was still; the moon was on the waters, and nothing moved between sky and sea. Then he came.

All was still now. It was near midnight. The moon rose slowly over the weald. Its light raised a phantom castle upon earth. There stood the great house with all its windows robed in silver. Of wall or substance there was none. All was phantom. All was still. All was lit as for the coming of a dead Queen. Gazing below her, Orlando saw dark plumes tossing in the courtyard, and torches flickering and shadows kneeling. A Queen once more stepped from her chariot.

'The house is at your service, Ma'am,' she cried, curtseying deeply. 'Nothing has been changed. The dead Lord, my father, shall lead you in.'

As she spoke, the first stroke of midnight sounded. The cold breeze of the present brushed her face with its little breath of fear. She looked anxiously into the sky. It was dark with clouds now. The wind roared in her ears. But in the roar of the wind she heard the roar of an aeroplane coming nearer and nearer.

'Here! Shel, here!'* she cried, baring her breast to the moon (which now showed bright) so that her pearls glowed like the eggs of some vast moon-spider. The aeroplane rushed out of the clouds and stood over her head. It hovered above her. Her pearls burnt like a phosphorescent flare in the darkness.

And as Shelmerdine, now grown a fine sea captain, hale, fresh-coloured, and alert, leapt to the ground, there sprang up over his head a single wild bird.

[313]

'It is the goose!' Orlando cried. 'The wild goose. . . .'*

And the twelfth stroke of midnight sounded; the twelfth stroke of midnight, Thursday, the eleventh of October, Nineteen hundred and Twenty Eight.

Orlando Index

INDEX

THE END

EXPLANATORY NOTES

Note: Comments attributed to Nigel Nicolson (NN) are taken from a copy of *Orlando* marked up by him. A list of abbreviations to books frequently cited will be found at the beginning of this volume. Historical proper names are given in a separate list after the Notes.

5 *Preface*: 'This Preface, of course, is all spoof. Not a single person thanked was consulted' (NN).

Defoe ... Walter Pater: With the relative exceptions of Emily Brontë and Pater, these names are all those of writers frequently cited in Woolf's essays as models.

13 *slicing at the head of a Moor*: Ariosto's *Orlando Furioso* (1532) involves a rivalry between European and Moorish (North African) knights.

some chivalry: the literalization gives a new twist to the word.

14 *Happy the mother ... happier still the biographer*: the gendering of this pair, confirmed in the next sentence, indicates already a question about the relation between the roles of the recording, monumentalizing man who writes a life and the mother who begins it.

15 *The red of the cheeks ... his temples*: 'All this an exact description of Vita' (NN).

Directly we glance ... Directly we glance: the juxtaposition brings out early on *Orlando*'s stress on the way that a biographer's perceptions are mediated by existing literary styles which set the terms for what he sees.

16 *'Æthelbert: A Tragedy in Five Acts'*: in her teens, Vita Sackville-West wrote six novels and three full-length plays, regularly based on stories associated with her family's history. Orlando's are enumerated in more detail in Chapter II, p. 73.

[318]

17 *a trifle clumsy*: 'As was Vita' (NN).

Stubbs: 'Actual name of Knole's head gardener' (NN).

18 *a place crowned by a single oak tree*: 'An eminence in the park at Knole called the Mast Head, where Vita often wrote' (NN).

one could see the English Channel: 'No!' (NN).

Snowdon herself showed mountainous: '!' (NN).

21 *But there, sitting at the servants' dinner table ...* : this figure recalls the legend of Shakespeare's visit to Knole, false according to Nigel Nicolson.

hodden brown: hodden is coarse, woollen cloth, and the word comes to mean a natural, rustic colour for dye.

22 *the waxworks at the Abbey*: VW wrote about Elizabeth I's in Westminster Abbey in a brief essay published in the *New Republic* in April 1928, just after she completed *Orlando*.

the finest legs: 'Note the continuous reference to Orlando's legs, which were the feature VW most admired in Vita' (NN).

23 *stiletto*: a short dagger.

she heard the guns in the Channel: 'Vita had just told VW about hearing from Knole the WWI bombardments in France' (NN).

so tradition has it: 'This was all true of Knole' (NN).

24 *a sad embassy to the unhappy Queen*: Thomas Sackville was dispatched by Elizabeth in 1586 to inform Mary, Queen of Scots that she was to be executed.

30 *the Court of King James*: James I succeeded Elizabeth in 1603.

31 *Clorinda*: Nigel Nicolson identifies her with Rosamund Grosvenor, a childhood sweetheart of Vita's lover Violet Trefusis. Clorinda, Favilla, and Euphrosyne are all typical classicizing names that might have been used in poems of the period.

drugget: a coarse material, all or mostly of wool.

32 *the Great Frost*: in 1608. Almost all the details of the following account—including trading on the ice—are authentic, taken from Thomas Dekker's pamphlet about this exceptional winter when the Thames froze over; VW knew this from Edward Arber's nineteenth-century anthology, *An English Garner*.

34 *six or seven miles*: as an indicator of a middle-range number, VW almost always uses 'six or seven'.

telling stories of the north-west passage and the Spanish Armada: Elizabethan explorers, in particular Martin Frobisher, set their sights on finding a sea route along the north coast of North America that would connect the Atlantic and the Pacific Oceans. The Spanish Armada dispatched by Philip II in 1588 was eventually defeated by English naval forces. These stories VW generally got from Richard Hakluyt's *Voyages* (in full, *Principall Navigations, Voiages, and Discoveries of the English Nation*, published in 1589 and then in much revised and enlarged form between 1598 and 1635. She read it first in her teens and then again in 1918.

35 *the corantoe and lavolta*: the first of these dances is French, identical to the courante; the second is described as 'a lively dance for two persons consisting a good deal in high and active bounds'.

37 *The stranger's name*: 'Sasha = Violet Trefusis' (NN).

38 *'Je crois . . . la sienne'*: all the French in this section was supplied by Vita. The translations are as follows: 'I believe I met a gentleman related to you in Poland last year'; 'The beauty of the ladies of the court of England fills me with delight. There is no more gracious lady to be seen than your queen, nor a *coiffure* more beautiful than hers.'

39 *speaking French with a perfect accent*: 'So did Vita' (NN).

40 *comme une grande perche mal fagotée*: 'like a tall, badly decorated pole'; there may also be an innuendo in the choice of the unusual *fagotée*.

43 *a white Russian fox*: 'In fact a Russian bear, Ivan, which was given to Vita, aged 19, by an admirer, and kept at Knole' (NN).

43 *bit him so savagely that his father had it killed*: 'true' (NN).

reach: the part of a river between two bends; whence a bay, headland, or promontory.

44 *the philosopher is right*: if this is a reference to Robert Burton, author of *The Anatomy of Melancholy* (1621), then the parenthesis is confusing, since Burton was an Anglican who expressly took a distance from 'Anabaptists, Brownists, Barrowists, Familists, but a company of rude, illiterate, capricious, base fellows' (vol. iii, Everyman edn. (London: Dent, 1964), 339). Conceivably, 'Anabaptist' is no more than a hint at the 'Anatomy', or 'cutting up', of the 'knife-blade' separation of happiness from melancholy.

46 *palanquin*: a covered litter.

48 *tree-planting*: gardening was one of Vita's passions.

this day sennight: a week from today; 'sennight', like ''Twas' (above, p. 35), is an example of VW's occasional pastiche of the language of the period through which Orlando is currently passing.

51 *something rank in her*: slipping via 'coarse flavoured' to 'peasant born', the word becomes an ironic pun.

52 *the stags . . . would stray into the great hall*: 'true, once, at Knole' (NN).

53 *cressets*: iron containers for grease or oil to burn as lamps; usually mounted on the top of a building.

54 *cony catchers*: a cony catcher is one who catches rabbits or 'conies', dupes; thus a cheat, sharper, swindler. The term was made famous by Robert Greene (1560?–1592), one of the obvious avatars of Nick Greene in *Orlando*, who makes his first appearance in the Elizabethan period. Robert Greene published two tracts on what he called conny-catching; the first, in 1591, inaugurated the word with the title: 'A notable Discovery of Coosnage Now Daily Practised by Sundry Lewd Personas, called Connie-catchers, and Crosse-biters'.

ostlers: stable-boys' grooms.

dishclout: dishcloth.

55 *'Methinks it should be now . . . Should yawn'*: Shakespeare, *Othello*, v. ii. 102 ff.

'Jour de ma vie!': 'Light [literally, 'day'] of my life'; 'the motto of the Sackvilles, referring to the Battle of Crécy (1346), where one of them fought' (NN).

57 *Hastily putting the horses under cover . . .'*: 'This is all a fantasy of Vita's elopement with Violet [Trefusis]' (NN).

61 *Irish rebels*: the first five years of James I's reign in England were marked by heavy expenditure on defence in Ireland; the specific allusion here is to O'Donaghy's rebellion, the same winter as the Great Frost.

65 *But the doctors were hardly wiser then than they are now*: VW's hostility to psychiatrists is also evident in the portrait of Sir William Bradshaw in *Mrs Dalloway* (1925).

67 *Grimsditch . . . Dupper*: all the names in this paragraph are those of servants at Knole in the early seventeenth century, listed in *Knole and the Sackvilles*.

68 *he must descend into the crypt where his ancestors lay*: 'Not at Knole but at Withyam church, Sussex, where Vita's own ashes lie' (NN).

69 *a writer called Thomas Browne*: Browne, whom Woolf much admired, and to whom she often referred in her essays, was a medical doctor; his literary works include *Religio Medici*, and *Urn Burial*, which Orlando seems to be thinking of here.

he was singularly methodical: 'true of Vita' (NN).

70 *foully murdered*: alluding to *Hamlet*, I. v. 27 f.: 'Murder most foul, as in the best it is;/ But this most foul, strange, and unnatural.'

71 *the pollen of the asphodel*: in Greek myth, the gods dwelt in fields of asphodel, an immortal flower.

73 *a great inlaid cabinet*: 'This belongs to Vita, and she kept all her most intimate letters in it' (NN).

74 *the cupboard behind his mother's bedroom*: Orlando's

mother is associated once again with his literary labours on p. 108.

74 *Thus had been written . . .* : 'Exaggerates but true of Vita's childhood' (NN).

One he had had printed: *Chatterton*, printed privately in Sevenoaks in 1909.

75 *rainbow and granite*: VW also used this conjunction as her starting-point for an essay called 'The New Biography', published in 1927, just after she had begun writing *Orlando*.

(the first of November 1927): this really was the 'now' of the period of *Orlando*'s composition, between 8 Oct. 1927 and 17 Mar. 1928.

78 *shawms*: the shawm was a medieval wind instrument.

79 *the vales of Tempe*: the valley of Tempe in Greece is often used as the type of the beautiful place in Latin poetry.

one Giles Isham: 'An actual name, and man, friend of VW. Shakespearean actor, but of Northamptonshire, not Norfolk. Sir Gyles (not Giles) Isham' (NN).

80 *Lady Winchilsea's fan*: Lady Winchilsea was Anne Finch, the Countess of Winchilsea (1660–1720), author of *The Spleen* and other poems; she appears also in *A Room of One's Own*. The presence of her fan is presumably prompted by the title of Oscar Wilde's play, *Lady Windermere's Fan*.

81 *Nicholas Greene*: this figure is partly based on the dramatist Robert Greene, a contemporary of Shakespeare's (see note to p. 54 above), and partly on the literary critic Edmund Gosse, a contemporary of VW's. Nick Greene also turns up in *A Room of One's Own*, the year after *Orlando*, where he is the actor-manager who 'took pity' on Judith, the fictional sister of Shakespeare with similar theatrical aspirations, then fathered her child, and is later cited as the author of Johnsonian opinions concerning the ludicrousness of women seeking to go on the stage.

Flodden and . . . Agincourt: the battle of Flodden Field, in which English forces defeated James IV of Scotland who had invaded from the north, took place in 1513. At the battle of

Agincourt in 1415, the English army of Henry V defeated a
French army that had intercepted their retreat back to Calais.

83 *the Malmsey*: a strong, sweet wine from southern Europe.

88 *provided they were written three hundred years ago*: in the
manuscript, this is followed by a passage which substantiates
the legend of Shakespeare's visit to Knole, and also makes
the biographer guilty of the destruction of the too explicit
'impure' letter in which Shakespeare revealed all about his
relations with the Dark Lady of the sonnets.

89 *teg*: a sheep in its second year, between weaning and first
shearing.

92 *midden*: dunghill; manure heap.

93 *elk-hounds*: 'Vita had two elk-hounds then, Cnut and Frya'
(NN).

   gave birth that very night: 'this did happen at Long Barn
[Vita and Harold's house near Knole]' (NN).

94 *Here he came then ... nothing whatever happened*: this
entire paragraph is a self-parody, of the 'Time Passes' section
at the centre of *To the Lighthouse*, the novel written immediately before *Orlando*. In the manuscript, it is followed by a
passage on the impossibility of biographical comprehensive-
ness.

96 *deserts of vast eternity*: Andrew Marvell, 'To His Coy
Mistress', l. 24.

98 *fleets*: vanishes, fades.

   satyrs: in Greek mythology, hybrid woodland creatures,
part man and part animal, associated with lust.

   *a man who never thought twice about heading a charge or
fighting a duel*: not, in fact, activities we have seen Orlando
perform.

99 *budget*: a pouch or bag, whence a bag's contents; a bundle.

100 *scrolloping*: the *OED* entry for this word could not be more
specific: '[Fanciful portmanteau formation by Virginia
Woolf, prob. combining SCROLL *sb*., LOLLOP *v*., etc.] Characterized by or possessing heavy, florid ornament. Also

[324]

transf. and as *pres. ppl.*, proceeding in involutions, rambling.'
There is a second occurrence of the word in Chapter V,
p. 220.

101 *There it lay* . . . : 'Vita said that this wonderful description
of Knole made her weep' (NN).

104 *the odious Parliament days*: a reference to the republican
'Commonwealth' period between 1649 (the execution of
Charles I) and 1660 (the accession of Charles II).

three hundred and sixty-five bedrooms: Knole, the Sackville-
West estate near Sevenoaks on which all the descriptions of
Orlando's estate are based, was indeed rumoured to have a
room (not, as Nigel Nicolson points out, a bedroom) to each
day of the year, as well as 52 staircases. Similarly, the
'shopping list' of purchases in the next paragraph is derived
from an authentic document reproduced in *Knole and the
Sackvilles*.

107 *sconces*: lanterns attached to the wall.

the blue and green arras: 'The sixteenth-century Flemish
tapestries in the Venetian Ambassador's bedroom depicted
scenes from Ariosto's *Orlando Furioso*. Did VW take the
name from them?' (NN).

Daphne flying: according to the classical myths, Daphne was
a nymph who fled from the advances of the god Apollo, and
was changed into a laurel.

108 *a round schoolboy hand*: 'like Vita's' (NN).

110 *the Archduchess Harriet*: 'Harriet is Lord Lascelles, who
wanted to marry Vita in 1910, but married Mary (d. of
George V) instead' (NN).

113 *King Charles*: Charles II.

Ambassador Extraordinary to Constantinople: Harold
Nicolson, Vita's husband, was a Secretary in the British
Embassy at Constantinople from 1911 to 1914.

117 *this wild panorama*: 'Refers to Vita's journey over the
Persian mountains, described in her *Twelve Days* (1927)'
(NN).

118 *Janissaries*: the Turkish Sultan's guard.

119 *The same ceremonies were gone through* ... : 'All this reflects Vita's letters to VW about diplomatic life in Teheran, 1926–7' (NN).

121 *his Dukedom*: 'Earls of Dorset promoted to Dukes by George I' (NN).

123 *Tunbridge Wells*: in Kent, not far from Knole.

124 *negus*: named after its inventor, Colonel Francis Negus (d. 1730), negus is a mixture of wine, especially port or sherry, and hot water, sweetened and flavoured.

126 *blue-jacket*: a sailor.

127 *A washer-woman ... no more could be seen*: with its lovers' embrace and drawn curtains, this paragraph parodies many similarly structured scenes of voyeurism in VW's novels.

128 *Rosina Pepita*: Vita's mother Victoria was the daughter of a Spanish dancer called Pepita, whose story Vita would later write in *Pepita* (1937).

bastinado: a beating with a stick, a cudgelling.

130 *brindled*: streaked, tabby.

131 *'Horrid Sisters, go!'*: these ominous females, horrid in their virtuousness rather than in their foulness, seem to be weird descendants of the three witches in *Macbeth*. As in the play—Lady Macbeth's 'Unsex me here'—their appearance precedes a disturbance of sexual identity; but here, they try in vain to prevent the change in Orlando which so threatens their loudly capitalized values.

still unravished: 'Thou still unravished bride of quietness' is the opening line of Keats's 'Ode on a Grecian Urn' (1819).

heights of Surrey: VW always lights on Surrey, already in the twenties becoming an affluent rural residential area for businessmen working in central London, as her exemplary site of a despicable middle-class respectability, characterized below by 'Wealth, Prosperity, Comfort, Ease'.

134 *Orlando was a man till the age of thirty*: in psychological

rather than fictional mode, Freud at this time was making an equivalent suggestion to VW's about women's development of a feminine identity. For him, too, it came about only as the sequel to a first identity that was masculine. See also the note to p. 233, below.

But let other pens treat of sex and sexuality: Jane Austen, Mansfield Park, ch. 48: 'Let other pens dwell on guilt and misery'.

her Seleuchi hound: In 1926, Vita stayed in Baghdad with Gertrude Bell, who was then political adviser to the Iraqi government. She decided she wanted a saluki hound as a present for Harold; a phone call by her hostess brought round 'a regular pack. . . . And they are all still here on approval', as she put it in a letter to her father. 'Vita wanted them all,' says Victoria Glendinning; 'on Miss Bell's advice, she picked a young yellow bitch called Zurcha. (She turned out to be irredeemably stupid, and the only really unsatisfactory dog the Nicolsons ever had.)' (Glendinning, 155–6).

135 *orient*: a pearl of orient is one from the Indian seas, as opposed to the less beautiful ones obtained from European mussels.

Broussa: 'the only town outside Europe which VW ever visited (in 1911)' (NN).

136 *hunch*: 'a thick or chunky piece, a lump, a hunk' (OED).

142 *a descent of four or five hundred years only*: in the letter to Vita of 9 Oct. 1927 in which she first pours out her fantasy of the book she might write about her lover, VW writes: 'Your excellence as a subject arises largely from your noble birth. (But whats 400 years of nobility, all the same?) and the opportunity thus given for florid descriptive passages in great abundance' (*Letters*, iii. 429).

Howards and Plantagenets: old-established noble families.

143 *Whigs and Tories, Liberal party and Labour party*: not long before the time of VW's writing, the relatively new Labour Party, which she supported, had won its first General Election when Ramsay MacDonald became Prime Minister in 1924.

144 *Four hundred and seventy-six bedrooms*: there seems to be a discrepancy with the 365 given (in figures, not words) just a little over a page ago (p. 143). The difference is precisely 111, obtained by adding one to each of the three digits of the original number—which may be significant, or may not.

burnous: 'a mantle or cloak with a hood, an upper garment extensively worn by Arabs and Moors' (OED).

148 *paduasoy*: 'a strong corded or gros-grain silk fabric, much worn in the 18th century by both sexes' (*OED*).

149 *Which is the greater ecstasy? The man's or the woman's?*: in Greek mythology, this was the question put to the prophet Tiresias, who had attributes of both sexes; his answer gave the advantage to the woman.

shiver: in the sense of 'fragment, chip, splinter', the noun could just about be applied to a tiny piece of meat. Its use here would seem to be motivated by a double attraction—to 'sliver', and to what the 'delicious tremor' in response to the Captain may be supposed to have sent down Orlando's spine.

pleasaunce: a pleasure-ground, usually a separate enclosure adjoining a mansion or garden, with features such as shady walks, statues, and ornamental water.

150 *staying*: putting on stays, corsets with whalebone stiffening.

151 *walk in procession ... D'you take sugar?*: processing down Whitehall, and performing the afternoon tea ceremony, are standard characterizations in VW of the respective conventional roles of masculinity and femininity. In the manuscript, there is an even more acerbic allusion to 'playing at soldiers in Pall Mall'.

152 *dress up like a Guy Fawkes*: although *OED* underlines the grotesqueness associated with effigies of Guy Fawkes paraded around the streets on 5 November, the anniversary of the 1605 Gunpowder Plot against James I, and by extension that of 'guys', its examples often seem to be more positively sartorial, as is implied here, where women's praise is the outcome.

154 *mantilla*: a large veil worn over the head and covering the shoulders.

156 *samphire*: the plant *crithmum maritimum*, which grows on rocks by the sea. Its aromatic, fleshy leaves may be used to make pickles.

mopping and mowing: grimacing, mocking. Each verb on its own means 'to grimace'; *OED* cites the whole phrase, 'to mop and mow', as a regular usage.

half Yorkshire: see note to p. 172, below.

158 *St Paul's which Mr Wren had built*: Christopher Wren designed the cathedral which was built between 1675 and 1710 to replace the medieval building destroyed in the Great Fire (1666).

a plague and a fire: the Great Fire of London in 1666 put an end to the plague which had spread throughout the country.

160 *The Captain must have been mistaken ... we let it stand*: Addison, Dryden, and Pope would not have been in the same coffee-house at the same moment (unless one of them was exceedingly precocious), as a reference to any listing of their life-spans, such as the one at the back of this edition, will show. And they would not have been found in the Cocoa Tree, which was the coffee-house associated with Tory politicians; intellectuals and writers frequented Will's, and later—at Addison's instigation—Button's.

they were Papists: Dryden, having written *Religio Laici* (1682) in defence of the Anglican *via media*, converted to Catholicism on the accession of James II, and then wrote *The Hind and the Panther* (1687) in support of his new faith. Pope was brought up as a Catholic. Addison was never anything but an Anglican.

161 *her home in Blackfriars*: Vita's mother lived in Dorset House, now demolished, in this part of London.

162 *Canute*: 'actual name' (NN); see note to p. 93, above.

165 *a little book ... which had been held by Mary Queen of Scots*: there was such a relic at Knole. In gratitude for his sensitivity in delivering her the news that she was condemned

[329]

to death, Mary, Queen of Scots gave Thomas Sackville a carved wooden triptych of the saints and the procession to Calvary. (See *Knole and the Sackvilles*, 47, also the note to p. 24, above.)

168 *High battlements of thought* ...: when she received her copy of *Orlando* on the day of its publication, Vita wrote in a letter to VW: 'There are a dozen details I should like to go into,—Queen Elizabeth's visit, Greene's visit, phrases scattered about, (particularly one on p. 160 beginning "High battlements of thought, etc." which is just what you did for *me*,)' (Louise A. DeSalvo and Mitchell A. Leaska (ed.), *The Letters of Vita Sackville-West to Virginia Woolf* (New York: William Morrow and Company Inc., 1985), 288–9).

172 *Falling on his knees* ...: 'This was true of Lord Lascelles who inherited Harewood House in Yorkshire and a vast fortune' (NN). The courtship of Lord Lascelles had been the topic of an exchange of letters between Vita and VW in October 1927, at the beginning of Woolf's 'researches' for *Orlando*. In response to the question 'What used you and Lord Lascelles to talk about?' (*Letters*, iii. 433), Vita wrote 'I try to remember what I talked to Harry Lascelles about. He was always very tongue-tied, so we didn't get very far. He had nice hands' (*Letters of Vita Sackville-West to Virginia Woolf*, 242).

the gape: 'a disease in poultry, etc., of which frequent gaping is the symptom' (*OED*).

174 *a game called Fly Loo*: 'played at Knole' (NN).

175 £40,885: 6: 8: six shillings and eightpence was exactly one-third of a pound (twenty shillings, each of twelve pence) in what is no longer 'our own money'.

178 *siren*: in the *Odyssey*, the female voices of the Sirens attempt to distract Odysseus and his crew as they sail between the perils of Scylla and Charybdis.

so dark, so bright, so hard, so soft, was she: a near quotation from Ben Jonson's 'A Celebration of Charis', 'O so white, O so soft, O so sweet is she!'

182 *to travel south is to travel downhill*: 'and insisted that the Nile must flow uphill' (NN).

183 *the heroine of the celebrated lawsuit*: a reference now to the trial of June–July 1913, in which the family of the late Sir John Murray Scott ('Seery'), who had been a close friend of Vita's mother, sued Lady Sackville over the large inheritance he had left her. The trial was heavily publicized in the popular press, and Vita, who gave evidence, figured as 'Kidlet', a name 'Seery' had called her.

184 *billets*: short written documents; notes.

routs: fashionable gatherings, generally evening parties or receptions, of a kind much in vogue in the eighteenth and early nineteenth centuries.

187 *Pippin*: 'A real name' (NN).

191 *The hostess is our modern Sibyl*: 'Joke at the expense of Sibyl Colefax, the London hostess who pursued VW' (NN).

194 *Link-boys*: employed to carry links (torches) to light people's way along the streets at night.

200 *'Whether the Nymph . . . at a Ball'*: Canto II, ll. 105–9 of *The Rape of the Lock* (1714), by Alexander Pope.

congee: a bow of departure.

201 *the following passage from the Spectator*: this passage is not from the *Spectator*, but from the *Tatler*, no. 116 (3–5 Jan. 1710); there are a few minor alterations of punctuation. In quest of a *Spectator* passage, however, the editor confesses to having spent several hours in the library, during the course of which she did come upon many related allusions to both hoop-petticoats and global sources of female adornment (see especially nos. 69 and 127 of the *Spectator*). To Neil Saccamano of Cornell University, who hit upon the solution, she is infinitely grateful. But the fruitless search produced another result, one perhaps more momentous in its implications than the simple location of a missing reference could be: it revealed quite unambiguously the meaning of the wild goose that appears at the end of *Orlando*.

a passage from the voyage to the Houyhnhnms: Jonathan

Swift, *Gulliver's Travels* (1726), ed. Robert A. Greenberg (New York: W. W. Norton & Co.), 241–42. The list continues for as long again. There are a number of minor copying errors, mostly of punctuation. But 'find' in the opening sentence should be 'feel' and 'splenetick tedious Talkers' at the end should be 'spleneticks, tedious Talkers'.

202 *Round Parlour*: 'The Poets' Parlour at Knole, hung with portraits of the 6th Earl's literary friends' (NN). The literary friends of the sixth Earl of Dorset, Charles Sackville, included Pope, Congreve, Dryden, Rochester, and Wycherley.

204 *Lord Chesterfield whispered it to his son*: in a letter of 5 Sept. 1748: 'I will therefore, upon this subject [women], let you into certain *arcana* that will be very useful for you to know, but which you must, with the utmost care, conceal; and never seem to know. Women, then, are only children of a larger growth; they have an entertaining tattle; and sometimes wit; but for solid, reasoning good sense, I never in my life knew one that had it, or who reasoned or acted consequentially for four and twenty hours together.' (Lord Chesterfield, *Letters, Sentences and Maxims* (London: Sampson Low, Marston & Co. Ltd., n.d.), 76–6.) In the manuscript, a link is made at this point to Arnold Bennett and Orlo Williams, author of the book reviewed by Bennett in the *New Statesman* piece which prompted a riposte from Woolf ('The Intellectual Status of Women').

205 *a certain famous line in the 'Characters of Women'*: presumably the second line of Pope's 'Epistle to a Lady; Of the Character of WOMEN' (1735), which begins: 'Nothing so true as what you once let fall,/ "Most Women have no Character at all".' The Argument states: 'Of the CHARACTERS of WOMEN, *treating of this sex only as contradistinguished from the other*. That their particular Characters are not so strongly mark'd as those of Men, seldom so fixed, and still more inconsistent with themselves.' The implicit understanding of character as fixity, drawn out literally in the poem as the scoring of a mark on a malleable substance, is potentially less misogynistic than it might seem (or than

[332]

Pope might have intended) and is closely connected with the question in *Orlando* of the fixing of character and its relation to age and sex (see pp. 134 and 233, and the notes).

Orlando, to cool her cheeks . . .: there is an allusion here to an incident between VW and her brother-in-law, Clive Bell, which took place in April 1928 during a journey north from the south of France to the port of Dieppe: 'And there was Nessa [Vanessa Bell] & Duncan [Grant] & Clive (who smacked me in public—curse him for an uneasy little upstart.)' (*Diary*, iii. 179; see too *Diary*, iii. 182; *Letters*, iii, no. 185).

206 *let herself secretly out of doors*: Vita enjoyed strolling in cities at night dressed as a man. Her first experiment was in 1918, when as 'Julian' she wandered round Mayfair with Violet Trefusis.

208 *the plain Dunstable of the matter*: 'Dunstable', referring to the Dunstable Road, was used in proverbial phrases to mean plain or downright.

209 *Several were the natural daughters of earls*: as was Lady Sackville, Vita's mother.

210 *Mr S. W.*: 'Edward Sackville-West, Vita's cousin, made a great fuss about this, thinking it referred to him. VW assured him, mendaciously, that she meant Sydney Waterlow' (NN).

212 *fled with a certain lady . . . the lady's husband followed them*: at a climactic moment in Vita's affair with Violet Trefusis, the two women eloped to Amiens in northern France, whither they were pursued by Harold Nicolson and Denys Trefusis; the two men had actually chartered a plane for the purpose.

218 *the brothers Adam*: the four Adams brothers were eighteenth-century architects who pioneered the construction of terraced housing, focusing not on the individual house, but on the single imposing edifice that could be achieved through their grouping together. Their written works were published from 1773, eventually in three volumes, under the authorship of two of the brothers, Robert and James.

219 *obfusc*: this word seems to be VW's own concoction from 'obfuscation' and 'subfusc', the local word for a dark outfit worn for examinations by students at Oxford University. Unlike 'scrolloping' (see next note), it has not been sanctified by inclusion in *OED*.

220 *scrolloping*: see note to p. 100, above.

222 *crystal palaces*: the Crystal Palace in South London was built for the 1851 Great Exhibition.

bassinettes: a bassinette was an oblong wickerwork basket with a hood over one end, used as a cradle for babies; the word was also used for a type of pram with this shape.

224 *to conceal the fact; the great fact; the only fact;*: the stop-start semi-colons suggest that 'the fact' was itself a conceal-ment of sex, by the Victorian insistence on motherhood as the only function of femininity.

225 *bombazine*: twilled or corded dress material made of silk and worsted; in black, it was much used to make mourning clothes.

226 *She had been working at it for close on three hundred years now*: 'true that Vita took 6 years on The Land, and VW mocked her for it' (NN).

It was time to make an end: this is much extended in the manuscript draft, which included a quotation from Thomas Sackville's poem, 'Induction to the Mirror for Magistrates'.

228 *'I am myself . . . Murmur' . . . 'She was so changed . . . of the tomb'*: the 'quotations' appear to have been invented by Woolf for the occasion.

Was it the damp . . . : in the manuscript, this sentence is followed by a general rumination on literary whys and wherefores with the biographer concluding that it was indeed 'the damp that did it' in this case.

229 *the vast solitary emerald which Queen Elizabeth had given her*: 'An emerald given to Vita by HN [Harold Nicolson]'s mother' (NN)

230 *pinchbeck*: an alloy invented by Christopher Pinchbeck, looking like gold and used to make cheap jewellery.

233 *a year or two past thirty, indeed, the lines of her character were fixed*: as with the move from masculinity to femininity, there is an apparent parallel here to Freud's contemporary constructions of the story of female development. In the quotation from his lecture 'Femininity' (1933) cited in the Introduction (above, p. xlv), Freud too makes 'about thirty' the moment of feminine character-fixing; but in VW's novel, this does not appear to inhibit the continuing multiplicity of *Orlando*'s innumerable selves.

234 *he had married a very great lady*: Lord Lascelles married George V's daughter, Mary.

sacks in Botany Bay: in other words, he had been transported to Australia.

235 *Canute and Pippin*: the names of Vita's elk-hound and Virginia and Leonard's dog.

236 *Sir Bedivere flung the sword of Arthur*: when Sir Bedivere throws Excalibur, the sword of the dying King Arthur, into the lake, an arm appears above the water, catches it and vanishes with it below the surface.

240 *He had a castle in the Hebrides*: an allusion to the Nicolsons' Scottish origins.

'For the Horn': the account of Marmaduke sailing round Cape Horn is taken from Hakluyt's description of Sir Francis Drake's circumnavigation of the globe, and the nineteenth-century retelling of it by J. A. Froude.

242 *Peelers*: policemen, so named after Sir Robert Peel, the minister who set up a national police force in the 1840s.

243 *'The lawsuits are settled'*: the story of Orlando's lawsuits draws on the much publicized legal battle over the inheritance of Knole in 1909–10, which was settled in favour of Vita and her mother; but there was also a second sensational trial, in 1913 (see note to p. 183, above).

244 *[Horses were put into carriages . . . and her own, etc.]*: this paragraph is an exaggerated version of Vita's and Victoria's triumphant homecoming in February 1910, following their

victory in the trial. The Bull and Stag are the actual names of pubs in Sevenoaks at the time.

245 *Mar*: the pet name by which Vita was known to her mother and husband.

252 *And then I came . . . like Egyptian girls*: the quotation is from V. Sackville-West's prizewinning poem, *The Land*.

254 *the Hogarth Press*: the small publishing house founded, run, and operated by Leonard and Virginia Woolf.

256 *Love, the poet has said, is woman's whole existence*: alluding to Byron's lines from *Don Juan*: 'Man's love is of man's life a thing apart/'Tis woman's whole existence.'

think of a gamekeeper: as Lady Chatterley was to do shortly afterwards (Lawrence's novel was published in 1930).

257 *Let us go, then . . .*: this entire paragraph is transposed into verse form in an anthology of poetry called *Another World Than This*, which V. Sackville-West published in 1945.

260 *the invention of the steam engine*: the exploitation of the steam engine for the purpose of railway travel began in the 1830s.

She had bought another in Mayfair: Victoria Sackville-West, Vita's mother, bought a house in Hill Street.

266 *lived long in America*: Edmund Gosse, the model for Greene's nineteenth-century version, lectured in America in the 1880s, but did not live there.

267 *Addison's Cato*: produced in 1713.

Thomson's Seasons: published between 1726 and 1730 in four books, one for each season, with an introductory 'Hymn'. Sackville-West's poem *The Land*, the 'source' of Orlando's long-running composition 'The Oak Tree', is similar in format and subject-matter.

269 *hansom cabs*: low-hung, two-wheeled vehicles holding two people inside, with the driver mounted behind in a dickey, or elevated seat, so that the reins went over the roof.

barouche landau: a four-wheeled carriage with the driver's seat at the front, and two facing double seats inside.

cypher language: 'It was called Unicode, which Vita and Harold used in telegrams to and from Persia' (NN).

273 *what Tupper said about Smiles*: making types of two Victorian writers, Martin Farquhar Tupper (1810–89), a noted hack, and Samuel Smiles (1812–1904), the originator of the philosophy of self-help. A further catalogue of nineteenth-century nonentities occurs on p. 277, below.

274 *'It's sunk!'*: this scene on the Serpentine has much in common with a childhood memory VW recounts in 'A Sketch of the Past': 'There was the great day when my Cornish lugger sailed perfectly to the middle of the pond and then, with my eyes upon it, amazed, sank suddenly ... To make the wonder complete, many weeks later in the spring, I was walking by the pond and a man in a flat-boat was dredging the pond of duckweed, and to my unspeakable excitement, up he brought my lugger in his dredging net ... and I ran home with this marvellous story to tell' (*Moments of Being: Unpublished Autobiographical Writings*, ed. Jeanne Schulkind (New York: Harcourt Brace Jovanovich, 1976), 77).

eight-hour bills ... factory acts: referring to the unprecedented quantity of legislation during this period which was aimed at regulating working conditions.

275 *four-in-hand*: a vehicle with four horses, driven by one person.

victoria: a light, low, four-wheeled carriage with a collapsible hood, seats for (usually) two people, and one in front for the driver.

277 *a mass of Alexander Smiths ... Jamesons*: see note to p. 273, above. In the manuscript, there is a much longer passage on the decline by expansion of literature in the nineteenth century. In place of this particular list of names as a simple background to the greatest, the forgotten second-rate writers are represented as the only possible companions for Orlando, on account of the seclusion of the exceptional: 'But genius being inaccessible, she was forced to consort with the writers who managed to write without a trace of it: the Smiles, the

Tuppers, the Smiths, the Prossers, the Hemans, their names are legion: and all forgotten now'. Further on, there is an allusion to one Volumnia Fox, frequently attacked by the 'brilliant' Arnold Bennett; 'her real name was Virginia Woolf'. In 'real' life, Volumnia Fox was a character in a novel about Bloomsbury by Marjorie Strachey.

277 *wrap a ten-pound note round the sugar tongs*: the manuscript has longer reflections on the cessation of patronage relations.

the Influence of this upon that: in *To the Lighthouse* (1927), Mr Ramsay's student Charles Tansley is said to be writing a thesis about 'the influence of something upon somebody' (rpt. London: Hogarth Press, 1955, p. 24).

280 *outrigger*: this adaptation of the word to mean outdoor clothing is not attested by *OED*; it corresponds to 'outrigging' in the sense of 'that with which anything is rigged out'.

282 *Orlando was safely delivered of a son*: 'We said to VW: "But there are two of us! Which one is this supposed to be?" "Both of you", she replied' (NN). The coincidence of the birth of a first child and the publication of a first book is common to the lives of both Orlando and Vita, whose first book of poetry was published by The Bodley Head just after Ben Nicolson was born, in 1914.

283 *to go and visit a certain lady opposite*: Mrs Keppel, the mother of Vita's lover, Violet Trefusis, was Edward VII's mistress.

286 *Marshall & Snelgrove's*: a major London department store at the time. In 1930, just before Christmas, VW had her bag snatched there; the incident is described in her diary (*Diary*, iii, 339–40).

287 *Louise then*: 'Louise Gamoux, Vita's French maid at Long Barn' (NN).

288 *another war*: the 1914–18 World War.

now thirty-six: Vita was born in 1892, so she too was 36 in 1928.

291 *the Dictionary of National Biography*: edited by VW's father, Leslie Stephen.

292 *she was an expert driver*: VW was impressed by Vita's driving. In a 1924 diary entry, she writes: 'Vita was here for Sunday, gliding down the village in her huge new blue Austin car, which she manages consummately' (*Diary*, ii. 313).

Thursday, the eleventh of October 1928: the publication date of *Orlando*.

296 *that don't count*: Orlando is given the upper-class dialect of the time.

297 *A prize*: in March 1927, Vita was awarded the Hawthornden Prize for her long poem *The Land*.

298 *A porpoise in a fishmonger's shop*: 'VW's often-repeated teasing description of Vita' (NN). In a letter of 7 Feb. 1927, for instance, VW writes: 'Aint it odd how the vision at the Sevenoaks fishmongers has worked itself into my idea of you?' (*Letters*, iii. 326).

With my guineas I'll buy flowering trees . . .': 'With her prize-money she planted a store of nut-trees at Long Barn' (NN).

302 *Spanish wine*: 'always Allella' (NN).

305 *Flodden and Poitiers*: the battle of Flodden Field took place in 1413 (see note to p. 81, above). At the battle of Poitiers in 1356, during the Hundred Years War, Edward the Black Prince, the son of Edward II of England, defeated a French army.

309 *old Greene getting upon a platform the other day*: John Drinkwater presented Vita with her prize for *The Land* in June 1927. VW had attended the event without pleasure, recording in her diary: 'My word! how insignificant we all looked! How can we pretend that we are interesting, that our works matter? The whole business of writing becomes infinitely distasteful . . . I felt there was no one full grown mind among us. In truth, it was the thick dull middle class of letters that met; not the aristocracy. Vita cried at night' (*Diary*, iii. 139–40, Saturday, 18 June, 1927).

313 *'Here! Shel, here!'*: 'How Harold flew from Paris, and

landed on the cricket-field at Knole. I remember how she cried, "Here, Hadji, here"' (NN).

314 *'The wild goose . . .'*: Readers from V. Sackville-West onwards have wondered about the possible significance of this creature appearing at the end. After chasing around after scholarly references for this book which is partly a joke against scholarship, this editor was satisfied that she had solved the mystery. (See further the note to p. 201, above.)

LIST OF NAMES

Note: Except for the date of their death, reference is not made to the subsequent lives of individuals alive at the time of *Orlando's* writing.

Addison, Joseph (1672–1719). Essayist.
Anne, Queen (1665–1714). Reigned from 1702.

Bell, Clive (1881–1964). Artist; husband of VW's sister, Vanessa.
Bell, Julian (1908–37). Son of Vanessa.
Bell, Quentin (b. 1910). Brother of Julian.
Berkeley, Bishop George (1685–1753). Philosopher.
Berners, Lord (1883–1950). Musician, artist, writer; acquaintance of VW.
Birrell, Francis (1889–1935). Literary journalist.
Boswell, James (1740–95). Friend and biographer of Samuel Johnson.
Boxall, Nelly. Cook and housemaid to Leonard and Virginia Woolf from 1916.
Brontë, Emily (1818–48). Novelist.
Browne, Sir Thomas (1605–82). Writer and doctor.
Browning, Robert (1812–89). Poet.
Burghley, Lord (William Cecil, 1520–98). Minister of Elizabeth I.

Carlyle, Thomas (1795–1881). Essayist and historian.
Cartwright, Mrs. Worked at the Hogarth Press, run by Leonard and Virginia Woolf, from 1925 to 1930.
Case, Janet (1862–1937). Classical scholar who taught VW Greek.
Cecil, Lord. *See* Burghley, Lord, *above*.
Charles II, King (1630—85). Reigned from 1660.
Chesterfield, Lord (1694–1775). Statesman and paternal letter-writer.
Cicero (106–43 BC). Roman politician, lawyer, and philosopher.
Colefax, Lady Sibyl (d. 1950). Society hostess; friend of VW.

Davidson, Angus (b. 1898). Art journalist; friend of VW.

Deffand, Madame du (1697–1780). French salon hostess; correspondent of Horace Walpole.

Defoe, Daniel (1661?–1731). Novelist.

De Quincey, Thomas (1785–1859). Writer; opium eater.

Dickinson, Violet (1865–1948). Close friend of VW.

Donne, John (1571–1631). Poet.

Drake, Sir Francis (1540?–96). 'Circumnavigator and admiral' (*DNB*).

Dryden, John (1631–1700). Poet and dramatist.

Eliot, T. S. (1888–1965). American-born poet; friend of VW.

Eliot, Vivienne (1888–1947). Friend of VW; wife of T. S. Eliot.

Elizabeth I, Queen (1533–1603). Reigned from 1558.

Fletcher, Thomas (1666–1713). Poet.

Forster, E. M. (1879–1970). Novelist; friend of VW.

Fry, Roger (1866–1934). Art critic, painter; friend of VW.

Gladstone, William Ewart (1809–98). Prime Minister.

Grenville, Richard (1541?–91). Naval commander and explorer.

Gwyn, Nell (1650–87). Actress; mistress of Charles II.

Hawkins, Sir John (1532–95). Naval commander.

Hudson, Nan (1896–1957). Painter; friend of VW, who stayed with her and Ethel Sands in Dieppe in July 1927.

Hutchinson, St John ('Jack', 1884–1942). Barrister; friend of VW.

Hutchinson, Mary (1889–1977). Friend of VW and especially of Clive Bell.

James I, King (1566–1625). Reigned from 1603.

Johnson, Samuel (1709–84). Lexicographer, poet, friend of James Boswell.

Jonson, Ben (1572–1637). Poet and dramatist.

Keynes, John Maynard (1883–1946). Economist; married to Lydia Lopokova; friend of VW.

Lopokova, Lydia (1892–1981). Russian dancer with Diaghilev's ballet company; married to Keynes; friend of VW.

Lucas, F. L. (1894–1967). Cambridge classicist and lecturer in English; friend of VW.

Macaulay, Thomas (1800–59). Historian and essayist.

MacCarthy, Desmond (1882–1953). Literary journalist: 'Affable Hawk' of the *New Statesman*; friend of VW.

MacCarthy, Molly (1882–1953). Literary journalist.

Marlowe, Christopher (1564–93). Dramatist.

Melbourne, Lord (1779–1848). Prime Minister.

Milton, John (1608–74). Poet.

Mirrlees, Hope (1887–1978). Poet and novelist; friend of VW.

Moray, Earl of. From the period of his mention, it would seem that the reference must be to the third or fourth in the line of Stewarts to hold this title; the *DNB* does not deem him worthy of an entry.

Morrell, Lady Ottoline (1873–1938). Society hostess; friend of VW.

Mortimer, Raymond (1895–1980). Critic and journalist; friend of VW.

Nelson, Admiral (1758–1805). Naval commander.

Nicolson, Harold (1886–1968). Diplomatist and author; husband of Vita Sackville-West.

Palmerston, Lord (1784–1865). Prime Minister.

Pascal, Blaise (1623–62). French mathematician and philosopher.

Pater, Walter (1839–94). Art critic.

Pope, Alexander (1688–1744). Poet.

Raverat, Jacques (1885–1925). Painter; friend of VW, who had been touched by his appreciation of her *Mrs Dalloway* shortly before his death.

Rossetti, Christina (1830–94). Poet.

Rylands, George ('Dadie', b. 1902). Cambridge academic; friend of VW.

Sackville-West, Edward (1901–65). Occupant of Knole; Vita's cousin.

Sackville-West, Victoria ('Vita'). (1892–1962). Poet and novelist; friend of VW from 1922.

Sands, Ethel (1873–1962). American-born painter; friend of VW (*see also* Hudson, Nan, *above*).

Sanger, C. P. (1871–1930). Barrister; friend of VW.

Scott, Sir Walter (1771–1832). Historical novelist.

Shakespeare, William (1564–1616). Actor and playwright.

Shelley, Percy Bysshe (1792–1822). Poet.

Sheppard, John Tresidder (1881–1968). Classics lecturer; friend of VW.

Sitwell, Osbert (1892–1969). Poet; friend of VW.

Snowden [*sic*], Miss M. K. (1878–?1966). Art-school friend of Vanessa Bell, VW's sister; subsequently an acquaintance of VW, who wrote a character sketch of her (*D* iii. 289).

Stephen, Adrian (1883–1948). Psychoanalyst; brother of VW.

Sterne, Laurence (1713–68). Novelist.

Strachey, Lytton (1880–1932). Biographer; friend of VW.

Swift, Jonathan (1667–1745). Satirical writer.

Sydney-Turner, Saxon (1880–1962). Treasury civil servant; friend of Leonard Woolf at Cambridge.

Taylor, Valerie (b. 1902). Actress; lover of Clive Bell, VW's brother-in-law, in 1927.

Tennyson, Alfred, Lord (1809–92). Poet.

Thomson, James (1700–48). Scottish poet.

Tomlin, Stephen (1901–37). Sculptor; friend of VW.

Vere, Sir Francis (1560–1609). Soldier; promoted in this novel to the rank of Lord.

Victoria, Queen (1818–1901). Reigned from 1837.

Villiers, George (1592–1628). Favourite of King James I.

Waley, Arthur (1889–1966). Translator of Chinese and Japanese works.

Walpole, Hugh (1884–1941). Popular novelist.

Wellesley, Lady Gerald (Dorothy, d. 1956). Poet; dedicatee of V. Sackville-West's poem, *The Land*.

Williams, Anna (1706–83). Poet; friend of Dr Johnson.
Winchilsea, Lady (Anne Finch, 1660–1720). Poet.
Wordsworth, William (1770–1850). Poet.
Wren, Christopher (1631–1723). Architect.

The Oxford World's Classics Website

www.worldsclassics.co.uk

- Browse the full range of Oxford World's Classics online

- Sign up for our monthly e-alert to receive information on new titles

- Read extracts from the Introductions

- Listen to our editors and translators talk about the world's greatest literature with our Oxford World's Classics audio guides

- Join the conversation, follow us on Twitter at OWC_Oxford

- Teachers and lecturers can order inspection copies quickly and simply via our website

www.worldsclassics.co.uk

American Literature

British and Irish Literature

Children's Literature

Classics and Ancient Literature

Colonial Literature

Eastern Literature

European Literature

Gothic Literature

History

Medieval Literature

Oxford English Drama

Poetry

Philosophy

Politics

Religion

The Oxford Shakespeare

A complete list of Oxford World's Classics, including Authors in Context, Oxford English Drama, and the Oxford Shakespeare, is available in the UK from the Marketing Services Department, Oxford University Press, Great Clarendon Street, Oxford OX2 6DP, or visit the website at www.oup.com/uk/worldsclassics.

In the USA, visit www.oup.com/us/owc for a complete title list.

Oxford World's Classics are available from all good bookshops. In case of difficulty, customers in the UK should contact Oxford University Press Bookshop, 116 High Street, Oxford OX1 4BR.

ANTHONY TROLLOPE

An Autobiography

The American Senator

Barchester Towers

Can You Forgive Her?

The Claverings

Cousin Henry

Doctor Thorne

The Duke's Children

The Eustace Diamonds

Framley Parsonage

He Knew He Was Right

Lady Anna

The Last Chronicle of Barset

Orley Farm

Phineas Finn

Phineas Redux

The Prime Minister

Rachel Ray

The Small House at Allington

The Warden

The Way We Live Now

Women's Writing 1778–1838

WILLIAM BECKFORD	Vathek
JAMES BOSWELL	Life of Johnson
FRANCES BURNEY	Camilla
	Cecilia
	Evelina
	The Wanderer
LORD CHESTERFIELD	Lord Chesterfield's Letters
JOHN CLELAND	Memoirs of a Woman of Pleasure
DANIEL DEFOE	A Journal of the Plague Year
	Moll Flanders
	Robinson Crusoe
	Roxana
HENRY FIELDING	Joseph Andrews and Shamela
	A Journey from This World to the Next and The Journal of a Voyage to Lisbon
	Tom Jones
WILLIAM GODWIN	Caleb Williams
OLIVER GOLDSMITH	The Vicar of Wakefield
MARY HAYS	Memoirs of Emma Courtney
ELIZABETH HAYWOOD	The History of Miss Betsy Thoughtless
ELIZABETH INCHBALD	A Simple Story
SAMUEL JOHNSON	The History of Rasselas
	The Major Works
CHARLOTTE LENNOX	The Female Quixote
MATTHEW LEWIS	Journal of a West India Proprietor
	The Monk
HENRY MACKENZIE	The Man of Feeling
ALEXANDER POPE	Selected Poetry

A SELECTION OF　　OXFORD WORLD'S CLASSICS

SHERWOOD ANDERSON	Winesburg, Ohio
WILLA CATHER	O Pioneers!
JAMES FENIMORE COOPER	The Last of the Mohicans
STEPHEN CRANE	The Red Badge of Courage
THEODORE DREISER	Sister Carrie
F. SCOTT FITZGERALD	The Beautiful and Damned The Great Gatsby
BENJAMIN FRANKLIN	Autobiography and Other Writings
CHARLOTTE PERKINS GILMAN	The Yellow Wall-Paper and Other Stories
NATHANIEL HAWTHORNE	The Scarlet Letter
HENRY JAMES	The Portrait of a Lady The Turn of the Screw and Other Stories
JACK LONDON	The Call of the Wild White Fang and Other Stories
HERMAN MELVILLE	Billy Budd, Sailor and Selected Tales Moby-Dick
EDGAR ALLAN POE	Selected Tales
HARRIET BEECHER STOWE	Uncle Tom's Cabin
HENRY DAVID THOREAU	Walden
MARK TWAIN	Adventures of Huckleberry Finn The Adventures of Tom Sawyer
LEW WALLACE	Ben-Hur
EDITH WHARTON	The Custom of the Country Ethan Frome
WALT WHITMAN	Leaves of Grass
OWEN WISTER	The Virginian